NEIL WHITE
NEXT TO DIE

sphere

SPHERE

First published in Great Britain in 2013 by Sphere
This paperback edition published in 2014

A CIP catalogue record for this book
is available from the British Library.

ISBN 978-0-7515-4946-1

Typeset in Meridien by M Rules
Printed and bound in Great Britain by
Clays Ltd, St Ives plc

Papers used by Sphere are from well-managed forests
and other responsible sources.

MIX
Paper from
responsible sources
FSC
www.fsc.org   FSC® C104740

Sphere
An imprint of
Little, Brown Book Group
100 Victoria Embankment
London EC4Y 0DY

An Hachette UK Company
www.hachette.co.uk

www.littlebrown.co.uk

Acknowledgements

My name appears on the cover, but writing a book is never as simple as just sitting at a computer and tapping out a story. Mistakes are made and ideas sometimes need rethinking, and so the advice and help I receive along the way from the hardworking people at Sphere is invaluable, and particularly from my two editors Jade Chandler and Thalia Proctor. A special large thank-you has to go to my agent, the wonderful Sonia Land from Sheil Land Associates, who made it possible for me to work with the people at Sphere.

As for the rest, the people who had to put up with my tired eyes and crabbiness and permanent distraction, I know who you are. I will always be grateful.

One

He paced backwards and forwards, apprehensive but excited. This was it, where he wanted to be, part of his plan, a new start.

It was quiet, apart from the scrapes and shuffles of his feet, but it seemed like a respite, a pause, because the night had been all about shouts and screams, someone fighting and struggling, angry voices. The morning was different. It was all about new beginnings.

He had to focus on that. Starting over. A new life. He stopped pacing, his hands on his hips, looking down. He noticed his shoes, plain brown, no laces, no shine to them, scruffy and worn, so that they melted into the uniformity of the floor, almost as if he couldn't see them anymore. He moved them around, made small circles, just so that they remained visible. The soles made soft sweeping noises.

He sat down and hunched forward. He was ready for it. He had to be ready. He took a deep breath and put his hands over his face, drawing his skin down, making it red, blotting out the view in front of him for a moment. Blissful darkness, except it soon became filled with their faces, all blurred features, open-mouthed, eyes searing. Their bodies thrashed and fought but it was never enough.

His eyes snapped open. His breaths were quick and sweat moistened his forehead. How had he got to this point? He knew how it all started, but this was not where it was meant to finish.

He pulled his hands away from his face and held them out, palms up. Just skin and muscle and bone. He turned them over slowly, his palms downwards, so that instead of the ingrained dirt making the lines stand out in relief, he could see just slender fingers. The nails would have been dirty but they were chewed down, and the skin alongside, so that all he had were short stumps surrounded by swollen fingertips. But what they had done still amazed him. So ordinary, but so much power, the boundaries they had crossed. How could they look so normal?

Just hands, except that it wasn't just about them. It was her. It had always been about her.

He closed his eyes again. He had to forget about her, but it was going to be hard, because whenever he tried to banish her all the others came back to him. Their hair over his fingers, soft and long, like gentle kisses on his skin, static crackling like tiny sparks. He swallowed.

But the memories were vivid, so that they flashed back into his mind and filled the room with the noise of struggles, and whimpers, and then the screams that were muffled into near silence.

His breaths became short as his mind raced through the memories. An empty space, echoing, soft hair on his hands, the rustle of the plastic, the legs of the chair on the floor, the wood knocking on the concrete. He clenched his hands around his knees as he thought of it. He had to stay in control, because he couldn't think like that anymore. That was in the past. He had to move on. This was a new beginning.

Day one.

Two

Joe Parker was swinging in his chair and looking out of his window, watching the square come to life.

He had made the calls to the police stations in Manchester and a few of the nearby towns, just to check for the latest prisoners. The margins in criminal law weren't large. The firm needed some of the daily grunt work, the drunks and overnighters, to fill the gaps between the bigger cases, and getting it was all about making your name known. So every morning Joe called every custody desk within a fifteen-mile radius, just to see if his name had been mentioned. It hadn't, as was usual, but every day he made the small talk, finding out whether any big cases had come in. Murders. Child killers. Rapists. It was his daily slog through Manchester's slurry. If nothing else, it helped to spread a reputation. There were some big players in the city and Joe had to fight to stay noticed. For his bosses in the commercial and civil departments, with their cut suits and tight smiles, the law was only ever about the money. For Joe, it was about the fight, the drama.

Joe swung his chair back towards the window. His view was a small park, a patch of grass and trees and tarmac paths on the site of an old church, an area of calm surrounded by high redbrick buildings that housed law firms and barristers' chambers, accountants and surveyors. High sash windows and white wooden lattice frames looked towards green iron railings brightened by the pink of rhododendron bushes, the monument in the middle of the park just visible, a stone cross on a plinth to commemorate the bodies still buried under there, surrounded by benches in a tight circle.

Joe started each day like this. He had been in the office since before seven, like most days, doing the work still piled on his desk, his plans disrupted by clients, whose chaotic lives deemed that appointments meant nothing. Most weren't kept, except for those on Friday afternoons, when a visit to his office was usually just an excuse to beg for some cash to get them through another weekend of their wretched lives. The Law Society objected to criminal lawyers giving gifts to clients, but Joe tried to do what was right. The rules were just about not getting caught.

He watched the city come to life in front of him. Geraniums and roses and marigolds framed the lawns in yellows and purples, and the trees were bursting with the green of early summer. It was a small piece of calm away from the shops and traffic, where workers and shoppers squeezed into the city centre, along roads that tried to fit around the remains of the industrial revolution.

There were some contradictions, like the high glass of Beetham Tower, built against all wisdom, high and thin, ready to be blown over, incongruous against the redbrick viaducts and the grime of the canals. When it was windy, the high glass blade on top hummed like a flute-chorus. The shops around it were crammed into the ground floor of old warehouses, the past morphing into the future, but as the city changed and reinvented itself each year, the small square remained the same.

Joe had been with Honeywells for a year, his first stop after walking out on Mahones, one of the bigger criminal practices, where advice was dispensed by a team of lawyers who worked hard but never made partner. He had started out as fresh-faced and naive, straight from law college, nothing but certificates and eagerness to his name. He had wanted to change the world and right some wrongs. Mahones had made him realise that it wasn't about how good he was; it was just about how much money he brought in.

Joe didn't mind that, because he thought he could do both. He knew he was a good lawyer. He had known this ever since his childhood, when he argued with his neighbour about how he should be allowed to kick his football against his fence, because children are supposed to play outdoors, and anyway, he was only kicking the ball against his own side. Joe remembered the old man going indoors, shaking his head and muttering something about him being a 'cheeky kid', but what gave him the glow was the winning of the argument.

He watched as Monica, the firm's trainee, crossed the park, skirting around a tai chi session, a frequent morning ritual, office workers trying to inject an alternative vibe into the middle of the city, and it worked. Monica stopped to watch, although Joe guessed it was more about avoiding the office than it was about the view.

As she turned back towards the office, Joe looked away from the window. It was time to concentrate on the day ahead.

The door opened. It was Gina Ross, a retired detective who had joined the firm at the same time as Joe, as an investigator. Like most coppers, she missed the game when she retired, and was too young at fifty to spend the rest of her years watching the clock move. She bore none of the scars worn with pride by some of her male colleagues. No bruised knuckles from one too many Saturday night tours or broken veins creeping across her cheeks from war stories in the pub. Instead, she wore the traces of grey in her dark hair with grace, kept short and neat, side-parted, her figure trim, with lean legs that belied her age.

It wasn't her looks that got her the job though. Joe knew that the best way to spot the police tricks was to employ someone who had used most of them, and Gina had been an expert at it. A flirt and a smile got the prisoners on her side, so that they were listening to her, not their lawyer, all too willing to tell their story despite the advice to stay quiet.

Gina had been more than just a pretty woman in a police station though. She was smart and hard-working. She had also been the lead detective in a case involving Joe's own family, the murder of his sister Ellie, a few years before he became a lawyer. Her death was a shadow over Joe's life, and for that he owed her, even though the investigation had come to nothing in the end.

She was holding a piece of paper in her hand, a small sticky note.

'Morning, Gina,' he said. 'What have you got?'

'Just had a call from the cells at court. One of the prisoners wants to transfer to us.'

Joe grimaced. Cell swaps were usually a waste of time. Those who had their bail refused at the custody desk often lashed out, and sometimes against the law firm who had left them there.

'Who did he have for his interviews?'

'Mahones.'

Joe raised an eyebrow and Gina smiled. 'I thought that would interest you more.'

'I smell trouble though. Why the swap?'

'I don't know, but there's only one way to find out.'

'Needs to be one hell of a good reason. Mahones don't give up their clients easily.'

'You're sounding more keen now.'

'You know how it works, but yes, I'm listening.'

'You'll be even more interested when I tell you what sort of case it is.'

'Go on.'

Gina passed over the note. 'It's a murder. And he wants you.'

Joe almost whistled. A murder. Mahones won't want to let that go, at any cost. Murder cases don't pay the best, because they don't have the page-count compared to a complex fraud case, where the volume of paperwork makes the bills a lot higher. A murder case is really just a bad assault case with one less witness, but they are highly prized as a boost to a firm's reputation. He looked at the note. There was just a name on it: Ronnie Bagley. 'Should I know him, if he wants me?'

'You'll have to ask him,' Gina said, and went to leave the room, pausing in the cloud of scent she trailed behind her. 'Maybe he's got a birthday card for you.'

Joe looked up. 'Thanks, Gina. You remembered.'

'Are you going to see your mother?'

'What, and spend the day suffocating slowly?' He lifted the piece of paper. 'I'll go once I've been to court.'

'Your sister hit her hard, Joe. Your father too. I was there, remember. It must be a rough day for her.'

Joe paused as he felt his mood slump, bad memories rushing at him. 'It is for me too, Gina. We have to fight it in our own way.'

Gina nodded at that and left the room.

Joe twirled in his chair once more and looked back towards the square. Monica was gone, now in the building somewhere, and the tai chi session was coming to an end. He turned away and caught his reflection in the glass of a framed picture on the wall – some Victorian judge, hung there to add gravitas. For a moment, Joe saw himself as others saw him. Suit, tie, cufflinks. A 'Lawyer'. Successful.

It was a façade, all of it. Joe had a secret, a darkness that he kept to himself. He fought against it, but there were times when it overpowered him.

He pressed his fingers to his temples. He had to shut it out for the next few hours. He had to go to court.

Three

Joe approached the City Magistrates Court, a high glass and red sandstone block at the back of Crown Square, once an open paved space that was the last dash of freedom for many, the Crown Court at the other end. Not anymore. The old magistrates court had been torn down and replaced by trendy shops and restaurants, so that the area had some big city vibrancy, providing the buzz for the lawyers and accountants and bankers, who sat outside and drank expensive coffees and ate overpriced granola bars.

It created a strange mix of defendants and high-flyers, side by side. A young couple walked past. She was skinny through addiction, in black dirty jeans and T-shirt. He was lean and muscled, in a white vest, tattoos on his arms, although his physique spoke more of threat than keep-fit. They brushed past two men in suits, large watches gleaming from their wrists, their clothes made to fit. They had a different type of swagger, confident and brash, meant to attract glances. The young couple stared and intimidated, designed to make people look away.

Monica was with him, walking quietly alongside. She couldn't do anything in the courtroom, not until her training contract was finished, but she could pass on messages, let ushers know when Joe would arrive, often double-booked in different courtrooms, or collect papers from prosecutors. It helped her face become known, so that when she qualified her early days as a lawyer were packed with fewer nerves. She had already done her time behind barristers in the more refined atmosphere of the Crown Court, making notes and understanding how it played out in the serious cases, but if she wanted to do criminal law it was the daily grind of the Magistrates Court that would keep her busy.

'So which area of law do you fancy when you qualify?' Joe said.

'I don't know,' Monica said. She tucked some stray hairs behind her ear, her other hand clutching a small briefcase that really served as a handbag. 'I like personal injury. And probate.'

Joe shook his head dismissively. 'Just paper shuffling. Crime is more fun.'

'Fun?'

'Yes, fun,' he said. 'No one chooses crime for the money, but you'll never be short of an anecdote. I could do with some help. Think about it.'

Monica smiled. 'Thank you. I will.'

She kept her smile until they walked into the Magistrates Court, where they queued behind defendants and their supporters to get past the security guards, even though they all knew Joe's name. Wearing a suit didn't help him jump any queues.

Monica looked at ease as she walked past the clusters of defendants, the usual crowds of deadbeats and hard-times, with their slumped shoulders and scowls, bad luck etched into the smoke-tinged lines on their faces and brown stubs of teeth. It was her presence that had attracted Joe to her when he first saw her around the office. She looked demure and poised in her dark suits and white blouses, always the same look, but Joe had noticed the green and red edge of a tattoo emerging from the collar of her blouse, along with the microdots of piercings that ran along the edges of her ears, the earrings left out for the day job. She would stand out and attract the punters. What good was one more grey suit?

They rode the escalator to the second floor, rising in the brightness made by the high glass roof and on to the open concourse, like a glitzy office complex, to where the lawyers from Mahones strutted around. It was one of the biggest firms in Manchester and it came with a status, so the eager young lawyers shook hands and flashed slick smiles, doing whatever they could to make their clients think that they were not really nice middle class kids whose legal career had dumped them in the bargain basement of law.

Joe pushed his way through the small crowd that blocked the entrance to the court cell complex, busy on a Monday morning. Young women talking to their boyfriends' lawyers, wanting to know when they would come home. A couple of reporters hoping to pick up on something, a case with an angle. Benefit fraud or illegal immigrants always sold well, but mostly it was just a sift through life's debris. Drink, drugs and violence – the dependable trinity of criminal law.

As he got closer to the door that led to the court cells, the Central Detention Centre, there was someone hovering outside with a Mahones file cover under his arm. Matt Liver. Thinning hair and narrow glasses, he thought being a lawyer was about the shine of his shoes.

Matt stiffened as Joe got closer.

'Morning, Matt,' Joe said. 'Looks like you lost one.'

'Ronnie isn't with you just yet.'

'So why are you here? I thought you'd be in court, putting in your legal aid form. You don't want anyone to swipe your client before you get your name on the court file.'

Matt's lips went tight at that.

Joe's eyes widened and he laughed. 'Didn't you get the forms signed? Old man Mahone won't like that, especially when Ronnie comes to me.'

Matt stepped closer. 'All weekend, Joe. I was there on Saturday night for him, and yesterday. Where were you then?'

'You need to get some more sleep,' Joe said. 'I can smell your tiredness on your breath.'

Before Matt could respond, Joe tapped on the window next to the door that led to the cells. As it slid open, Joe smiled at the wide man in the white shirt, a chain hanging from his belt loop. 'I've come to see Ronnie Bagley.'

'Hello, Joe. He's been waiting for you.'

The door buzzed and Joe and Monica went through. Matt tried to follow, but Joe put his hand out. 'Don't demean yourself. I'll tell the old man you did your best.'

Matt was swearing as the door closed, the final click of the electronic lock bringing welcome silence.

The guard turned round to say, 'He's been getting pretty worked up.'

'What, Matt?' Joe said. 'He needs to learn that it's just a job. He'll never make partner at Mahones.'

'Is that why you left?'

Joe didn't answer that. The reason for his leaving was nothing to do with his career path. Instead, he passed over a legal aid form. 'Can you get Ronnie to sign that in the usual place, Ken?'

'No problem,' he replied.

It wasn't protocol, but Joe knew who to keep on his side. The ones who transported the prisoners around were the people who might mention his name to those who didn't have a lawyer. Bottles of whiskey at Christmas, and he made sure he knew their names.

Joe was shown to the kiosk in the corner, where he squeezed in with Monica. Her perfume filled the small space, the view ahead an empty chair behind a glass screen.

'I've never met a murderer before,' Monica said, her voice quiet.

'We don't know if he is one yet.'

Monica pursed her lips. 'But if the police think he murdered someone, there must be some good reason?'

'We are lawyers. It's about proof, about evidence. You'll learn to rationalise it; we all find our own ways. Just don't become one of those lawyers who take sides, because often they can't see where the line is, so get dragged over to the wrong side and become just a crook's lackey. I do things I shouldn't, but it's all about knowing which ones will come back to bite. Be nice but keep your distance, because most of them would sell you out if they get into trouble.'

Monica's training session was brought to a halt by the sound of someone talking to the guards on the other side, and then a dishevelled man sat down in the chair on the other side of the glass. He had all the averages. Height, build, pale complexion and his hair short but not crewcut, sticking up on top, the result of two nights on the vinyl mattress in a police cell.

'Ronnie Bagley, I'm Joe Parker. This is Monica Taylor.'

Ronnie rubbed his head. 'I know who you are, Mr Parker. I asked for you, remember.' His voice was tired and defeated. When Joe didn't respond, he said, 'What did you expect? Big smiles? I'm locked up for murder.'

'Okay, let's start again,' Joe said. He wouldn't take it from clients normally, but he could only guess at the stresses Ronnie was under. 'Tell me why you want me and not Mahones.'

'I thought I was getting you when I asked for Mahones.'

'I've left.'

'Yeah, I know that now. So what happens next?'

Joe considered Ronnie Bagley. He seemed angry, not nervous or scared, almost impatient to start the process. That wasn't usual for murder suspects. Most just wanted to tell everyone how innocent they were, even when it wasn't true. Joe started to notice other things. Ronnie clasped his right

12

palm with his left hand, his thumb rubbing all the time, betraying the nerves. There were tattoos between his finger and thumb, homemade, like small grey lines, just coloured scratches.

Ronnie scowled and, as Joe let the silence grow, he sat back and then hunched forward again, his body in perpetual motion. There was a rugged sort of handsomeness in his face somewhere, but it was being eroded by the knocks and bangs of life, his mouth showing the puckered lines of too many cig-arettes, his eyes sunken by dark rings.

'Nothing much will happen today,' Joe said. 'You'll go to prison tonight. Tomorrow, or probably the day after, a judge at the Crown Court will think about bail, but he won't grant it. Then you'll wait for your trial.'

Ronnie swallowed and looked down. 'Is it for definite I won't get bail?'

'Yes, because you're charged with murder.'

'Don't people accused of murder ever get bail?'

'Not usually. I'm not going to raise your hopes, Ronnie. I can tell you the truth or I can tell you what you want to hear, but the facts won't change.'

Ronnie kept his eyes on the floor and nodded, almost to himself, as if it was the news he had expected to hear. When he looked up again, his gaze shifted to Monica, who put her hair behind her ears again and shifted uncomfortably. 'And you are?'

'I'm Monica Taylor,' she said, clearing her throat. 'I'm the trainee.'

Joe tapped on the glass. 'Eyes this way, Ronnie,' he said, pointing to himself. 'Talk to me about your case. Who do they say you killed?'

Ronnie lingered on Monica for a few more seconds, and then said, 'My girlfriend, Carrie, and Grace, our daughter.'

Joe made a note of that, although it was really just to

take it in. His own child. 'What did you tell the police?' Joe said.

'I didn't say anything to them. Why should I? There aren't any bodies. If there aren't any bodies, how can I be guilty of murder?'

Four

So now it was all about the waiting. He put his head back against the wall. It was cold.

The uncertainty ahead was the hardest part. Was he doing the right thing? He was doing it for the right reason, for love, but what if it was the wrong way? There had been thrills, he knew that, but he had to stop it all. It was out of control.

But quiet moments made him think back; there were so many memories to keep him occupied, and his mind drifted back to the first one.

The first time had been his selection. That had been the promise when he agreed.

He had seen her coming out of the hairdressers, a small salon opposite the blackened walls that ran alongside the railway station, permanently in the shadow of what was once a high grassy outcrop, now scarred by millstone cottages and the slow climb that led to the top part of the town. She was brightness against the dark, somehow wasted in the gloom.

Her hair had been just how he liked it, long and straight, not kinked and spoiled by chemicals and colour. It was as it was meant to be, natural and soft, although the tips had been severe, so that he could almost see the clip of the scissors. He had tried to resist, because he had promised himself he would, but he couldn't, the urge was too strong. It started as a whisper, but then it turned into a growl, so that his head felt tight, blood coursing around his skull so that he had to release the pressure.

So he had walked behind her. All he could hear was the brush of her hair against the nylon of her top, just soft crackles, swaying from side to side, mesmerising, hypnotic. He moved to the other side of the pavement whenever she paused to look in a shop window or check her phone, worried that he had been spotted, but it had only ever been about her reflection. She had flicked at her fringe, her hair cut straight across and long down the sides, so that it framed her face.

He remembered the coldness of the scissors, small in his pocket and tight around his fingers, but he could keep them concealed in his hand right up until they were slicing across their target. So his fingers went into the grips, ready, just hoping that the chance would arise. A busy shop, or perhaps a bump on the street, his hands quick, like a pickpocket.

Then she had stopped. His heart had drummed in his chest. She was at a bus stop. The perfect way.

He stopped next to her. She hadn't noticed him.

When the bus came, he listened to where she was going and got a ticket to take him further. He would see where she went.

The seat behind her had been vacant, and so he slid in behind her. Her hair had hung over the edge of the seat and, as the bus rocked, he watched it move in front of him, his breaths like quick gasps, his mouth dry. No one behind him, just an old woman in front, but she wasn't looking. She wouldn't remember him.

So he had pulled the scissors out of his pocket. They were his tools, short and sharp, oiled so that they made no sound, the blades keen so that there was no pull. Just one quick, clean cut.

As they came to a stop, her hair had stopped moving. His hand reached up, the scissors ready, his other hand underneath, ready to catch.

It had taken just one snip, the blades coming together, and an inch-wide strip of hair fell into his hand, soft and light, just tickles on his fingers. He clenched his fist and felt the strands in his grip.

He remembered how his vision had blurred, the need to get home, to spend time alone with it, but then she had flicked her hair and everything had seemed to move more slowly, the long strands swaying like the slow waft of a curtain in the breeze, because he had seen it, just a glimpse, but enough. It was the soft nape of her neck, where her hair was softest, those fine hairs almost like down.

He had leaned forward. It had been a risk, because she might feel his breaths on her neck, but he had to get closer. He loved short hair, bob-style, but high at the back, so that he could imagine the hairdresser's clippers buzzing over skin, sending hair to the floor, tumbling off the back of the chair, the bristles soft against his fingers. Short hair made it too difficult though, because he might nick the skin and so draw attention to himself and his scissors. The clippings he collected were a consolation, because it was the nearest thing he could get without touching.

Her nape had made it harder to think clearly.

She stood up to get off the bus. Her top crackled as her hair swished across it, clean and gleaming, flowing down her back and then swaying with the soft rock of her hips, although not all of it stayed neat. There were those small strands that rubbed against the shoulders, static making it dance. He wanted more. He had watched her as she got off the bus, as she turned into a long street of stone houses. There were only open fields at the end, so that meant she must live on the street.

That had been the moment when he had known he would go further, because he had her hair and knew where she lived.

She had been the first one.

Five

The scene at the court corridor was the usual one: blank faces waiting around for their hearings, sitting on stained blue chairs bolted to the floor as prosecutors made their way past with laptops under their arms. Most of the defence lawyers were young, with their firms emblazoned across the top of their files, instructed to hold them so that the firm's name was visible, so that they acted like a sandwich board, free advertising.

Monica trailed behind him as Joe moved towards the courtroom. Joe let the conversations in the corridor wash over him, defendants reliving whatever had brought them to the court, although their lawyers would repackage and sanitise the stories and pack them full of remorse, ready for the courtroom. He scanned the faces quickly, just to check if there were any clients he recognised, particularly old clients from Mahones. It didn't take much to get them to swap; sometimes just a bottle of cheap sherry, but there was no one who looked familiar.

'So what happens now?' Monica said, her voice almost a whisper.

'We get the papers from the prosecution and then later we go see him in prison. All Ronnie has got now is a long wait to find out what happens to the rest of his life.'

The chatter faded as Joe pushed at the door and the courtroom hush took over. Rows of wood-effect desks ran towards the front of the room, stopped by the raised platform used by the magistrates, justice dispensed from below the court crest. The lion and the unicorn. The Royal Standard. *Dieu et Mon Droit*. Defence solicitors filled the desks. Some were talking. Others were reading their files or doing the crossword. Joe groaned. It looked like there was a queue. He checked his watch. He had somewhere he needed to be.

He thought for a moment of leaving, not wanting to be delayed, but Ronnie's case was too important. The darkness came back over him, like a sudden swamp of his mood, because he knew what would come later in the day, when the memories flooded him and the secret he had carried for fifteen years rose to the surface once more. But that was for later. Ronnie was the here and now.

He gestured for Monica to sit at the back as he went to speak to the prosecutor. When he saw it was Kim Reader, he smiled. Kim was an old friend from law college, although they had once been more than that, a couple of drunken nights bringing them together. Her expression was weary as she turned round, expecting another bout of moans from a defence lawyer, but when she saw it was Joe, her face brightened.

'Joe Parker,' she said. 'It's good to see you.'

'Yeah, you too. What are you doing here? I thought you played around in the big courts now.'

'I've got a murder case and so I'm keeping hold of it, except that I get the rest of the list too,' and she grimaced and pointed to a tablet computer on a lectern, the morning's cases loaded on and ready to be presented, next to a small pile of white file covers, the overnighters.

'Ronnie Bagley?' Joe said. 'He's mine.'

Her eyes widened. 'You've got that one?' She turned round and nodded at two people sitting on the seats at the side of court, a man and a woman. Detectives, Joe guessed. It was obvious from the way they were dressed. Pastel shirts, well-pressed, and clean suits. Lawyers went for either well-worn or expensive pin-stripes.

They got up and walked over, their identification swinging from blue ribbons around their necks.

'DI Evans,' the woman said, smiling, although Joe could see it was forced. For now, he was the enemy.

The man behind said, 'DS Bolton,' and held out his hand to shake. Joe took it, even though he knew why it was being done, to try to make him grimace, to admire the firmness.

'Inspector, good morning,' Joe said.

'I thought Bagley was with Mahones?' Evans said.

'Not any more.'

'I'm not surprised. They told him to stay quiet, but if he had something to say, he should have said it. He might not have been charged.'

'So you'll believe whatever he says, Inspector?' Joe said, mock surprise on his face. 'If you want, he'll say how he didn't do it and you can let him out.'

Evans flushed at Joe's sarcasm. Before she was able to reply, a door opened at the side of court and the magistrates walked in – two pensioners in suits and a young woman too glammed up for a courtroom. Everyone rose and gave their ritual bow, and then the court was filled with the noise of a key jangling in a lock. Joe turned towards the back of the courtroom and looked at the dock. A bedraggled man in his fifties appeared behind the toughened glass screen, handcuffed to a security guard, the first overnight drunk of the day, his sweatshirt and jogging bottoms showing the rigours of a night in a cell.

As the court clerk started to speak, to check the man's name and date of birth, Joe realised that he needed Ronnie Bagley, just for a distraction from the everyday trawls through broken lives.

He went to sit down, but as he did, he saw the detectives talking in whispers, nodding, staring over at him. They stood to go and, as they left the courtroom, Joe got the unerring sense that his involvement in the case had somehow become more important.

Six

Joe looked up at his mother's house and his fingers gripped the steering wheel a little tighter.

From the outside, the house was a quiet semi-detached with large windows and a small garden wall, a driveway running towards a garage with a battered wooden door. He knew what it would be like inside: birthday banners, cakes, family fun. Except that it was all faked, all designed to keep up the façade that everything was fine, that they were a happy family. Only those in the family knew how deeply fractured they had been by Ellie's murder. His father sank into a depression that he never got over and sought comfort in a bottle. A stroke ended his life five years later. Joe's mother had carried on the drinking where he left off, and since then the house had started to decay.

His parents had bought the house from the council at the height of a property boom, expecting it to be an investment, but they'd never had the income to maintain it. The other ones on the street received the regular touch-ups from the council, but his mother's house had grass growing from the gutters, so that water poured out when it rained, and window frames that were starting to look rotten, the paint almost gone. He had tried to get her to hire a decorator, had even turned up himself one day with a paintbrush, but she hadn't wanted anything touching. It was as if she couldn't stand the thought of moving on, even though there was Ruby to consider.

The concern for the house was for a different day. What was waiting for him in it was part of the charade, and so he got ready to smile, to pretend that he didn't want to be another year older, the number forever getting bigger. But it's what they did, the Parker family. They celebrated everything together, as if they would somehow fall apart if they didn't join together for the big events.

It was more than that, though. It was about Ellie. Every day since then had been about his sister.

The memories came back, and they hurt, as always, the dark blanket ready to smother him. His birthday was always about holding back the grief. He had expected the steady roll of time to take away some of the pain, but instead it had become magnified. It was his own fault, because he fought to keep her memory alive and felt angry when he thought he was about to forget and move on.

He glanced in the rear-view mirror. He had to be ready, best smile, but he knew that whenever he walked into the family home, the grief seemed as raw as it had been back then. Especially on his birthday, the anniversary of when she died.

No, that was wrong. It wasn't as clinical as that. She hadn't died. She had been killed. Cold and brutal.

He shouldn't dwell on it though. His diary had been kept light, because it was the same every year, his birthdays following a pattern, as his mother tried to make it a celebration, despite knowing the day wouldn't stay like that.

The day was warm as he stepped out of the car. Manchester was damp too often, plagued by grey skies from whatever rain Ireland hadn't managed to soak up. This was one of those rare late-spring days, when the birds sang and the Pennine hills that loomed over the city seemed to glow rather than brood. The metal gate let out a clink as he opened it, and as he walked up the drive and the twin tracks of paving slabs along the side of the house, his sister, Ruby, appeared at the window. She waved. He waved back and then got his best smile ready as he saw her outline through the glass in the door.

Ruby was all teenage excitement and long limbs. At just thirteen, there was a large gap between them.

'Happy birthday,' she squealed, and then planted a kiss on his cheek. 'I thought you were never going to arrive.'

'How could I miss this?' he said, and laughed, despite himself.

She led the way, pulling on his hand, and as he got into the house he was assaulted by the sights and smells of his childhood: the aroma of home-baking coming from the kitchen, the holiday kitsch ornaments on a shelf next to the television: an ashtray from Malta, a bell from Spain, some shot glasses from various places in Scotland. There were photos of him and his brother on the mantelpiece, along with pictures of Ellie, his first baby sister.

He focused on Ellie's picture. His birthday celebration was always early, the morning for him, because the rest of the day was for Ellie. She had died on his eighteenth birthday, raped and strangled and left in undergrowth not far from her school. So every birthday he had was about Ellie, and so they had to get him out of the way first.

It struck him how much Ruby was like Ellie. It was the way she smiled, sort of mischievous, a glint to her eyes, her tooth biting her lip. It took him by surprise sometimes. He felt that kick of sadness and had to remind himself that Ruby was her own person, wasn't just a substitute for the sister he had lost.

'You made it then?'

It was his brother, Sam.

'It is my party,' Joe said, as he turned around. 'I'm supposed to be late. It's fashionable.'

Sam flickered a smile. 'Happy birthday, brother.'

He was a detective, although he wasn't like most Joe knew. Sam was quiet and thoughtful, slim, with his hair neat and short, but he was nervy, his eyes shielded by glasses. He was the family conscience, the one who tried to keep everyone together, as if life was a series of obligations. So on birthdays, holidays, and sometimes just because there was a good weather forecast, the same small group was asked to turn out and mumble at each other.

'Yeah, thanks,' Joe said. 'Where's Mum?'

'In the back room, fixing food. You know how it is. Just let her stay busy.'

'What time are you going to the cemetery?'

'Aren't you coming?'

Joe sighed. It was the same old argument. 'I'm working.'

Sam didn't say anything at first. He glowered for a few seconds, cricked his neck, and then said, 'It wouldn't hurt one year. Just for Mum.'

Joe stepped closer, so Ruby couldn't hear him, and spoke in a whisper. 'I think of Ellie all the time, but I prefer to think of her in happier times, like when it's her birthday, not on the day she died. I want to remember her for the right things, not how it ended.'

'That's bullshit.'

Before Joe could respond, his mother came into the room, a plate of sandwiches in her hand. As she put them down next to the sausage rolls and scotch eggs, the plate rattled against the table. The shake to her hand was getting worse.

Her smile was weak as she came towards him. Joe could tell she was trying too hard. He had to lean down to let her put a kiss to his cheek. Her lips felt cold, and she trembled more than she used to.

'Don't you look handsome,' she said, taking his hand, her fingers cold and brittle in his. 'My youngest boy, thirty-three. Who would have thought it? It makes me feel old.'

'Worry when you start to look it,' he said, making her laugh.

It was a lie, they both knew it, but it made her feel better.

For years, he thought she hadn't changed. Her style hadn't altered – skirts and jumpers. Her hair was still cut short and only the colour had changed, as the grey started to take over before being replaced by a series of light browns. Some looked natural, others didn't. Now she was starting to look like the woman she would become. Older, more frail. There were broken veins under her eyes and her cheeks were acquiring a permanent flush. Joe knew it was the booze, but there was no point in saying anything. She drank to reach oblivion when she needed it, and Joe knew that his birthdays were always the toughest. She put herself under pressure to make it a good day for him, even though he had told her often that it didn't matter. But if they didn't do this it would become solely about Ellie, and she needed the drink to get her through the day.

'Come this way,' Ruby said, interrupting, pulling him to a chair by the fire. Even though it was May and warm outside, the fire was on a low heat.

He let Ruby lead him, and sat there as they sang him 'Happy Birthday'. Joe did his best to look cheerful, for Ruby's sake, and then Ruby disappeared to bring in the small pile of presents. He made a show of delight as he unwrapped them, laughing at the jokes on the cards, expressing all the right amount of gratitude for each gift. Shirt, a mug, beer and socks.

'Happy birthday,' his mother said, and a tear rolled down her cheek.

'I've got to go soon,' Joe said, and then winced at the hurt that flashed across her eyes for a second. He wished he could take the words back, but they were out now.

'So which low-life is more important than your family today?' Sam said.

'It sounds like you're the one who's still on duty,' Joe said, sighing. 'Try not being a copper for a day. You might like it.'

'Go on, tell me how they're just people, like you and me.'

'Let's not have this conversation again.'

'I've seen how your clients really are, when they're spitting and snarling in their handcuffs. You get the cleaned-up version, when they're pleading for bail or whatever.'

'They *are* still people.'

'Don't fight, boys.' It was their mother.

They both smiled at her, trying to make it out like it was all a joke, just a brotherly wrestle, except that the passing years had made it more verbal than physical.

'His work is more important,' Sam said.

'Joe's work *is* important,' she said. 'I'm very proud of him.'

Sam clenched his jaw. He locked them up, Joe set them free, but in her world success was measured by the price of your suit, not the good work that you did.

'I'll call in later, I promise,' Joe said.

His mother's smile was even more forced. She knew he was avoiding the graveyard trip.

Sam's phone rang. He turned away as he answered but Joe listened in anyway.

'I'm not working today,' Sam said. He listened, and then his voice seemed to raise a notch when he said, 'I'll be there as soon as I can.'

When he turned back around Joe said, 'What is it?'

Sam looked back at his phone and said, 'I've got to go in. They want to speak to me about a murder case.'

'I thought you were on the financial unit?'

'I am,' Sam said.

'So why a murder?'

'I don't know.'

Joe didn't get an answer when he reached for a sandwich and said, 'It's not good when work gets in the way, is it?'

Seven

Sam Parker checked his tie in the rear-view mirror and straightened it, but it just became more twisted than before. He straightened it again, so that it ended up how it had started. Sam didn't feel ready to go in so soon after visiting Ellie's grave, but an inspector on the Murder Squad had summoned him. He couldn't ignore it. The Murder Squad wasn't the official name, it was now the Major Incident Team, but Sam knew that the egos preferred the old moniker.

He looked up at the building. Stanmoss police station was old and built in redbrick with wings at either end. Rings of sandstone wrapped around it, so that it looked like it was wrapped in gold, although it looked jaded, with the brickwork bearing decades of traffic fumes like fatigue.

Try to stay calm, he told himself, it might be nothing. But if a murder case needed a financial investigation, this could be his opportunity to impress.

It would be better on a different day though. All through his career he had worked towards this moment, a brief glimpse into the Murder Squad, but the memory of the cemetery took away any sense of satisfaction. Ellie was always there, the little sister he had last seen as he went to university that day. A clingy, cute fifteen-year-old, snatched away from her life by someone who cared about it so little. It was corny, he knew it, but Ellie needed someone to fight for justice. And not just for

27

her, but the people like her, the ones who left their homes but never made it back.

One more deep breath. Whatever this involved, it was just another case. Murders and frauds are the same. It's about what stands out as unusual, a change from the routine. A different spending pattern, or a different route to work.

Sam had done his share of frauds. They were a lot of effort for not much reward. People went to jail, but not for long. Sometimes it felt like it was worth it, like when a pursuit of the paper trail led to houses bought by laundered money, so the fraudster lost his gains. But most of the time it was just people trying to work out ways to provide money for gambling, or to entertain the women they had lied to about their money. Perhaps this was his chance to get involved with something bigger, the reason why he had joined the police. This was for Ellie.

He jumped at the sound of his phone. The screen said it was a withheld number. He thought about not answering, because he guessed it was the call he had been getting for a few weeks, but it was the number he gave out to witnesses so he knew he had to answer.

'Hello, DC Sam Parker.'

There was a pause, and for a moment he thought it might be an automated message, a promise of compensation if he had ever tripped or had a car crash. But it wasn't. The sounds came as they always did. A struggle, cries, muffled grunts of exertion, and then the sound of a scream, cut short by a slap and followed by sobs.

He clicked it off and thrust the phone back into his pocket. His guess was that it was the soundtrack from some post-midnight horror film, because it was recorded. He put it down to being a detective, being targeted by people who hadn't enjoyed his work. He had seized a lot of dirty money from a lot of bad people, and some of them got angry.

The calls weren't every day, but they came in flurries, so that he might go for a few days without a call, and then he would receive four or five a day for a few days, the message never changing.

Sam let the sun perk him back up as he stepped out of the car, and then checked his appearance again in the reflection as he walked slowly towards the front door. His suit was grey and sharp – he'd gone home to get changed – with a cornflower blue shirt and dark blue tie. It made it look like he was going for a job interview, but that was how he felt.

The door echoed as it closed and he roamed high-ceilinged corridors lit by dirty strip-lights, the covers filled with dirt and dust, the radiators thick with years of paint. He was looking for something that resembled an Incident Room, but most of the rooms seemed empty, used as storerooms, with boxes piled high and desks dismantled, ready to be taken away. As he walked, he started to think that someone was playing a joke on him, but then he heard soft mumbles of conversation. He followed the noise, and as he turned a corner he saw an open door ahead. The shirts and ties visible ahead told him that he had found the Murder Squad.

Sam swallowed as he got closer, and as he tapped on the door, everyone turned to look.

The room was filled with desks in clusters, screens flickering on each one, casting blue reflections over files and notebooks. There were bits of paperwork stuck to the wall and on white noticeboards, with dates and names scrawled on in green.

No one spoke, so Sam said, 'I'm DC Parker. I'm here to see DI Evans.'

Everyone looked towards the back of the room, to a woman speaking on the telephone. She glanced up at him and then carried on with her conversation, so he took in what was around him. There were posters on each wall of four teenagers, two of them not even eighteen. He recognised them because they were posted in every police station in the county. In the Incident Room, they felt more prominent, alongside more pictures and larger images from the posters.

The sounds in the room seemed to recede as he got closer to them, to look more carefully, the chatter replaced by that crushing sadness whenever he thought of what the families must be enduring. Four young women from different parts of Manchester, with no connection between them that had been made public, and all of them missing, presumed dead. The last woman went missing two months earlier. There must be a pattern. It was just a question of seeing it.

But they were all so very different. Two of them were white, one of them tall and redheaded, the other brunette, her hair long and curly. There was a young black girl, only fifteen, although the flirt to her smile made her seem older, along with an Indian girl, the dark lushness of her hair giving a glow to her photograph. What weren't people seeing?

There were footsteps behind him. DI Evans. He turned to her. She was small and petite, with short grey hair and some steel to her smile.

'Sam Parker?'

'Yes,' he said, and when he saw the slight flare of the nostrils, he added, 'ma'am.'

'I'm Mary Evans,' she said. 'Call me Mary in here. I'm glad you could make it.'

'I know, I'm sorry,' he said, guessing that he had already taken too long. 'I'm on a rest day.'

'You're here now. Follow me.'

She walked past him and led him away from the Incident Room, along the corridor to a smaller room that seemed to serve as her office. There was a dirty coffee cup and a framed picture of a young woman. The office looked temporary though, because there were lever arch folders in a pile by a cabinet that were browned with age, as if she'd had to clear out the remnants of the previous occupant before she could use the room. The papers on her desk were strewn around, and he had to fight the urge to reach over and stack them neatly, so that she would find it easier to read them.

'Sit down,' Evans said, pointing to a chair that looked on the verge of collapse, the legs starting to splay. It swayed beneath him as he sat down.

She stared at him for a few seconds, and he fought the urge to shuffle in his seat. 'Is it about the four missing women?' he said, and pointed to the room next door. 'I saw all the posters.'

'No, it isn't,' she said. 'Have you heard of Ronnie Bagley?'

Sam's mind flicked through the files in the cabinet next to his desk, picturing it like an address book, a list of names, and then when he came up with nothing he tried to skim through all the villains and wasters he had dealt with through the years. Finally he shook his head. 'No, ma'am. It doesn't sound familiar.'

'He is to your brother.'

Sam was confused. 'Joe?'

'Yes, Joe Parker. He's a defence lawyer, right?'

'Yes. Used to be with Mahones. With Honeywells now.' He frowned. 'What does this have to do with me?'

Evans hesitated before she spoke, staring at Sam, as if she was trying to unsettle him, remind him who was in charge.

'I want you to get some information from him,' she said eventually.

'In relation to what?'

'One of his clients.'

Sam's eyes widened. 'You want me to spy on my brother?'

'That's one way of putting it.'

Sam exhaled loudly. He wasn't sure he was going to enjoy the rest of the conversation.

Eight

Joe had collected Monica from the office and driven straight to the prison. He made small talk on the way, to take his mind from all the reminders of Ellie's death, and it worked. Monica was filled with all the eagerness he'd once had as a lawyer starting out, and he enjoyed the bounce of her conversation, her ready smile.

Strangeways took the shine away, with its high walls and old redbrick core. It was no longer the prison it had once been, when the cramped conditions and constant lock-up ended up with the prisoners taking it over for twenty-five days, but still it made for a brooding shadow on a major route into the city. The layout was like spokes on a bike wheel and on the outside it had been given a modern look, clad in bright new bricks and with a visitors' centre by the main road. That was all gloss however, because behind the high walls there were still remnants of the Victorian gloom. The tower and those parts of the prison furthest away from the main gate still showed its history, of executions and riots, through chipped and scarred redbrick.

Joe didn't do as many prison visits as he used to, as Gina took care of those, but he had learned the hard way that he had to ignore most things said to him when speaking to a captive prisoner. A client once told him that he wanted to plead guilty, the bars and the locks making him want to do anything to get out. The prosecutor was informed and the witnesses were told to stay at home. After a weekend with amateur lawyers on the prison wing, the client changed his mind. Joe lost a client and earned the scorn of the judge. Lawyers make mistakes all the time. The good ones don't make the same one twice.

This time was different. The visit to see Ronnie Bagley wasn't just about getting his story, but about keeping him as a client. Ronnie had already walked out on the first firm in the case. Joe didn't want Ronnie to walk out on him too.

'It's a horrible place,' Monica said, staring up at the walls. 'It's always the part of the bus journey I hate most, whenever I come into town.'

Joe looked at her. He didn't know if it was the aesthetics she found objectionable, or the thought of people being locked up.

'You better get used to it,' he said. 'You'll see inside it often enough.' He smiled. 'Enjoy the human drama – there aren't many who get something they don't deserve. There isn't much innocence in the courts; just different shades of guilt.'

They stayed silent through the security checks and a trip through a scanner, the stern glares of the guards ensured that, and then they were led upstairs to the section set aside for legal visits.

There were two rows of glass kiosks. Lawyers didn't have to endure the noise of the main visitor centre, where partners and children tried to squeeze a week's worth of conversation into an hour, but they weren't trusted enough to have complete privacy. The guards had a good view of whatever went on in the lawyers' kiosks. Not that Joe could blame them. He knew many defence lawyers who played it straight, but he knew too many who were prepared to do whatever it took to keep their clients on their books; after all, the drugs have to find their way into prison somehow.

Joe drummed his fingers on the table. A young woman walked past in a short skirt, a file under her arm. She was from Mahones. There was a whole team of them just like her, pretty and young, whose only role was to follow a barrister around. They didn't know much about the law, but their clients went back to their cell with a greater glow than Joe could provide.

'What are you going to say to Ronnie Bagley?' Monica said.

'I'm going to get his story.'

'Do we know anything about the case yet?'

'I've been given the paperwork, and I've read the summary, but I want to hear what he has to say before I read the detail. Let's get his story and see if it stacks up with the evidence.'

'Is this the normal way? I thought we'd be going through the statements, because don't the prosecution have to prove the case?'

'The problem with murder cases is that they never go away,' Joe said. 'People don't just serve a bit of time and then every-one moves on. Families have still lost someone. A prisoner still bears that guilt of taking someone's life. Or at least the stigma, knowing how people hate him. So they get appealed and examined, and when you have long forgotten about it, it will end up in the Court of Appeal, your mistakes being picked over. The things you overlooked, the enquiries you didn't make. One of the first things they will try is poor representation, and he will blame me for putting the words into his mouth that convicted him. So let's hear his story first.'

Before Monica could say anything further, a door opened at the end of the room and a prison guard walked towards them. There was someone walking behind him. Ronnie Bagley. His eyes darted around, his shoulders hunched, as if he was trying to make himself small, inconspicuous almost. No one wanted to stand out on the first day in prison. Joe saw the fear in his eyes as he got closer. There was no threat or danger from him, although Joe wasn't sure why he was surprised by that. He had seen enough murderers to know that there is no type. Sometimes the calmer the person, the more threat there is, because real evil doesn't shout its presence.

The guard opened the kiosk door. Ronnie nodded his thanks to the guard and sat down at the table.

'How are you doing, Ronnie?' Joe asked.

'Not good,' he said, and shook his head. 'There's a presentation later today, like an induction. What's the point? Just put me in the cell and leave me alone.'

'Stay strong,' Joe said. 'We need to start getting your case ready. I've spoken to the court listing office and got them to list your case tomorrow, and so I need to know everything by then.'

'Why bother?' Ronnie said.

'Because the only other choice you have is giving in. You haven't got time for the self-pity. You've got to see me as your only friend, because no one else will give a damn about you. So you have to talk to me. Don't let this place swallow you up.'

Ronnie clenched his jaw as he considered that. 'The looks I get, from the guards, it's like they don't think much of me.' His eyes filled with tears. 'I didn't kill them. I didn't kill anyone. But I won't get out, will I?'

'You're charged with murder. If you want my opinion, you'll be going nowhere until the trial is over.'

'And you're going to go back to your swanky apartment and let me spend another night in a prison bed. I didn't do it.'

'That's the law, Ronnie. I didn't make it.' Joe picked up his pen and made a show of clicking it on. 'So why do people think you did it?'

'I'm the obvious one, I suppose, but how can they even know that I've murdered anyone when there aren't any bodies? There has to be a dead body for a murder, right?'

Joe shook his head. 'No, there doesn't. So tell me your story. I need to know everything.'

Nine

'Does that bother you, spying on your brother?' Evans said.

Sam almost laughed. Yes, it bothered him. He pushed his glasses further up his nose. 'I know you won't like what he does, because he helps criminals,' Sam said. 'But tapping him for information? That seems, well, not right.'

'I'll tell you what isn't right, Sam, and that is people like Ronnie Bagley walking away from killing his girlfriend and his child. Why? Because someone like your brother will devote his life to making sure that killers like him escape justice.'

Sam understood her, and he'd had the same argument with Joe, but they were brothers, and Sam wasn't going to talk him down.

'It's Joe's life, not mine. We've talked about it, but he's proud of what he does. I'm proud of him, ma'am, in my own way. He's made a good life for himself.'

'But?'

'I don't know what you mean.'

'I sensed a "but" in there.'

Sam paused as he thought about that, and then said, 'I'm proud of who he is. I just wish he had chosen a different path as a lawyer. A prosecutor, or something like that.'

'So you try to lock them up, and he tries to get them out.'

'Something like that.'

'I want to change that,' Evans said. 'I've come across your

36

brother too many times, and you can be as loyal as you like, but he thinks different rules apply to him.' Sam was about to say something, but Evans raised her hand to stop him. 'I know, defence lawyers do that, but he goes further.'

'But what has this got to do with me?'

Evans leaned forward. 'Ronnie Bagley is a murderer. He killed his girlfriend and his baby. He attacked them in their flat and then somehow got rid of the bodies. We can't find them. He must have killed his daughter to make it look like his girlfriend had run away. We've managed to get the CPS to charge it but, like us, they know the case will be a hell of a lot stronger if we find the bodies.'

'You've got a murder case without bodies?'

'Yes, and so you see how important it is that we find them. You don't want Ronnie to walk free just because he's buried them well, do you?'

Sam closed his eyes for a moment as he felt the slow rise of disappointment, that this was nothing to do with him but all about Joe. 'So what do you want me to do?' he said, his voice quiet. He knew where this was leading, and he didn't like it.

'We thought Bagley was represented by Mahones,' Evans said. 'But then your brother turned up this morning to represent him.'

'How do you know that?'

'We were there. And your brother is with him now, at the prison.'

Sam pressed his fingers tightly against his forehead. His disappointment was replaced by anger, because that was why Joe couldn't attend the cemetery, because he had to go see a murderer.

'We can make our case better, Sam, through you, because you give us access to Bagley's lawyer. We need to find the bodies.'

Sam shook his head. 'Joe won't tell me anything.'

'So he's the one with the scruples, not you?'

'I don't understand.'

'You said that he wouldn't tell you, when I thought you might have said that you wouldn't ask him.'

'That isn't fair, ma'am.'

'Neither is being murdered in your flat, along with your baby daughter. You must know how to get him to talk. Perhaps you've just never asked the right questions.'

'But spying on my own brother?'

'All lawyers talk, especially to other lawyers and cops,' she said. 'They think they're in safe territory, because everyone has war stories.' When Sam looked down, she leaned forward again, her voice softer. 'I know it's difficult, but remember your loyalties. Do you think you should be more loyal to your brother's client or to the force? To the victim?'

Sam looked up. 'So this is all you brought me here for, to ask this?'

'What do you mean?'

'I thought you wanted me on the team, that you were going to get me transferred to this unit.'

'Is that what you want?'

'It's what I've always wanted. But not like this.'

Evans sat back again. She paused, her eyes narrowing, until she said, 'You can't be on it officially.'

'What do you mean?'

'Think about it. What if Ronnie Bagley is found not guilty and it becomes common knowledge that his brief's brother was on the squad? We'd get crucified.'

'So what am I?'

'Just a detective ready to report anything you hear, that's all.' She pulled out a small silver tin from the top pocket of her jacket. She clicked it open and took out a business card. She handed it over. 'Call me if you hear something. Whatever it is, if he mentions Ronnie Bagley, I want to know what he says.'

Sam turned the card over in his hand. 'And if I say no?'

'You're just a detective who'll get a black mark on his report card. Don't be that person, Sam. Think of your own career.'

He stared at her, disbelieving, but she met his stare. At that, Sam got to his feet. He tried to control the anger in his voice. 'Am I excused, ma'am?'

'As long as we understand each other.'

He nodded. 'We do.'

As he headed out of the room, he glanced along the corridor to the Incident Room. No one looked his way. He wasn't part of their world.

He turned away, his cheeks flushed and red, his footsteps quicker than before, his hand banging against the doors as he headed out to his car.

Ten

Ronnie Bagley looked at his hands, one thumb rubbing at his palm. When he looked up again, he said, 'No one knows if they're dead. How can I have murdered them if they might be alive somewhere? I mean, just because they've accused me of murder doesn't mean that I've got to be found guilty.'

Joe pursed his lips. The lack of bodies didn't stop a murder case, but it made it a whole lot harder to prove.

'Juries like mysteries, especially murders,' Joe said. 'It means they can play detective and solve the case. But this isn't a burglary or a pub fight. The prosecution thinks two people have died. If the jury thinks the same, they'll want to catch the killer. If I can't prove that you aren't the killer, you will be convicted.'

'I thought I was innocent until proven guilty.'

'This isn't legal theory; it's about how juries work. They're just people, like you and me, and they don't like to see a killer walk free. It will take a lot for you to get a not guilty verdict. So talk to me. Go back to the last day you saw Carrie alive.'

Ronnie took a deep breath and swallowed. He looked nervous, but Joe wasn't sure if it was due to his memories of the day, or because this was his chance, his rehearsal for the trial, to see if he could convince someone of his innocence.

Joe glanced at Monica, who was sitting forward, and he could sense her excitement at her first involvement with a big case.

'Carrie was shouting at me,' Ronnie said, wiping his eye. 'Carrie did that a lot. We live in a flat, on the ground floor of some dump of a place. I had a job, but it was hard to make the money stretch. And Carrie drank a lot. Too much really, even though we had a baby.'

'Had?'

'What?'

'Past tense, Ronnie. You mean *have*.'

'You know what I mean,' he said, his cheeks becoming red.

'And so will the jury, because the prosecution will ram that at you all day. It will be the word they use in the closing speeches, and the jury won't forget it. They'll see it as you knowing that Carrie and Grace are dead, just a small detail and slip-up that gets you locked up for life.'

Ronnie nodded that he understood and said, 'Our life is like one long argument. We were together because of Grace. Carrie didn't love me, I knew that.'

'*Doesn't*, Ronnie, not didn't.'

Ronnie scowled.

'And do you love her?' Joe said.

'More than I can say,' and then his voice broke. He used the heel of his palm to wipe his eyes. 'I wouldn't hurt her. She's everything to me. Pretty and fun and, well, you know ...'

'How old is she?'

'Thirty.'

'So tell me about the shouting.'

'It was just money stuff, you know how it is. Carrie was ...' He stopped, to correct himself. 'Carrie *is* crazy with money. She applies for any credit card she can and then just buys rubbish, like clothes and shoes and anything that makes people look at her, and so we had these credit card bills and food to buy, rent to pay. So that last morning, we had no money left on the electric card and she was telling me that I wasn't good enough, how it was all my fault that we don't have anything. But she was the one drinking all the time. It had got so that it was the first thing she did when she woke up, pour herself a drink. She had nice clothes but she looked a mess.'

'You don't like her much.'

'What do you mean?'

'You love her, but I'm not sure you like her much. Perhaps you even hate her.'

'Not enough to kill her.'

Joe scribbled some notes. 'I've had a quick look at the file, at the summary. Someone called Terry Day told the police about the arguments. Who is he?'

'Our landlord. He lives on the top floor. Creepy bastard. Was always hanging around at the front of the house, just watching the street. He couldn't wait to tell the police he heard us arguing.'

'Don't call him a creepy bastard in your trial,' Joe said. 'You can't afford to sound vengeful. It's got to be a wide-eyed plea that it's all a misunderstanding.'

Ronnie nodded and said, 'We shouted at each other, and then I left for work.'

'Where were you working?'

'Why don't you know all this?' Ronnie looked across at Monica, and then back to Joe. 'Didn't Mahones tell you?'

'I want to hear it from you. I won't be there to hold your hand in the witness box. You've got to do the work.'

'You're trying to trip me up.'

'You haven't seen anything yet, Ronnie. Wait until you get into that courtroom and the prosecution barrister rips into you. Pack in the self-pity and tell me the story.'

Ronnie folded his arms. 'You don't believe me, I can tell.' He turned to Monica. 'What about you? Do you think I could kill someone?'

Before Monica could say anything, Joe leaned forward across the table and lowered his voice. 'It doesn't matter what we think, Ronnie. I could believe that you were nothing but a cold-blooded murderer and I would do the same job for you. I'm not interested in making you feel better in your cell. I'm interested in defending your case.'

'That's what the man from Mahones said.'

Joe got the hint – that the last person to say it lost the case. He got to his feet. 'It's time to go,' he said to Monica, and so she stood as he put the papers into his briefcase.

'Where are you going?' Ronnie said, his eyes wide.

'If all you want is someone to hold your hand and tell you how unlucky you are, find someone else. You might have a long time to regret that.'

'Wait!' Ronnie said.

'Don't start pleading to be believed. I'm interested in defending your case and nothing else.' He indicated to Monica that they should leave.

Before they could, Ronnie reached out and put his hand on Joe's briefcase. 'Please, don't go.'

Joe paused. He'd bluffed and won. 'Those are my rules,' he said. 'You listen to my advice. I'm your lawyer, not the voice of your conscience.'

Ronnie sulked for a few seconds, and then said quietly, 'All right, I'm sorry. I was working where I do every day, in a packing factory, on a production line. It doesn't pay much, which was why we were in that crappy flat.'

Joe looked at him and then sat down. 'Keep going.'

Ronnie stared, his mouth set, and then he said, 'My line manager said I seemed distracted.' The words came out with a little more snap.

'Were you?'

'Sort of.'

Joe sat back and threw his pen onto the desk. 'You don't sound like you're doing that well here. Go on, tell me what "sort of" means.'

'You sound just like them.'

'Them?'

'The police,' Ronnie said. 'I kept on dropping things, that's all, not getting the boxes on the line in time, so they kept on having to stop the line. We got behind in the order and so the line manager got stressed.'

'That doesn't sound good. They're building-blocks for the prosecution, you being distracted.'

'I was upset. We had been shouting at each other before I went to work.'

'I thought you were always shouting. Why was that morning any different?'

Ronnie looked at the table and rubbed his hands together. His teeth clenched and unclenched. Eventually he looked up and said, 'I shouted that I wished she was dead and, well, I hit her.' He glanced at Monica, and then looked away, blushing with shame.

Joe closed his eyes for a moment. Ronnie wanted to swap because Mahones had told him the same thing, that the prosecution were building a good case, that it was time to tell everyone where he buried the bodies and try to get a manslaughter plea, go for diminished responsibility.

'So it was more than just the usual argument?' Joe said, opening his eyes again.

'Yes, it was, but I'd never hit her before, you've got to know that,' Ronnie continued, his gaze flashing between Joe and Monica. 'I've said bad things about her, even said that I could kill her, but those were just words. It doesn't mean that I did it.'

'Tell me about you hitting her.'

'I lost it, that's all I can say. She was screaming at me, and so I punched her, on the nose. Blood flew all over the place. On the wall. On the fireplace.'

'Did you clean up the blood?'

44

'Yes. I had to go to work but I did it anyway. I was ashamed of what I'd done. When I came home, she wasn't there.'

'No note or text?'

'Nothing.'

'Does anyone else live in the building?'

'No, just the landlord. He lives on the top floor. The flat between us is empty.'

'What did you do when you got home and saw that she had gone?'

'I just thought she'd gone out, or gone to her mother's or somewhere. She did things like that, would take off. But I suppose things were different. I'd hit her.'

'So what did you do to find her?'

'Nothing at first. I was ashamed. Then as time went on, I got more worried. I couldn't find her. I rang her friends, her mother.'

'How long after she walked out?'

'Three weeks. She had Grace with her and I didn't know how she would cope with her. I started getting all worked up, and when I get all worked up, I don't think straight. I imagine stuff, and I start to convince myself about the things that scare me. So I started wondering ...' He paused to take a deep breath. 'I started wondering whether I had done something, about whether I had left work earlier than normal and that I had killed her.'

'Why do you think that?' Joe said. 'Do you forget things? Have a history of black-outs?'

'Sometimes. It's just the way I get when I panic. I get gaps in my memory.'

'Have you ever been violent during these black-outs?'

'I don't think so, and killing someone is way out there, but what if I had but blanked it out? And so I was worried about Grace, about where she might be. So I did something stupid.'

45

'I get the impression I'm not going to like this.'

'I went to the police and told them I'd killed Carrie.'

Joe couldn't hide the surprise from his voice. 'You did what?'

'I wasn't thinking straight, like I told you. I didn't know if I had or not. It was all just so . . . ' He shook his head.

'Can you remember what you said?'

Ronnie exhaled loudly. 'Not really. It's a blur. Something like "I might have killed my girlfriend".'

Joe sat back. 'So the evidence against you is that you were shouting the odds in the morning, how you wished Carrie was dead. You left her blood in the flat and then acted strangely at work. You didn't do anything at first, and then you walked into a police station and confessed to murder.' He held out his hands. 'Have I got that right?'

'That's about it, yes.'

'I've heard enough,' Joe said.

'What, you don't want the case?'

'I didn't say that. I need time to read the case properly, that's all.'

'I need you,' Ronnie said, his voice more pleading now. 'I didn't kill anyone. I know that now. It looks bad, I know, but you've got to help me. I thought I could handle prison, but I can't.'

Joe looked at him, and for a moment saw the desperation in his eyes. Joe realised how draining the case was going to be. The big ones were always like that, because they consumed him.

'I'll see you tomorrow in court,' Joe said. 'All I can say is keep your head down.'

A guard appeared in the corridor that ran between the glass booths. Ronnie got slowly to his feet. A tear ran down his cheek. It was either guilt or grief, and it would be some time before Joe knew which one.

Just as Ronnie left the booth, he turned to Joe and said, 'You don't remember me, do you?'

That made Joe pause. 'No, I don't. Should I?'

Ronnie shrugged. 'I suppose not.' And then he was gone.

Eleven

Sam Parker found himself driving past the station where he worked, more modern than the one used by the Murder Squad: a long brick building that shouted its police credentials with bright blue window frames and fencing, high and spiked to keep out those who fancied some revenge. It was on one of the routes out of Manchester, opposite an open patch of grass dominated by a grey stone church, although the view was spoiled by tower blocks that popped up on the horizon. He decided to call in. The visit to the Murder Squad had put him in work mode, but as he went inside he knew his mood wasn't right, still angry and embarrassed that he had been wanted for just one reason: his brother.

Sam worked from a small office along the middle floor, sandwiched between two report-writing rooms, with a view over the car park at the rear. The road outside was quiet as he climbed the stairs, where he could see through the windows that went to the height of the stairwell, so that it felt exposed and vulnerable. The view would be much different in an hour, when it would be just a nose to tail drag for those who lived on the east of Manchester.

The window was open in his office, to let out some of the heat, and so the vertical white blinds knocked against the glass in the light breeze. He tapped on the open door with his fingernails. Helen, one of the financial investigators, looked up.

She had been poring over spreadsheets, her wire-framed glasses falling down her nose, as always, so that her reading became a constant twitch of her glasses being pushed back. As Sam looked in, he saw it for what it was: a nerd's refuge.

Helen was surprised. 'I thought you were on a rest day.'

'I am,' he said, and was about to tell her about his meeting with DI Evans, but then decided against it. It had amounted to nothing. 'I was passing, that's all, and I remembered that there was something about the bus case that was bothering me.'

'Wouldn't it have waited?'

'Probably,' he said, and then went to his desk. He looked at what was there. A cup filled with pens. A photograph of his wife and two daughters in a frame. Everything was safe, ordered and neat.

'And how is your bus case?' Helen asked.

'As dull as yesterday,' he said.

He didn't turn round to look at the files, lined up neatly on the shelf behind him. He had come into the office to remind himself of the career he had ended up with. He was good at it, he knew that, but he got the cases no one else wanted. No blood, no interest, that's the mantra for most cops, and so anything that involved accounts and forms and paper trails landed on his desk. His bus case was like that – a dreary case involving fraudulent claims of fuel duty rebates, where the owners of a bus company overstated the route mileage to claim more fuel duty than they were due. It was a collection of forms and accounts, and then a pursuit of the money so that it could be claimed back if convicted.

The only positive side was that he had his own desk, a space for his things, but he hadn't joined the police to pursue money trails.

He looked at Helen, and for a moment saw himself how others saw him: bookish and quiet. The longer he stayed where he was, the more he would end up like Helen. That wasn't what he wanted.

He felt his resolve grow. That was why he had gone to the office, to check whether he preferred this, the paperwork, the dullness, or whether he wanted more, even if it meant doing what DI Evans had asked.

'I've changed my mind,' he said.

'What, about your bus case?'

'Yes. I can save it for another day. It's my brother's birthday. I ought to say hello. He shouldn't be on his own tonight.'

And then he smiled as he turned to go. As the door closed behind him, it felt like a metaphor for his career – that he was moving on. He went down the steps more quickly than he had come up, and when he burst out into the car park, he felt determined. He would do what he needed to impress Evans, because the Murder Squad was where he had always wanted to be.

It was his time.

Twelve

Joe's thoughts were on Ronnie Bagley as he walked into the gardens near his office. There was enough evidence to justify an arrest. Enough to persuade the prosecution to charge him with murder. And enough for a judge to keep him locked up until his trial.

He felt that churn of self-doubt, the one he kept to himself. He knew it was the wrong day for a case like Ronnie's, because the anniversary of Ellie's death had made him think too much of lives stolen too young. He tried to shake it away. Ronnie was entitled to a chance. That was the system he had been trained into, the bargain he had made with himself, that he would help, not judge.

He glanced over at Monica walking beside him, looking for a distraction. 'It's not as glamorous as you think,' Joe said. When she looked confused, he added, 'I know we only saw a couple of corridors, but I could see the way you looked around as we walked through.'

'The prison?' she said, and laughed. 'I wasn't thinking it was glamorous. It was just something new.'

'I used to find it exciting, like I was on the sharp end of all the cut and thrust, dodging the police.'

'And now?'

'Just a big building full of broken lives. Some perhaps got heavier sentences than they deserved, and perhaps some are

51

even innocent, but you can bet that most of them in there have got away with more than they have been caught for.'

Monica blushed. 'You make me sound naive.'

'I don't mean to, but you're from a nice background, different to the people in there. It's bound to seem exciting, but glamour on the inside is just crime on the outside.'

'Will Ronnie get out?'

'Probably not.'

They walked past the flowerbeds, late lunchers filling the benches, and as they crossed the road to the office, he said, 'What do you think of Ronnie?'

'I don't know. He didn't seem threatening or like he had done something bad, which surprised me. He seemed pathetic, really.'

'Pathetic people are murderers too.'

'I suppose so.' She smiled. 'Go on then, what did you notice?'

'Grace,' Joe said.

'The baby? What do you mean?'

'He hardly mentioned her,' Joe said. 'If you think about it, there can be only one of two truths. He either killed Carrie or he didn't. If he killed her, then he must have killed Grace too, because she can't survive on her own. So think what he would be like if he hadn't killed her. What he knows is that Carrie is nowhere to be found, and so neither is Grace. Wouldn't you expect him to be a little more frantic? His child has been taken away; he might never see her again. But we didn't get that. Just self-pity and confusion.'

Monica was silent for a moment and then said, 'So you think he did it.'

'What I think doesn't matter.'

'But it does matter.'

'Does it? Do you think justice means truth?' Joe shook his head. 'Justice is an outcome, that's all, and all I have to think about is what outcome I can get for Ronnie. That's the deal you make with yourself when you become a criminal lawyer. You help wicked people get away with awful things.'

Monica didn't respond to that, and Joe knew that the hard truth of his job stripped away a little more of his humanity every day, and it had become just a challenge, a way to test the system, because as far as Joe was concerned, the system had failed him and his family. More importantly, it had failed Ellie.

'Ronnie seems to think you ought to remember him,' Monica said.

'I've had a lot of clients. He'll get over the hurt.'

'It's not just that though.'

'What do you mean?'

'Well, I know where you live, and you do live in a swanky apartment.'

'Why is that important?'

'Because Ronnie knew that you did. He said you would go back there tonight.'

Joe paused and then gave a small shake of the head. 'A lucky guess,' he said, although he started to wonder if there was something he wasn't quite seeing.

They slipped into the building by a side door. The firm specialised in commercial work and family law, but kept a crime practice out of habit. The clients who paid the private fees used the double oak doors that sat between white pillars at the front, the reception tiled in black and white. It had been built for grander times, not for the daily grind of a city centre law firm, except that the main entrance wasn't for his clients. The criminal department had always been the poor relation, made to work out of a side entrance, so that thieves and sex offenders didn't share the main waiting room with businessmen and sobbing divorcees.

'Have I missed anything?' Joe said to Marion, the receptionist, a woman in a smart business suit with a sharp tongue, who let clients know what was acceptable banter and what wasn't. No one got past Marion if she didn't want them in the building.

'It's been quiet,' she said. As he headed for the stairs, she added, 'Happy birthday, Mr Parker.' When he turned round, she was smiling, even blushing a little. 'I always remember, you know that.'

Joe returned the smile and then went quickly up the stairs that curved to the first floor and to a corridor filled by doorways, each office small, remnants from the day when the buildings were designed to be grand houses. Honeywells occupied two buildings next to each other, four storeys tall, knocked through into one complex of corridors and small rooms.

'So what do I do now?' Monica said.

'You must be hungry; you missed your lunch. Take a break.'

Monica looked deflated by that, as if she wanted to stay with him, but Joe turned away. He needed some time to himself.

As Monica left, he settled into his chair. The green leather cushion felt familiar and comfortable, and for a moment he closed his eyes. He should persuade Monica to do something else. No one came into crime anymore. Not anyone with any sense, anyway. There was still some money to be made, by learning all there was to know about road traffic laws and hoping you got clients rich enough to pay your bills, but for most young lawyers, it was all graft and no reward. He should treasure Monica's enthusiasm and then send it elsewhere, for her sake.

He opened his eyes when Gina came into the room.

Gina's office was two floors above, in the old roof space, squeezed below the sloping timbers with all the law clerks. She was there to keep an eye on them, to report back on who was really interested in impressing, or who was just seeing out a training contract. Sometimes the noisy and the brash get noticed the most, but it was the ones who did the billable hours that the firm would keep on.

'How was Ronnie Bagley?' Gina said, leaning against the door jamb.

Joe tapped his fingers on the desk for a few seconds and then said, 'I don't know.'

'You think you might have an innocent one?'

'I always believe that they might be.'

'That's one of your failings. You're always looking for the client who will redeem you, because you saved him, proof that the system isn't just about people getting away with it.'

'And you've still too much of the ex-copper in you.' He sighed. 'None of that matters when they look at the figures, does it? We will decide what is best for Ronnie, and we get paid along the way.'

'That's the game, Joe. That's what you keep telling me. And I've spoken to the prosecution. They've got some more papers for us. What you were given in court was just a summary. They're arriving by courier later, so you can read them before tomorrow.'

'Call me when they arrive. I'm going to draft Monica in on it.'

'I thought you might.'

'What do you mean?'

Gina laughed. 'Come on, Joe, I've seen how you look at her. I can't blame you. She's a pretty young woman.'

'I don't look at her in any way,' Joe said, a blush creeping up his cheeks.

'I'm a woman, Joe. I know how men look at other women. Just promise me one thing: don't make a fool of yourself,' and then she turned to walk away.

He didn't answer that. He just looked away as the door closed slowly, listening as Gina's footsteps receded faintly down the corridor.

Joe turned in his chair to look out of the window. Monica was on a bench eating some salad in a plastic tray, a book open in front of her, her hand constantly pushing her hair back behind her ears as she dipped her head to eat, so that it was like a routine, her fork going to her mouth and then her hair teased back, and then it would fall forward again as she looked down to her tray. Joe smiled to himself. He had enjoyed her company during the day.

She looked up and he pulled his head back quickly, panicking that she might see him watching, not wanting her to get the wrong idea. He closed his eyes. It was his window, with a good view, so everything was normal.

Joe eased himself back in front of the window, and he saw that she was on her feet now, walking across to a litter bin, her food finished.

He was about to turn away again, but then something attracted his attention. He leaned closer to the window and scoured the park. Then he saw it. It was a man sitting on a bench further along from Monica. He looked smart, in a blue V-neck and grey slacks, his hair parted neatly. But it wasn't his clothes that had caught Joe's attention. It was the way he was looking at Monica.

No, that wasn't right. It wasn't just that he was looking at her. He was studying her. He was sitting bolt upright, with his hands on his knees, his head turned towards her, watching as she put her food in the bin and started her walk back to the office.

Joe kept watch on him as Monica went through the park gate and crossed the road to the office. As she skipped up the office steps, the click of her heels reaching up through the open window, the man got to his feet and walked away.

Thirteen

Joe noticed the silence as he clicked the door closed in his apartment. No tick of a clock or the sound of conversation from another room. There were noises from elsewhere in the building – the mumbles of a television from the apartment above, and someone was shouting a few doors down – but his home had none of that.

He was carrying a box filled with papers, Ronnie's file, sent over from the prosecution an hour earlier. It was no way to spend his birthday.

He walked through to the living room and put the box on the floor. The low evening sun flooded in as he opened the blinds. The apartment was sleek and minimalist, although more by accident than design. He wasn't interested in decorative clutter. A sofa. A television. A computer. It was all he needed, because it was the view that he came home for.

The apartment was in Castlefields, once the heart of the industrial revolution, the hub of what had built England, where waterways and railways converged, with the end point for the world's first industrial canal, the stopping point for the cotton sent over from the Deep South, unloaded at Liverpool and sent along the canals to the Pennine towns that stretched all the way into Yorkshire, where deep green valleys became choked by smoke, and moorland grasses were replaced by long stretches of terraced housing, like deep gashes across the countryside.

The history had created a landscape of reclaimed warehouses and wharf buildings, some of it new but built to the same design, to blend in, but a lot of it was the modern crammed into the old, creating a beautiful knot of water, brick and steel all built on the footprint of the Roman fort of Mancunium. The city centre and busy roads were just on the other side of the apartment block, but his view was the tranquil stillness of canal water and pleasure barges, two willow trees gently sweeping at the surface, the calm disturbed only by the rumble of the trams as they went back and forth over the viaducts.

Manchester had been built on textiles, but it had been a tough upbringing. The city had grown too quickly, meaning people had been crammed into small houses, a family to a room, sometimes more, so that for a while the whole city choked on fumes and human debris, the streets nothing more than a network of slums and factories that killed its inhabitants too young, cholera thinning the population. Joe knew it as a proud city though. The squalor had grown the labour movement and the Manchester people had almost starved when they supported the cotton blockade of the Southern States during the American Civil War. They knew what was right and stood up for it. The mills and factories were gone now, and the few that remained were just brick shells used for art studios and craft fairs, but it was that mindset that had framed Joe's upbringing.

It was the canal that had drawn Joe to the apartment. He enjoyed evenings on his small balcony, watching the sunset shimmer across the water, the murky water gleaming as the light caught it.

He opened his fridge and found a sauvignon blanc, the product of an internet wine club he had joined a few months before and hadn't bothered to leave. The swish of the balcony door as he opened it brought in the sound of early evening. The clink of glasses and sound of laughter from the open restaurant in

Catalan Square on the other side of the canal mixed in with the creak and squeal of the tram wheels.

He poured himself a glass and then went back for Ronnie's file.

As he set the box down on the balcony, he picked up his glass to toast it. 'Happy birthday,' he said, and then sat down, pausing to take a sip.

He let the late-evening warmth bathe him for a moment, knowing that he would lose it soon, because once he started to read he would become immersed in the case. It was always the way, that he thought of nothing else but winning. It didn't matter what type of case, from a minor fight to a murder like this one. It was the result that counted.

There was a buzz on the intercom. He wasn't expecting anyone. He thought about not answering, but then curiosity got the better of him. He went back inside to the panel, and when he pressed the button, he heard his brother's voice, Sam.

'Joe, it's me. You can't have your birthday alone.'

Joe wondered whether to answer. He guessed that Sam wasn't there for his birthday, and that it was about what had happened earlier, when he hadn't gone to Ellie's grave with him. But Ellie's memory had been with him all day, and so it was good to hear a voice from the family.

He pressed the button to let Sam into the building and then opened his apartment door to let him walk right in.

Joe returned to the balcony. When Sam appeared, he was holding some beer cans, smiling.

'Happy birthday. Again.'

'I don't normally get all this.'

'We parted badly earlier,' he said. 'I thought I should try to make amends.'

Sam pulled a can from the ring and offered it to Joe, who held up his wine glass and said, 'I've got this.'

'I thought you were a beer drinker,' Sam said, looking at the can in his hand and then at the wine glass.

'I am, but I like a glass of wine sometimes.'

Sam sat down on the chair opposite and put the cans on the floor. He tried to slot the can back into the ring, and Joe watched amused. Once the four-pack was reassembled, Sam frowned and said, 'You're changing.'

'People do.'

Sam looked at the view and then back at the wine glass. 'You can't reinvent yourself, Joe.'

He took a deep breath. 'What are you talking about?'

'This,' Sam said. 'Apartment on the canal, wine, like you're some kind of city sophisticate. You're just like me, from the same bland part of the city, our family trashed. This isn't you.'

'You're turning my booze preference into a class war,' Joe said. 'It's not like that.'

'Are you sure?' Sam said. 'Is that why you wouldn't come to the grave today? You're moving onwards and upwards, leaving us behind.'

'Don't be stupid,' Joe said. The smile disappeared. He could feel the darkness tugging at him. Ellie. A woodland path.

'I just think our family should matter more,' Sam said.

'It does matter, it's just that . . .' and then Joe paused. There were too many things he carried around with himself, a secret he couldn't share with Sam. 'I had to be somewhere. It's work, Sam. It's what I do. It pays my bills.'

Sam sighed. 'I worry about Mum. And Ruby. Mum can't cope with her. She goes out all the time, doesn't do her homework, and Mum just ignores it, because she can't stomach the fight.'

'Should we speak to her?' Joe said. 'Teenagers left to make their own decisions get into trouble, and I don't want to get called out to the police station for her.'

'Yes, I think we should.'

Joe let the silence grow as Sam looked out over the water. There was something troubling him. Finally Sam said, 'Talking to Ruby would make a change from talking to a murderer, I suppose. That must sit heavily, after what happened to Ellie.'

Joe took another sip of wine. There it was, the reason for the visit. 'You said "murderer".'

'Yes, I did.'

'Do you mean Ronnie Bagley?'

'Well, yes.' Sam sat back. 'Why was he more important than your family today, so that you had to squeeze us in before a prison visit?'

'It's not a competition,' Joe said, and put down his glass. 'How did you know I'm involved in Ronnie's case?'

Sam looked surprised by that. 'Well, you are, aren't you?'

'From today I am, but how did you find out?'

Sam didn't answer at first, and so Joe waited, knowing that Sam would fill the silence.

'Someone mentioned it at the station,' Sam said eventually. 'They asked me what was going on.'

'And what did you say?'

'Nothing. What else could I say? I don't know anything about your cases.'

'How did they say it to you? The last I heard, you were on the financial unit, shuffling papers. So what was it? An email, or a phone call? Or just whispers in the canteen?'

'It wasn't like that.'

'I'm not stupid, Sam. I've had one court hearing and a prison visit and you find out, when I can't think of any reason why you should. So why? Is my involvement making people nervous, because I get results?'

'Don't be so bloody arrogant.'

'Or is there something about the case that you don't want people finding out?'

'Now you're being ridiculous. Someone just mentioned that

you had picked up the case, that's all. You being my brother is a conversation piece, something to say when you pass people in the corridor.'

Joe didn't respond. Sam wasn't going to reveal anything.

'I don't know how you can do it anyway,' Sam said.

'If you're saying what I think you are, we've had this conversation before.'

'It still needs saying. You defend murderers and rapists and thieves and fraudsters. How can you do that? How can you go to sleep at night, knowing the people you help keep on the streets?'

Joe closed his eyes and took a deep breath.

The question bored him. It was the one all defence lawyers got, especially from the police. His answer changed, depending on who was doing the asking. Sometimes he gave the truthful answer, that he thought that it was a mark of civilisation that people could have a fair trial, because the crook would be convicted if there is proof, regardless of what he did. The police had to follow rules, just like everyone else did, and the rules gave everything order. Other times, he went for the shock value and said that he didn't care, that it was fun, rocking the system, but he didn't really think like that. Cases did keep him awake sometimes, when he had to walk past the families of the victims when the person who took away someone precious walked free, but those were the exception. As much as he tried, most of his clients took a long walk down the cold steps, and some would never walk back up them to the harsh blink of freedom.

But this was Sam asking.

'You mean how could I do it after Ellie?' Joe said, and his thoughts flashed back again to fifteen years earlier, sitting there surrounded by birthday cards, *18 Today* banners pinned up around the living room, the house filled with police officers and the sound of his mother's screams.

'He's still out there,' Sam said, his fingers tapping out a rhythm on the table, a sign of his agitation. 'And when he's caught, he'll get someone like you to help him get away with it.'

Joe didn't respond at first. There were secrets he had kept for fifteen years, and it was too late to change things now.

He took another sip of wine, a longer one this time. 'I don't have to defend myself,' he said. 'I'm beyond all that. I just help people.'

'What do you think Dad would say if he knew?'

Joe turned to him, anger flashing in his eyes. 'That's a low blow, and you know it.' When Sam responded only by looking at the floor, Joe said, 'It's time for you to go.'

'What, we can't enjoy a birthday drink together?'

'You didn't come here for that.'

Sam looked at him, stern-faced. 'If that's how you want it.'

Joe kept his gaze focused on the water as Sam scraped his chair back.

'Don't leave your family behind,' Sam said, and then his footsteps faded as he went through the apartment.

When he heard the apartment door close, Joe reached across and took a beer can from the holder. When he popped the ring pull, he raised it in salute. 'Happy birthday, Joe Parker.'

The evening was spent lost in paperwork, and it was nearly eleven before he took the box back inside. The beer was gone, as was the wine, and the wobble he felt as he walked back in told him that he would feel the booze in the morning.

The case was just as he had first gleaned from Ronnie – that it was conjecture and guesswork, because Carrie and Grace's bodies hadn't been found – but the evidence was stronger than Ronnie hoped.

Ronnie and Carrie lived on the ground floor of a tall Victorian house, with stone-silled bay windows and stained glass around the front door. The crime scene photographs made it look grim and cramped, with just one bedroom, Grace's cot in one corner, squeezed in alongside the double bed. The other main room was the living room, with a kitchen beyond, the bathroom just a small room at the other end of the kitchen. The doors were plain and flat, the paint on them bubbled at the bottom, the white now a dirty cream.

The living room was dingy, everything in brown shades, the light provided by a window opposite the fireplace, although they looked like they were cleaned rarely, with dust and cobwebs on the outside. The carpet was faded brown swirls, with worn out patches from the door. Carrie had made some effort to make the flat look nice, with some flowers in a vase on an old dresser, although the varnish on the wood was cracked and old. There were photographs of a young baby Grace in clip-frames, but the pictures looked dulled by cigarette smoke even though Grace was only two years old. The ashtrays were piled high with old butts, and in the bin in the corner of the room there was the neck of a vodka bottle, the red label just visible.

The crime scene investigator had been thorough. The flat surfaces of the doors made for good fingerprints and acted like a blank canvas for the blood splatters. The attack had started at the entrance to the bedroom, because there were smears on the door, as if someone had made a bad job of cleaning up. It was the same on the fireplace, with contact marks and then tiny spatters that were consistent with Carrie's head being banged on the granite hearth. The landlord's statement was graphic, making the argument seem beyond the routine bickering they normally engaged in. The prosecution case was simple: Ronnie had killed Carrie in their apartment and then removed her, dumping her somewhere. They just didn't know where he had taken her, or his daughter. If they found Carrie, they expected to find Grace buried alongside her.

And then there was the visit to the police station, when Ronnie walked in and said that he had killed his girlfriend. That gave Ronnie a problem. All the jurors needed to believe was that Ronnie killed her. The lack of a body was a problem, but juries don't like to let killers go free.

Joe closed the sliding doors, so that the low hum of late traffic disappeared and all that was left was the fan of his computer.

He went to his desk and moved the mouse to fill the screen with the desktop picture of a scanned family photograph, his favourite of them all together, taken on holiday in Portugal. They were on a beach, all of them in shorts and T-shirts, the soft sandstone of the Algarve cliffs behind them, his parents grinning, their arms around Ellie's shoulders, Joe and Sam on either side. It made him pause for a moment. Although he saw it every time he went to his computer, the conversation with Sam brought back the memory of the holiday. Ellie was dead less than a year later.

He took a deep breath and then clicked on his internet browser. He knew what he was going to do. Sober, he never went there, but when he felt the jangle of booze in his fingers, he went looking for company.

Internet dating. He had registered but always ignored the requests for a meeting. It just made him feel like he was back in the game, which was what he needed, but he had no desire to commit. He browsed the pages and read the profiles, imagining what would happen if he got in touch, just to feel that tingle of anticipation that had long since disappeared.

He got up to close the curtains, but as he stood at the window, he paused. There had been a flash of something on the other side of the water, as if the lights along the canal bank had caught the gleam of something metallic. Joe remembered the man outside the office earlier in the day. He clicked off the light so that he got a better view outside, and as he pressed his

65

face against the glass, there was movement – someone moving quickly.

He stepped away from the glass. Someone was watching him.

Fourteen

His sobs blotted out the sounds of the morning. No birdsong, no shouting, no hum of the traffic from outside. Just his own steady moans, his arms over his head trying to keep out the noise of his memories, because they had been coming all night, waves of screams and cries, making sleep impossible. Was this how it would always be, never able to forget? Was it too much to ask that he could wipe away what had happened, so that he didn't have to be tormented by their final moments? The fear in their eyes, their end incomprehensible. He had wanted to say he was sorry each time, that he had never meant it to be like that, but in those final few seconds it was meaningless.

So he craved the silence that never came.

It wasn't just the memories that frightened him. It was the arousal he felt when his mind dwelled on what had happened. It had taunted him all night, the build up of a few hours looking back on it all, it cheated even that small pleasure from him because it was wrong to be aroused by it. What sort of monster had he become?

It was his way of dealing with it, though, rooting it in pleasure, but those few minutes trapped in fantasy were always replaced by shame and disgust. He called it the dead phase, when the passion had gone and all he had left was the panic of discovery or the sweep of remorse.

Instead, he watched the slow spread of daylight across the

floor, cold and harsh, the slow finger of judgement creeping towards him. He pulled his bedding over his shoulder and tried to curl up and get some moments of sleep, but as he stared at the wall, he knew the chance for sleep had gone.

It was all so wrong, he knew that, and so he hoped that his memories would be enough to maintain him, but remembering everything wasn't the same as experiencing it, where the need for someone new drove him on.

He closed his eyes and tears tickled at his eyelids, his cheeks burning red. It was there again, remorse, that dark shadow that crept into his thoughts and eroded the pleasure. For every silky feel of hair, he remembered a screech of fear or panic. Struggles against the rope, the terror of the blindfold, until those final muffled moments, the fast thrash of the legs, and then stillness. He clenched his teeth as they came back to him. It hadn't been about that, it never had, but how could they be allowed to leave when they would bring an end to it all?

Loneliness would get him in the end, because there was no one to ease his pain, to provide the words that had helped him to function, the inspiration behind it all. Beautiful, tender, passionate love had driven him to it. Didn't that make it better, that it wasn't all about him?

He sat up, let the bedding fall to the ground. He needed to be stronger. This was supposed to be the new beginning.

The words seemed hollow. He wasn't strong enough.

As the strip of daylight widened across the floor, he clamped his eyes shut again and wrapped his arms around his head. He had got it wrong. He couldn't do this.

Fifteen

Sam was awoken by the buzz of his phone on the small set of drawers next to his bed. He glanced across at the clock. Only 5.30. He rubbed his eyes. Too early.

He reached for his phone. He was about to click the answer button when he saw that it was another withheld number. He sat up and held the phone in his hand. It vibrated against his fingers. Alice stirred next to him, but still he left it, until eventually it fell silent as it transferred to voicemail.

He lay back on the pillow and tried to forget about the call. It would still be there when he got up. It might be something else, a cold call about an accident claim or a fake computer virus, but he couldn't turn his mind away from it, the thought of it like an itch, and the more he tried to resist it, the harder it became to ignore it. So he watched the day get brighter through the curtains, more awake with every minute, Alice's slow breaths the only sound as he resisted the urge to check his voicemail, to see if it was the same message.

He turned over and bunched the sheets under his chin, tried to get back to sleep, but his mind went back to the night before. It had ended sourly, but Sam couldn't stay angry with Joe. They were brothers. That meant something.

Alice stirred. 'What's wrong?' she said, her voice a drawl.

He thought about not saying anything, but the way she propped herself up on her elbows, her tangled hair trailing on the pillow, told him that she would keep asking until she got an answer.

'It's nothing. Just work.'

Alice didn't respond for a while, and then she said, 'Is it something to do with Joe?'

'What do you mean?'

'You seemed a bit distracted when you came back from work, and you weren't there long, but I thought going to see Joe would have shaken it off. It was your rest day but you came back even worse. You hardly said a word to me, and even when the girls were playing with you, it was as if you didn't want to. That isn't like you.'

Sam didn't know what to say to that. Emily had been in the bath, three years old and all curls and smiles, with Amy, just crawling, playing in the room next door. It was normally his favourite time of the day, relaxing with his daughters. He couldn't even remember how he was the night before.

'I'm not on the squad, but the inspector wanted me to do something, and I didn't like it. She wanted me to spy on him.'

'On Joe?' Alice sat up. 'Why, what's he done?'

'It's one of his clients. He's been charged with murder. He killed his girlfriend and daughter, but we can't find the bodies.'

Alice looked shocked. 'Can you do that, have a murder case without a body?'

'Provided we can be sure the victims are dead.'

'And so what do they expect from Joe?'

'That he'll talk, breach his client's confidence just because I'm his brother. He won't, and I should have known that. If it came out that he'd told me his client's secrets, he would be struck off.'

'So what about the inspector?'

'I'll just tell her that Joe won't talk, that he's a better man than she gives him credit for, and then it's back to my little office.'

Her arm went over his chest, and he felt the warmth of her body alongside him. 'You're a good man, Sam Parker.'

They lay like that for a few minutes, Alice's breaths getting slower as she drifted back to sleep. Sam tried to join her, but every time he glanced towards the clock, he saw the green light blinking on his phone. A voicemail message.

His curiosity kept him fully awake and so after five more minutes of sighing and fidgeting he slid away from Alice. He swung his legs out of bed and searched for his clothes, before grabbing his phone.

He went downstairs to the computer. It was in the dining room, tucked into a corner so that they could pretend it wasn't there. Alice used it for shopping and looking at houses abroad she dreamed of buying but knew she never would. As the computer started, he scrabbled around for a cable that would connect the earphone socket on the phone to the computer. All the cables were wrapped up neatly in labelled bags to stop them tangling, but there was still a small loose collection in an old biscuit tin. Right at the bottom, he found it. A small black lead, jack to jack.

He found the microphone socket on the computer and put in the lead. He scrolled through the programs until he found the recording software that came with the computer and changed the settings to get the right input. He was ready.

He dialled his voicemail to check that it was what he thought it was, and straight away he felt the jolt in his chest as he heard the screams, the pleading. He plugged the lead straight into the phone, pressed the record button on the computer, and then replayed the message. He watched as the meter flickered up and down as it recorded the call, mostly green, but the occasional red peaks were like small stabs to his stomach, until the peaks became longer and he watched the seconds go by. Twenty. Then thirty. He had normally ended the call by then. After fifty seconds, the meter went still so he clicked the stop button.

Sam unplugged his phone and held it to his ear. The voicemail was going through the options. He clicked to save the sound file. Whatever the message was, he had it on his computer.

He was tired but the nerves in his stomach stopped him from wanting to go back to his bed, where the warmth of Alice's embrace would be preferable to what he knew would be stored on the hard drive. He heard the click and whoosh of the central heating as it came on, the summer not yet taking hold. Birds were singing outside, a joyous start to the day, but Sam's only focus was the hum of the computer fans.

He sought out some headphones, put them on, and then scrolled through to the music folder, where he had saved the sound file. His finger paused over the mouse button for a second as he readied himself, and then he clicked the play button. He closed his eyes. If he was going to listen to it properly, he had to blot out everything else.

It was the sobbing he heard first, but it wasn't through misery. It was wretched, part pleading, part terror. Then the first scream came. He flinched. The scream was cut short, as if there had been a gag, because the struggle he could hear was muffled. Then another scream, louder this time, higher-pitched, more desperate.

He threw the headphones onto the desk. His hands were trembling. Sweat flashed across his forehead and he felt the tingle of goosebumps over his body. The screams were real, he knew that. It was no film soundtrack, where a scream is just a loud noise, a one-note pitch. You can never properly replicate that fear, because it comes from deep within, something uncontrollable.

He couldn't avoid it though. He had to listen again. If it was something real, it was being sent to him for a reason. He was a cop, but he was about money and frauds and secreted accounts. This was something different, violent.

As he placed the headphones on his head once more, he focused his mind on staying with the call. He clicked play and put his head down. The sounds were just the same, the first scream hitting him like a jolt of electricity. He clenched his jaw and carried on listening. There was the gagging, the muffled gasps, but he could make out something else, like a second voice, and small shuffles, like the sound of a struggle, before the second scream burst into his ears. It made him sit bolt upright, his eyes wide, as if he was feeling the terror himself, transported away from the corner of his dining room to wherever it was taking place.

There was the rumble of an engine. Near a road? But it was moving slowly. A noise too. Like a regular beep.

The call ended and Sam put the headphones back onto the computer desk. His chest was rising and falling with the pace of his breaths and his mouth was dry. The call meant something, and it was aimed at him.

He knew it was going to be a bad day.

Sixteen

Joe cupped his hand over his mouth and blew. Stale booze. He had bags under his eyes and his mind felt lethargic. He should have eased off with the drink, but it had been his birthday. He had to get his head together for the court hearing. Judges can tolerate poor advocates. What they can't tolerate is a lawyer who isn't prepared, so he had to appear sharp.

The clicks of Monica's heels were loud as they marched through Crown Square, the noise only partly drowned out by the loud whirring of the street cleaner as it swept up the debris from the Swiss restaurant in the centre. He looked around as he walked, checking behind him. Nothing suspicious. Just the suits whose breakfasts came as coffee in foam cups and small groups of people gathered near the entrance to the court, huddled and nervous, families and supporters, the defendants obvious in their suits that didn't quite fit, pulling hard on cigarettes.

'What's wrong?' Monica said. When Joe looked at her, she blushed. 'I'm sorry, I didn't mean to speak out of turn. You just seem a bit on edge.'

He shook his head. 'No, I'm fine,' he said, smiling reassurance, although he remembered the man outside his office, and the feeling that he was being watched the night before.

They were heading for the Crown Court. It was within sight of the Magistrates Court, but it was a whole different legal world. The Magistrates Court was chaotic, all the low level crime dealt with at high volume, where a court appearance was nothing more than an interruption to many people, carried out with a relaxed swagger. The Crown Court was the serious court, where the lawyers wore wigs and gowns and people went to prison for a long time. Even the regular players loitered nervously.

The building was modern on the outside, trapped into a seventies frame, with plenty of concrete and a high glass front, so that people outside could always see who was on the corridor. Not every courtroom entrance was visible from Crown Square, but there was enough exposure to take away someone's privacy. Once inside the courtrooms, though, it turned traditional, windowless and wood-lined.

Joe went straight to the computer terminal so that he could book himself in for Ronnie's case.

'Who's prosecuting?' Monica said. 'I'm going to have to get to know these people.'

Joe checked the screen. 'Kim Reader, same as yesterday,' he said, and he couldn't help but smile.

'Who is she?'

'Just an old friend. It's her case.'

'Does that help?'

'No. There are no favours here. Kim fights hard so don't be fooled by her friendliness. She is ambitious, and she's good, and if it helps her case, she will make you look small in front of the judge.'

'Has she done that to you?'

'Oh yes, and I soon learned not to be taken in by her. She plays it straight, but don't expect her to ignore a weakness.'

'You sound like you know her pretty well.'

Joe tried not to give away how well he had got to know her when he said, 'We were at law school together, that's all, but she has her sights set higher than I do.'

'What do you mean?'

'You've still got your head filled with the law, I can tell. I was like that. Your job is not about the law now. Once you've finished all your training your job will be to make money for the firm. It's as simple as that. Kim Reader is different. She's a prosecutor, doesn't do anything else, and so she can think about being a lawyer. She's got a weakness though.'

'Which is what?'

Joe smiled. 'She's all about control. Kim will want to do the trial herself.'

'Can she do that?'

'She can, but she will only get the trial as junior. A QC will handle the trial strategy, but she won't back away from the tough stuff. And that control thing means something else: she doesn't like losing. She will fight hard, but if she thinks the case is a loser, it's gone. Not all prosecutors are like that. Some like to hang on for a slim hope of something. Sometimes that works. Most often, it doesn't.'

'What about you?' Monica said. 'Will you do the trial yourself, as junior?'

Joe shook his head. 'I got my higher rights last year, but I haven't done enough trials to do a murder case. This is serious stuff, not an ego trip. Come on, let's go find Kim.'

They went to the robing room, just another plain door along a corridor, but the numbered keypad gave it away. Joe paused before he went inside. This was where the hardest fights were won, where the right attitude could rescue a settlement from the battle lines. This was also an arena for old-fashioned class war, with solicitors slowly but steadily taking over from barristers, who once enjoyed exclusive rights to practise in the higher courts, so that the old guard gathered in cliques, with their cigar-stained wigs and faded black cloaks, a dirty and ragged badge of honour against the pristine outfits of the solicitor-advocates. It meant the Crown Court had gained some street sense but lost some of its refinement.

The people inside turned to look at him as he opened the door. Most turned away. He didn't mind that. It was what he expected.

The room was long and narrow, with lockers on one side and shelves of law books on the other. Desks ran the length of the room, and most of them were occupied, papers spread in front of the barristers, their horsehair wigs next to them, dancing a delicate balance between protecting their own interests and not pissing off those who sometimes instructed them. Except that Joe had heard them talking, whenever they thought no one else was there, about how people like him were interlopers, superfluous, just intermediaries, without the craft and guile that a well-trained barrister brought to a case. There was some truth in that – a good barrister is worth every bit of their bill – but Joe had seen too many cases thrown away by those who thought trials were there just to build up a fee and then plead it away. If Joe wanted a fight, he expected a fight, and the side that was going to give up wasn't going to be his, because it was Joe who'd had to deal with the day-to-day moans of the clients, about delays or seemingly inconsequential things, like prison food.

He threw his bag onto a chair and pulled out his starched winged collar. As he fastened it with a gold stud to his plain white shirt, he looked along the room and shouted out, 'Anyone seen Kim Reader?'

There were shuffles as people looked up and then went back to their own papers, but then he heard a shout from the other side of the room. 'She's gone to court.'

He pulled on his black gown and headed for the door, nodding at Monica for her to follow him.

The clothes felt unfamiliar, the first decade of his career spent patrolling the corridors of the Magistrates Court in a cheap suit. The archaic and formal dress sense of the Crown Court felt uncomfortable and stifling. At least he was spared the indignity of the wig, although as he reached the court corridor, he saw that his discomfort wasn't shared by the young men who walked quickly, their gowns hanging from their shoulders, the rolled-up bundles of paperwork under their arms, tied up with pink ribbon. The older ones were less urgent; just slower, scruffier versions.

Kim Reader was further along, talking to two men in suits, detectives, although not the same ones as the day before. Kim was elegant in a dark suit and patent heels, her wig bright against the sheen of dark hair that flowed onto her shoulders.

Joe slowed down to pop a mint into his mouth and then turned to Monica. 'Did you get hold of Ronnie's mother?'

'Yes, she said she would be here,' she replied, and then pointed to a small lady sitting on her own, her handbag on her knees, looking warm in a large brown coat, despite the brightness outside. 'She would be my guess.'

The old lady glanced up as they got closer, and so Joe went over. 'Mrs Bagley?'

She nodded.

'We represent Ronnie.' When she didn't answer, Joe asked, 'Can Ronnie stay with you?'

'What, you think he might get out?'

'Probably not,' Joe said, 'but I'd rather know in advance, just in case.'

She looked at Joe, and then at Monica. 'Yes,' she said, her voice hesitant. 'Fine, all right then. And my name is Winnie.'

'All right, Winnie, thank you,' he said, and then went towards Kim Reader.

She looked away from the detectives and smiled as he got closer, moving her papers to her other arm so that they stopped acting as a shield. 'So, Joe, you still haven't told me how you muscled Mahones out of this one.'

'Client's preference,' Joe said, nodding a greeting at the two men in suits. They didn't return it. 'I'm just Ronnie's servant. Does he get to walk out today?'

Kim gave a small laugh. 'Murderers don't get bail, you know that.' That brought smiles from the detectives.

'Perhaps the judge will feel creative,' Joe said, and then pushed at the door to the courtroom. He had to get some kind of argument ready, if only for the show. Clients expected their lawyer to bang on the table, even when it was pointless.

Monica followed him, escorting Winnie Bagley to the public gallery. He didn't want Kim to know what he had planned, and he let the door close so that she was left outside with the police. He needed some time on his own in the courtroom first. There were things he needed to find out.

Seventeen

When Sam Parker walked into the Incident Room, his eyes already starting to feel the tiredness from the early start, DI Evans was in a huddle in the corner of the room, talking to two men in dark suits. Sam recognised them from the day before. Sergeants, he guessed, from the way their suits were a little sharper than the rest in the room, in their rolled-up shirtsleeves. Evans looked over as he walked in and then whispered to the men next to her. Both turned to look at Sam.

'How did you get on with your brother?' she said. 'Did you learn anything useful about Ronnie Bagley?'

'No, nothing, I'm sorry,' he said, shaking his head. 'Joe won't talk about his clients, which I guessed. I told him that I'd heard he represented Ronnie Bagley, but he just clammed up. As far as he was concerned, that was the end of the conversation.'

'A lawyer with morals?' Evans said, rich with sarcasm, and then, 'I expected that. It was worth a try.' As Sam stood there, unsure what to say, Evans exchanged glances with her sergeants and then said, 'Come into my room.'

Sam followed her into the small office he had been in the day before. It was even untidier, with food wrappers and two coffee cups added to the mess of papers. She pointed to the chair, and when he sat down, she said, 'Do you want to know why I asked you to come in to tell me that in person?'

'I did wonder,' he said. 'I presumed you wanted to see the

whites of my eyes, so you could tell whether I was being too loyal to my brother.'

'And were you?'

'No, I don't think so,' Sam said. 'And I shouldn't have been asked, ma'am.'

Evans sat back and pursed her lips, making Sam shuffle in his chair, but he held her gaze. Eventually she said, 'You're right, I know, I shouldn't have put you in that position. It was a charade really, a chance to check you out, and your brother turning up for Ronnie gave me that chance.' She sat forward again and put her arms onto the desk. 'The real reason I wanted you to come in is because of Ben Grant.'

The name surprised him. 'What, *the* Ben Grant?'

'Is there another? And as it was your moment in the spotlight, you'll remember it well.'

Sam exhaled loudly. 'I haven't been allowed to forget it,' he said, and straight away his mind flew back to a night shift eight years earlier, just another routine patrol in a marked car, before he became a detective. The whole force had been on high alert after the bodies of three young girls, two aged ten and one nine, had been found in parks around Manchester. Each had been abducted and strangled and raped, their clothes removed, so that they were left naked and bloodied, discarded like rubbish, fly-tipped into the bushes. There were more missing children, their bodies undiscovered, and the atmosphere around the city was tense.

Sam had been driving past a park, just south of the city centre, when he had seen some movement in the bushes furthest away, at the bottom of a railway embankment. It hadn't been much, just a flash of something pale and the rustle of greenery, but it had been enough for him to spot it.

It could have been something innocuous, like someone needing the toilet, but instinct told him that it was something else. He had jumped out of his car and sprinted over, barking into his radio. As he got closer, Ben Grant emerged slowly from the bushes, his arms out, compliant, and for a moment Sam had wondered whether he had read it wrong, because Grant didn't try to run or fight. He just turned to Sam, took one last look into the bushes, and then walked slowly towards him.

Sam had got ready with his PAVA spray and barked at Grant to get down. He had expected a bolt through the park, but Grant just sank to his knees and held his hands out to be hand-cuffed. Sam thought that he heard something near the embankment, that there was some movement on the edge of his vision, but all of his focus had been on Grant.

Once cuffed, Sam had shone his torch into the bushes, and when he saw the light reflect against pale white skin, he had trembled and almost dropped his torch.

The torch beam had reflected against the lifeless legs of a girl, her clothes removed and shoved into a plastic bag. It had been Sam's first dead body, and as he had struggled to stay calm, his hands shaking, sweat on his face, Grant had remained still, almost serene.

The dead girl was the fourth murdered by Grant that they knew for certain, coaxed into his van, strangled and raped, and the murders turned him from a factory worker into a tabloid hate figure. His notoriety hadn't just been about the crimes though, as awful as they were. It was the way he enjoyed the attention, grinning and waving towards the cameras that caught him on the short journey to the prison van, and then using his trial to describe how he snatched each girl and murdered her. He didn't have a defence. He was just insistent on everyone hearing him gloat.

Sam received a commendation, but he saw no pride in it, because anything similar to his own sister's murder didn't seem worthy of a celebration.

He looked at Evans. 'Why Ben Grant? He's locked up.'

'You've seen the young women on the posters around here?'

'They're in every station,' he said, as he recalled them from the day before and the television appeals and reconstructions.

'All four missing, presumed dead,' Evans continued. 'We thought there was no real link when the first two went missing, that if they were taken by the same person, it was just random, but we think differently now, because there is one thing that links all of them. If we talk about it, it must stay within these walls, because we haven't gone public, but it involves you.'

Sam's eyes widened. 'Me? Well, yes, I understand, of course.'

She lowered her voice as she spoke. 'They are all connected to someone involved with the Ben Grant case.'

'Connected? How?'

Evans reached for one of the posters, which had been lying on the floor next to the desk. She pointed to a pretty smiling redhead. 'Samantha Crane was the first one. One of the detectives on the case was Jimmy Crane. Ben Grant wasn't even in our thoughts. Samantha was a girl missing from the family of one of our own. That was all that mattered.' Evans pointed to a young woman in a ball-gown, blonde hair gleaming against the bright blue silk of her dress. 'Then there was Gilly Henderson. One of the prosecution barristers was Bill Henderson. Still it didn't click. Ben Grant's case wasn't the only one they had worked on together, and why would we think of Ben Grant? He's locked up and will probably never get out.'

'So what made you change your mind?'

'Emily Brooker,' Evans said, and pointed to a black girl on the poster, her hair curly and long, her teeth bright white, her face fun and flirty. 'She's the daughter of one of the crime scene investigators. That was when we worked out the connection. We knew something was going on that involved the police, and so we got a list of all the cases where Emily's mother and Samantha's father had worked together. We gave the list to Gilly's father, the barrister, and when he went back through his briefs, the only match was Ben Grant. We had a link.'

Sam thought about that, then said, 'Have you spoken to Grant?'

'We tried, but he won't speak to us. We can't force him, because we don't know if he has any information.' Evans gave a small laugh, although it was bitter. 'We could hardly arrest him, because being in prison the whole time makes his alibi pretty strong.'

'What about the fourth victim, the young Indian woman?'

'Arshafi Devi,' Evans said. 'If we thought for a moment that the connection had been just a strange coincidence, Arshafi took that idea away, because her father was one of the jurors who convicted him. A juror's daughter? That was a link too far.'

'When was the last one, Arshafi?'

'Two months ago,' Evans said. 'Like with the other ones, the trail went stale. All we know is that she didn't go home again, and we don't know where she had gone that evening. But then something changed, and this is why I wanted to check you out, have a look at you.'

'Go on,' Sam said, caution in his voice.

'Yesterday we got a call. It was the prison. Grant had changed his mind. He would talk to us, at last, but it came with a condition.'

'What has made him come forward now?'

'I don't know,' Evans said. 'We're hoping you can find out.'

Sam was confused. 'I don't understand.'

'His condition is that he will talk, but only to you.'

Eighteen

Joe sat in the courtroom, his forearms on the desk, calm on the surface, but his feet tapped out a fast rhythm. Monica was behind him, watching, learning.

It was almost ten o'clock. The silence was awkward. The usher paid Joe no attention, but the court clerk flushed above the white lace of her formal blouse every time he glanced her way. Kim was further along the front row, reading something on her phone. He knew why she was doing it, so the police couldn't accuse her of being too cosy with the defence. The shield stayed up when there were other people who could report back.

The courtroom was made up of rows of long wooden desks and flip-down chairs, rising to the dock behind, the public gallery beyond that, two rows of plush red fabric. Ronnie's mother was there, staring ahead, as if she was disbelieving, unsure of what was going to happen to her son. Joe turned and gave her a small nod of reassurance, a smile, but she didn't respond.

Joe's eyes went to the television mounted on the wall. Once a case was before a judge, prisoners made their court appearances by video, although at the moment it showed just a grey curtain and a sign for HMP Manchester in front of it – the official name for Strangeways. A few minutes of silence passed and then Ronnie appeared, wearing a grey sweatshirt. His eyes stared at the camera, red and strained. From the inset image on the screen, all Ronnie could see was the empty judge's chair.

Joe looked around the courtroom again. It was a statement on how pathetic Ronnie's life had become. Joe had seen the real excitement of the Crown Court, with gun-toting police officers manning the doors, everyone wary of a hardcore criminal or a revenge attack. Ronnie was facing a life behind bars and the only people to see his first step were his mother, two lawyers, a trainee, and two court employees.

Then there was a noise. Joe turned round and watched as a man entered the room and shuffled along the back row of the public gallery. He sat in the corner, as if he had wanted to be anonymous, but he stared at Joe when it was obvious he had been seen. Joe felt a jolt of recognition. It was the man who had been outside his office the day before, watching, looking up.

'Do you know him?' Joe said. When Kim looked up, Joe nodded to the back of the courtroom. 'The guy sat in the corner.'

Kim turned back and then shook her head. 'No. Is it important?'

Joe paused as he thought about that, and then shook his head. 'No, it's all right.'

Kim pointed to the television screen. 'They never look how you expect,' she said. She knew that Ronnie couldn't hear them. The microphone was showing a mute symbol.

'What, killers?' Joe said, turning to look back at Ronnie. 'He isn't one yet.'

'Let's not play games, Joe. Fight hard when Ronnie can hear you, but between us, let's be more realistic. Proof of guilt is different to proof of innocence, you know that. I always expect the guilt to be visible, like a stain or something.'

Joe returned the smile, some of his poise returning. It was just a pre-court joust. 'They don't wear badges,' he said. 'Killers live next door and move amongst us. That's just how it is. You can't predict it.'

'His baby though? Poor thing. How callous can he be?'

'You're sounding naive, Kim. With every murder I've ever dealt with, I've never got the full story. There's what you can prove, and there is what people will tell me. What really happened is only ever known between two people, and one of those isn't here.'

Before Kim could respond, Joe said, 'So how are you going to keep him in custody?'

Kim scoffed. 'Bail? Are you kidding?' She leaned further in. 'He's a fucking murderer, Joe. You don't bail murderers.'

Joe had to suppress a smile at the sound of expletives spoken with the refinement of an expensive education. 'Fine,' he said. 'Watch the judge let him walk instead, because if you don't agree bail, I'm asking for the case to be thrown out.'

'Bullshit. You can't do that.'

'I know that, and I'll get shouted down, but I might be able to cement in the judge's head that it's a weak case. You know how a judge can wreck a case, that if he decides he doesn't like it, he will pick it apart, piece by piece, until you've nothing left to give to the jury. So your case ends up as a loss, and all because of what I say here.'

Joe could see her thought processes in the flare of her nostrils and the twitch of her lips. She was trying to decide which would turn out worse for her – Ronnie getting out because she agreed it, or the judge turning against the case.

'You've got to justify bail in a murder case, you know that,' she said.

'That's easy. You've got a weak case, and until you find the bodies, it will stay that way.'

'We've got enough.'

'Have you? So this is it? You're not expecting any more evidence?'

'Making the case stronger doesn't mean it's weak to start off with.'

'No,' Joe said, 'but all you've got is a jigsaw. Lose a piece, and you haven't got enough left to finish it. Take the blood. That's just one piece of the jigsaw, and Ronnie has an explanation for it.'

'I bet he has, Joe. And when did this recall happen? Just after you took over the case? Why didn't he tell the police all that?'

'That's Mahones for you,' Joe said. 'You can't punish a man for his bad representation.'

Kim was silent for a while, and then said, 'So what is it, this explanation for the blood?'

He shook his head. 'Not yet, but do you agree that if he has got an explanation, your case becomes too weak?' Joe was trying to persuade her that she had no case. It wouldn't end it yet, but it might make it easier to persuade Kim to drop the case later if she started out with less confidence. He pointed to the television. 'You were looking for the stain of guilt. Do you think that person there could have killed his own child? Really?'

'They come in all guises. That's what you were saying two minutes ago.'

'Killing your own child is different. That would lead to some kind of darkness. With Ronnie, there's nothing. He's scared, because of this case, but he doesn't seem haunted by anything.'

Kim didn't have time to respond because the door behind the raised bench opened and the judge walked in, with his horsehair wig and red sash over his silk clothes, like some extravagant dandy. It was the Recorder, the senior judge on the circuit who supervised all the most serious cases. Joe made a mental note that it was 'my Lord', not 'your Honour'. The words were habit-forming, a way of filling the gaps in speech, but when it resulted in bad etiquette, it gave the judge an excuse to try to make him look small.

Everyone rose to their feet and waited for the judge to nod that they should sit down. Joe fastened his suit jacket. It was supposed to be fastened, but he always made a show of it, just so the judge spotted his respect. It was the little things that won arguments. Once in his place, the judge looked towards Joe with a scowl.

They rushed through the preliminary matters. Ronnie's name. The charge. Ronnie's plea of not guilty. Joe was able to set out which witnesses he wanted. When it came to fixing a date, they needed to know whether Ronnie would stay in prison. The trial would come around sooner if he stayed behind bars. The judge waved for Kim to stay seated.

'Do you have an application, Mr Parker?'

Joe understood the shorthand. *Don't waste my time with a bail application.* But Joe was more interested in Ronnie's feelings.

Joe rose to his feet. 'I do, my Lord.'

The judge raised his eyebrows, thick and white under his wig. 'I've read the papers.'

'I'm pleased, my Lord, because the flaws in the prosecution case are obvious.'

The judge sat back and seemed amused. 'Please enlighten me.'

Joe glanced towards the screen. Ronnie was leaning forward, his expression keen. The detectives were sitting back, smirking, thinking that they had the judge on their side. What they didn't know was that Joe had been first into the courtroom and a warm smile from him had made the court clerk let slip that the judge wasn't impressed with the case. Perhaps not enough to let Ronnie stay free until his trial, but at least it gave Joe a chance.

'The case is built on three things,' Joe said. 'Blood, an argument, and a confession.'

'And two missing people.'

'That's the crucial word, my Lord. Missing, not dead. What

if my client spends months incarcerated and then the deceased walks into the court, his daughter in a pushchair? It has to be a possibility. The blood? We've got smears, that's all. Nothing to age it yet, and his girlfriend lived there too. There was an argument, and not for the first time. It is a real leap to say that he must have killed his girlfriend, and then his own daughter.'

'What about the confession?' the judge said. 'He walked into a police station and admitted killing his partner.'

'It depends which confession you mean,' Joe said. 'I counted at least three. So which one is it? "I've killed her"? "I think I've killed her"? Or "It's my fault, I've killed her"? We don't want another Derek Bentley case of "Let him have it, Chris", where people lose everything on a nuance. Does the prosecution have it recorded anywhere?'

The judge turned to Kim. 'Miss Reader?'

She rose to her feet, Joe giving way to her. 'If your Lordship means whether it is captured on CCTV, the answer is no.'

'But three accounts?' the judge said.

'One account from the person who heard it, and two accounts from people to whom he recounted it. Their recollections may be flawed, but we have an account from the person who heard it.'

'Who might have got it wrong, by the sounds of it.'

Kim didn't respond.

'And the blood?' the judge continued. 'Can you prove it is recent?'

'I'm told we can age the blood. We will seek to do that, but it is too early in the case to have that evidence available.'

'So at the moment you can't age the smears?'

Kim shook her head. 'No, my Lord.' A flush developed in her cheeks.

'So we can't be sure what was said and we can't be sure how long the blood has been there?'

'No, my Lord,' Kim said, her voice getting quieter.

'And so all you have is an argument and two missing people.'

Joe felt a glow of anticipation that the case was turning his way. The judge paused and looked up at the television, at Ronnie craning forward, anxious.

Joe scribbled on a piece of paper and slid it along the desk to Kim.

Kim glanced down and read it. *Agree bail and I won't say anything else about the evidence. Let it go to trial.* She took a couple of deep breaths and turned to the back of the court-room, to the detectives who were now leaning forward, their arms over the brass rail of the public gallery. She looked at Joe, who winked. He knew his words were still in her mind, that he could try to get the judge to dislike the case from the start.

'My Lord, the prosecution haven't asked for the defendant to be remanded in custody,' she said. Her voice was quiet, and she blinked at the sound of the two detectives walking briskly out of court, their moods discernible from the thumps of their hands against the door. 'Bail would be appropriate, with conditions, if your Lordship approves.'

'Does he have any convictions?'

'A minor assault a few years ago.'

'And does he have somewhere to live?'

Joe rose to his feet. 'He can stay at his mother's address, in Marton. She is at the back of the court.'

The judge nodded to himself. 'So be it,' he said eventually. When Joe bowed his gratitude, the judge added, 'I hope this man's partner walks into a police station soon, but if any bodies are found, the prosecution will succeed in getting your client's bail revoked.'

Joe bowed his gratitude again. 'I hear you, my Lord.'

He swivelled round to Monica, who was beaming her

admiration, and when he looked at Ronnie, his mouth was open, shock on his face. Ronnie was getting out.

As Joe looked around, his eyes went to the back of the courtroom. Whoever the man was who had been watching, he had gone.

Nineteen

Sam was confused. 'Ben Grant wants to speak to me?' he said to Evans. 'Why me?'

'Because you caught him, is my guess,' Evans said. 'He knows who you are, and your importance to the case, although he might think you're still a uniformed constable and so you'll be a soft target, be taken in by him. Ben Grant is all about his ego.'

'I'm okay, I can deal with him,' Sam said, nodding.

'Good, I'm glad to hear it. I'm not going to rush it though, because what Grant will hate is being ignored. He might tell us more if he gets desperate to tell us. So familiarise yourself with these four missing girls. Know all about them, read everything, get the facts in here.' She tapped the side of her head. 'Places, dates, so that if he says something that you know is plain wrong, we can discount it, put it down to what we think it will be, Ben Grant being grandiose, but if he tells you something that we haven't released, then you'll know it's important. More than that, he might tell you something we don't know.'

'I can do this,' Sam said.

'You mustn't share anything with him though. You are not going to see him so that he can indulge in sick fantasies, something for when he's on his own in his cell. The flow of information is going one way only.'

'I understand, but there is something I don't get.'

'Go on.'

'The coincidence. You drag me in because of Ronnie Bagley, because my brother became his lawyer, and now Ben Grant wants me too. I can't understand why I've become so popular.'

Evans drummed her fingers on the desk for a few seconds and then sighed. 'It's no coincidence.'

'What do you mean?'

'There is a link with Ronnie Bagley's case, although not an obvious one,' Evans said. 'Bagley killed Carrie Smith, his partner, along with their child. That's our case, except that Carrie is something significant to Ben Grant. Does her name sound familiar?'

Sam curled his lip as he thought about it, and then said, 'No, it doesn't.'

'Carrie used to work with Ben Grant,' Evans said. 'Her name came up a few times in Grant's case, because there were rumours he had a girlfriend, except he wouldn't admit it.'

'And the rumours pointed to Carrie?'

'Yes, and guess what: in the last five years, Carrie has been visiting Grant in prison. She was the only person he ever allowed to visit.'

Sam was surprised. 'Why would anyone want to visit Ben Grant? Girlfriend or not, he raped and killed children, for Christ's sake.'

'I don't know, and we'll never find out now, because we think Ronnie killed her, but she's another link to Ben Grant, and we haven't found her body either.'

'But if she is another missing woman connected to Grant, couldn't she be another victim of the same person who has made the others disappear?'

'Perhaps, but we don't think so. She's a different type of victim. She's a lot older, for a start. And there is other evidence linking Ronnie to her murder. The blood. A confession. Threats. Carrie is different from the others because she was actually connected to Grant. The other missing girls are just connected to people who put Grant away. A barrister. A detective. A crime scene investigator. A juror. It seems almost as if they are some kind of revenge for Ben Grant. Carrie's murder is different.'

'So what can Grant know? And who would do it for him?'

'Sam, cast your mind back to when you discovered Grant, in those bushes. You are the only person who can know the answer to this, because you were alone when you caught him.'

'Okay.'

'You said in your original statement that you were totally focused on Ben Grant.'

'I was. I just knew something dangerous was happening. I was watching him totally. I'll admit it, I was scared.'

Evans looked Sam in the eye. 'Think carefully, Sam. Could there have been someone else in the bushes?'

He was surprised, but his mind went back once more. Dark greenery, with only his torch to illuminate the scene. He had kept it trained on Grant. There were noises, soft swishes. 'I heard something, but no voices, no shouting, no one running. Just some movement, like rustling. Are you thinking that he might have had an accomplice?'

'Maybe. These four missing girls aren't copycat, because the bodies haven't been found, but it is connected. They all have relations connected to the Ben Grant case. Now his most frequent visitor is missing, presumed dead.'

'More than *presumed*,' Sam said. 'Someone is charged with her murder.' When Evans didn't answer, he asked, 'Are you thinking that Ronnie Bagley was his accomplice?'

'It's possible.'

Sam thought about it. He had followed the Ben Grant case, because of his interest in it, and Ronnie Bagley's name had never come up. 'But if Ronnie was on some kind of revenge mission for Ben Grant, why would he kill Carrie? She was his girlfriend, the mother of his child.'

'We've asked ourselves the same questions. It might be just

a coincidence. Ronnie's case looks like a domestic killing, an attack in their flat, and perhaps it is just one of those things that Grant's most frequent visitor was murdered at a time when these girls were going missing.'

'Do you believe that?' Sam said.

Evans shook her head. 'No good copper likes a coincidence. Which is more likely, that it is pure chance, or that it means something? Carrie knew Grant. She was his confidante. Is that how she got to know Ronnie, because of his connection to Grant? Was she was going to expose him as Grant's accomplice? Had Grant told her something that no one else knew? Had Ronnie been attracted to Carrie because he could keep in touch with Grant through her? There are so many scenarios that we don't know where to start. So go and see Grant; your job is to make him desperate to share.'

'I'll do what I can,' Sam said, although as Evans nodded her approval, he wondered how he would deal with meeting someone who had done just what someone else had done to Ellie, fifteen years earlier. It wasn't something he relished.

Evans smiled. 'Good to have you on board.'

Sam thanked her. This was his chance.

Twenty

Joe stood and waited by his car outside Strangeways, Monica next to him, with Ronnie's mother still sat in the back, her bag on her knees, confusion in her eyes, just like she had seemed at court. His car was parked awkwardly, so Joe had one eye on the prison gate, the other on the traffic patrols, hoping not to cop a ticket. It was a rare thing for Joe, because it wasn't his job to give prisoners lifts home, but then again, Ronnie was a murder suspect so he got special treatment.

'Can I ask something?' Monica said. Her voice seemed hesitant.

'Yes, anything,' Joe said.

'I don't mean to be rude, and I'm sorry if you think I am, but, well,' and she smiled nervously, 'I like you and I think I can talk to you.'

Joe returned the smile. 'Just say it. You won't offend me.'

'You've been quiet ever since we left court. I just thought you'd be happier, because you did your job well. You got Ronnie out of prison when most people wouldn't. Is it because he's accused of murder so you worry you've done the wrong thing? I need to know how I'll be able to cope with things like that, helping people who've done bad things.'

Joe was surprised. He hadn't realised he had seemed distant, although he had been brooding. The stranger at the back of court had unnerved him, the same person who had been outside his office the day before. It meant there were things happening that felt out of his control. He didn't like that.

But he didn't want to share any of that with Monica.

'It's a responsibility,' Joe said. 'There are no guarantees when he leaves prison. He has promised to turn up for his trial and keep out of trouble, but empty promises are easily made.'

He was saved from any further discussion by a noise, a creak of hinges. A small grey door opened, next to the large steel ones where the white prison vans drove in. A guard looked out first, a bald head and bright white shirt, and then Ronnie stepped into freedom.

Ronnie blinked and shielded his eyes at first. He looked around, shocked, as if he hadn't expected his day to turn out like that. When he saw Joe he waved, although it seemed hesitant.

As he got closer, Joe said, 'How are you feeling?'

Ronnie took a deep breath. 'I don't know. Pleased to be out of there, I suppose, but it's not over yet.'

'So you need to do whatever I say,' Joe replied. 'If the trial goes badly, you'll be back in there, except this time with no privileges.'

'I want a drink.'

'You've time for that later.'

'No, now, just one,' Ronnie said. 'I've had a rough night. I deserve one.'

Joe sighed. He needed to speak to Ronnie anyway. Getting clients in for their appointments was one of the many challenges the job created, because they lived chaotic lives and didn't go by a normal clock. Every day was just another hard slog to get through, and so a meeting a week later was often nothing more than a niggle that they knew they had somewhere to go that day. He hoped it would be different with Ronnie, but he wanted to avoid the possibility.

'All right,' Joe said, 'but then straight to your mother's afterwards.'

'Is she in there?' Ronnie said, nodding towards the car.

'She's the key to your freedom,' Joe said. 'If she hadn't turned up today, you wouldn't have got out.'

Winnie put her face to the car window. There was no gesture from Ronnie, no smile or wave. He walked round to the other side and climbed in alongside her. She turned to say hello but Ronnie just mumbled in reply. When Joe climbed in, he looked into his mirror and said, 'So where to, Ronnie? Your call.'

'Can you take me to Marton?' When Joe agreed, Ronnie said, 'Good. I'll tell you when we get there.'

Joe exchanged a curious glance with Monica, but it was Ronnie's freedom, not his. The least Joe could do was let him choose where to drink his first pint.

Marton was a small town outside of the Manchester ring, one of the last stops before the sprawling moorlands of the Pennines. The journey started as inner city clutter, with adult shops and bargain off-licences, before it opened out into semi-detached suburbia and then the small towns just outside the motorway that looped around Manchester. The journey was quiet, with Ronnie's mother silent all the way there, and Ronnie either looking out of the window or down at his phone, which had been in his hand ever since they left the prison.

The nearer they got to Marton, the greener it became, with the last part of the journey a long climb lined by low stone walls and trees that grew over the road. The branches clattered against buses and made shadows across the tarmac, and the hilltops were just barren glimpses between the trees.

The mood changed as they drove into the town. The redbrick of Manchester was replaced by the grey stone of the Pennines, where the doorways were smaller and the streets ran much steeper. The sun tried to give it some rustic charm, reflecting brightly against the polished steps on the rows of cottages that fronted up to the road. But up here the winds blew hard, and even on the warmest days a grey cloud always seemed to be nearby, ready to take away the brightness.

Joe checked his mirror to look into the back seat. Ronnie was staring forward, at Monica, suddenly less interested in his surroundings.

'So where are we having this drink, Ronnie?' Joe said, as the houses gave way to shops.

Ronnie peered through the windscreen and then pointed. 'There. The Brittania, near the station.'

Joe followed the gesture and saw a pub on the main street, draped in St George bunting with a couple of bench tables outside. There was a view along the main street, and Joe guessed that the moorland crispness was just enough to take away the traffic fumes. It was Ronnie's drink though, not Joe's, and so he found somewhere to pull over. 'Can you drive?' he said to Monica.

She looked surprised. 'Yes.'

'Good,' Joe said. 'Take Mrs Bagley home and then come back here.'

Joe stepped out of the car and was joined on the pavement by Ronnie. As Monica drove his car away, Joe turned to Ronnie and said, 'You need to know that I'm not going to come running every time you call me.'

'But you're preparing my case.'

'That doesn't make me your babysitter. I'm the lawyer here, not you, and so what I say goes. If I need you to give me some information, you give it. If I call, you come running. Do we understand each other?'

Ronnie shrugged, his expression sulky.

'If I'm not there, call Monica Taylor.'

'Is that her name?'

'She's the trainee. She'll pass everything on, so don't worry, I'll be making the decisions, but it will be quicker that way.'

As they walked into the pub Ronnie became more agitated, looking around, swallowing.

'You look like you really want this drink,' Joe said.

'Yes, I do. Can we start preparing now?'

'Why not,' Joe said, but then he looked around, his voice a whisper. 'But wait until we get outside.'

The pub was dark inside, with deep red carpets and paintings screwed to the walls. There was a smell of food in the air, pub fare, and there was a decent lunchtime trade. An old man with a newspaper. A group of workmen in dayglo bibs eating from plates piled high with chips. A woman with dark hair staring quietly into her drink.

Joe ordered the drinks and then followed Ronnie back outside. They settled on the wooden benches, Joe's orange juice on the table in front of him. He watched as Ronnie took a long, slow sip of his drink, a creamy bitter.

'So, Ronnie, how was it last night?'

He looked into his drink for a few seconds, and then said, 'I thought I'd be able to handle it, but . . .' He stopped and shook his head. 'Do you ever think about it, when your clients go to prison?'

Joe thought on how to answer that. The truth was yes, he did, because he took it as a failure, but Joe knew the system wasn't perfect, not by a long way, but it tried its hardest to work. Prison was part of that game, and once the prison van pulled away, he consoled himself with the thought that justice had taken its course.

'Yes, all the time,' Joe said.

'Until you've experienced it, you can't really know,' Ronnie said, his eyes down. 'It's the noises, echoes. The floors are all so hard, and the walls, so every sound seems to bounce around. You can't just hide away, because it feels like it's coming right at you.' He shook his head slowly. 'I thought I could do it.'

'So make sure you keep in touch,' Joe said. 'If you don't want to go back there, we need to plan your case properly. And your mother looked pleased to have you back.'

'That's a lie and you know it. She's doing it because you asked.' Ronnie took another drink. 'So what now?'

'You spend tonight with your mother. If I need to speak to you, I'll call you, so keep that phone charged up. I don't know when I'll need you.'

'What are you going to do?'

'I'm going to get my team together later and plan for everything.'

'I need to ask you one thing,' Ronnie said, looking Joe in the eye.

Joe held his gaze. He knew what was coming.

'Do you think I did it? That I killed Carrie and my baby?'

Joe had been right. The quest for reassurance, that someone was fighting for him.

'It doesn't matter what I think,' Joe replied. 'It's about the evidence, about whether you should be convicted.'

'But I'm entitled to know, because you must have an opinion, and if it's about me, I should know it.'

Joe considered what to say, and then he shook his head. 'No, I don't think you did it.'

Then Joe looked away, because the truth was that he didn't know, and what frightened him most of all was that if Ronnie had done something so callous, killed his own child to cover up another crime, the lack of remorse in his eyes made him a very dangerous person.

Twenty-One

Sam sat at a desk by a window, the only vacant one, because there was no blind to stop the sun from bleaching out the computer screen, and already the heat of the steady glare was sticking his shirt to his back. It gave him a view over the Incident Room, so he could work out who might help him, and who would do their best to not. Squads like this were always that three-way mix of jaded old-timers, canteen braggers, and those with talent on the rise. The canteen braggers were the ones to avoid, who thought that noise and fake camaraderie, wrapped up in tight pastel shirts, were the keys to success.

Sam watched the movement in the room for a few minutes, to judge who was liked and who wasn't, looking for the smiles that quickly disappeared when the joke ended, and then logged into the police computer. He found the summaries of each case.

There was nothing remarkable about them, nor anything unusual about the girls. They were all a similar age, mid to late teens. Not children, but not really women either. All disappeared, with no warning, no trace. There must have been a weapon if they had been abducted, like a knife and a threat. The call logs for each night they disappeared had been collated, and as he scrolled through them he saw there had been no reports of struggles or screams. That made the connection seem more obvious, because it was another link. Not just Ben Grant, but also the way in which they disappeared.

People went missing and it wasn't always foul play, Sam knew that, but these seemed different. In most cases, you could look to a reason. A history of running away or run-ins with the police. Drugs. Perhaps a boyfriend or the wrong crowd. If there were no calls about a fight or screams, they were either runaways or else they went willingly. But, in these cases, runaways didn't seem likely. Their backgrounds showed no signs of anything being wrong. They weren't from bad families. There were no concealed drug problems or boyfriends who made the family nervous. All they knew was that their daughters went out one evening and never returned. There were headlines for a few days, with media appeals and soundbites from those closest to them, and then the story dwindled as news of each missing person faded, rehashed only when there was another disappearance.

Sam remembered how they had been swamped after Ellie's murder, and that was before instant headlines on the internet were the norm. Cameras outside the gate, reporters shouting for a quote, their deadlines more important than the family's grief. But how could a few words summarise what they felt? The victims in these cases were not children, but the first two were pretty and white, and that had got the press interested.

He thought again of Ellie. Her murder had shaped his adult life. He had been a university student when she was killed, studying English, but Ellie's death changed everything. He dropped out so that he could look after his parents, the eldest boy. That was the year his career changed, because he saw what the police did for his family, and he joined within twelve months. If any good had come from it, the fact that he had done the right thing in his career was it.

It had been different for Joe, almost as if Ellie's death was something he wanted to get away from. It had always been Sam, not Joe, who had been there for his parents, held their hands through their darkest time, helped them somehow carry on with their lives. Joe just headed off to university and left everything behind. Sam had resented that at first, but maturity had taught him that people dealt with grief in different ways. Ellie's killer had done despicable things to her in her final moments, and to Sam it had seemed that Joe's way of coping with that had been to try not to dwell on it.

Sam tried to focus on the case again. Four attractive young women, with long flowing hair and bright smiles, but there was nothing else to link them apart from the Ben Grant case. They were from different parts of Manchester, different backgrounds, and none of them were friends. If it hadn't been for the Ben Grant connection, it would have seemed like just random bad luck that they came across whoever made them disappear. None of them had given any clue about where they were going. Two had just left the house and never returned. One had gone missing after running an errand. Another had lied about where she was going.

There was a noise in front of him. He looked up. It was one of the detectives he had noticed the day before. He was in just a shirt, his jacket draped over a chair, but he needed a larger one, because his biceps pushed against his sleeves. He was carrying a tray filled with cups. 'Hello, new boy,' he said.

He glanced back at the room when he said it, so Sam knew that he was about to be the butt of a joke.

'It's not "new boy",' Sam said, pushing his glasses up his nose. 'My name is Sam Parker. And you are?'

'You can call me Ged,' he said, and put the tray on the desk, making the cups clatter. 'Fresher's privilege. You get to make us all a drink.'

Sam looked behind him. Some of the men were watching, waiting for his reaction. It was a test, he knew that, to see how he would fit in. Sam wasn't interested in canteen politics. He was either good enough or he wasn't.

'I'll tell you what, big boy,' Sam said. 'Seeing as though I'm the guest, why don't you be a good host and make me one. You just need to find me a cup.' There was a moment of discomfort and then someone sniggered. Sam looked back towards his screen, smiling. At least someone had enjoyed it.

Then there was the sound of a phone slamming down. Everyone looked round. It was DI Evans, and her jaw was clenched hard. She stared at Sam, and for a moment he wondered what he had done wrong.

'He's out!' she shouted.

'Bagley?' someone asked.

'Yes, this morning. The judge gave the prosecutor a hard time and so she buckled and let him go.' She kicked at the leg of a desk. Everyone stayed silent, although all eyes turned to Sam.

He was about to say something when Evans shook her head. 'No need. It's not your fault.' She was taking deep breaths through her nose. She closed her eyes. 'Fuck!'

Sam went back to the screen, as refuge rather than interest. The detective who had spoken to him before was staring at him more intently, holding the tray he had brought over.

He felt the excitement of the investigation fade, replaced by resentment. He shuffled and went red, but it wasn't embarrassment. It was frustration. It was about Joe, as always, not him.

Twenty-Two

Joe waited in his office for Gina and Monica to join him.

He was standing by the window, gazing towards the park, his mind occupied with how he was going to organise Ronnie's case, when he noticed something. There was someone sitting on a bench on the side furthest away. The same man as before, the one who had turned up at court, in a grey V-neck, his legs crossed, facing towards the flowerbeds, but his head was cocked towards the office.

There was a creak behind him, and as he turned, he saw that it was Gina. Monica was a few steps behind, bringing with her the aroma of fresh coffee, a tray of drinks balanced on her arm.

Joe looked back to the window, to point out the person he had seen to Gina, but the bench was now empty.

Gina took the chair nearest to Joe's desk and said, 'How did it go with Ronnie?'

Joe thought about that for a few seconds and then said, as he took a cup from her, 'Monica, what do you think?'

'I thought he'd be more pleased to be out. I mean, he loosened a bit after that drink, but when we dropped him at his mother's house, he seemed, well ...'

'Hesitant?' Joe said.

'Yes, that's it, as if he didn't really want to go in.'

'That's what I thought,' he said, and Monica blushed,

pleased to hear that she had assessed it correctly. 'We need to know more about Ronnie Bagley. Can you do that, Gina? Try to tap some of your police sources.'

'I can, but the prosecution can't spring any traps, you know that,' Gina said. 'Whatever they are going to use, they have to show us.'

'I'd rather know before they tell us, so that we're ready to fight back. We might even find something out that helps us, like a reason why he comes across badly. He doesn't come across as dangerous, but it feels like he's holding something back all the time. We have to accept that juries might not like him. We can put him in a suit, but he'll look uncomfortable, and if he gives evidence, he'll come across as surly.'

'Do we know why Mahones told him to stay silent in his interviews?' Gina said. 'It makes him look guilty from the off. All he had to say was that he didn't know where Carrie had gone.'

'Not yet,' Joe said. 'Stick to what he tells us. If we tip them off, they might alter their notes, to make their advice look better. We can spring that just before the trial.'

'What if he told them he did it, that he had killed Carrie and his daughter?' Monica said.

'Then we feel happy that he hasn't told me that yet.'

Monica sat down. 'That doesn't make me feel good. I believe him, because I think he would seem different somehow, if he had killed his daughter. I don't mean I like him, but I believe him.'

'If you stay in criminal law, clients will shock you for the rest of your career, whether you believe in them or not,' Joe said. 'But you can't let it affect what you do. If you can't cope with that thought, then you're in the wrong line of business. You will free rapists and killers, and make excuses for all the low-lifes who won't care about the misery they cause. Tough. That's the bargain you make with yourself when you take on the job.'

'Can we stop the philosophical debate for a moment,' Gina said, impatience in her voice. 'How are we approaching Ronnie's case?'

'We have to dismantle it,' Joe said. 'The clues aren't obvious. There's no body in the basement, no eyewitnesses. The prosecution have had to build the case and make it fit in with their version of events. We have to take each strand of their case and unravel it, because we can't rely on Ronnie to talk his way out of it. By the time Ronnie steps into the witness box, if he does, our case will be as good as it gets, because when Ronnie starts talking, it will just get worse. He will have to admit violence, and he will have to explain away his confession. So we need to knock down the prosecution case so that the judge throws it out before it even gets to Ronnie's turn.'

'So how do we go about that?' Gina said.

'The blood is the first problem. We've got smears, not blood spatter analysis, but it makes it sound like mopping up. The police seized more things with brown stains on them that they think might be blood, which includes a saw. If it is blood, and it is Carrie's, they've got a theory about the bodies being disposed of.'

'It could be worse than that,' Monica said quietly. 'It could be little Grace's blood.'

That made everyone pause, until Joe said, 'So let's hope it isn't, not just for Ronnie's sake, because he goes straight to jail if it is Grace's, but for our own. There are some things I don't want to think about. Until then, we defend him. If it is Carrie's blood on that saw, we need another explanation for it. Gina, I want you to talk to him about it. If it is blood and it is Carrie's, we need a damn good story for why her blood ended up all over that blade. The prosecution's case, that there is only one possible explanation is all speculation. We need to provide some different options.'

'But it's cumulative, all the strands pulled together,' Gina said.

'I know that, but a number of explanations gives a number of possible outcomes. Our job is to create doubt, that's all.'

Joe started to pace, thinking about the case. It was the part he liked best, when he saw the challenge, the evidence against him.

'Monica?'

She sat up in her seat, attentive.

'Hit the experts' directory,' Joe said, his voice more urgent. 'Find someone who can examine blood. Could it be old blood? We don't need to prove how old it is, just that it could have been there longer than the prosecution say. We need to destroy the case so that Ronnie doesn't have to get in the witness box.'

As Monica made some notes, Joe turned back to Gina. 'We need to find Carrie. That's the most important thing. If we can prove that she might not be dead, there is no case at all. The police have spoken to her family and friends. Speak to people who might want to avoid the police, like anyone she's been in trouble with. Trawl the gutters. Speak to people in the red light areas. We need to check she hasn't just run away and is holed up somewhere, earning money.'

'What about you?' Gina said.

'I'm going to speak to the landlord tomorrow. The other angle is that there might be more than one suspect. The landlord is a witness, not a suspect, but I might be able to change that. Or he might know of other people who visited Carrie, perhaps when Ronnie was out. She was a drinker and had no money. She might have found other ways to pay for the booze.'

'Wouldn't the police have uncovered that?' Monica said.

'You'd think so, but the police tend to look at proving a theory, whereas we are looking at disproving it. We have to be more creative.'

'You need to be careful,' Gina said. 'You could destroy the landlord's reputation if people end up thinking it is him.'

'Right now, it's Ronnie I'm concerned about.'

'Why are you leaving it until tomorrow?'

'Because there's someone I need to see.'

'In relation to Ronnie's case?'

Joe nodded. 'There's something that's bothering me, about the prosecutor this morning.'

'Like what?'

'She gave in too easily, which isn't like Kim.'

He pulled out his phone and went to a number he kept in his address book but rarely used. He pressed dial and then waited. When he heard her voice, he fought hard to keep the smile from his face.

'Kim, it's me, Joe Parker. Do you fancy a drink?'

When she agreed, he arranged a place and then rang off. He had some questions, and he wanted Kim to answer them. He tapped his phone against his chin. He reckoned the day was about to get really interesting.

Twenty-Three

The City Arms was one of Joe's favourite pubs, a small place of wood and guest ales behind a typical Manchester exterior of old green tiles. The music was set on low, so that the air was filled with the sound of conversation and the clink of glasses. The long wooden tables were clear, the after-work crowd spilled onto the pavement outside.

He checked his watch. Kim Reader was late, but she had always been like that.

Someone came in, and he looked up, expectant, but it wasn't her. He took another drink. Warm bitter, the pint glass ringed by white marks, each one showing where he unwound a little more, like the slow loosening of a belt.

He was just checking his phone, wondering if Kim had backed out, when she walked in. She was a little breathless, as if she had walked quickly from her office just a few streets away.

Joe got to his feet to buy her a drink but she waved him down. When she came over, she was carrying two drinks. A small lager for her, and another beer for him.

'It's not a sign of weakness, me buying the drinks,' he said, smiling.

Kim shook her head as she sat down. 'It would be regarded as hospitality, you know that, and I'm not allowed any from a defence lawyer. So if I buy, it's just two old friends having a drink.'

He smiled and drained his glass, sliding the new one over. 'Thanks for coming. I appreciate it.'

Kim looked around. 'I would have thought we could have met somewhere nicer.'

'What's up with the place? I like it.'

'You choose like a drinker. I choose, well, like I need a bit of glamour.'

'You meet more interesting people in real pubs. Anyway, I thought you might prefer the darkness, in case you were seen.'

'By whom?'

'Your bosses. Your beau.' He took a drink and watched her reaction. Her blush told him that it was her boyfriend she was worried about. 'Like you say, it's just two old friends enjoying a drink.'

'It's not like that,' she said, and then tried to stop the blush from spreading. It was exactly like that. 'It was good to see you today.'

'And you.'

'How's business?'

'Good, and for as long as you don't lay off charging people, it will stay good.'

'We've no plans to do that.'

Joe sat back to lean against the old leather pads at the back of the high bench. 'How is your boyfriend? Is it Sean?'

She looked into her glass. When she looked up again, her eyes had lost some of their shine. 'We pass in the hall sometimes.'

Joe rolled his eyes, laughing. 'You're not about to give me the "my partner doesn't understand me" spiel, are you? I thought it was men who came out with that stuff.'

'I'd be more direct, you know that,' Kim said, and as she looked at him, the light flecks in her green eyes were crowded out by the spread of her pupils.

For a few moments, the prosecutor, in her dark suit and

manicured fingernails, was gone and back came the student Joe had known, the happy young woman he had stared at across a lecture hall, always in denims that hung from her hips and a baggy old jumper. He tried not to think how he had seen her sometimes, her clothes on the floor, her eyes closed, two young people in bed. Those memories were clouded by drink, because that was how it had happened, that sometimes they went home together when they had been drinking. There were times when he had just walked her to her house, supporting her when she was drunk, and there were others when she had invited him in, to the mattress on the floor in a student room that smelled of marijuana.

'You haven't changed, you know,' Joe said. 'Except when you're in court.'

'What do you mean?'

Joe took a drink, avoiding the answer, but when Kim raised her eyebrows at him, he said, 'You're much tougher, like everything's a moral crusade. I remember how you were, and that must have been the real you, because you didn't have to play a part.'

'Perhaps this is the real me, and I needed the job to bring it out.'

'No, we've become what we wanted to become, but that is different to how we are. Are you this tough at home, away from the office?'

Kim looked down, and Joe knew he had upset her.

'Sometimes it's hard to switch off,' she said. 'I make decisions that ruin lives, whichever way the decision goes, and it weighs heavily, but Sean expects me to come in and be all sweetness, be some kind of domestic goddess, when I'm just so tired most of the time.' She took a deep breath and raised her glass. 'I need this too much, I know that, but I know what it will be like when I get home.' Once she'd taken a drink, she said, 'You've changed.'

'How?'

'More grown up, I suppose. More serious. You don't laugh as much as you used to.'

'Maybe life isn't as funny anymore,' he said, and took off his jacket and put it on the seat next to him.

'So come on,' she said. 'I'm sure you haven't invited me out to mull over how our lives have got worse, so let's get it out of the way. Ronnie Bagley.'

'What do you mean?'

'We see each other often enough and you don't usually ask me out for a drink. What's different about today?'

Joe thought about denying it, but he knew it was obvious why he'd called her.

'Okay, Ronnie Bagley,' he said.

'Is this off the record, or should I make a note?'

'It's just a talk,' Joe said.

'If any of this is used in the case, whatever I say, we'll never talk again.'

'You know I fight hard, but you know that I'm never underhand.'

Kim paused as she thought about that, and then said, 'Okay, what do you want to know?'

'It's about this morning,' Joe said.

'What, the court hearing?'

'Yes.'

'What about it?'

'It's about you, really. I've known you as a prosecutor ever since we both qualified, and if I know anything about you, it's that you are a fighter.'

Kim looked in her glass for a few seconds, swirling the froth around. 'There are some things you can't win.'

'No, that's wrong. Ronnie Bagley is charged with murder. I was blowing hot air, making a noise, acting up for Ronnie's benefit. I didn't expect you to cave in like that.'

'I didn't cave in.'

'You did. You got wind that you were losing the judge, and rather than talk him round, you gave it up. And you would never allow a man who you think murdered his girlfriend and baby to walk out of prison, just to avoid a judge turning against your case. That's not you, Kim. You could have fought it, because if you really believed in your case, you could have convinced the judge better than I could.'

'What are you trying to say?'

'That there was something else going on, and it's been bugging me all day.'

'What like?'

'There are only two possibilities. That you think Ronnie didn't do it, and just for a moment your conscience shaped your decision, except I've seen the evidence, and it looks okay.'

'So what other reason can there be?'

'That you want Ronnie out, even though you know he's guilty.'

'Why would we want that?'

'So it's *we* now?'

'You're not making sense anymore.'

'I don't think it was Kim the lawyer making the decision this morning,' Joe said, 'but the Kim who works with the police, because I don't think it was a legal decision. You caved in to help the investigation, because you think that whoever made the decision to charge Ronnie did it too soon. You let me think that it was all my doing, that I talked the judge round, but you want to find the bodies, because if you can do that, it will be easier to convict him. You wanted Ronnie walking the streets so that he'll lead you to the bodies.'

Kim drained her glass. Her eyes had lost that shine, her expression cold. 'I can't talk about things like that,' she said.

'It makes me sound like I'm right.'

'Perhaps you made a good case, Joe. For once, it might have

been about you.' She got to her feet and reached down to collect her bag. 'I've got to go.'

'I didn't mean to end it so quickly,' he said, reaching out for her hand.

She smiled ruefully. 'I'd have come out if you'd just wanted to say hello, maybe even talk about old times. I can't do this though.' She kissed him on the cheek, her lips cold from her drink. 'See you around, Joe.'

As he watched her go and the coldness of her kiss faded, he slumped back into his seat, feeling empty. He was used to women walking out of his life. He just wished he could summon up some fight in himself to try to stop them. He raised his glass and said, 'Yeah, you too,' but the alcohol had lost its glow.

Twenty-Four

He closed his eyes and put his head back, stretching out his back. He took a long, deep breath, inhaled the cold air of the night around him, daylight gone, just the blue darkness of an early-summer evening. He tried to reclaim the silence, after his day filled with noise.

He was back where he belonged. This was his space, his world. The hum of the city wasn't far away, cars and trams, the occasional smash of a bottle or drunken shout. That was somewhere else, beyond the walls, high and safe. He had no control out there. Here, it was different. It was his space, where he knew the shadows and had been into the dark corners, broken its peace with the echoes of his footsteps.

He went there to be with them, long nights with his memories, as if to stay there meant they hadn't really lost their lives, that his presence somehow kept them alive. He was their guardian, looking after them until nature took them back and turned them into dust.

The air tasted of beautiful familiarity. Cold steel, rusted iron, damp brickwork, the sweet smell of the ferns that grew through the concrete. Scents that reminded him of all those nights spent alone there, where he paced, marked out, sometimes jumping at the noises in the shadows that kept him on edge until the slow spread of daybreak pushed back the threats, receded until the following night, when they would creep out once more, each time more daring.

It was more than just those nights though, because not every night was long and lonely, with just darkness and imagination to keep him company until morning. It was the other nights. The screams. The chases. The struggles. Thrashing bodies under his hands, flickering eyelids, memories like strobe lights.

He opened his eyes. Stars shone through the gaps in the roof, just dots in the gloom, the full spread broken by the jagged edges of broken metal, the corrugated strips smashed in places, sometimes through vandalism, other times through simple decay. Where he was standing had been undisturbed for more than sixty years, except for the slow progress of time, reclaiming it, taking it apart piece by piece. Each time he visited, it filled him with awe; that this could exist at the heart of the city, its heartbeat still, frozen, just waiting for some attention. It said so much, was symbolic, that behind all that was new and modern was disease and dereliction, forgotten glories left to crumble.

It wasn't an easy place to be though. It was the shadows that plagued him, the way a bright moon made the light come through in patches. Some parts in front of him were shifting patterns of grey, insects caught in the light, whilst others were nothing other than pitch black.

He closed his eyes again. He wanted the noises. They helped to bring the place alive. Some of them were real, some of them distant. Sometimes it was light scratches, claws on concrete, scampering, dashing for the long grass that had taken over in places. Or the crack of flapping wings, birds nesting in the roof space, the sound of flight bouncing and swirling above him, so that he had to turn quickly to know the source of the noise, ready for when the wings brushed too close and he felt dirty feathers in his hair.

The thought made him shudder, and his mind went to the

119

other sounds, soft to the ear, never loud enough to blot out the constant noise from the other side of the walls, but he could hear them. They were ghosts of the past, the memories embedded in the brickwork. The movement of people, like a constant murmur. Feet on concrete, shouts, the turn of the large wheels, whistles like screams.

He stepped forward, just to hear the crunch of his footsteps, to break his thoughts, because he could feel the tremble in his fingers as he knew where his mind was going, to his own memories. He couldn't go there, not yet. He hadn't broken the spell.

There was a flurry of wings, birds swapping places on the rafters, making him turn quickly, his torch flashing upwards. His heart beat quickly. It made him jump. He laughed to himself and then raised his arms upwards and outwards, claiming ownership, his kingdom, an oasis of nothing.

The sound of fear drifted towards him. It came as soft whimpers, muffled by the gag. He looked over.

She was under a shaft of light from the moon that shone through, like a silver spotlight, her hair streaming down her back, the light bouncing off it like water. He swallowed. She had been there for nearly an hour, her cries muted to sobs of fear. He had wanted to get away from this, but as he looked over, he knew he was being drawn back in again. She rocked on the chair, the wooden feet knocking quickly on the concrete.

He looked down at his own feet for a moment. Mortal, weak, just brown shoes, soft soles, hazy against the grey concrete floor. He knew what would happen next.

His feet made no sound as he walked over, moving softly, slowly, not wanting to alert her. His torch was off. It was the not-knowing that frightened them the most. There was a dark cloth around her eyes, pulled tight and tied at the back, digging into her skin, the edge wet where she had cried tears of fear.

The gag around her mouth was a small cloth rammed between her teeth and kept secure by a larger rag tied around it, digging hard into her cheeks.

It was something else that attracted him as he got closer though. It wasn't the gag, or the rise and fall of her breasts as her lungs tried to keep pace with her panic. It was her hair. It was long and dark and luxurious, falling like a dark stream down her back.

He put his face closer. She must have felt his breaths because she jolted and recoiled, and then her head thrashed around, trying to see him through the tightness of her blindfold. His hand reached out and he felt the crackle of static as he let her hair fall across his fingers, the strands lifting in the air. Her skin flashed into goosebumps and he saw the glisten of sweat. She was whimpering, struggling, the clatter of the chair on the floor getting faster.

He put his mouth next to her ear and whispered, 'Do you want to go home?' His voice was a hiss.

She screeched at first, but then as the words sank in she nodded, uncertain at first, but then more desperate, her approval coming as grunts through the gag.

He looked past her, to the figure by the wall. When he got the nod, his hand went to the knife in his pocket. The blade was sharp. He reached down to the rope that bound her arms to the chair and slashed at it. Her arms flexed as she was released from the pressure, although her hands were still tied behind her back. He knelt down to her ankles and cut the rope there, her feet kicking outwards. She was free from the chair, bound at the wrists, blindfolded and gagged.

'Fly, little bird,' he said.

As he stepped back from the chair, silent again, so that she wouldn't know where he was, he looked over once more, asking for approval. He got it. A smile.

It was time for the game.

Twenty-Five

Sam Parker's eyes opened quickly when he heard the telephone. He looked at Alice, who moaned softly before turning over. The clock radio said it was 6.30.

He thought about leaving it, expecting it to be another withheld number, another bout of screaming, but he knew he had to answer it, because wanting to know who it was would make him get up anyway. He scrambled under the pile of clothes from the night before until he found his phone. He flopped back onto his pillow before answering.

'Hello?' His voice was thick was sleep.

'It's Mary Evans.' Sam sat up, jolted awake. 'Someone else has gone missing,' she said. 'Another girl. You need to come in.' And then the phone went silent.

He wiped the tiredness from his eyes. He hadn't slept much the night before, the images of the missing girls on his mind. All long hair, innocent smiles. But he couldn't dwell on that, because then he would think about Ellie, or about how he would feel if it was one of his own daughters. That wasn't the way to think about it. Go in, do his job, impress. His own memories and fears would cloud things.

Alice stirred and put her arm around him. 'Don't tell me,' she murmured. 'You've got to go in.'

'I'm sorry,' he whispered, and kissed the top of her hair. 'Another girl has gone missing.'

Alice pulled away at that and propped herself up on her elbows. Sam saw her glance towards the bedroom door, to their own daughters' bedrooms.

'Are you all right doing this?' she said.

'Absolutely,' he said, and slid out of bed, pausing only to stretch. 'It's why I joined the police.'

'Just saying it doesn't convince me, Sam.'

He didn't answer as he got ready. A quick shower and he would skip breakfast. DI Evans had called him early because she wanted him there, and if he took too long, she would think that he didn't really want to be a part of it.

The journey in didn't take as long as usual, the rush hour not yet in full flow. When he got into the station, he sensed an increased feeling of urgency. It had been busy the day before, but it was something different. There were uniformed officers standing in groups on the corridor, in black boots and navy blue boiler suits, talking in whispers. Search teams. In the main squad room, a group of senior detectives were talking by the window.

Sam turned to the nearest person, Ged, the detective from the day before who had taunted him with the coffee. 'What's going on?' Sam said. 'Has a body turned up?'

'No. Just missing, but we're thinking the worst.'

'Connected?'

Ged looked like he wasn't going to answer, still bristling at the way Sam had stood up to him, but after a few seconds he said, 'Yes. She's called Julie McGovern. Her father is a local councillor, and he was one of the magistrates who first remanded Ben Grant in custody. And it looks like someone has tipped off the press, because they're gathering outside.' He shook his head. 'We've lost control now.'

The detective went back to his computer screen and Sam stood and looked over his shoulder. He recognised the blue banner of Facebook. The profile picture was of an attractive brunette, her wide smile showing teeth that were bright and even, with thick lustrous hair that swept down over her shoulders. As he looked down the page, there were photographs showing groups of girls with their arms around each other and comments posted underneath.

'Pretty girl,' Sam said.

'I'm watching her profile page,' Ged said, 'just to see if anyone posts something we don't know about.' He looked up at Sam. 'About yesterday. I was only joshing, you know how it is.'

'It isn't about us, it's about them, but thanks.' Before the detective could answer, Sam walked over to Evans, who was organising some paperwork. There was a map, and it looked like she was sorting the search teams or door-to-doors.

She glanced up as he got closer, but then held up her hand. Sam stopped. She was busy and wouldn't welcome the intrusion. He turned and went back to his desk. He remembered what Evans had said the day before, that he had to know everything about the case, so he went looking for the logs from the night before. He paused when he heard footsteps behind him. He turned round. It was Evans.

'You'll need to know about Julie,' Evans said. 'We've been on to the prison again this morning. We can't wait around for Grant now. Julie McGovern going missing has made it more urgent.'

'So what happened with Julie?'

'She went to meet a friend, but that was a lie. We spoke to the friend and there was no arrangement to meet.'

'Has she got a boyfriend?' Sam said.

'No, nothing steady. She's a good student, nice kid, if her profile is any guide. Works hard, listens to music, all the usual stuff.'

Sam looked at the pictures around the room of all the young women who had gone missing. Nice girls from good families.

'It could just be some mistake, like she has a boyfriend no one knows about, and so used a friend as an alibi,' Sam said. 'Families are complicated. Did things get out of hand and she stayed out later than she promised? Now she daren't come home because her father is a bigwig, and right now she's with her boyfriend, wondering what to do.'

DI Evans frowned. 'That's one scenario we've already thought of, and I hope you're right, but something tells me you're not. The connection with Ben Grant's case is too strong.' She cast her arm towards the search teams, dark blue boiler suits crowding the room. 'This might be all premature, but they'll slam me if I do nothing and turn out to be wrong.' She looked Sam up and down. 'Your inspector knows you're with us for the day, doesn't he?'

'He does, ma'am.'

'Good. Stay here then. We could do with the manpower.'

'Thank you. I'd like to help.'

'You're on the phones to start off with. I want you with Ben Grant today, so you've got to know everything about the case. We're just waiting for the nod from the prison.'

She walked off quickly to speak to the groups of boiler suits. Sam allowed himself a small smile. It might be just answering the phones, but it was much better than a slow slog through financial statements.

The morning had arrived brightly, the sun rising just after four, and had moved on slowly towards rush hour, the city beyond the walls gradually coming to life. His chest was pumping deep breaths, the hours before long and exciting, except that now he was in the climb-down and so had to fight back the shame, try to hang onto what happened at the height of the thrills.

She was on the floor, her body twisted, her white blouse dirty and torn, blood on the elbows and front. Her jeans were wet where she had pissed herself, her hair matted with sweat and dust from running around, being taunted, chased. She was still now, lifeless, her hair scruffy, all of its shine gone, bedraggled and lying across her face. She had been so different not long before, when she had been trying to cling onto the last shreds of life.

He reached down to move her hair from her face. His touch was tender as he lifted it from a wound, where it had stuck to a deep gash where she had run into an old pipe, the end jagged and broken. That had sent her to the floor, gasping, squirming in pain. The blood was drying now, no longer pumping. He moved her hair so that he was tidying her up. Her body should have some dignity in death.

He took a deep breath and sat back on the floor. He ran his hands over his face and wiped away the sweat. The start of the day made it seem so different. It became too stark, too real.

'You're being too soft.'

He looked up, shielding his eyes against the sun. 'Yes, I know,' he said, taking in the dead girl's swollen ankle from where she fell from one of the raised platforms, tumbling four feet to the ground. The cut on her forehead where she had run into a pillar. Her hands scrubbed red, cuts on her palm from scrambling across glass.

His eyes caught the pale skin of her breast, visible through a rip in her blouse. He looked away. It wasn't about that. It hadn't been about that for any of them.

'Come on, we need to get rid of her.'

He scrambled to his feet. He reached for her hair again and this time pulled it into a ponytail, tying a knot in it to keep it neat. He reached into his pocket and took out a pair of scissors. They were small and sharp, and as he cut across the ponytail he smiled as the long pieces of hair came away in his hand. It felt silky in his fist.

'Get her in the ground.'

'Okay, okay,' he said, and he grabbed her hand and dragged

her to a hole he had dug further along. Next to the others. He pulled her body so that she slithered into the ground and then dragged the dirt over her with the spade. He pressed it down with his foot and stepped back. The weeds would reclaim her soon. Nature did that. It cleansed, started again.

'I wanted to get away from all of this,' he said.

'Tonight again.'

'It was supposed to stop, you know that.'

'It was never going to stop.'

He clenched his jaw. He knew that was right.

'You can make it your choice, if you want.'

His eyes widened at that. 'Can I?'

'Yes. Tonight is for you.'

That pleased him. 'Good, thank you.'

'Do you know who it's going to be?'

'Yes, I do.' There was tightness in his chest. And excitement. 'I definitely do.'

Twenty-Six

Joe drove to the street where Ronnie Bagley had lived, to what the prosecution called the murder scene. It was a long street of Victorian bay windows, cobbled, the stones worn and shiny, with a busy road at one end and a dead end at the other, where a steep grassy bank fell away to a factory in the valley, the ridges of the corrugated roof a grey stain between the green hills. The morning peace was broken by the backwards and forwards of a forklift truck.

It struck him as it always did when he visited a murder scene. It was so ordinary, yet he expected some kind of sign, like a shadow over the building, the source of so much anguish, with a life rubbed away behind one of those windows. Every time he went past the path where Ellie was killed, it seemed darker down there, even though he knew it was his imagination. Ronnie Bagley's street was just another normal street in a quiet northern town.

Joe had skipped the professional etiquette of calling the prosecution first. It wasn't a hard rule, and he wanted the reaction of the witness, not the prepared answers he would get from an arranged visit. Joe didn't seek out a bad reputation, but he wasn't bothered if he ended up with one. There was a risk that the witness might tell lies about him, accuse him of making threats, but it would be one word against another, and unlikely to go anywhere. Reputations were built on results. Anything less wasn't looking after your clients.

The house Ronnie had lived in with Carrie was three storeys of blackened stone with large bay windows, the frames painted white and covered by dirt and cobwebs, the net curtains yellowed.

He strode up to the large wooden door, the paint faded blue, and was about to knock when he saw three doorbells. The bottom two buzzers had no names on them, but the top one read: Terry Day.

Joe pressed and waited and then turned to look at the street. It was quiet. There were cars parked in the road but there was no activity. It wasn't an affluent area, but it was no inner city blight either. The cars were family cars, nearly-new Fiestas and Nissans, and there were flowers in some of the windows.

Joe turned around as the door creaked open behind him, and he was met by a tall man with a stoop, thin grey hair combed over a bony skull and small wire-framed glasses. He looked surprised at Joe and started to close the door. Joe put his hand out.

'Terry Day?'

He faltered and looked along the street. 'Yes?'

'My name is Joe Parker. I want to speak to you about Ronnie Bagley. I'm his lawyer.'

A blink, and then, 'Yes?'

'Can I come in, so we can talk?'

The man didn't answer.

Joe had expected the door to be closed on him, but this was even more frustrating. He clicked on the dictation machine he had put into his pocket earlier. If there was to be a complaint about his visit, he wanted to be able to produce evidence of the real conversation.

'Is it Terry Day?' Joe handed over a business card. It was taken from him without being looked at.

The man pursed his lips and then glanced down the street. 'Yes, I'm Terry Day. What do you want?' His voice was quiet but precise, as if he wanted to enunciate every consonant.

'To speak to you.'

'Do the police know you're here?'

'No, they don't.'

'Can I refuse to speak to you?'

Joe paused. He had been talking with Terry Day for just a few seconds, and already he knew that it was all coming to an end.

'Of course you can,' Joe said, and he smiled, trying to put the man at ease. 'I'm not here to cause you any problems. I just want to ask you a few questions.'

'And if I refuse?'

'I will call the police and ask for permission to come back.' Joe stepped forward. 'So we might as well get it out of the way. Do you want the police involved again?'

Terry Day stared at Joe, and then said, 'I'll wait,' before slamming the door.

Joe considered the door for a moment, just inches from his face. Terry Day's evidence might look good on paper, but Joe didn't think he would be as convincing in the witness stand. He needed to exploit that.

He turned and walked down the stone steps to take him back to the street, clicking off the dictation machine.

A young mother was struggling with a toddler as Joe walked back to his car, trying to get him into a small buggy. She glanced up as Joe got closer and then looked back at Terry Day's house. 'Are you from the council?' she said.

'No, I'm not,' Joe said, and clicked his key to unlock his car door. Then something struck him, like a sense that her question was more than idle curiosity. 'Why do you ask?'

She looked back to the house again. 'Are you a friend of Mr Day?'

'No, I'm not.'

She looked Joe up and down. 'No, you don't look like it.'

'What do his friends look like?'

'He doesn't have many, from what I can see,' she said, scowling.

'Tell me about him.'

'What is there to say? No one likes him.'

'Why do you say that?'

'Because of the way he behaves.'

Joe followed her look back towards the house. 'What do you mean?'

'Ask anyone round here, they'll tell you. It's like he's put himself in charge of the street, telling people what to do, what they can't do, and if you stand up to him he makes a nuisance of himself.'

'How?'

'Just stupid stuff. Stands outside his house taking notes on what we do, as if he wants to report us for something, but if you don't know what he's writing, then you can't do anything about it. But it's creepy.' She tilted her head. 'So who are you?'

'I'm the lawyer for Ronnie Bagley, the man who used to live in the bottom flat.'

The woman's face turned red and she started to walk down the street quickly, the buggy's wheels making loud clacks on the uneven pavement.

'I shouldn't be speaking to you,' she said over her shoulder. 'You should have said who you are.'

'Why?'

She didn't say anything else. She just walked away, and as Joe watched her go, he realised that there were things going on in Ronnie's street that needed further investigation.

He turned to look back at the house and glanced up towards the top floor. He could see Terry Day in his window, staring down at him.

A jolt of unease made Joe shudder. Something wasn't right.

Twenty-Seven

Sam looked down at the growing press pack spreading along the street outside the station. The story was getting bigger, and the chance to print a picture of another missing pretty girl was too good to turn down. One of the photographers looked up and Sam turned away, his eyes scanning the room instead. There had been some joking the day before, but that had now stopped. People concentrated on their screens or telephones, some trying to contact the people on Julie McGovern's Facebook profile, most of whom had added their phone numbers.

He opened a notepad he had found on a nearby desk. He numbered the first page and underlined the date with a ruler, before going to the police logs of when the calls first came in. DI Evans wanted him to answer the phones, but the calls weren't coming in too quickly. Sam went to the first log. The police had been contacted at 11.30 the night before, when Julie's parents had called round all her friends and found out that she wasn't anywhere they knew about. The other missing girls had made enough headlines to ensure that Julie's parents feared the worst. She had left the house at 8.30, so there were three hours unaccounted for.

It wasn't a high priority at the time, but it had been circulated so the police had been looking out for her. The description had been too vague, though. Five foot seven, green eyes, long brown hair, wearing a white shirt and jeans. As Sam considered a mental map of Manchester, with all the public transport and motorways, Julie could be anywhere. The search teams were cosmetic. They might turn up something, but it was more about reassuring the family they were doing something.

He was distracted by the buzz of his phone in his pocket. He looked at the screen. It was Alice.

'Hi, I'm busy,' he whispered. 'Is everything okay?'

'Yes, sorry, but I've had your mother on the phone. Can you call round tonight? She's heard about the girl on the news, the one who's gone missing. It's reminded her of Ellie and she's feeling low. She wants Joe to go too.'

'Yeah, no problem. I'll call him soon.' A pause. 'You don't mind? I thought you were going out tonight.'

'I was, but you go see her.'

'All right, thanks.'

There she was again, Ellie, always with him. The press would move on to a new story and people would forget, but for the people left behind, it never ended.

The phone on the desk flashed red, a number displayed.

'Sam Parker, Major Incident Team,' he said, his pen poised.

There was some rustling and giggling on the other end of the phone, and then a teenage voice said in a whisper, 'I've got her all wrapped up here, nice and warm,' before there were more giggles and the phone clicked off.

He made a note of the caller's number that had flashed up on the screen. Most appeals brought out the idiots. They didn't realise that if the police got the number, they would get a visit, under the pretence of pursuing the lead but really intending to frighten. Most often they found people who suddenly understood why it had never been funny in the first place.

He looked up as Evans shouted his name. She tilted her head as an indication that he should join her. The other detectives tried to pretend that they weren't watching as he walked over, but he could feel their gaze on him as he went.

'Yes, ma'am?'

He went to put his hands in his pockets but then took them out again and clasped them together in front of him.

She stepped closer, checking around, and then said quietly, 'Remember what I said, that if Ben Grant agrees to speak, you'll need to go down straight away. So I want you with me today. Come on, let's go.'

Sam was surprised, but there was only one answer if he was going to stay on the team. 'I understand.'

Evans turned to walk out of the squad room and Sam followed her. As he got to the door, he glanced back into the room. A few people were watching, and Ged, the detective with the muscles, glowered at him. Sam thought they had cleared the air, but for Ged it seemed like it was a short truce. Sam gave him a small nod. He wasn't going to be bullied off the team.

As they walked along the corridor Sam asked whether there had been a press conference yet.

'No. I need to talk to the family again, just to finally rule out another possible explanation. We get enough routine runaways each year to make sure we don't jump to conclusions. They usually turn up around Piccadilly in a short skirt, but they are not normally from families like this. We need to brief them before we put them in front of the cameras, because they've got to be able to stop any questions.'

'Is someone with them now?'

'Yes, the FLO. We'll see if she's got anything to tell us.'

Sam nodded. The Family Liaison Officers were seen by some as hand-holders, but they were experienced detectives sent in to be a constant presence. Most murders happen within the family, and so the FLO look out for things that make them suspicious, all under the guise of sympathy and quiet reassurance.

Sam knew what would come next. They would take apart Julie's room, and then take apart her life. Her friends would be spoken to, her college, her computers checked. All her intimate secrets would be revealed.

'Were there any leads from any of the other girls when you went through their stuff?' Sam said.

Evans shook her head. 'We hoped the computers might show up something, like some stalking or grooming, but nothing has turned up.'

'So what do you think, ma'am?'

'My guess?' Evans said. 'They've been snatched, except they haven't turned up yet, which is unusual. If someone has gone missing and been killed, they usually turn up in woods somewhere.'

Sam's jaw clenched and he felt the jab of grief rush at him. Just a casual remark, cop to cop, but she was there again. Ellie. He had to learn to lock her away, although it always felt like a betrayal when he thought like that.

He followed Evans out of the back of the station to the car park, where they got into her silver Astra. As they set off, Evans said, 'Don't say anything. We've got to look grimly determined when we pass the reporters.'

Sam stared straight ahead as the car emerged onto the street. Some of the reporters turned round, but as there were no sirens and lights it didn't interest them too much. Once they were clear of the press, Evans said, 'I'll keep the family talking. I want you to search Julie's room, and I mean a proper search.'

'If Julie is dead, that room will be all they have left,' Sam said.

'So don't disturb anything. Just make sure that you look everywhere. Under the mattress, in all of her drawers. Look for any kind of a diary, the kind of thing that she might have hidden away. Scraps of paper. Go through her computer. Just find anything that gives us an idea that she had secrets.'

Sam tried not to smile as Evans drove away from the station. He was at the heart of the investigation. Now it was up to him to impress, whatever enemies he might have made in the squad. He knew he was seeking some kind of redemption for Ellie, that he was the older brother who lived every day with some residual guilt for not protecting her. But if that stopped another murderer from going free, his reasons were not important. All that mattered was that no one else died.

Twenty-Eight

When Joe got back to the office he went quickly to the top floor, to where Gina worked in a cramped room with the slope of the roof as a wall, just across the corridor from where the trainees and clerks flirted and joked and sometimes worked.

He walked straight in, breathless from the rush up the stairs, but then he raised his hand in apology when he saw that she was on the phone.

Gina put her hand over the receiver. 'Where were you?'

'I went to see a man about his evidence.'

She held up her hand to indicate that she had to finish her call. He paced as she said her goodbyes. When she hung up, Gina said, 'I'm trying to line up a QC for the trial. I know it's early, but like you said, we need to try to scare off the prosecution early.'

As Joe nodded approvingly, she asked, 'So what's got you all excited?'

'I've got our back-up plan.'

'What do you mean?'

'Our main defence has to be that Carrie and Grace are still alive. That's what I want you to focus on. Search for her. Speak to anyone who knew her and just follow the trail. If she's run away because Ronnie hit her, then she won't want to be found. Try to get funding for an enquiry agent, someone who will sit outside a house all night in case one of Carrie's friends is keeping her hidden.'

'And if we can't find them?' Gina said.

'Rely on whichever blood expert Monica comes up with.'

'But Ronnie gives an explanation for it.'

'Yes, and it sounds like he's making excuses,' Joe said. 'We have to keep picking at the prosecution case so that Ronnie doesn't have to make his excuses. We need to get the case thrown out, not rely on Ronnie to explain himself out of it.'

'Got any ideas who we should use?'

Joe thought about that. 'Concentrate on a lab we haven't used before.'

'Why? They might give us an opinion we don't like.'

'They won't, because they will want to please us, so that we give them more work. The ones we normally use won't mind giving an unfavourable opinion, because they give us enough of the right ones. Someone new will see this as a chance to show us what they can do. Find someone who trades on their own, not as a research spin-off or part of a big consultancy. If they don't need our money, they won't give us what we want.'

'Sometimes this job makes me feel dirty.'

'You're not in the search for truth anymore,' Joe said. 'You're in the doubt-building business. Truth doesn't come into it.'

'So is that your back-up plan? A blood expert who'll give dodgy opinions?'

'No,' Joe said, and then he grinned. 'Like I said, I've been to see someone.'

'I get the feeling I'm not going to like this.'

'We want to show that Carrie and Grace are alive, but if the jury thinks that they're dead, we have to provide other possibilities. It doesn't have to be Ronnie.' When Gina didn't respond, Joe added, 'Terry Day, Ronnie's landlord.'

Gina sat back and frowned.

'What's that look of disapproval for?'

'I might work for you now, but I was a cop for thirty years.'

'Go on, give it to me,' Joe said, his eyes rolling. 'Lay the guilt trip.'

'It's not that,' she said. 'He's a witness. You can't keep on approaching him directly.' When Joe went for his pocket, Gina waved her hand. 'Don't get the voice recorder out. It doesn't record how you behave, just the words you use. It won't work for everything.'

'Come on, Gina, it's not just that, is it? You're getting a pang of conscience about Terry Day, I can see it.'

'Well, maybe, because Ronnie's landlord might just be an innocent in all this, and from my time working with victims and witnesses, what they all say is that the criminal process left them feeling dirty, as if they were somehow to blame.'

'And it bothers you that we're going to throw a few red herrings around?'

'Yes, it always has, but you know that. To you, it's just a tactic, something opportunistic. To Terry Day, it will be a stain that will hang around him for the rest of his life, and even if Ronnie is convicted, in ten years' time someone will try to claim that it was a miscarriage of justice, and so Terry Day will be brought up again.' She sighed. 'I'm sorry, Joe, I know I'm supposed to think differently now, because I work for you, but I saw the effect of defence tactics on witnesses and victims, and it's not pretty.'

'Don't apologise,' Joe said. 'It's human, don't lose that, but we've got a case to win, and we've got to do it.'

There were a few moments of silence, then Gina said, 'So what do we do then, about Terry Day?'

'We find out what we can. I want to know about his past, his full adult life. If there is anything about him – and I mean *anything* – that we can use, I need to know about it.'

'Do we have his convictions yet?'

'Too early. We'll need to do our own digging, and you're the best person for the job. Use that soft voice you used when you were still in the police. Ask around. People open up to you.'

Gina shook her head and then laughed. 'Okay. It will get me away from here for a while.'

'Remember you're not a cop anymore. This is even dirtier.'

'And what about Monica?'

'I'll let her work with Ronnie. He seemed to like her.' And then he left the room.

As Joe headed for the stairs, he felt his cockiness slip. His thoughts weren't too far from Gina's. All he had done was train himself not to listen to them.

His phone buzzed in his pocket. He looked at the screen and saw an unfamiliar number.

'Joe Parker,' he said.

There was a small laugh. 'You sound very official.'

It was Kim Reader, using her office phone.

'Hang on, let me get back into my room,' he said, and walked quickly through the building until he was able to close his office door for some privacy.

'Sorry, Kim. What can I do for you?'

'I'm just calling to apologise for last night.'

'You've no need.'

'I have. We've been friends for a long time, and sometimes more than that, and I just ... well, work got in the way of that.'

'I saw it the other way round, that our friendship got in the way of work. I was exploiting our friendship, and so I should be the one who is apologising.'

'I didn't see it like that.'

'We can't rewrite our history, Kim, and talk about work and pretend that our past doesn't exist. It's the same with our present. We can't just meet up and ignore the Bagley case.'

'Why not? We should be able to meet up as old friends and talk about something other than work.'

Her voice was hesitant, and Joe was silent for a moment as he listened to the words she hadn't said but which hung heavy in the conversation. The invitation, the desire to meet again. Before he could stop himself, he said, 'I would like that. Tonight.'

'Good. I'd like that too. Not the same place though.'

Joe could hear the smile in her voice. 'What, you're not a real ale fan? Okay, you pick.'

'How about Duke 92?'

Right across the road from his apartment. 'Not there,' he said. 'Meet in The Ox and we'll go from there.'

'I'll look forward to it,' Kim said, before hanging up.

He stared at the handset. He knew he was heading towards something that was wrong, but there had been no part of him that wanted to say no.

The phone on his desk rang. When he picked it up, it was Marion, from reception.

'Mr Bagley is here.'

'Send him up.'

Twenty-Nine

Sam walked behind DI Evans as she approached the door to Julie McGovern's home.

The house was large and detached, with gravel in place of what had once been a front garden, and fake Tudor beams fastened to the first floor. There were some reporters by the gate, blocking the way, so that anyone entering or leaving had to work their way through the scrum. As the front door opened, the sound of camera shutters disturbed the peace, desperate to capture the delivery of bad news.

The Family Liaison Officer opened the door. She was an older woman, a detective seeing out her career, where her experience became expertise.

Once they were safely inside, Evans said quietly, 'How are they?'

'Julie's mother is upstairs, sitting on the girl's bed, crying. Her father is pacing, trying to be strong, but getting angrier all the time.'

'Get the mother downstairs. We need to search Julie's room.'

The FLO turned and went upstairs, and so Evans went into the main room. Sam followed.

The faked ageing of the house continued on the inside, done out like a cottage, with wooden flooring, a blackened fireplace, yellow walls and flowers in rustic vases dotted around the room. It looked like something from a magazine article, rural in a suburban setting.

Julie's father turned as they went in.

'You took your time,' he barked, his hands on his hips, a purple tinge to his cheeks, dressed in grey trousers and a yellow golfing top.

Evans paused before she answered, and when she spoke, her voice was calm. 'We are setting up search teams and speaking to all of her friends.'

'And is there any news?'

Evans paused. 'Not yet.'

A woman walked in. Julie's mother. She was wearing a grey T-shirt and saggy jogging bottoms. Her face looked bleached out and her eyes were red. She looked at her husband but he turned away from her, so she went to sit down. The FLO walked in and gestured with her head towards the stairs that the coast was clear.

'This is DC Sam Parker,' Evans said. 'He's going to look through your daughter's things.' Sam nodded a greeting to them. 'Are you all right with that?'

Mrs McGovern was about to say something, but Sam stopped her by saying that he would be respectful. She smiled thinly, her eyes watering, and so he went towards the stairs.

Julie's bedroom was at the back of the house, overlooking a long lawn shaped in curves, with a greenhouse at one end and bright bursts of flowers in the beds. The room itself was the curious age-mix of a young woman still at home, with remnants of her childhood slowly replaced by her adult life. There were stuffed bears on the pillow and a statue of a ballerina on the dresser, with a make-up bag and a box of tampons further along.

Sam went to the dresser first, feeling to the back of the drawers, ignoring the expected contents and trying instead for anything unusual, like paper or a notebook. Nothing there.

The other drawers were just the same. Jumpers and T-shirts and jeans and shorts. He took out the bottom one to look in the space between the drawer and the floor, where she might keep her secret things, but it was just that – an empty space. He straightened and went towards the bed, clicking on the computer as he went past it. There was a shelf above it, lined with Harry Potter and Twilight books. He lifted out each book to check for anything in them, but they were just books. He lifted the mattress. Nothing there.

Julie's computer sat on a desk by the window. It was tidy, but more than just neatness. It seemed like there was attention to detail. When he looked at most desks, they made him uneasy, because there were usually papers strewn across, or pens lying haphazardly. Julie's was different. The mouse mat was placed in the centre of the desk, exactly in the middle and parallel. There were two pens, one blue and one black, lined up next to each other. A notepad was on the corner, perfectly positioned. Sam was no psychologist, but it didn't seem like the desk of someone who would do something rash or impulsive. Julie wanted order in her life, some kind of plan.

There were two drawers in the desk. Neither was locked. Sam looked in the top one. There was a pencil case to one side and next to it an address book.

He lifted out the address book and placed it on the desk. He would look through it at the station.

The computer had finished its whirring and was showing a desktop picture of three girls in an embrace, all grinning at the camera, Julie in the middle. Three happy teenagers, looking forward to life.

Sam went to the email software first. He scanned the messages but there wasn't anything that aroused suspicion. He was looking for any discussions about Julie feeling low, or any meet-ups planned for the night before. There were just receipts for a few online purchases and routine chatter between friends. He scanned through the documents folder but nothing stood out as unusual. He went to the computer folders, to see whether she had hidden anything away, but none of the folder titles gave any hints.

He clicked on the internet browser and checked the history, looking to see where she had looked on the internet, whether she had visited any suicide websites or suspicious forums. Or even whether she had been trying to find accommodation somewhere. A hotel or hostel. It was blank, cleared out. That struck Sam as unusual. He expected teenagers to be a little secretive about their internet history, but it meant that Julie had cleared it before she went out. Was that relevant? The computer experts would go through the hard drive later, to look for what she had searched for, or the trail of her chat programs, but that would take time.

None of that was good. If there was something that hinted at deeper problems, then she could end up as a runaway, someone who would go through difficult times but would be alive. But as the alternatives run out, you are left with just one: that she had been abducted and murdered.

He stopped when he heard a shout from downstairs. He went to the landing and looked over the rail. It was Evans.

'Yes, ma'am?'

Evans came up the stairs and spoke in a whisper. 'I've just heard from the prison. Ben Grant has said yes. Now is the time. Can you do it?'

'Yes, ma'am, you can trust me.' And in that moment, as the words came out, for the first time he really meant it.

Thirty

'Ronnie, come in,' Joe said, and pointed to the chair in front of his desk.

As he walked into the office, Ronnie seemed uncomfortable. He looked towards the paintings on the walls, pictures of old Manchester hung against bright stripes of gold and white, like an Edwardian drawing room. There were law books in a bookcase, All England Law Reports going back through the years, but they were just for show. The textbooks Joe actually used were accessed through his computer.

The room was intended to impress, because criminal clients don't want to put up with the guy above the estate agency. They want to think they have the best lawyer, and so a plush office in a city centre building goes part way to convincing them.

There was a creak as Ronnie sat down. Joe sat opposite, the barrier of the desk between them. Some firms went for sofas, so the client could be put at ease. Joe didn't agree with that, because his clients wouldn't get an easy time in the witness box. They had to answer questions under pressure, and that started in his office.

Joe picked up his phone and called for Monica to join him.

'Do you want a drink, Ronnie? Just tea or coffee though.'

He shook his head. 'Can I smoke?'

Joe thought about saying no, but then remembered how

Ronnie had been all too keen to swap firms. He didn't want to risk another defection over some passive smoking. Joe went to the window to open it, and Ronnie rummaged in his pocket for his cigarettes. Joe was about to lift the sash when he saw him. In the park, on a bench, looking up. Same as before. The man in the courtroom. As soon as Joe caught his eye, he got to his feet and started to walk away.

'Wait there,' Joe said to Ronnie, and then rushed out of his room, bolting down the corridor and the stairs. As he emerged onto the street, he looked along, up and down. There wasn't anyone walking away. He went towards the park, the gate clanging loudly as he pushed through it and headed towards the bench where he had seen the person. It was empty.

Joe put his hands on his hips, feeling exasperated. Someone had been watching the office again.

He trudged back across the road and into his office. Ronnie was still sitting in the chair when he walked back into the room, but the blinds were crooked, as if he had been looking out. Monica was there too, sitting on a chair at the side of the room, her legs crossed, a notepad open in front of her.

'What had you seen?' Ronnie asked.

Joe was panting from the rush up and down the stairs. 'I saw a client I needed to see, that's all.'

Ronnie sat upright. 'So this is where we start, is it? What do you think about my case?'

Joe looked towards the pile of papers on the edge of the desk. 'Yes, this is it.' He tried to keep the focus on Ronnie's case. 'How are you feeling, Ronnie? You've got a long haul ahead.'

'Tired,' he said, which surprised Joe. Ronnie didn't seem happy to be out of prison. He hadn't at any point. Most people would have stayed in prison until their trial. Ronnie seemed to treat his time inside as if it was a momentary inconvenience.

'So what's our defence?' Ronnie asked.

'If you didn't kill Carrie and Grace—'

'I didn't,' Ronnie interrupted.

Joe held up his hand. 'If you didn't kill them, the fact that they are still alive is our defence.'

'Can you prove that?'

'Not yet,' Joe said. 'We're going to try.'

Ronnie looked down.

'What's wrong, Ronnie?' Joe said. 'They are still alive, right?'

'Well, I didn't kill them,' he said. He looked over at Monica. 'You believe me, don't you?'

Monica glanced at Joe, and then said, 'Our job is to defend you. That's what we'll do.'

'We need to prepare for the worst though,' Joe said. 'What if Carrie and Grace are dead? The jury might think that, so we have to look at other suspects. Tell me about your landlord, Terry Day.'

'No.'

Joe was surprised. 'What do you mean, no?'

'Just that,' Ronnie said, his lips pursed. 'Leave Terry out of it.'

'There is enough evidence to convince a jury that Carrie and Grace are dead,' Joe said. 'If it wasn't you, then it must have been someone else. What about the lonely man on the top floor who listens out for arguments? Did he go downstairs to comfort her, because he was worried about her, and things got out of hand? Did he come on to her? Did Carrie come on to him?'

'No, Carrie wouldn't.' Ronnie's voice was getting angry.

'Why not? You're out at work all day, and she's lonely because life is hard. You've got a young baby and things aren't good between you. Did she miss the physical side, the strength of a man? Did Carrie come on to him and he pushed her away, making her bang her head?'

'No!'

'Or maybe he saw her and knew how lonely she was. He heard the argument and saw it was his chance. He went down there. He comforted her. He read too much into it and tried it on and they fought. He killed her. And he had to get rid of her before you came home.'

Ronnie was shaking his head violently. 'No, no,' he said, wagging his finger at Joe. 'What about Grace, my daughter? Where does she fit into it?'

'The same way the prosecution say it fits into your case, Ronnie. People panic. If he killed Carrie, he couldn't leave Grace on her own. He had to make it look like Carrie had run away, so that people would think that she had left you. When you walked into that police station, it was his chance. Someone else would get the blame, not him.'

Ronnie sat back and looked down, clamped his hands under his thighs. 'We can't do that. We can't blame Terry.'

'It's a case theory, that's all,' Joe said. 'It doesn't have to be true, as long as it might be.'

'It's not my case theory,' Ronnie snapped. 'Leave Terry Day out of this.'

Joe thought about that. He was the lawyer and he was the one who made the decisions, but he couldn't ignore his client.

'So if we don't go after Terry Day, all we can do is pick at the prosecution case, except that it's a decent one. If we ignore Terry Day, your defence gets weaker.'

Ronnie shrugged.

'Okay,' Joe said. 'Let's go through it. The bloodstains. How hard did you hit Carrie?'

'I don't know. What do you mean, how hard? It was a punch. How hard is a punch?'

'And did she stay on her feet?'

Ronnie thought about that. 'I don't know.'

'How can you not know? It's the first time you hit her, so you say.'

149

'Like I said, I don't know.'

Joe slammed his hand on the desk, making Ronnie jump. '"I don't know" won't work, Ronnie.' His voice was angry. 'Carrie is missing. Grace is missing. Carrie's blood was on the door and on the walls, smears where you wiped it up. The jury will think it was from when she was killed, so if we can't come up with an alternative theory, you're finished.'

Ronnie looked at the ceiling and closed his eyes. He squeezed them tight, as if holding back tears, but when he looked down again, his eyes were dry.

'I punched her, that's all,' he said, his voice soft.

'Why?' Joe said. 'What had she done that made you snap?'

'She was, well ...' Ronnie shook his head. 'I found out she had been having men round when I was at work. To, well, you know, entertain them. That was the argument Terry Day heard.'

'She worked as a prostitute?'

Ronnie nodded slowly.

Joe made a note in his notebook. 'Who were her clients?'

'I don't know. I wasn't her pimp, you know. I was just some poor sap who went to work as she fucked men in our bed to get vodka money.'

'Who was her pimp? Who organised it?'

'She didn't say. The argument was too angry to get into the detail.'

'And you hit her.'

'Yes. I'm not proud of it, but she was taunting me. I just lost it. Can you imagine what it must be like to find that out?'

Joe swung round slowly in his chair as he thought about that, facing out of the window. He had felt the red-hot stab of infidelity, but not on the scale mentioned by Ronnie. He glanced towards the park, just checking, but there was no one there.

He turned back to face Ronnie. 'This could go two ways, you know that?'

'How?'

'It might be enough. Did you want Carrie to stop?'

'Yeah, of course. Who wouldn't? Sleeping with men, with Grace in the flat. It was wrong.'

'And you asked her to stop?'

'I told her to stop.'

'So perhaps Carrie had handed in her notice, so to speak?' Joe said. 'And there we have it, another case theory. Her pimp hits her, or one of his men, and kills her accidentally. They panic and get rid of the body. But there is one thing that stands out in all of this.'

'Go on.' Ronnie was grinding his teeth as Joe looked at him.

'If this might be true, you have to accept that whoever killed Carrie also killed your daughter.'

Ronnic took a deep breath. 'I understand.'

'And there's the other side to it,' Joe said.

'Which is what?'

'That you were so angry at what Carrie was doing, how she was sleeping with men when you were out at work, that you attacked her. It might give you an explanation, but it also gives you a motive.'

'For killing my own daughter?' Ronnie sat back and folded his arms, scowling. 'How sick do you think I am?'

'How long had she been a prostitute, Ronnie?'

Ronnie started to shake his head slowly. 'Not long, I don't think.'

'You don't pick up an application form at the job centre. If she was working from home, she knew her way around. So maybe Grace isn't yours,' Joe said, and he watched as the blood rose in Ronnie's cheeks. 'Is that what happened? She argued and taunted you, and then it came out that Grace was a punter's child? So you flew in a rage and then took it out on poor Grace, that sweet, defenceless little girl.'

'You bastard.'

'No, Ronnie, I'm not. I'm just giving you a flavour of what you've got ahead if we go with this case theory. For all that it explains away the evidence, it gives you a motive. A damn strong one.'

Ronnie didn't answer.

Joe dipped his head to try to catch Ronnie's gaze. 'Ronnie?'

He looked up.

Joe softened. 'I've told you nothing you haven't thought yourself, have I?'

Ronnie pulled a face. 'So what do we do now?'

'We find out more about Carrie, about how she worked, and who sent her clients. If we can find some people to testify about how she was moving in dangerous circles, we have a case theory.'

Ronnie looked more encouraged.

'It won't be easy, though, remember that. Expecting prostitutes to give evidence against a violent pimp, to help out someone they've never met, who plied her trade in a warm flat, not under the arches around Piccadilly, will be hard.'

'But it's all we've got,' Ronnie said.

'Yes, it's all we've got.'

Thirty-One

Sam took a deep breath. Ben Grant was in the room ahead. He remembered his instructions. Let Grant do the talking and don't give anything away. Grant wanted Sam, but Sam didn't want to fuel his fantasies. Let Grant masturbate over someone else's words.

It had been the trial when Sam had last seen Grant, with Sam as a policeman in his parade dress in the witness box, Grant watching from the dock. Sam had not detected hatred from him, no resentment at being caught. Grant had seemed amused by the trial, his moment on the front pages, a tabloid anti-hero, but that only fuelled his arrogance. What would hurt Grant more would be when someone even more vile came along, making Grant's chapter in a true crime compilation a few pages shorter.

The guard opened the door and Sam walked in. Ben Grant was standing by the window, his hands on the window ledge, watching the slow drift of the clouds painting white trails across the blue of late spring.

Sam set his notebook on the table and pulled back the chair. Grant knew he was there. It was just part of his game. It was only when Sam sat down that Grant turned.

Grant looked at Sam, and then at the notebook, before a smile spread slowly across his face. 'It's good to see you again, after all these years.' He tilted his head. 'I had to ask for you,

153

because I knew they wouldn't send a woman. They think it's control, because it's denying me, like a game.'

'It's not always about you,' Sam said, looking at his notebook, trying to sound disinterested, writing the date and time at the top. 'I came because you asked for me, but don't read too much into it.' When Grant pursed his lips, Sam smiled. 'That's right, you're not so important anymore.'

Grant leaned against a wall, his arms folded, his jaw clenched.

Sam looked up and saw how he had changed. Remnants of the famous image were still there, the police photograph showing a round, boyish face and a small flick of dark hair across his forehead, with small eyes staring from behind dark-framed glasses, but there had been some changes too. Grant had lost some weight and the hair had grey tinges and was now cropped short. The glasses were gone too. He looked less of a threat, but Sam knew that size could be misleading.

Grant flicked his hand towards the window. 'You're thinking that I was dreaming of freedom when you came in. That's what makes you sleep better, isn't it, that monsters like me are kept away.' It was his voice that had always been the biggest surprise. It was quiet, soft, almost with a hiss and the slightest hint of a lisp, but his eyes remained fixed, staring, his head tilted forward.

'I wasn't thinking anything.'

'I don't believe that,' Grant said, shaking his head. 'You see those bars as protection, maybe even revenge. I don't. They are reminders of how many of us there are out there.'

'"Us"?'

'Beasts,' Grant said, and a malevolent grin spread across his face, his voice acquiring a deeper snarl. 'That's the word you like, I suppose, because it makes me seem less human, as though I'm not like you.'

'You are nothing like me,' Sam said. He was trying to keep

the hostility out of his voice, but it was hard, because thoughts of Ellie kept coming back to him, the victim of someone just like Ben Grant. 'Sit down, please.'

Grant stayed on his feet for a few seconds, but then relented and scraped the chair on the floor as he sat down. He sat bolt upright, his hands on his legs. 'So what do you want to know, Sam? You don't mind first names, do you? You can call me Ben.'

Sam thought about what he could say about the missing girls, but then he thought of a different way to broach it. 'What do you know about Carrie Smith?'

Grant's eyelids fluttered for eyes a moment. 'Carrie?'

'Yes, Carrie. She was your most frequent visitor.'

'You've just said it. She was my most frequent visitor. There you are, no secrets in this place.'

'She's gone missing.'

'You say dead,' Grant said, his tongue darting across his lip. 'I read the papers. Ronnie has been charged with her murder. And Grace. Poor little thing. Never quite got to that perfect age.'

'Do you know Ronnie?' Sam asked, ignoring Grant's attempt to goad him.

Grant didn't say anything for a while. He rocked on the chair, staring at Sam, his eyes narrowing, a smile always just twitching at the corners of his mouth.

'You insisted it was me,' Sam said. 'I'm here, so talk. What do you know?'

'I'll come to that,' Grant said. 'Let me tell you a story first.'

'I'm not here to listen to you reminisce,' Sam said. 'If you haven't got any information, I'll go. I'm not here for your ego. I'm here to cover our backs, that's all, so that if this is the one occasion when you had something to say that was worth writing down, I can make a note.'

Grant's eyes were suddenly wide and fierce. 'Fuck that, Detective. You're here because I demanded it, and if you don't speak to me with some respect, then I stay silent, and so remember that protecting yourself isn't just about turning up. It's about listening, and treating me with the fucking awe that you feel.'

There it was, Sam thought, the quick flip of the murderer, the menace just beneath the surface.

'Awe?' Sam said.

'Yes, awe,' Grant snapped. 'I can guess your excitement today, coming back into my world. Tonight, you will go home and say, "Guess who I spoke to today", and that pretty wife of yours will be so impressed that the answer is Ben Grant, and that's why you'll tell her, to impress her. She will want to know about me. What am I like? Did I scare you?' He tapped his fingers quickly on the table, like a drum roll. 'And she will get herself a little turned on by it, and so when she climbs on you tonight, all wet and horny for the first time in a while, she won't be thinking of you. She will be thinking of this meeting, of me, wondering what it would be like to be here, locked in a room with me. So enjoy it, Detective.'

Sam leaned forward, both of his arms on the desk, his fingers clamped into tight fists. 'Or maybe I will look at my daughters and thank God that you are in here, so that they are a little bit safer.'

As soon as the words came out, Sam knew he had given away too much. Grant's eyes narrowed and a small flush crept up his cheeks.

'What are they like, your little girls?' Grant said, smiling, his mouth just a thin mean slit. 'Would they be my type?'

Sam took some deep breaths. Stay in control, he told himself.

'You don't know anything, Grant,' Sam said, and closed his notebook. 'Carrie will stay missing. That's fine. I don't want to be here. You can get your kicks with someone else.'

As Sam got to his feet and went towards the door, Grant said, 'Things have changed now.'

156

Sam stopped. 'What do you mean?'

'Another girl has gone missing. She looks nice. Long dark hair. Likes horse riding. Good family.'

Sam turned round.

'You're not here about Carrie, I know that,' Grant said. 'You want to know about the missing girls.'

'How do you know about her family?'

'I saw the news. I've got a television in my cell.'

'There's only been a release of her name and a photograph. How do you know the rest?'

'I knew her father,' Grant continued. 'He's a councillor, and a magistrate, and so he will have the ear of your Chief Constable and have strong words about you if you walk away now.' Grant smirked. 'So sit back down and indulge me, if you want to find her. She might still be alive, but not for long. Don't you be the one who messes things up.'

Sam knew Grant was playing with him, making him think that he knew more about Julie McGovern's disappearance. A formal press conference had not been held yet. There had been just enough information released to make the news bulletins on television and radio, a name and a photograph and her last known location, hoping that it might be enough to generate the right phone call. The media buzz would give the news conference proper coverage, and then it would hit the social networks. Launching a public appeal needed the brains of an advertiser.

Sam placed the notebook back onto the desk and sat down again. 'This had better be good.'

'It will be,' Grant said, enjoying his moment.

Thirty-Two

Joe needed a break. He was already becoming consumed by Ronnie's case. He had read the papers over and over, each time hoping something new would jump out at him, but it didn't. All he saw was a strong circumstantial case. It just needed two bodies to make it airtight. Joe just needed two live people to make it disappear.

He put his head in his hands and as he closed his eyes, Ellie came back to him. She did that when he wasn't expecting it, almost as if he could only keep her away if he willed it that way. She was the shadow over his life, the wrench of guilt that threatened to overwhelm him if he didn't focus on keeping it at bay.

He thought of that day fifteen years earlier, and he saw her again, Ellie walking, her headphones on, oblivious, turning into the gravel path that took her between the trees that would lead her back to their house. Joe had been a long way behind her, but he had seen her. And there was a man there, and each time Joe thought of him, his image burned into his mind a little more. Sharp blue eyes, like squints, and a blond fringe under his hood, turning to follow Ellie. And it wasn't just the image of the man that burned into his memory. It was his own weakness, how he had watched her and had done nothing. That was his shame. His secret.

He jolted as he opened his eyes. His forehead felt clammy.

The memory did that to him. It didn't fade with time, a smothering wave of darkness that engulfed him whenever he forgot to hold it back. He could have stopped her killer. He could have saved her.

Joe allowed his breaths to slow down as he tried to focus on Ronnie's case.

Monica had been given the job of driving Ronnie home, Gina with her, so that they could speak to Terry Day's neighbours on the way back. They might know more of what went on that day, when Carrie went missing. If someone else had carried Carrie's body out of the house, someone might have seen it. More importantly, he wanted to know what they might say if the police ever got round to speaking to them. And despite what Ronnie said, Joe wasn't ready to give up on Terry Day.

Ronnie's information about Carrie selling her body gave Joe a new angle. He tried to work out how he could find out more about that. His mind skimmed through the active files he had, whether he could exploit any of them to get access to the seedier side of the city. Then he smiled. There was one.

He went to his cabinet and pulled out the file he was looking for. It was an assault case and the victim had called Joe a fortnight earlier, wanting to drop the case. It wasn't as simple as that though, because the prosecution might force the victim to go ahead if they were tipped off about his reluctance. Joe had backed off from speaking to him, it might be a set-up, but he had told his client, who had told him to set up a meeting. The assault case was routine, but Joe's client moved in the right circles to know what was going in with the prostitutes in the city. If Joe could arrange the meeting, where the options could be more easily explained, his client would owe him a favour.

Joe scoured the file for the victim's number and then dialled. When it was answered, he said, 'Daniel? It's Joe Parker, from Honeywells. You called me not long ago. I've spoken to my client. He is willing to listen to you. Can you get into town now?' When Daniel agreed, Joe said, 'Go to the Acropolis café, behind Bridge Street.'

When he hung up, he called his client and told him where to be. They had talked about this but Joe had advised him against it. The risks were too great. There was something in it for Joe now.

It would be some time before the meeting, and Joe found it hard to concentrate. He could do some work on other cases, but alone in his office, his fingers tapped on the desk and his mind went back to the evening before.

His feelings towards Kim had moved on from memories of their few college intimacies and been replaced by their occasional conflicts as lawyers on opposing sides. There had been coffees together and parties at barristers' chambers, and he had spent plenty of time with her in court, enjoying tense exchanges and then a flirt and a talk between cases, but the evening before had been the first time since college that it had been just Kim. Had it reawakened old feelings, or was it something else? The gap in his life that made him browse singles' websites?

Joe stared at his phone. He wanted to call Kim, just to check that they were still on for later, that nothing had changed, but then he stopped himself. What was he hoping for? That she would change her mind, and then he could remind himself that romance just wasn't for him? That was nothing to do with Kim. But when he thought of her, as he had done through the day, he felt that familiar crawl in his stomach and butterfly flutters. The images of Kim in his head, how he saw her whenever they came across each other in the courtroom, were all mixed up with older memories, of her heavy breaths, of her moving on him, the comedown afterwards, Kim lying naked in his arms.

Then he realised something else – that for as long as he thought about Kim, he felt some of his darkness lift.

Thirty-Three

Sam opened his notebook and gestured with a twirl of his fingers for Grant to continue, who was grinning, showing bright white teeth.

Grant must have spotted him looking, because he said, 'Nice, aren't they, my teeth? My others were hurting, so I said, and they were unsightly. They undermined my confidence, which isn't good for my rehabilitation. Like the glasses. They had to go. Laser treatment. Now, I look pretty. I feel more of a person, you see. They can't deny me that. It's my human right.' When Sam flinched, Grant said, 'That was the fun. The papers loved that one. *Monster Grant Gets Makeover*. It was worth it for the headlines. Don't they ever learn?'

'What do you want to tell me?' Sam said, trying to keep the meeting together. He tapped his pen on the notebook page. Grant was playing him.

Grant was still grinning when he said, 'I'll tell you a story of how to grow a monster. It's in all of us. Everyone has their thing, their quirk. Me? I liked them young. But what about other things?'

'You've nothing to tell me, Grant.'

'Hair,' Grant said quickly, his grin fading as his eyes darted to Sam's notebook. As Sam paused, Grant added, 'There's a story about hair, how it helps to build a monster. That's what you want to know, isn't it?'

Sam considered Grant. For all his taunting, he wanted to talk. 'Go on.'

'Imagine how it would be if hair was your thing,' Grant said. 'If all you wanted to do was touch some, feel it flow through your fingers. You'd want to keep some then, because just touching wouldn't be enough, and so you'd want to take some, to have a piece of them, something private. It had been theirs, but then it became yours, but what next?' He leaned closer, before saying in a whisper, 'You'd want the rest of them.'

When Sam didn't respond, Grant said, 'You can understand that, can't you?'

'No, I can't.'

'Come on, Sam, don't be shy. You know what it's like to want more. Are you telling me that you've never looked at a woman and wondered what she would be like naked?' Grant's look darkened and he sneered when he spoke. 'You thought it, and wanted it, but didn't have the nerve to do anything about it. I did. Me. Ben Grant. So pay me some respect.'

Sam swallowed. He was here to find out what Grant knew, his first real assignment on the Murder Squad, but he was faced with boasting arrogance, and in his eyes, Sam saw the spit of venom that had ended his sister's life. He had to ignore that though. He couldn't waste his chance, and so he closed his eyes for a moment, just to make a silent apology to Ellie, for not reaching out and squeezing the last breath out of Grant. And it wouldn't make him as bad as Grant, because Grant would be just a casualty in the battle to make the world a better place.

Sam opened his eyes. 'You can't say that just because some things on the scale of desire are normal, then everything else is allowed. You have to put down markers.'

Grant was pleased. 'You're debating, I like this, but you're wrong, because it's so artificial. Murder for politics is fine – go fight a war – boys, but murder for pleasure is wrong? You know nothing.'

Grant raised his hands and held them out. When he spoke, his voice was a whisper. 'It's special, you know, when life disappears, that hiss of the last breath under the squeeze of your hands. It's part fear, part relief, because after everything that has been inflicted, death is a release. A beautiful, joyous ride into the afterlife, an escape from what preceded it. I miss it so much, Detective. You see, some try to persuade you that they are cured and so are safe to be let out. Not me. You need to keep me locked up, because I will kill again, I know it, because I dream of it, that bliss, the tremble in my fingers, the shudder in my groin, everything in sharp focus. But it has to start somewhere.'

'Does it?' Sam said, his disgust evident in the curl of his lip. 'Perhaps it's just faulty wiring and you were always going to end up like this?'

Grant shook his head. 'No, there is always a trigger.' His eyes went distant for a moment, as if he was caught up in some memory. 'Back to my hair story, and big sister Sally.'

'Whose sister? Your sister?'

Grant got closer again so that Sam could feel the warmth of his breath. 'Sally was a little older than me. Five years. I was eleven, Sally sixteen. That's when I first noticed her hair. She was like them all at that age, all flirt and tease but no idea how to use it, and her hair was long and dark and she flicked it all the time, or played with it, twirled it into pigtails. My hair was short and scruffy, and sort of pointed in all directions, and whenever it was time to wash it, my mother grabbed me, but it was rough and it hurt. We didn't have a shower, and so it was always done over the sink with a cup, and she would grab my neck and splash the water, and soap went into my eyes.' He swallowed and his tongue darted over his lips. 'Then one day, I walked in on Sally.'

'Do I need to know this?' Sam said.

'Are you worried about the time?' Grant said. 'There's no need. I've got plenty of it. And yes, you need to know it.'

Sam sat back as he detected an increase in Grant's breathing.

'So I walked in on her,' Grant continued. 'She was in the bath, beautifully naked, washing her hair, and it was different to how mine was washed. It was slow and luxurious. She didn't know I was there at first, but I couldn't move. I was stuck, transfixed.'

'She was your sister, for Christ's sake.'

'That doesn't mean anything. That's your problem, Detective, that you see boundaries where I see opportunities. She was a woman to me. Slim, but she had curves, you know, with a peachy arse and perky little tits.' He grinned. 'Your sister was just getting to that age.'

The air seemed to rush out of the room. Sam's chest tightened and his mouth went dry. He couldn't speak or make a response.

'Yes, I know all about her,' Grant went on. 'I make it my business to know about my enemies. And tell me, do you ever think about her? I don't mean family stuff, like old photographs. I mean, how she was, you know, when she was all alone.'

Sam exhaled loudly. 'Are you enjoying yourself?' he said, his voice hoarse. 'If this is just for show, so I can find you disgusting, you've no need to try. You already disgust me.'

'You keep denying it, Detective.' He smiled. 'Back to big sister Sally. It was her hair that did it, you see. I thought you would want to know about that, because you need to know to find out about the missing girl. It all starts somewhere, and Sally, well, she was the start. She had a nice body. Her skin was pale and perfect, the water making it red and hot, and so I watched, couldn't stop myself. I stared at her breasts. They were small but not flat, so that her hair seemed to sort of rise and fall over them.'

'Okay, so I'm playing your game,' Sam said. 'What happened when she noticed you?'

'She jumped, like she was shocked, but then I asked her if I could wash it for her.'

'Did she let you?'

Grant swallowed. 'Yes. She knelt down in the water, and so I stood over her and poured water onto her head, watched as it ran down her hair and then back into the bath. I couldn't breathe but I didn't know why then. All I knew was that the feel of her hair under my hand felt like sparks on my fingers and the flushed pink of her body made my stomach turn over. I was eleven. I didn't know what that meant.'

'So where did it go from there?'

'So you do want to know, Detective,' Grant said, a gleam in his eyes. 'I knew you couldn't resist.'

'No, I'm just playing along, waiting for you to get to the relevant part.'

'I can live with that,' Grant said. 'It's a long story, because it became our thing, Sally and me, a pattern. It made Sally feel special, like playing a salon game, because our parents couldn't afford for her to have a proper wash and cut. We lived in a small terrace, where the front door opened straight into the living room and there were just two bedrooms upstairs. Twice a month she let me wash her hair, when there was no one else in the house, and it became my treat as well as hers, so that I would look at her hair and dream of the next time.'

'So you blame all of what you've done on your sister engaging in some silly game with her little brother?'

Grant shook his head. 'It changed when I touched her.'

Sam closed his eyes for a moment. He could hear Grant's excitement rattling as fast breaths through his nose.

'You touched her?' Sam said eventually.

'Yes, I touched her. How could I resist? I had no control then. And do you know how she responded?

'I've got to listen anyway, I suppose.'

'That's right, you do,' Grant said, and then, 'She giggled.'

Sam sat back and folded his arms, but Grant continued anyway.

'She had been leaning back as I was washing her hair. I was sweeping it backwards, like they do in the salons, pulling it back, and I was looking right down her body. At her breasts, her stomach, and there in the water, I could see the hair between her legs, and I just stopped. My mouth was open, my little cheeks red, and Sally opened her eyes to see what was the problem. When she saw where I was looking, she said I could touch her. So I did. Just a gentle touch, more like a brush with my fingertips, and Sally's cheeks flushed, I saw them, and I wanted to keep on touching, but she stopped me.'

'So she had some sense.'

'Or maybe she liked it too much. Like I said, people see limitations and boundaries. Not me. I see desires, goals. So I finished washing her hair, and then that was it, the last time. I had done something wrong, and she didn't let me into the bathroom after that. Instead, all I had was watching her brush her hair before she went to bed, both of us on opposite sides of the smallest room, and sometimes the street light would come in from outside and make her nightdress almost invisible, so that I could see the long stretch of her legs and the outline of her breasts. The light outside would catch loose strands of her hair.'

'You were kids, making discoveries,' Sam said, contempt in his voice. 'That is no excuse for what you did. For all your talk of bravery, you hide behind your story.'

'Maybe,' Grant said. 'But it burns, rejection. I was fourteen when she left home. She became pregnant by a man she had started to see at work and got herself a flat over a small shop. She never mentioned what had gone on, because she acted like it was just some dirty secret, and I didn't say anything either, but the thoughts of it were always there, those days spent in the bathroom and the soft luxurious feeling of her wet hair.'

'So you moved on to killing young girls because your sister walked away from you?'

Grant started to laugh, shaking his head. 'You don't get it, do you?'

'Get what?'

'Sally was my first one. My virgin kill.'

Thirty-Four

Joe waited inside the dark interior of the café, one of the oldest in the city, where an old Greek man served up milky coffees long before someone else renamed them latte. The seats were padded PVC, bright green, below Formica tops that bore coffee rings on their surface like wrinkles and the sugar was poured out of glass jars, all against the backdrop of a blue-tiled mosaic of the Acropolis. The owner, Andreas, made his name on big breakfasts for manual workers, or omelettes for professionals who thought that going greasy spoon kept them in touch with the common man.

For Joe, it was a simpler equation. Andreas let Joe's clients use the back door, a favour for helping him with a speeding ticket a couple of years earlier that avoided a driving ban and so kept his business going. That's what I do, Joe thought. He kept people's lives going when they hit a bump, and this was the payment, to be allowed to use the café to meet people who didn't like to be seen coming in or out of busy places.

Andreas appeared behind him. 'When is your boy coming?' he said, the words rolling around his mouth, his Greek accent still strong.

Joe checked his watch and tapped the table with a coin. 'Not long, I hope,' he said, and then turned to the front door as the bell tinkled and a young man walked in. He looked out of place, glancing around nervously, his eyes searching the dark corners of the room. Joe recognised him from the injury photographs sent by the prosecution.

Joe raised his hand in the air and the young man walked over.

'Perfect timing,' Joe said to Andreas, who grinned from under his grey moustache, tinged with brown from the cigars he smoked at the back door when the café was quiet. 'Another coffee please.'

The young man was in chinos and a hooded top, the hood down, his dark hair glossy and clean, his skin healthy from a good upbringing. There was none of that pinched hardness worn by the people who came to see Joe with charge sheets in their pocket.

'Mr Parker?' he said as he sat down.

'Hello, Daniel,' Joe said. 'Can I call you Daniel?'

The young man nodded and smiled nervously. Well-mannered but scared.

'Good,' Joe said. 'I want you to remember that you asked to speak to me.'

'But not here.'

'No, it had to be here. I wasn't seen coming in or out, and so I might deny ever having this conversation.'

'That sounds threatening.'

'It wasn't meant to be,' Joe said, aware of the situation. The young man had been the victim of an assault by one of his better clients, a local thug who thought that selling pills to clubbers made him the big man. He hadn't realised that the really big men let him carry on because he attracted the police attention and kept it away from them. 'So, Daniel, what is it you want to say to me?'

Daniel looked down at the table, his arms folded, rocking forward slightly. 'I want out of it,' he said eventually.

'What, out of the case?'

Daniel nodded.

'Why?'

'Do I have to give a reason?'

'It makes me curious, that's all.'

'I don't want to go to court.'

'Have you spoken to the police?'

'I tried to, but they weren't interested. They said I had to go to court, and that they could force me if they wanted, and I've got my parents telling me to do the right thing, that justice is important.' He shook his head. 'I don't know what to do.'

'If you don't go, he'll get away with it,' Joe said. 'You know that, don't you? You're the only witness to what happened.'

'Yes, I know.'

Joe reached into his jacket pocket and took out an envelope. He placed it on the table.

'If you keep pushing at the police, telling them that you won't go, they can make you with a witness summons,' Joe said. 'If you ignore that, a warrant, and you'll sit in a prison cell until the trial, even though you're the victim.'

Daniel paled. 'So what do I do?'

'Play along, tell them that you'll be there at the trial, and then just don't turn up. The prosecutor will try to get it adjourned, to find out where you are, but they won't succeed, because the court has targets to meet, and a case delayed looks bad for their figures. So without you, the surprise no-show, the case comes to an end.' He slid over the envelope. 'My client feels bad about your nose. You're a good-looking young boy and he didn't mean to break it like he did, but you know the truth about what was going on, don't you, Daniel.'

Daniel's eyes narrowed. 'What do you mean?'

'You were bitching about the deal you'd just bought, because you were bulk buying and had hoped to make a bit on top for yourself, but because you were already too tanked, you got your sums wrong. You lashed out and so you got thumped, except you didn't tell the police that. They think it was unprovoked, but we know different. Is that why you're reluctant, because of what might come out?'

Daniel's cheeks flushed and Joe knew he had hit home. He had sanitised his version and didn't want his parents to know what was going on.

'Like I said, no witness and the prosecution have no case, and we all get to move on,' Joe said. 'If you decide not to go, my client wants you to be compensated for what he did. So take the money, two thousand pounds, and take a holiday.'

Daniel swallowed. 'And if I don't?'

'Nothing. No one is going to hurt you. To my client, you're just a kid who got carried away, but he's on a bender and so wants to avoid that being activated.'

'Bender?'

'Suspended sentence. For violence. So you can see his worry. No one is threatening you. He is just trying to do the right thing.'

'Won't the police try and persuade me into going?'

'Go away, somewhere beyond their reach. Have you got a friend you can stay with? Don't answer your phone unless you know the caller.'

Daniel's hand went to the money, nodding, taking a deep breath. When he slid it across the table, he said, 'Thank you. I appreciate your advice.' He stood to go, putting the money in his pocket.

Before he left the table, Joe said, 'You've taken the money and it's yours. But my client will need it back if you turn up at court, you know that.'

'Yes, I understand.'

Daniel turned to go, and once the door closed, there was movement behind him. Joe felt strong hands on his shoulders. It was his client, short and wiry in a black suit, his head shaved bald to help with the image.

'Thank you, Joe. I appreciate it. You're taking a risk though.'

'No, I'm not, because I was giving him what he wanted. There is always a way that keeps everyone happy. I found it in this case.'

'I like it. So what now?'

'You turn up at court next week, suited and smart,' Joe said. 'You look surprised at the no-show, and then you go home.' As his client nodded, Joe added, 'Now it's your turn for a favour.'

'Shoot. What is it? Coke? Pills?'

'No, none of that. I don't touch it. It's about a case. It's a murder case, except I'm not sure the victim is dead.'

'That makes it unlucky for someone.'

'Yeah, that was my logic. She's a drinker and spends money she hasn't got. There are rumours that she was topping up her income by selling herself from her flat. If she has just run away, she's going to have to find ways to earn her money, and she's already built a client base.'

'You want me to ask around?'

'I know you use some of the street girls to deliver for you.' When his client raised his hands in innocence, Joe said, 'I'm your lawyer. I don't judge when I'm in my work clothes. So ask them if someone new has turned up. Tall blonde. Carrie. She'll have a young child with her. Here's a picture.' Joe passed over the clipping from the newspaper from the day before, where Ronnie's case had found its way to one of the middle pages. 'If someone knows her, the name of her pimp would be good too.'

His client smiled and put it in his pocket. 'I'll get back to you.' Then he walked out of the café, his strut telling Joe that the day had ended well for everyone.

Thirty-Five

Sam paced the corridor in the prison. He had left Grant on his own in the room as he called Evans, except that he had been trying for more than thirty minutes, her phone constantly engaged. When she eventually answered, Sam said, 'Grant is saying nothing. He's just boasting, like he's pleased to have an audience.'

'What about?'

'Killing his sister.'

'Really?' Evans said. 'I've not heard of that before.' A pause, and then, 'What are you thinking?'

'That he's making it up. He's just spinning some fantasy, to deflect us. It doesn't even have any point to it.'

'Stick with it,' Evans said. 'Let's see where it leads us.' And then she hung up.

As the corridor fell into silence again, Sam braced himself to go back into the room. He wasn't enjoying spending time in there, but he had to keep going, just so that he would have something to take back with him.

When he went back into the room, Sam said, 'So you killed your sister?'

'You haven't read about that, have you?' Grant said, and he winked. 'You should pay attention to detail, because that's where the answers always are, in the detail.'

'So tell me about her.'

'Sally knew I watched her when she was in bed.'

'How?'

'By my breaths.'

'And she didn't tell you to stop?'

Grant shook his head.

'And so you killed her for that?'

'No, no, no. Do you think it's so simple? It taught me patience, that's all, because I had taken a risk in touching her and it had ended up as a mistake. So watching became the important thing, it's better to take your time, because taking risks leads to mistakes. It wasn't easy for Sally though. I was always there, watching as she came out of the bathroom, or getting changed, or just doing her homework. So she did the cruellest thing.'

'What was that?'

Grant sat back, his arms behind his head. 'I had been lying in bed. Sally was in the bath, and it was like a taunt, because with every splash of the water I felt the shame of her breast, how I had responded, how she had rejected me, that it was all something dirty. Except that as I thought of her, I felt the stir of excitement stronger than I had ever felt before, because I was at that age when manhood starts to burst through. When Sally came out of the bath, she was wearing just a towel, and she must have seen something in my eyes, maybe something she had seen in other men, because Sally knew her power by then. So she let the towel slip, and my eyes tracked downwards in line with the towel, to the flatness of her stomach, and then as it dropped to the floor she watched me. She let me look.'

'So is that when you killed her?'

He looked at Sam and tutted. 'There you go, rushing again. No, it isn't. I did something much simpler. I touched myself. I couldn't stop it and Sally saw me. I don't know what I did, gasped or jolted or something, but she shouted out. She had

174

been grinning in the bedroom, although it was nasty, victorious, spiteful, but as she ran out, covering herself up with her towel, she sounded angry. She shouted down the stairs that I was touching myself, because of her, and that I was a dirty little pervert.'

Grant shook his head as if lost in memory.

'My mother sprinted upstairs. She dragged me to the bathroom and held my head under the tap, making my hair wet, the water cold. How do you think I felt?'

'Humiliated,' Sam said. 'Most of all, angry.'

'You're getting it, because it was always there, in the background, everyone's dirty family secret. My father tried to make it right, said that it was normal, because everyone is confused at that age, but it wasn't forgotten, from the sideways glances I got sometimes, or from the little sneers I got from Sally. And she told people at my school. I was the quiet boy in the class, but I tried to fit in. I noticed things. How some of the boys showed off when the girls were around, and how some of them responded, as if they liked that stupidity. So I tried a joke sometimes, to try to join in, but the girls just looked at each other, embarrassed, and then the boys would tease me, and it always came back to the same thing, that I thought of my sister when I played with myself.'

'So what did you do?'

'Like I said, I had learned to be patient. Sally left home and had her baby, but still I was prepared to wait. When her little boy was six months old, her boyfriend left her. So she was always alone, and I kept watch. There was a park opposite her flat, and when it went dark, I sat there and watched. She didn't know I was there.' Grant's eyes narrowed, his breaths were getting shorter, his arousal growing. 'Isn't that just the best bit? The build up. The watching. I knew what I was going to do before I did it, and I didn't try to fight it, because you shouldn't fight your desires. That's what separates me from the flock.'

'We call it society,' Sam said, 'where people don't do cruel things because it would be just that – cruel.'

'Bullshit,' Grant said, slamming his hand on the table, making Sam jump. 'You're scared of the consequences, that's all. Men rape and murder all the time when it's allowed, like in war zones, so don't give me the high and mighty bullshit.'

'Go on then, tell me how you killed her. I will check this out, and so if you're lying to me it's a waste of time. If you just want to tell the world, there are enough true crime writers out there who could do it for you.'

'Like I said, I'm giving you the answers for the missing girl. My story is about Sally.' Grant lowered his voice. 'It was the onset of autumn that had done it. It's the best season, all that long hair swirling around woollen scarves, caught by the wind, damp and wild. Summer is too manufactured, because sunlight wrecks the colours, makes them dry and light. When the heat fades, so does the fake bleach, and so all you see are beautiful young women, just how they are supposed to be. Except that back then, Sally was always there, making me feel ashamed. I had to do something about it.'

'So what did you do?'

'I was in the park opposite. It was dark and so she couldn't see me, but I could see her, just a blurred outline through the glass, but it was enough. I could see her fingers dancing through the strands as she showered, teasing out the shampoo, stretching it.' Grant's fingers started to tap on the table again. 'The door was unlocked, and so I crept upstairs, my footsteps light. She couldn't hear me. I pushed at the bathroom door. Her baby was asleep in the room next door, face down in a light blue sleepsuit.' He laughed. 'I almost lost my nerve at that point. Even I have weaknesses.'

'Or humanity. That boy was your nephew.'

'He meant nothing to me, because all I could hear was the water running over her. It's all about focus.' He tapped the side of his head, his teeth gritted. 'I pushed at the door and I saw her. She was facing away from me, standing in the bath, her hands running down her hair from the overhead shower. Her skin was pink and wet, her bottom wider than it had been when she had lived at home, but still it set off that churn in my stomach.'

Grant clapped his hands together, making Sam jump.

'I ran at her. I grabbed her hair and yanked it. Sally screamed, but I was pulling hard, and then she was falling backwards. Her head cracked when it hit the bath. It was louder than her scream. I heard it above the slip of her feet in the water. It was like a dropped melon and a gasp, and then she was quiet. All there was left was the smack of the water as it drummed against her stomach.'

'Is that how you had planned it?'

Grant laughed. 'No. I was going to strangle her, because that had been the image that had excited me as I had imagined it, but as I watched the water turn pink as it ran towards the plug, as I felt for her pulse, for a heartbeat, and felt just damp skin, I knew that it was perfect. She had slipped in the bath. No one would know.'

'How old were you then?'

Grant paused and closed his eyes, the small nods of his head giving away his mental arithmetic. 'Sixteen. I was sixteen.'

Sam was silent for a few seconds, and then said, 'Why have you told me this, after all these years?'

'Investigate it and discover the truth.'

'We could charge you with it if we can prove it.'

'It will just make me more popular.'

'Popular?'

'Oh yes, you should see my fan mail. Young women, old women. They like a bad boy. Nude photographs, requests to meet. Deluded young men, or even people who think like I do, so they want to meet me, like I'm their idol.'

177

Sam shook his head. 'I'm bored of your ego. Now can we get on to the missing girl?'

Grant looked smug, as if he had just won a game that Sam didn't know was being played. 'I've told you all I've got to tell you,' he said. 'The answers are all there. It's up to you to work it out.'

Sam gathered his notebook and pen. The chair flew back as he got to his feet. He pointed at the window. 'Take a look out there, Grant. I'm parked along the road you were looking at. I'll be walking to my car, smelling the scent of freedom. You think about that back in your cell.'

'Or maybe I'll think about your sister instead.'

Sam closed his eyes for a moment, just to steel himself. He should have been ready for the taunt. 'Leave my sister out of this.'

'Why? Because she went the same way?' Grant leaned back in his chair and folded his arms, grinning. 'Someone just like me enjoyed her. Did you enjoy her too? Just little peeks when she got ready?'

Sam went to the door and banged on it. He had to get out.

Grant laughed. 'Or what about your other little sister?'

That made Sam whirl round. 'What did you say?'

'Little Ruby, although she isn't that small now, is she? All long legs and hair. Sweet.'

Sam felt the blood rush through his head, had to fight against the clench of his fists, the need to attack Grant, to see some fear in his eyes, some pain. His heart was hammering, sweat on his forehead.

The door opened and Sam rushed through. As the door started to close slowly on its hinges, Grant shouted, 'Don't forget to mention me to your wife. She'll give you the time of your life.'

As the door finally closed, Sam set off at a jog, just to get away as quickly as he could, but all he could hear was the sound of Grant laughing, loud and manic.

Thirty-Six

Joe checked his watch as he got back to the office. Five o'clock. It was time to meet Kim.

He had gone to his office to drop off his dictation machine. It had recorded the café meeting, just in case. He checked his reflection in the glass of a picture frame. There were dark rings under his eyes and some sag to his cheeks, but it was the end of a long day. It was the best he could do.

He headed for the door when Gina burst through, Monica just behind her.

Gina checked her watch. 'It's early for you, Joe.'

'It's been a long couple of days,' he said. 'Sometimes you can only read the same words so many times.'

'I've found a blood expert,' Gina said. 'He does blood spatter normally, but he can age it to some extent. Bloodstains get a black border round them after a couple of months, and this border will increase in size all the time, until it gets to about nine months old.'

'And we can prove Carrie and Grace were alive more than two months ago,' Joe said. 'So if we can show a black border, we can eliminate it from the morning of the argument?'

'Exactly,' Gina said.

Joe grinned. 'I like it.' He turned to Monica. 'How were Terry's neighbours?'

179

'Interesting,' Monica said. 'Terry Day isn't popular on that street.'

'Tell me more,' Joe said. He had gleaned that himself, but had been lacking in detail.

Monica opened the notepad she had taken with her. 'He's awarded himself the job of some kind of neighbourhood warden. Except that it isn't anything official, and the hardest thing is finding out any facts about his background, because it's all gossip. Most people haven't been there very long. It's turned into a rental area, and there's a high turnover of tenants. The gossip is that he has lived there all of his life. The house used to belong to his parents, but when they died it was too big for him. He retreated to the top floor and let out the other floors, and it appears that he wasn't a great landlord. Most of his tenants used to bitch about him to the neighbours.'

'About what?'

'About being creepy. One of the neighbours across the road used to be one of his tenants, until another flat came free. She moved out because he was odd. When she first started renting, he used to let rooms, like in a shared house, but he wouldn't allow them use of the kitchen. He put a small stove in each room, like a camping stove, and they had to wash their plates in the bathroom sink. She said that wherever she turned, he always seemed to be there, just watching. After that, people kept on leaving and so he turned them into flats.'

'What does he do for a living?'

'Nothing, it seems. There are rumours that he lives off a big inheritance. He cycles into town and just hangs around cafés and pubs. When he's not doing that, he bangs on neighbours' doors, harassing them about some problem or other. Bikes left on the pavement, a late party, things like that.'

'A local oddball. Nothing wrong with that,' Joe said, pacing now, knowing that there was something extra.

'How about a deceitful fantasist?' Monica said.

180

Joe stopped. His eyes widened. 'Go on.'

'He had a reputation as some kind of war hero,' Monica said. 'He used to go to the Remembrance Sunday marches every year, in his blazer and his beret. No one else on the street has been there long enough to remember him as a young man, and so they thought he was a Falklands veteran or something. He's, what, mid-fifties? So he used to walk round, ordering people about, and they put up with it, because he had that military bearing.'

Joe started to smile. He could see where this was going.

'You're right to smile, Joe,' Gina said, taking up the story. 'It all came crashing down for him. I met a few people like him in my police days, those who lied about their exploits just for the attention. They'd get a weekend in the cells, until we found out they had nothing to do with the crime. The problem is that they get greedy with their fantasies, because even they get bored with the one they have created for themselves. That's what happened to Terry Day. He enjoyed his fantasies but boasted too much about his adventures and started to wear too many medals. And none of it was real. All he had was a blazer and second-hand medals, but someone took a picture of him and sent it to the paper, wondering about this local war hero with a chest full of glory. He was everyone's favourite veteran for a couple of days, until some real soldiers saw it and realised he was a fake.'

Gina looked towards Monica, who responded by pulling a sheet of paper from an envelope she had been holding in her hand.

'We went to the local library,' Monica said. 'They remembered the story, because in towns like Marton, they remember the gossip. They found the back issue of the local paper and let me copy it.'

She put the piece of paper on the desk.

Joe picked it up to read.

181

The main photograph was a picture of the man he had disturbed earlier in the day, except that he was more smartly dressed. The Terry Day he had met had been in scruffy jogging bottoms and his hair unkempt. The Terry Day in the photograph wore a sand-coloured beret with a dagger and flames insignia and a smart navy blazer, pride burning in the set of his jaw and the stare of his eyes through dark-rimmed frames. Across the breast pocket was an array of medals, and it looked impressive, a testament to bravery that was in excess of the men marching behind him. Old men wearing poppies, their expressions a mix of pride and sadness, the day about remembering those less lucky than they had been.

Underneath the picture was a list of medals worn by Terry Day. They ranged from the South Atlantic Medal to the NATO medal, along with medals for distinguished service and meritorious service, and many others. Seventeen in total, all lined up. Marton's own war hero.

'None of it is true,' Monica said. 'He was trying to impress a woman in the next street and it seems like he got carried away, began to enjoy the attention. He made up war stories in the pubs and cafés, but once everyone found out, life got pretty tough for him. He was shunned. He goes to the same pubs, but he sits on his own.'

'This is good,' Joe said.

'But being a liar doesn't make him a murderer,' Gina said.

'No, it doesn't,' Joe said. 'It makes him untruthful though.'

'So we keep on looking into Terry?' Monica said.

'And don't stop until there's nothing left to know,' Joe said, looking at the piece of paper again, smiling. The case had just got a little better.

Thirty-Seven

Joe looked around as he got close to the pub. It wasn't a usual meeting place for him, but he didn't want to go any place where he would be seen. He was in The Ox, a white-painted corner pub near the Science Museum, so that the street was filled with tourists and school groups, not the lawyers and accountants who fleshed out the pubs along Deansgate.

Kim Reader was already in the bar when he walked in. She was sitting in front of the window, the light blocked out by dark stained glass, which made the inside of the pub look gloomy. There were tables outside, filled with some of the after-work crowd, but it seemed that Kim had thought the same thing he had – that it was better not to be seen together.

Kim was staring down at the table, drinking from a bottle. When he slid in alongside her, squeaking on a burgundy leather bench, she looked up.

'I thought you were standing me up,' she said, and then she smiled.

'No, never,' he said, grinning. 'Do you want another? You can put it in your hospitality disclosure book, if you want.'

Kim thought about that, and said, 'Why not?' before draining it.

When he returned from the bar, two bottles in his hands, he said, 'So how was your day?'

'The same as all of them,' she said. 'Not enough time to do what I'd like to do.'

They talked through their day for a while, each of them avoiding Ronnie's case. For Kim, it was all office politics. Who had upset her over something trivial, the pressure to do more as staff numbers went down. For Joe, it was talk of business worries, of how getting paid for being a criminal lawyer was getting harder each year.

Then Kim said, 'Let's get it out of the way. It spoiled last night. We might as well deal with it now. Ronnie Bagley.'

'What do you mean?'

'It will come up, it is bound to, so let's talk about it now. Then we can have a drink as old friends. Nothing goes beyond this table though.'

'That depends on what you tell me,' he said. When Kim frowned, he added, 'You can't expect me to hold back something that will help Ronnie.'

'Okay, I understand, but don't worry, there's nothing I know that you don't or won't.'

'Let me try this then. Do you think he's guilty?'

'I've never prosecuted anyone I didn't think was guilty.'

Joe raised his eyebrows. 'Never?'

There was a pause, and then, 'Well, that depends on how you look at it, because there are different ways to believe in a case. Sometimes you have got to trust what the witnesses say. If they are telling the truth, then yes, I believe someone is guilty. Put another way: I've never prosecuted someone I thought was innocent.'

'What about during a trial? I've lost cases I thought I had won.'

'You're talking about innocence, not guilt.'

'No, you are,' Joe said. 'I didn't use the word "innocent". I'm talking about whether you think someone can be proved guilty.'

'That's your conscience speaking, Joe,' she said. 'It's how

you rationalise what you do. To you, guilt is a concept, that if we can't prove that a person did something bad, then it is some kind of moral vacuum, but real life isn't like that. Guilt is an emotion, not a verdict.'

'So you prosecute emotionally?'

'It's hard not to.' Kim leaned closer to Joe, her elbows on the table. 'Let me tell you about something you won't see, and that is how many times we have to say no to cases against really bad people just because we know that we won't get it past a jury, because a witness won't get involved, or because we can't get funding for a crucial forensic report. Those are the cases that keep me awake, not the Ronnie Bagleys of the world, where at least we have a go. Juries sometimes get it wrong. Hell, sometimes we do, because we miss something or don't spot a defence tactic, but at least we tried.'

'So you think Ronnie is guilty?'

'Yes, absolutely, and I mean guilt as in he did it, not whether we are sure to convict him. What about you?'

'Just between us, never to leave this table?'

'Of course.'

Joe smiled. 'I've got my work cut out, I know that, but I just don't think he killed them both. I don't see that shadow around him. The evidence tells me that he's guilty, but sometimes the evidence is not what it seems.'

'What do you mean?'

Joe took a drink. He wondered whether he should say anything about Terry Day. He would have to disclose what he had discovered at some point, as the law doesn't allow surprise attacks anymore, but was The Ox the right venue for it to happen?

Or he could find out whether Kim already knew.

'What about Terry Day?' he said.

Kim paused as her mind flicked through the witness list. 'The landlord? What about him?'

'How do you know he didn't do it? He's alone in the house with her all day. She used to drink a lot. Perhaps he did it.'

'The landlord's in the clear,' Kim said. 'He's got no record. A decent man.'

'So you've nothing to show that he isn't always truthful? Some man living on the top floor of some rundown building, a bit of an oddball?'

Kim sat back. 'Have you got anything to show that?'

Joe had got the answer he needed, that Kim didn't know what the neighbours saw, and he didn't want to let his client down by spilling secrets because he was faced with the long lashes of an ex-girlfriend.

'Just a notion,' he said, and then, to change the subject, 'It was good to see you last night.'

'Yeah, you too.'

She flushed, and there it was. Unfinished business. Joe saw it in the small flare of her eyes, the dark shadow of her pupils.

'There is one thing though,' he said. 'I don't mess around with people in relationships.'

'What do you mean?'

'What I said.'

Kim tapped the side of the bottle with her fingernail. 'Can I be honest with you, Joe?'

'I want you to be.'

'You've always been about bad timing. I know for you we were perhaps just a couple of fun times, notches on your bedpost, but I don't give myself up easily. I did for you, and, well, it was a big deal. Then I had to watch you carry on as if we were just drunken moments. Maybe we were the right people but at the wrong time.'

Joe was surprised. 'Yes, maybe,' he said. 'I didn't know you felt like that. I'm sorry.'

'Knowing doesn't matter. If you didn't feel it, there was no point in knowing it.' She patted his hand and took a drink. 'Don't worry, I'm no stalker. I knew we would both meet other people. I was with someone when you turned up in Manchester, and then you were with someone when I was single. It's just the way things are. This is how we turned out. I thought of you though, more than I should have done.'

'How do you know I didn't think of you?'

Kim gave him a look of reproach. 'I don't mean something you could use when you felt horny and alone. I mean something more than that. Something in here,' and she patted her chest.

'It's not that though,' Joe said. 'It doesn't matter what you feel; if you were happy with Sean, none of it would matter.'

'How do you know I'm not happy with Sean?'

'Because you wouldn't be here now, with me, talking about your feelings, if you were.'

'We're just two people who never see each other,' she said, and then she shook her head. 'Can we talk about something else, because we're staying as just friends, aren't we?'

'It seems that way.'

'And if I wasn't with Sean?'

'Don't promise to leave him, just to make me feel better,' Joe said, and as he looked at her, he recovered the memory of her from their student days. Her kiss. Her passion. 'If I come for you, you won't turn me away, will you?'

'No, I won't. I'll be there for you, Joe. I have always been there for you.'

He slid out of the bench seat. He had to use the gents, and, more importantly, he needed to work out what was going on.

The toilet was empty. Just a line of cracked porcelain urinals and an old sink on one wall. He settled himself in front of one of the urinals and thought about the conversation he'd just had with Kim. He felt that buzz of something about to happen, but he wanted to step back from it. Kim was with someone else.

He didn't pay any attention to the sound of the door behind him. He was zipping himself up as footsteps made soft sounds on the tiled floor. As he turned to go to the sink there was a sudden movement. The noise of clothes, the slide of footwear, and then a grunt of effort followed by an explosion in his head.

Everything went quiet, and the world tilted, his legs not going where he expected them to go. He was falling, and as he watched as the floor got closer, he knew that his arms weren't out and that his face was going to break his fall.

Then there was just darkness.

Thirty-Eight

Sam's daughters were in bed by the time he arrived home, Alice with them upstairs. That happened too often. He could hear Alice reading a story. He listened for a moment. It was a story for Emily, *Green Eggs and Ham*.

He thought about a beer, but he knew that there was no solace there. His father had tried his own escape down that route, and it ended in a stroke and a grave plot alongside Ellie. He threw his keys onto the kitchen top and put his head in his hands, and for a moment he enjoyed the stillness. The meeting with Ben Grant had made him feel dirty, that Grant had somehow managed to invade his life by talking about his sisters, and his wife.

He stood upright and leaned back against the wall, his head resting on the tiles. It was the part of policing he hated most, the way he brought things home. Even when he was doing the financial cases it was the same; he would wonder whether he had missed something, a link to an account that would reveal the undisclosed assets or the villa in Spain that was supposed to be a secret. And for what? So he could be taunted by sickos like Ben Grant while his own children went to bed without seeing their father? He was trying to do the right thing, that was all, a job that should make his children proud and feel protected, but it meant long hours. He couldn't just leave in the middle of an investigation, because there would always be those who would work for as long as they could. Sometimes it was just to get noticed. Other times, it was because they cared about the job. So it meant nights like these, where he got home to find his children saying farewell to the day.

He shouldn't think like that, though. It was destructive, a sign that Ben Grant was winning. He heard Alice come downstairs slowly, and as she hit the bottom, there were the shuffles of little feet on the wooden floor, followed by a squeal as his eldest girl saw him in the kitchen and ran towards him in a pink sleepsuit.

He knelt down to pick her up. She smelled of bubbles and talcum powder and so much innocence. She put her arms round him and gave him a toddler squeeze, where it was all cheek against cheek. She giggled some more as he tickled her and tried to inject some fun into his evening, but his day hung too heavy. Alice pecked him on the cheek. She was in late-evening baggy pants, her hair pulled back. She looked tired.

'Emily heard you,' Alice said. 'I knew I wouldn't get her to sleep until she'd said hello.'

That made him smile. 'I'm glad,' he said. 'Sorry I'm late. It's hectic.'

'How is it going?'

Sam was about to tell her about where he had been that afternoon, to see Ben Grant, to tell her what a vile human being he was, but then he remembered Grant's taunts, how Alice would enjoy hearing about him, that it would excite her.

'All routine stuff. Nothing much happening.'

She took Emily from him. 'There's a microwave meal in the fridge if you're hungry.'

And so went the rhythms of their life. Sam brought in the money, Alice kept their home life afloat. He wasn't always sure that was how she wanted it, but his job had been too good to give up when their first child came along, and it made more sense for Alice to be at home rather than paying for childcare.

190

But recently he had detected some boredom, and he worried that she spent too much time waiting for him to come home.

Their life was routine, but life was like that, long stretches of the mundane broken up by moments of happiness.

'Is Amy asleep?' he said.

'Yes.'

'I'll just go and say goodnight anyway.' He pulled at his tie as he walked up the stairs. As he went into Amy's bedroom, he saw she was on her front, her knees pulled up, foetal, her hair a thin blonde sprawl that flowed onto the sheet. Soft toys lined her cot, a world of innocence. He stroked her hair. He was about to lean down to kiss her when his phone chirped in his pocket.

He cursed the noise and looked at the screen. It was his mother. He remembered that he had promised to go see her. He backed out of the room to answer. 'Hi, Mum. I'll be up there in a bit.'

'Sam, you've got to come round now.'

His mother was shouting, distressed.

'Mum, what's wrong?'

She paused as she took some deep breaths, and then said, 'It's Ruby.'

He went cold. 'Ruby? What's wrong?'

'Ruby said that someone was following her. She's scared, Sam.'

He closed his eyes. His mind shot back fifteen years to the day Ellie never made it home from school, and that same sick feeling in his stomach was there again, the knowledge that danger lurked so closely. And he remembered Grant's taunt.

'I'll be right there,' he said, and then he ran down the stairs.

Monica was sitting on her bed, turning the pages of a magazine, the television blaring its mid-evening tedium of reality shows. Her nights were too often like this during the week, as the bare minimum of a trainee's salary didn't stretch to luxuries. Her surroundings were less salubrious than what she had hoped for when she was still a law student, living out of what her landlord called a studio apartment on Lower Broughton Road, an area of once grand houses turned into bedsits and student accommodation. In her world, it just meant that there was no living room, only a bedroom and a kitchen.

Her phone rang. She looked at the screen. The number was unfamiliar. 'Hello?'

'Monica? It's Ronnie.'

She was confused for a moment. It took her a few seconds to realise that she knew only one Ronnie, her mind having made that separation from her working day. When she made the connection, she remembered that she had given Ronnie her number, just in case there was a development. She was getting used to the fact that criminal law was conducted at strange hours. Criminals don't work nine to five, and don't even take time off for bank holidays.

'What can I do for you, Ronnie?'

'I need to show you something. It's important. It's about Carrie. I think I've seen her.'

'Really?' Monica sat up, suddenly alert.

'Yes, but you've got to come now.'

Monica looked down at her magazine, then at the view out of her window, towards a brick alley and a broken streetlight, the back yard crammed with the rubbish bins needed for all the flats in the building. Her evening wasn't unfolding with any excitement, and she realised that Joe would expect her to go. He wanted her to stay on after she qualified, but she had to keep on impressing him or else he might change his mind.

'How sure are you?' she said.

'Absolutely, and she had Grace with her, but no one will believe me. They'll believe you though.'

Monica knew he was right. There was nothing in it for her to lie. The firm would lose money if the case finished early.

'Where are you? You sound different. I can hardly hear you.'

'Outside Victoria station. That's where I saw her. I know where she might have gone, but I'm scared to go there in case I'm wrong.'

Monica thought about the rest of the evening, about how tired she was, but this was going to be her life, running around at a criminal's request. She had only been with the firm for a few months, but already she had got used to being a taxi and cigarette provider. And it was only a short drive to Victoria. 'I'll be five minutes. Wait there.'

She slipped her dictation machine and a pad of paper into her bag, and was about to head for the door when she thought about her camera. Photographic evidence would be even better.

She paused for a moment. Was she doing the right thing? She dialled Joe's number, just to check, but his phone went straight to voicemail. She had to go. This was a chance to end the case, to prove that Carrie and Grace were alive. She checked herself in the mirror, her hair pulled back into a pony-tail, wearing jeans and a long black jumper, and then headed for the door.

The evening was still warm, and she swatted away midges as she walked quickly along the crumbling path that led down to the pavement outside. The road became a race track at night, a long sloping curve connecting North Manchester to Salford, but it was quieter than normal. No one to bother her.

She was cautious though, because Ronnie unnerved her. She had caught him staring at her a few times, and it wasn't the usual flick up and down she got from men, checking out her figure. It was more intense than that, direct, in her eyes, and never looking down. And he had got too close at times, almost as if he was trying to smell her. She knew she was taking a risk, but she had seen Ronnie and knew she could handle him.

Her car keys were in her hand, her Mini parked on the road outside. She clicked the fob on her car and noticed that the lights didn't flicker. She must have left it unlocked. She gave a silent thank you to Ronnie, because her car wouldn't have made it through the night if she had left it like that. There were too many who had given themselves night shifts, patrolling the streets, checking front doors and car door handles. She had heard rumours of turf wars, streets and estates divided, with the old hands given the nice new estates built in the spaces left by closed down factories, where each driveway had two cars filled with iPods and satnavs. Her Mini wouldn't have got past midnight.

She climbed in and locked the doors, putting her bag on the passenger seat. Monica enjoyed the security of her car. It was the quiet stillness of the interior, the danger of the night just outside, but it was muffled, on the other side of the glass. She checked her hair in the mirror. Although she was in her own clothes, she was still representing the firm.

She slid her keys into the ignition. She stopped. There was a noise just behind her. A rustle, like something moving. She looked over to her bag. Perhaps it had settled.

There it was again. Then there was a giggle.

She gasped, a scream forming, and then there was the sound of fast movement.

An arm went around her neck, cutting off her scream. It was tight, making her choke. Her eyes flashed to the mirror. She saw just the gleam of gritted teeth. Hot breath was against her ear. Her hands reached behind her head, to try to grab, to fight, but something hit her on her temple. Everything went quiet, and Monica slumped to one side.

Thirty-Nine

Joe's world only started to focus properly at Gina's house. He remembered the coldness of the toilet floor against his cheek, being helped to his feet, being handed the remains of his phone, cracked and broken when he hit the ground. He didn't know who had taken him to a taxi, but that's where he ended up, his head leaning against Kim, her arm around his shoulder. There were words of encouragement, that he was going to be all right, and then frustration that he wouldn't go to a hospital.

He told Kim that he'd slipped, but she hadn't believed him. She said she had seen someone rushing out. Kim had tried to get him to call the police, but he refused. Kim didn't want to leave him on his own though, and so she got Gina's number and called her. There was a cut above his eye, but it was more swollen than bloodied, and there was blood coming from the back of his head.

Gina sat down next to him and pressed a cold cloth against the swelling over his eyes. Kim had gone.

'You didn't slip, did you?' she said, her voice soft.

He opened his eyes. She was still blurred, her voice fainter than it should be, but he could think more clearly.

'No. Someone hit me.'

'Did you get a good look?'

'I was at the sink. I just heard the rush, and the next thing I knew there were people around me.'

'Do you want me to call the police?'

Joe shook his head, but then winced. 'No, like I told Kim, you know how much they'll enjoy it, a defence lawyer as a victim.'

'Yeah, I can imagine it,' she said, and then, innocently, 'So before then, how did it go with Kim?'

Joe was able to raise a smile at that. 'We're old friends.'

'You're more than that, Joe. I could see it in her eyes when she brought you round here. But why didn't she take you to her place?'

'Her boyfriend might have objected.'

Gina tutted. 'If that's how you behave, I'm not surprised you got hit.'

'It wasn't a jealous boyfriend. I haven't seen the action to deserve it. There is one thing though: there has been someone hanging around outside the office.'

'You should have said.'

'It's a public garden. I can't start panicking every time some-one stares at the office.'

'But you spotted this one. How long has this person been there?'

'Since Monday. Or at least that's when I started noticing.'

'That's when you took on Ronnie's case.'

Joe thought about that, and then he remembered something else. 'He was at court yesterday. At the back, watching.'

'Joe, why didn't you say?'

'Because cases attract crackpots.'

'So what are you going to do?'

'About tonight?' He shook his head. 'Nothing. Let the bruises go down, and always check behind me when I have a piss.'

'You shouldn't make a joke of it. You could have been badly hurt. Next time it could be me. Or Monica.'

Joe tried to sit but pain came at him quickly, like a kick to his head.

'Take it slowly,' Gina said.

He waved her away and had another go.

'You're right, I'm sorry. I'm not calling the police, but you or Monica, you do whatever feels right. Be careful. I got a good enough view in court that I'd recognise him again. If I see him, I'll confront him.'

Gina didn't respond, and Joe knew that she wasn't happy with that answer.

Once he was in a sitting position, taking deep breaths, he was able to have a good look around.

He had never been to Gina's house before. It was a new-build box, all clean lines and bright doors. There was a small table at one end, a vase with a single flower in the centre, and the living room was grouped around the fireplace, rather than the television, which sat modestly in the corner. Candles were dotted around the hearth, and there was a bookcase against one wall filled with worn out spines. Joe imagined her with her feet lifted onto the sofa, a glass of wine in one hand, a book in the other, just peace and solitude.

'Nice house,' Joe said.

'Thank you.' She looked around. 'I used to think it was a bit lonely here, but now I don't like to think of anyone else in it, because it's become my quiet little place.'

'You're lucky,' he said. 'You've found your place.'

'What did Miss Reader have to say about the case?'

'Nothing much. She thinks Terry Day is a good witness.'

'What, you've told her what we found out, that he's a fantasist?'

'No, I'm not stupid. I just floated him as a suspect. She didn't seem concerned.'

'Did she give anything away?'

'She didn't get a chance. I was too busy being revived. Anyway, I didn't go for a drink to tap her for information. We're old friends, that's all.'

'Just that?'

Joe smiled. 'There were a couple of times.'

'I'm surprised she had it in her.'

'She's not how she seems at work. She's sweet.'

'Sweet?' Gina said, laughing. 'How hard did he hit you?'

'Not that hard,' Joe said. 'Thanks, Gina, but I'll go now.'

'No, stay,' she said. 'You've had a bang on the head.'

'Thank you, Gina,' he said, and then he sighed. 'I could really do with a drink.'

Monica struggled against her bindings.

She was tied to a metal chair, but she was fighting against it, the chair legs clattering on the floor. Her hands were fastened behind her back, her wrists bound together tightly, with ropes around her ankles. She was wearing a blindfold. It smelled of sweat and dirt and put grit into her eyes.

But it wasn't just the discomfort that made the cold finger of fear drag slowly down her spine. It was the disbelief, the way her night had changed beyond any way she could have imagined.

There was someone behind her. She tried to twist her body but it was futile. It was pure instinct, the need to know the direction of attack. There were footsteps, shallow breaths, the stench of sweat and alcohol.

Monica's breaths increased. 'Who are you?'

There was no answer. Her words echoed.

She was somewhere large and empty, but there was the hum of traffic not far away, and sometimes voices more distant. Even music drifted over, jumbles of conversation and songs that told her that there was nightlife nearby. And then there were the trains, the unmistakable steady rumble and the occasional blare of a tannoy, mixed in with the whirr and rattle of tramlines, very close by, the carriages screeching on the rails as they curved away.

Monica jumped as she caught the scent of someone different. It was less masculine, like a perfume, just a faded smell of flowers, and then she remembered the hand around her when she had climbed into the car. It had been slender and soft, even though it had gripped tightly. Not the coarseness she expected from a male hand.

'Who are you?' Monica said again, but softer this time, more pleading.

She jumped when the voice appeared in her right ear, a whisper, jolting her. It was a woman.

'Hello, Monica,' she said. The voice sounded cold and vicious, meanness in every snapped syllable.

Monica whimpered, she couldn't stop it, and then she was angry with herself and so gave her bindings another rattle. She was stronger than this. But whoever the woman was, she knew her name. This wasn't random and that scared her even more. And then she remembered the call from Ronnie. Or at least she had thought it was Ronnie, because that was the name she had been given, but he had sounded different somehow.

Monica strained against the ropes, her breaths fast, tears soaking her blindfold. 'Why are you doing this?'

There was a laugh, loud and strident, echoing again, and Monica got a sense of the emptiness of where she had been taken. Her head thrashed around, not knowing the source of the threat, but then she tried to gulp down deep breaths. She had to stay in control. She put her head down and tried to compose herself. But how was she supposed to cope with being punched until she was dazed and then dragged from her own car and into the back of a van parked just behind? She had tried to fight, but there had been two of them, and they had fastened the blindfold and tied her wrists and feet together. She had been tied to a chair and left there, with no idea of time, with every moment filled with terror, waiting for someone to come near her, unseen, so that she had jumped at the flutter of wings, the drip of water onto concrete, the creak and bang of a loose metal fence. There had been rustles in grass, like rodents.

Monica pulled against her ropes, but they were too tight. 'I want to go to the toilet,' she said, but when the woman laughed behind her, she realised that it had sounded like what it was: a pitiful attempt at misleading them.

'I'm not stopping you,' the woman said, sneering. 'You can sit there and piss yourself, if you think it will make you more comfortable, but it will weigh you down.'

'For what?'

'For what happens next.'

Monica yelped and flinched as she felt a hand on her neck. The fingers were rougher than the ones that had been round her before. It was a man's hand. Hardened dry skin rubbed against her, scratching, moistened only by the sweat that had popped onto her neck. She tried to pull away, to put her chin down, to protect her throat, but then she realised that the hand wasn't going for her neck, but for her hair. A rough finger tickled at the soft hairs at the nape of her neck, and then started to grasp the longer strands and run it through his fingers. Monica felt it as light tugs. The hand ran down the length of her hair, straightening it, and then hovered over her breast, where it ended. She moaned in fear, couldn't help herself.

There was a sound. Of metal blades clicking together.

'What's that?' Monica said, aware that there was something new, her terror increasing another notch.

Her hair was pulled tight. She gasped and then she heard the wet lick of a tongue on a lip, before the blades clicked together and the tension on her hair relaxed. There was a moan of satisfaction, and then she felt the warmth of someone's breath on the top of her head, the sound of someone inhaling. The smell of human sweat was in her face. A man, definitely. Sour, damp. She tried to turn her face, not sure what was going to happen, but nothing did, apart from the continued inhale and exhale from above her.

Monica closed her eyes and gritted her teeth. Her blindfold was sodden with her tears.

'Please, stop,' she said, her voice more pleading now, desperation evident. 'I'm scared. You've had your fun. Just let me go home. Please.'

'Fun?' It was the female voice, shrill and loud. 'Do you think this is it, tying you up? The fun has only just started.'

Someone knelt by Monica's ankles, and then she felt some tugging, before there was the surprise of her ankle coming free, first her left, and then her right.

Her head filled with a mix of hope and fear, that things were about to get worse, but perhaps about to get better, that she was going to be set free.

There was a kick to her chest, a booted foot that hit her hard, made her gasp in pain and in shock, and then she was falling. She braced for the collision. Her head jolted backwards as the chair hit the ground, momentum making it carry on to the concrete, the crack loud in the night. She was dazed and winced in pain, and the back of her head felt damp. The chair clattered away from her. Monica lay on the ground, panting, grimacing, her hands still tied behind her back, the blindfold still in place. She curled up her knees instinctively, to protect herself.

Someone knelt next to her. It was the woman again. Monica could smell her perfume.

'This is your chance to go home,' the woman said, her voice soft.

Monica didn't say anything at first. She lay there, sucking in deep breaths. She could feel dampness in her crotch. She had pissed herself as she was kicked over, the surprise of the unexpected blow making her lose control. The woman was watching her. She could tell from the steady pattern of her breaths, patient and slow.

'I don't understand,' Monica said, gasping. 'Why you are doing this?'

A laugh. 'You don't have to understand. You just have to play the game.'

'What game? What are you talking about?'

'This game. Our game. The one we always play.'

'This is no game,' Monica said, straining at her ropes, but it was no use.

'It's simple. In thirty minutes, we will kill you. The only way you can stop us is if you get away.'

Monica sobbed, tears making it past the blindfold. 'But I don't know where I am. I can't see anything.'

Another laugh, and then she whispered into Monica's ear. 'That, my little sweetness, is why we like it.'

Forty

Sam cursed as a traffic light turned red near his mother's home. He pulled out his phone and dialled Joe's number, but his phone was switched off.

'Joe, it's me,' he barked, once it went to voicemail. 'Get to Mum's as soon as you can. It's about Ruby.'

The lights changed to green and he threw the phone onto his seat. The journey had been too long, just a stream of red traffic lights and queues. The roads around Manchester never seemed big enough; there was never a quick route anywhere.

As he turned on to the street where he'd grown up he could see his mother in the window, pacing, looking out. Sam didn't bother locking his car. She turned towards him as he strode to the front door, and when he rushed into the house she had taken up a position on the sofa, holding Ruby's hand, who had been crying.

'What happened?' he said. He was out of breath.

Ruby looked at Sam, and then at their mother, before she said, 'I want to talk to Sam. Alone.'

His mother looked hurt as she struggled to get to her feet, but she knew that this had been her reason for calling him, that Ruby would confide in her big brother, the nearest person she had to a father figure. Sam knew from the purse of her lips and the glaze to her eyes that she wasn't as strong as she was trying to appear.

When the door closed, he said to Ruby, 'Talk to me.'

She started to cry straight away. 'I didn't do anything wrong.'

'I know that, but if you don't talk to me, I can't help you.'

Ruby pulled her legs onto the sofa, long and awkward, and wrapped her arms around her knees. Tears ran down her cheeks as she said, 'I went down the path,' her voice breaking.

Sam went cold. He sat on a chair opposite. 'The path?' he said, although he already knew the answer.

Ruby nodded.

Sam closed his eyes. The path where Ellie was murdered. Images of Ellie flooded into his mind. He had tried so many times to reconstruct the last moment he had seen her alive. She used to set off for school bright and cheery, tall and awkward, just like Ruby, a cloth bag slung over her shoulder, the one that ended up thrown into the undergrowth, her school books dirty and wet. He couldn't remember if that was how she had been that morning – it had been just an ordinary morning then, so why should he remember – but it was still something he clung on to, the idea of her smile and her goodbye as she went.

He opened his eyes to look at Ruby, who had stopped crying and was looking back at him over her knees with large, wet doe eyes.

'Why did you walk that way?' he said quietly. 'We've told you often enough.'

'Don't you think I don't know that?' she said, her voice angry. 'My life has always been about Ellie, but I never knew her. I want my life to be about me, so I don't see why I can't walk home that way. It's the quickest route.'

'Because it's dangerous,' he snapped.

'Lots of people go that way!'

'Not everyone has to visit a grave once a year because of that path!' He was shouting now.

Ruby ran out of the room, crying, and Sam groaned as he

listened to the stomp of her feet on the stairs. When her bed-room door slammed, he knew he had to go after her.

He went up the stairs and knocked lightly on her door. When she didn't answer, he pushed it open slowly.

Ruby was lying on her bed, face down, her head in her arms, theatrical, teenage. Sam understood her frustration. Her whole life had been moulded by what happened to Ellie, as if Ruby had only ever been her shadow. The replacement girl.

Sam softened. 'I'm not here because you used the path,' he said. 'Mum said you had been followed.'

Ruby didn't move.

'Tell me,' he said. 'It's you I'm worried about.'

She lifted her head to look at him, and then pulled herself up.

'Why do you care?'

'Because I'm your brother, and since Dad died, I know I've got to be there for you. So here I am.'

Ruby wiped her eyes and sat up. 'Okay,' she said. 'I left school just like normal. The roads were busy, and so I thought I would be all right down the path. It was just another normal day, and so why should today be any different?'

'What, you walk that way often?'

Ruby shrugged. That was her answer.

'Carry on.'

'I thought it was going to rain and the proper way takes so long. So I took the shortcut.'

'Who followed you?'

'I don't know, that's the thing. I didn't get a proper look. I turned in, and you know how it goes quiet, because the path bends round, and the trees make it private, so all I could hear were my footsteps. Then there was something else. It sounded like someone walking through the trees, like a rustling sound, as if someone was moving fast.'

Sam's hands tensed into fists as he tried not to show his

205

anger, some of which was aimed at Ruby, for doing what they had always warned her not to do.

'What happened?'

Ruby swallowed and her chin trembled lightly. 'I was scared. I looked back along the path, to see if anyone was there, but there wasn't, although I couldn't see the entrance anymore, because of the curve, so I didn't want to go back. I carried on ahead, but I walked more quickly. I looked into the trees to see if I could see anyone. There was something moving, but it was between the trees, like a blur, so I ran. I was crying and shouting, and the noises followed me for a bit, but when I saw the opening ahead, to our street, I sprinted.'

'Did anyone follow you onto the street?'

She shook her head.

'Could you describe this person?'

Another shake of her head.

'Not even height or clothes or hair colour?'

'No. Like I said, it was just a blur.'

Sam considered her for a few moments. Ruby had a history of attention-seeking. She played up, became provocative. He had to be sure.

'And are you sure someone was there?'

'What, you don't believe me?'

'I know it's been hard for you, Ruby, feeling like you have lived in Ellie's shadow, but you know that you mustn't say these things just to get our attention.'

Tears again. 'Well, fuck off then!'

'Ruby.'

'No, fuck off, Sam. All you care about is Ellie. Mum's the same.'

'That's not true, Ruby. It's just that sometimes people say these kinds of things to get attention, and I need to be sure that you're not. I know it's been hard because Dad isn't around, but you know I'm here for you.'

'I'm telling the truth,' she said, quieter now. 'There was someone there.'

Sam considered her. Her room still bore the remnants of a childhood she was leaving behind, with soft toys strewn over her bed, but the young woman she was becoming was taking over. Make-up, perfumes, hairdryer, a picture of a teenage boy, handsome and sporty, propped up against her radio alarm. Some boyfriend, Sam guessed.

He exhaled loudly. 'Okay, I'll see what I can find out. Do you promise me that you'll never go down there again?'

'Don't tell me what to do.'

'Ruby?'

'No, stop it. You can't run my life. You're not my father because, like you say, I don't have one, but that doesn't mean that you can take charge.'

Sam went over to her and kissed her on the top of the head. 'You are you, not Ellie, don't forget that. It's just that we couldn't face losing you too. So stay safe, for our sake.'

He left the room and went down into the kitchen, where his mother was adding some flour into a mixing bowl. Whenever his mother needed to distract herself, she made cakes. He put his arm around her shoulders. Music came on upstairs, the volume loud.

'Everything will be all right,' he said. 'Try not to worry.'

She nodded but didn't say anything.

'Has Joe called?'

She stirred harder. Sam guessed the answer.

'I'll speak to him,' he said.

She looked up at him. 'He works hard, you know that.'

'We all do, Mum,' he said. 'We all do.'

Forty-One

Monica took deep breaths and tried to clear the haze from her head hitting the ground. Her hair was damp and sticky from the blood oozing from the back of her head. Boots crunched next to her, and she yelped and shuffled along, her wrists still bound by rope. The boots followed her, another crunch, and she scrambled further, using her legs to move, like a snake, and then curling up to protect herself. Then there was laughter, low and mean, taunting.

She put her head to the ground. It was cold on her temple, grit sticking to her skin. She tried scraping her head along the concrete to dislodge the blindfold, but it was on too tight.

Her head swam with emotions. Terror. Pain. Disbelief that this was happening to her. She wanted it to end, and then was angry with herself for letting weakness creep in. She was a fighter, but she could feel the fight draining from her.

'Why are you doing this?' she asked, defeat in her voice. 'Just let me go. Please.'

Monica knew how she sounded; she wanted to be stronger, more defiant, but she felt terrified, fearful, unable to know what was happening.

The boots scraped on the floor again, near to her head. Then there were fingers in her hair and she yanked herself away. A laugh. The woman. She was further away. Watching, Monica presumed.

'Just tell me why,' Monica said.

A pause, and then the woman said, 'Have you ever experienced love?' Before Monica could say anything, she added, 'Not the kind of love you think of, with flowers and holding hands and all that romance novel stuff. I mean the real gut-wrenching, all-consuming, do-anything kind of love. Have you ever known that?'

'I don't understand,' Monica said, her breathing recovering.

'If you had known it, you would know what I mean. You wouldn't have to ask.'

'But how has this got anything to do with love?' Monica strained at the rope around her wrists.

'I don't have to explain anymore, because you don't understand.' Monica recognised the snap of anger in the woman's voice. 'No one understands. They just condemn. So all you have to worry about is staying alive, because the clock is ticking.'

Monica sensed a change in tone, which had switched from being reflective to something more sinister, and she realised that her chance to talk her way out had slipped away before she had even noticed it was there.

Monica scrambled to her feet, teetering a little, and put her feet apart to steady herself. She turned slowly, her feet reaching out, tapping at the ground, searching for obstacles.

Something went past her hair, a bird, perhaps a bat, or even one of her captors teasing her, making her step back quickly. She ducked, scrunching up her shoulders, and then stopped, wobbling, not knowing what was there. The blackness terrified her. All she had were noises, but they were moving around, so she never knew where they were going to be until she felt someone's breath or heard a whisper in her ear. 'Just let me go,' she said, pleading. 'I won't tell anyone.'

A laugh behind her, masculine, making her turn again, getting dizzy, disorientated. Then there was someone next to her.

The scent of stale perfume. Monica jumped when there was a voice.

'You need to keep on trying to escape,' the woman said, her voice a sinister hiss.

'Why not just let me go?'

'Because it wouldn't be the same.'

The woman's voice seemed to swirl around her, and Monica heard the soft shuffle of moving feet. Monica tried to track her, but she made herself dizzy again, with no arms that she could put out to steady herself.

There was movement towards her and Monica flinched. There was a sharp pain on her forearm, like heat, and then wetness, as the heat was replaced by pain that made her cry out, like shards that dug deep into her skin. She had been cut with something.

She backed away slowly, screeching and gritting her teeth in pain. 'What the fuck are you doing?'

'A little incentive to run,' the woman said. 'Don't stay and fight it. Some of the others tried it, but it never worked.'

'Others?' Monica heard the tremble in her own voice.

The woman laughed. 'Do you think you're so special? That you're the first?' Then she stepped closer, making Monica flinch. 'If you want to be the first to get away, keep running. That will make you unique.'

Monica felt her tears wet her blindfold again, and that was the moment when she knew that there was no choice. She winced again as the night air caught the slash on her arm, the blood turning cold on her skin. If she stayed, she would die. If she ran, she would die. But there was always the chance that she would get lucky, that she'd find some way to take off her blindfold and free her hands. If she wasn't bound, it became an even fight. And Monica knew she could win it.

Monica bolted.

She grimaced, waiting to run into something, but that was

better than staying there. She wasn't running fast though, she knew that, but as fast as she dared. All she could see was the blackness of the blindfold, and so she tried to run sideways on, so that her shoulder would take any collision. There were footsteps behind her, loud, deliberate, stamping on the ground, mocking her.

Monica screamed, loud and shrill. The noise bounced back from the roof. She hoped someone would hear.

The footsteps came quicker, running now. Someone slammed into her, sending her forwards. She couldn't put her hands out so she tried to curl her body to absorb whatever she was about to crash into, but it was no use. Her head hit something hard and metallic, a loud clunk, before she collapsed on the ground. She tried to suck in air to clear her head, but it felt like her face didn't move with it, almost as if her cheekbone fought against it. She went faint with the sharp stabs of pain. Her cheekbone was broken, she knew that.

Monica struggled to her knees again, willing herself through her daze, trying to shut out the agony. As she stood, she knew the world around her was swirling. Blood was running down her face.

'I'm not running,' Monica said, her teeth gritted, the words barely audible, blood spitting forward, sucking in air through her nostrils and sinking to her knees. 'I'm not playing your games.'

Then there were hands around her head, making her screech in pain, and then her blindfold fell loose. She blinked a few times, even though there was hardly any light to hurt her eyes. When she looked around, there was a high roof, holes in places, with metal pillars supporting it, along long concrete platforms.

There was movement. As she looked, there were two people there, just silhouettes against the moonlight.

'Who are you?' Monica said.

One of them stepped forward. It was the woman, obvious from the slender build of her shoulders, although all Monica could see was an outline.

'Let me go, please,' Monica said, and then put her head down, blood and tears dripping onto the floor.

The woman stepped closer. 'You are for him. My gift. I can't let you go unless that is what he wants.' She turned. 'Do you?'

Monica looked up again and as she saw the woman's face, her mouth hung open in disbelief, but then a sharp jolt from her cheekbone stopped it. She blinked a few times to try to clear the red haze in front of her, multi-coloured speckles brought on by the pain. When she was able to speak, Monica said, 'I don't understand. Why?'

The man got closer, but he was behind her and Monica couldn't see his face. 'This one is for you,' the woman said to him.

Monica closed her eyes and listened to the unbuckling of his belt just by her head. She started to shuffle away, but his hand went to her hair and gripped it, stopping her from going any further. She heard the acceleration of his breaths and knew what he was doing, the tremors of his rapid arm movements jolting her.

'Stop it,' Monica cried, disgusted, frightened, trying to pull her head away, but he carried on, moaning, tugging more on her hair, his body jerking faster. Monica looked towards the woman, but she was smiling, enjoying it, crouching, watching.

He gave out a long moan and then gasped, and as his hand relaxed, the woman rushed forward, a clear plastic bag in her hand. It went over Monica's head and was pulled tight.

Monica took a deep breath in shock, sucking the bag into her mouth, pulling it tight around her face, so that she wore it like a skin. She breathed out, pushing it away, but as she tried to suck in more air, it was hotter, and she felt the first ache of complaint from her lungs. She could see through the plastic, saw the man stepping away, buttoning his trousers.

It was the woman who took over her vision. Her teeth were bared with effort, her eyes were screwed up. Monica tried another breath, but it was getting harder. It was the end, she knew it. She wanted to say sorry to everyone, because she knew that pain would follow for someone. Her parents. Her brother. She felt the shake of her body as her lungs tried to capture air, but whatever was there was running out.

She tried to keep her eyes open, to take one last look at her life, but all she could see was the woman, her eyes wide, manic, gleeful, and then she started to fade. Her chest was pushing out for air but Monica started to feel peace. Her cheekbone didn't hurt anymore, and the scene started to fade in front of her, like someone turning up the brightness control. There was the sound of laughter, someone shouting, and a child crying, not far away. Another screech of a tram, city sounds, but as her vision faded, so did the noise, and as everything went white she felt herself start to fall backwards. As her body hit the concrete, it felt like it pushed through it, carrying on, a long tumble into darkness.

Forty-Two

The morning did little to make Joe's soreness go away. He tried to sit up and winced as jabs of pain shot across his head. He felt a hand on his shoulder.

'Don't get up, not yet.'

It was Gina, her voice soft.

He tried to focus, and as the room came into view, he saw she was holding a glass of water and some pills. 'Take these,' she said. 'They'll take away some of the ache.'

Joe swung his legs out from under the covers. 'I don't look my best at this time of the morning,' he said, his voice thick with sleep, and then he coughed, which made his head hurt more. He thanked her for the pills and swilled them down.

'None of us do,' she said, and then got off the bed to open the curtains.

He watched her go, squinting through tired eyes. She was wearing a nightdress, cream silk, short and sexy, so that when she reached for the curtains, it rode up, showing her white panties. Despite his headache, he marvelled at her figure. He looked away as she turned around, although the smile on her face told him that he'd been spotted.

'It looks like you've recovered enough,' she said, and then headed for the door. 'Breakfast in ten minutes. I'll see you down there.'

He laughed to himself and then creaked out of bed.

Joe was in Gina's spare room, the bed small, meant for emergencies only. He remembered the night before and he winced. Gina had opened a bottle of wine once she thought he had got over his dizziness. He didn't think it was sound medical advice, but the booze had dulled some of the pain, although not all of his sluggishness was down to being hit on the back of the head.

He stumbled his way to the bathroom. The mirror on the wall cabinet wasn't kind to him. His face was swollen around his eye socket and was turning purple. He would have to endure some questions, but there was no point in hiding away. He splashed water on his face, making him wince, and then he left the bathroom to get dressed. He put on his clothes from the night before. Gina had washed his shirt and hung it over the bedroom door to dry. The bloodstains were still visible, but it wasn't the horror show it had been.

When he went downstairs, Gina was dressed and frying up food. Bacon and eggs, with sausages under the grill.

He eased himself into a chair, grimacing, and sat back as Gina spooned fried food onto his plate.

'So what next?' she said. 'Have you thought any more about involving the police?'

'I told you last night, no,' Joe said. 'I've got a black eye and a sore head. Perhaps I deserved it. I don't know who did it, and I'm sure all the police will do is laugh at the smart-arse defence lawyer running to them as soon as things go wrong.'

'They're not that bad, you know,' she said. 'Most understand the game.'

'But they aren't the ones who will make the most noise.'

'*We* need to know, though,' she said. 'Me, Monica, and anyone else involved with Ronnie's case.'

Joe frowned. 'I know, I'm sorry. Just leave it with me, okay.'

He started to eat, realising that he'd had no food the night before, dipping his sausage into his egg, when Gina's phone rang. He could tell from the way Gina smiled at him that the call was for him. His phone had been smashed in the attack.

'It's for you,' Gina whispered.

When Joe answered, it was Kim.

'Are you all right?' she said, her voice a whisper.

'Groggy, but I'll survive. Where are you?'

'I'm at home. Sean is in the shower, so that's why I'm calling, because I won't get another chance until I get to work.'

'Don't get into trouble on my behalf.'

'I was worried about you, Joe,' she said, and he could hear her concern in her voice. 'You were attacked.'

Joe looked up to see Gina smiling at him.

He turned away.

'I'm fine, don't worry.'

There was a pause, and then she said, 'Joe, I want to see you later. Will you meet me again?'

'As lawyers?'

'No,' she said. 'As friends.'

He closed his eyes as memories came back to him. That tone in her voice, soft, gentle, not the brusqueness he had seen in court. Joe remembered the Kim from college, the soft murmurs in the dark, gentle moans and her hands on his back.

'Do you think we should, because of Sean, I mean?' Joe said.

'Don't you?'

A pause and then, 'No, I don't.'

There was silence on the other end, and then, 'Okay, I'm sorry. Take care, Joe.' The phone clicked off.

He stared at the phone and then exhaled loudly.

'Have you turned the lady down?' Gina said. When he didn't respond, she said, 'You're scared of women.'

'How do you work that out?'

'Because you go to too much trouble making sure that you don't get involved with any.'

Joe didn't respond. He could try to defend himself, fill the

216

silence with emotional stuff about how he had never found the right woman, the special one, but he knew that there was too much truth in what Gina said.

'She's got a partner already,' Joe said.

'What if she isn't happy? Isn't it for her to decide how to feel?'

Joe shook his head. 'I don't cross that line. It only ever brings trouble.'

'Do you want her?'

Joe didn't answer. He concentrated on his food instead.

Gina's hand reached across and gripped his. 'You're a better man than you think you are.'

He smiled at that. He had just acquired a virtue.

The morning had been a long time coming for Sam Parker. He had tried to sleep, knowing that he needed to be alert for his day ahead, but Ruby's account of being followed had made sleep impossible. He wasn't sure he believed her, but he needed to be sure, because he couldn't have it on his conscience if this was the one time that his hunch let him down.

So he had made his way to the path where Ruby said she had been followed, to see if anyone appeared who troubled him. He sat on a small bench near the end of the path, so that he looked like someone taking a rest, in plain sight, not obviously keeping watch.

It was a woodland space between two housing estates, with his mother's estate on one side and a modern redbrick on the other, built on the site of terraced housing that had been swept away in the rush to modernise the city. A gravel path ran through it, lined by trees, and a small brook trickled alongside, with a steep bank that ran towards the estate where his mother lived. He had a good view towards the trees, so he would be able to see if anyone was trying to hide in there.

His mind went back to Ellie and how she had once walked down the same path. It had been familiarity that put her in danger, because she had walked it so many times, and so what was just once more? She had been wearing headphones and wouldn't have heard the footsteps. The path twisted and curved, so that parts of it became hidden and sounds were soaked up by the small thickets of trees. It had been in one of those that Ellie had been found, dragged through the brambles and slumped against a tree, her knickers pulled to her ankles, her top ripped from her shoulders.

Sam closed his eyes. He tried to never think of that, but Ellie's body had been described to him and so he had constructed the picture in his own mind. That made him get close and see the scratches on her skin, pale and young, her face bloodied from where she had been hit. Just one wrong turn, the failure to heed the warnings, and his sister was gone forever. He wasn't going to let that happen again.

The pavements further along were filled by schoolchildren, their uniforms dark blue. Some used the path through the trees, and he fought the urge to tell them not to do so, but he knew how he would be perceived, a lone man talking to teenagers.

Sam thought he heard something. Crunches on the gravel. Then two pupils came into view, one of them using the quiet of the path to have a cigarette.

He sighed. It was pointless. It was just an ordinary path near a school, a frequent shortcut, but Ruby knew that it meant something else to him. He got to his feet. He was angry with her. She had used Ellie's memory to exploit his emotions and get his attention.

Sam set off walking back to his car, his hands jammed into his pockets, when he heard a scream.

Sam whirled round. Two school pupils were looking back down the path.

He bolted towards the noise. It had been a young woman, loud and shrill. He rounded the first bend in a sprint, just the twist of the path ahead, his head filled with the sound of his own feet and the rattle of car keys and coins in his trouser pockets.

He stopped when he saw what was ahead. It was a schoolgirl, lifted in the air by one of her friends, maybe even a boyfriend, shrieking and laughing.

Sam took some deep breaths to get over the exertion. He raised his hand in apology when they saw him, the girl who had shrieked now embarrassed, pulling her skirt back to her knees from where it had ridden up. They both rushed past him and he turned to watch them go.

This wasn't good, he knew that.

He started to walk back along the path, his head down, when he heard something in the woods to his left. He looked quickly. There was something there. The sound of movement, audible as swishes through the undergrowth, and he thought he could see a shape through the trees. Flashes of green, almost impossible to make out, but it was there. Someone running.

Sam set off again, his feet moving quickly over tree roots and uneven ground, but all he was following were shadows and the rustles of movement. He was panting quickly, too long spent at a desk looking at financial statements, but he knew the area well. There was a gate at the top of the slope that led to a small children's park, and beyond that the modern housing estate. It would give him a good view of whoever he was chasing as they broke into the open.

He tried to speed up, despite the ache in his lungs, but was looking forwards and not down. His right foot caught on a loose stone. He was falling, and as he hit the ground, a root winded him as it caught him in his ribcage. He groaned and held his side, and then looked up the slope. Whoever was there had got away.

219

He stamped at the ground with his heel and shouted, 'Fuck!' Then he thought about Ruby, and he knew now that she had been right.

Someone *was* watching.

Forty-Three

As Joe left his apartment, fresh from a shower and change of clothes, he tried to let the sunlight take away the heaviness inside his head. Whoever hit him the night before must have got in a good shot, because if he moved his head too quickly his vision seemed to lag, like a video buffering on a slow internet connection.

He followed his normal route. It started at the waterside, two willow trees trailing over the surface, the idyllic country scene out of step with the industrial backdrop, and then over a long metal bridge that connected the apartment blocks to the brick railway arches that rumbled with the passing trains and the electric squeal of the trams.

It was a walk he usually enjoyed, but he saw it differently now. What was once industrial history became dark bridges filled with shadows and echoes. Whoever had hit him must have been watching him, and so the threat might still be there.

Joe turned as he walked, felt himself speed up. It had been easy to shrug off the attack while he was still at Gina's, but now that he was alone and not far from where it had happened, his bravado slipped and his fear materialised as a burst of cold shivers. He was waiting for the sound of footsteps behind him, or a shout, or some blow to his back. Would it be more than a fist next time?

He made his way towards St Johns Gardens, where normally

he relished the green of the trees and the calm before the grind of the working day. As the gate closed behind him, the gardens seemed empty, with only the crunch of his shoes to disturb the birdsong. He would have enjoyed that on an ordinary day, but after the events of the night before, he saw it as a threat, and imagined people lurking behind bushes. It didn't help that it was also where he had been watched from the previous day.

He stopped and turned around and went back through the gate to walk to his office the longer way, around the gardens rather than through. When he went inside the building, Marion, the receptionist, stared when she saw his face but didn't say anything.

'I slipped,' he said, and headed for the stairs. As he got to the top, he heard the click of a keyboard. Marion was emailing someone about his eye, no doubt.

He closed the door to his office. He knew everyone would find an excuse to walk past to take a look if he didn't. He realised that his chest was heaving, and when he looked at his hands, they were trembling. He would save the sideshow until later.

He went to the window. Although it was partly out of habit he was also checking for the sight of someone watching. There was no one there.

He stepped away from the window. He had to forget about the night before. He tried to tell himself that it was just a punch in a pub, perhaps just a random drunk, or someone he had once cross-examined too roughly who saw a chance for revenge. Random events happen.

But the man at the back of the courtroom, and who had been outside his office, loomed large in his mind. And if he was at court, it was connected with Ronnie's case.

There was a knock on his door and Lisa, his secretary, came in, holding a coffee. She grimaced when she saw.

'Thank you,' he said, and then, 'I slipped.'

'So Marion said.'

Before he could even take a drink, the phone on his desk buzzed. It was Marion.

'There's someone for you in reception,' she said.

He checked his watch. It was just past nine. 'Can Monica see him?'

'She isn't in yet.'

That was unusual. 'Who is it?'

'He won't say.' Then she whispered into the phone. 'He said it's about last night.'

Joe went to rub his eye, but the painkillers were wearing off and he pulled his hand away, remembering how sore it was. 'Tell him to sit down and wait.'

When he put the phone down, Joe sighed. He didn't want to know anything about the night before, but now people were coming to the office to tell him what had happened.

Then he remembered Kim. If someone had seen him, then Kim had been spotted too, and he didn't want them to become the subject of gossip.

Joe went along the first floor and then to the long sweep of the staircase. It gave him a view towards the waiting area. He stopped.

It was a tall man, in grey trousers and a navy jumper, dressed up to see a lawyer.

Joe carried on towards him. As the man looked up and saw him, his hand went to his mouth and tears popped into his eyes.

'I'm so sorry,' he started to say.

Joe held up his hand to stop him and clenched his jaw. It was the man who had been watching the office, and who had been in the courtroom.

'You better come up,' Joe said.

Joe held the door open to his office as the man walked past him. He took another look at Joe's face and then turned away quickly.

Joe gestured towards a chair, and as the man sat down, Joe took his seat on the other side of the desk. He wanted it as a physical barrier, to prevent an attack.

The man fidgeted for a while, so that the only sound was the creak of the chair legs, and Joe let the silence build. He was going to let him start the conversation.

The man dropped his hands and said, 'I'm sorry, Mr Parker, about your eye.' A tear ran down his cheek and his chin trembled.

Joe was confused. 'I don't understand.'

'I hit you. I'm sorry.'

'Yeah, I get that, but what the fuck? Why did you do it?' The man didn't answer, and so Joe let him sob quietly for a while before he said, 'Okay, we'll start with your name.'

The man looked up and wiped away a tear with the heel of his palm. 'David Roberts.'

'I don't know it,' Joe snapped, his impatience showing.

'My son was Nat Roberts.'

Joe closed his eyes for a moment. He should have guessed. He had been receiving cards highlighting events Nat Roberts would have enjoyed had one of his clients not killed him in a pointless street-fight, if you could call it that. Nat had been in the wrong place and looked at the wrong person, who was angry, drunk and looking for a fight after being thrown out of a club. Nat had walked past him, and then there had been a shout, and whatever Nat had said got him a punch for his troubles, except that when he went down, he cracked his head on the edge of a pavement. Nat bled his young life away on a Manchester side street, and his attacker pleaded guilty to manslaughter. He received just five years in prison, and would have many decades of life in front of him when he got out – decades Nat would never have.

So Joe had received pictures of Nat's grave, and a birthday card on the day he would have been twenty, and photos of the niece he never got to meet.

'Nat would have been twenty-one on Monday,' David said. 'I came down here to tell you, to shout it at you, because you have no idea how angry I feel, how cheated. But I couldn't do it. I'm a coward.'

'I'm sorry for Nat,' Joe said quietly. 'I know you won't believe me, but doing my job doesn't make me less human.'

'You made Nat's death seem so unimportant, that it was just some argument, how we should be gentle on the person who killed him.'

Joe didn't respond. His client hadn't meant to kill Nat. It was a drunken punch, a routine Saturday night happening. David Roberts hadn't seen the tears cried by his killer, how he could never really look at Joe whenever they went through how Nat had died, but Joe knew that Nat's father didn't want to hear that. Not yet. Joe had made enough apologies for his killer.

David looked at the ceiling and more tears rolled down his cheeks. 'Now I'm just like him, that bastard who killed Nat. I was angry. I needed a focus. I can't get over losing Nat. I never thought being a parent would involve me burying my son, and I don't know how to deal with it except feel angry, and so I hated you, Mr Parker, for not giving me any kind of justice. It seemed like we were the people who mattered the least.'

'And so you were watching me?'

'I wanted to tell you how it was for me, to let you know what you did to me. What he did to me, your client, and Nat's mother, and his family. We are just left behind, and I don't know if I can carry on. Then I found out that you're doing it again, helping someone else get away with murder. I couldn't handle it.'

'So why last night?'

'Because I was going to confront you, at last, I was building up to it, just to tell you how I felt, so that maybe you'd understand. Then I saw you drinking and enjoying yourself, like freeing killers is just another day for you, and that people like me don't matter, the ones left behind. And so I couldn't stop myself. I followed you in and punched you, but you hit the sink. It was such a crack, and I felt sick, and you didn't move.'

'You don't have to say any more,' Joe said, holding up his hand.

'No, I do, because what I did was no different to what he did to Nat, which makes me just like him.'

'He's just like you, and me, and like anyone who did something stupid that turned out to be far worse than intended.'

David wiped his eyes. 'I understand now, and I'm sorry. I won't write again. I'll go to the police and tell them what happened.'

'There's no need. I haven't told the police.' David looked confused, so Joe said, 'If hitting me helped you understand a little more, and lets you grieve a little easier, then I'm glad you did it. Not as hard, perhaps, but it's all worked out.'

David swallowed and then nodded with relief. 'Thank you.'

Joe stood up and gestured towards the door to tell him that the meeting was over.

David moved away from his chair, but then stopped and said, 'I ought to warn you that I wasn't the only person watching you.'

'What do you mean?'

'When I was in the gardens yesterday. I didn't think anything of it at first, but I saw someone head towards your building, before backing away, as if he had changed his mind. He was pacing up and down. He seemed really nervous, looking up at your window all the time. I knew something wasn't right.'

'What did he look like?'

'Tall, thin, scruffy, except that he wore a blazer with some sort of crest on it. It didn't look right.'

'A blazer?'

'It looked worn out, but it didn't suit him, because it looked like he thought he was someone important, some kind of faded war hero.'

The description was familiar.

Joe went to his desk and the papers Gina and Monica had left the day before. He pulled out the news clipping of Terry Day, showing him on the Remembrance Sunday march, in his beret and array of unearned medals.

'Is that him?'

David squinted at the picture. 'Yes, that's him. He looks more like a real war hero in that picture, but he didn't look like that yesterday.'

Joe thanked him, and once he had the room to himself again, he sat down and pondered on what he had just been told. Terry Day was keeping watch on him, and it seemed like he wanted to talk. Why would he do that? He had learned the answer to one mystery, except that now it seemed like another one had just taken its place.

Forty-Four

Sam avoided the hard gaze of DI Evans as he went into the Incident Room. He could see from the greasy bags that had once held hot sandwiches that some of the other officers had been there for some time. He slipped into the chair he had been on the day before and tried to log on, but less than a minute passed before he felt a hand on his shoulder.

He looked up.

'Talk to me, Sam,' Evans said, her voice soft, and then she turned away, the signal to follow.

No one looked up as he threaded his way through the desks, although he could tell what they were thinking from the way they avoided his gaze – that he had blown it. The Major Incident Team expected dedication. A girl was missing and he had rolled in after nine as if it was some kind of quiet shift.

When he got in front of her desk, she made a show of looking at her watch and said, 'Explain.'

Sam had been looking down as he thought about what to say, but when he made his decision to talk, he looked Evans in the eye.

'I've got some information,' Sam said. 'I went to see Ben Grant yesterday, like you said.'

'Go on.'

'He referred to my sister, Ruby.' He took a deep breath. 'I had another sister, Ellie. She was murdered fifteen years ago.'

Evans went as if to say something but then faltered, before she gave a sympathetic smile. 'I'm sorry. I didn't know.'

'Ruby was born two years after Ellie was murdered. Grant knew about her.'

'Ben Grant is locked up. He will never get out.'

'I know that,' Sam said, 'but as you know, these cases are linked to Ben Grant's case somehow, and Grant mentioned her. Then Ruby came home from school yesterday and said that someone had been following her.'

Evans tilted her head, surprised, her eyes keener now. 'Why didn't you tell me this last night? You could have got my number from someone.'

'Ruby might have just got it wrong. She feels like she's always been in Ellie's shadow, so she does things to get attention, and two days ago was the anniversary of Ellie's death. It had all been about Ellie, and then Ruby made it all about her. I couldn't be sure.'

'Something has changed,' Evans said.

'I went there this morning. It's a quiet path that runs towards Ruby's school. It was where Ellie was killed.'

'And your sister still goes down there?' Evans said, her eyes wide.

'It's not the same to her. She never met Ellie. Anyway, I think she was right. I saw some movement in the trees, just like Ruby said.'

'What time did Ruby think she was being followed?'

'Yesterday. Four o'clock.'

'I'll call the school and ask them to remind pupils not to go that way,' Evans said. 'We'll put someone down there today, just to see if anyone turns up. It might be just some local voyeur, watching teenage legs from the woods, but whoever it is, I want him in this station to explain himself.'

Sam nodded, satisfied.

'So you're still okay to do this?' Evans said. 'You're the link we have between Ben Grant and Ronnie Bagley, through your brother, and as Grant wants you involved, he might spill something.'

Sam nodded again. 'I'll be fine.'

'Back to Ben Grant,' Evans said. 'Did he say anything useful?'

'For the case, no,' Sam said, shaking his head.

'Just an ego boost?' she said.

'Something like that. Like I told you yesterday on the phone, he told me how he started out because his sister used to let him wash her hair, until he killed her.'

'He was wasting your time.'

'I don't understand.'

'I looked into it after you called. Ben Grant didn't have any sisters. He was an only child.' When Sam appeared confused, Evans said, 'Forget about Ben Grant. He has nothing to tell us. The link is still there, but it doesn't seem to be anything he knows about.'

As he walked away, Sam remained deep in thought.

Ben Grant might not have had a sister, but the story meant something. He just had to work out what.

Forty-Five

Joe sat in his car and dialled Monica's number. He'd found an old phone in his desk and was able to use his SIM card. Still no answer. He dialled Kim Reader's number instead. He wasn't sure if she would answer, because she might be in court, but after a few rings, he heard her say, 'Joe, I can't talk properly right now. Not if it's about this morning when I rang. Look, I'm sorry, I shouldn't have said anything.'

There was noise in the background, and the echo told him that she was on the court corridor. For a moment, he imagined her in her gown and crisp white wings.

'This is a courtesy call, sorry,' he said. 'A professional obligation.'

'I recognise your court voice,' she said, and Joe heard a trace of disappointment in hers. 'Go on, what can I do for you?'

'Terry Day. I'm about to pay him a visit.'

There was a pause, and then, 'You can't do that.' The warmth had slipped from her voice. 'He's a prosecution witness.'

'There's no property in a witness, you know that,' he said.

'That's not the point, and you know that too.'

'And that's why I'm calling you, to let you know.'

'Joe, don't be an arsehole,' she said, anger in her voice now.

He sighed. He had wanted it to go differently, for her to shrug it off, but he knew she was a better prosecutor than that.

'I'm trying not to be an arsehole,' he said, his voice softer. 'I'll call you afterwards, to tell you if there's anything you ought to know.'

'Joe!'

'Don't worry, I've got Gina with me. She'll be a witness, to make sure I can't be accused of anything.'

'Or so you can both concoct a story to get yourself out of trouble.'

'You know me better than that,' he said, and then clicked off his phone.

He stared out of his window for a few seconds, his hand around the wheel, gripping it tightly, knowing that he had created a rift. It wouldn't last long, professional disagreements didn't, but it might make their non-professional relationship a little cooler.

'It sounds like the romance is over,' Gina said.

When Joe turned towards her she was smiling.

'I've always been good at getting it wrong,' he said, and then reached for his door handle.

'You didn't have to tell her. You didn't bother last time.'

'I think this visit might be different.'

He looked up at Terry Day's house again as Gina joined him on the pavement. She led the way, her hips swaying as she walked up the steps and pressed the doorbell. They waited a couple of minutes, and were about to turn to go when the door opened a crack and Terry Day's face appeared.

Joe smiled and said, 'Good morning, Mr Day.'

Terry Day didn't move at first, just looked between Joe and Gina, only a sliver of his face revealed. When Joe said, 'I think we need to talk, don't we?' Terry stepped back and let the door swing open.

Terry went towards the stairs, and so Joe and Gina followed. As they went past the first door, the entrance to Ronnie's flat, Joe made as if to go towards it, blocked off by crime scene tape, when Terry shouted, 'No!'

Joe stopped.

Terry swallowed and then said, 'The police told me not to let anyone in there, at least until after the trial.'

'Why did they say that?'

'In case the defence want to examine it.'

'I am the defence.'

'No, they meant an expert, bloodstains or whatever. They said that if I don't look after the scene, it might give the defence something to use, because it makes it look like it's unfair for them, as they can't examine it if it's been spoiled.'

Joe moved away from the door. It was a reasonable answer. As Terry started to climb the stairs, Joe said, 'So you're left all alone now?'

'I like it that way,' he said. 'I just wish I didn't need the rent money.'

Joe took another look towards Ronnie's flat and then followed Terry up the stairs and along the first floor landing. The middle flat wasn't self-contained, so the doors to all the rooms opened on to the landing. Terry hadn't made many alterations to his house so that he could let it out.

Terry carried on up the stairs to the second floor, and Joe felt the building close in on him. The daylight through the glass above the front door didn't travel far up the stairs, and the stairwell to the top floor was much narrower. The door at the top looked makeshift, as if Terry had just pinned a doorframe in between the ceiling and the floor, and so the whole frame moved as Terry went through it.

He gestured towards a living room on the other side of a small landing and muttered something about making a drink. Joe and Gina went in, and as Terry rushed off to make some coffee, they settled onto a sofa that was low to the floor and covered in a blue cloth, like a futon. The room seemed dingy from the small attic windows, made worse by the dark brown swirls of the carpet and the nicotine tinge to the woodchip wallpaper.

'I've got my pepper spray if he walks in with a chainsaw or something,' Gina whispered.

'All I know is that I'm not drinking whatever he's making,' Joe said.

After a few minutes, Terry came back into the room carrying a tray, with three cups and a small plate of biscuits. Joe took a cup and placed it on the floor. Gina did the same.

When Terry sat down, he pointed at Joe and said, 'What happened to your eye?'

'Don't you know?'

Terry looked confused. 'What do you mean?'

'You've been following me around, keeping watch on me.'

'No I haven't,' Terry said, although his cheeks flushed.

Joe nodded slowly. 'Yes you have. Someone saw you. So I want you to tell me why. What do you want to tell me?'

Terry looked at his drink cradled on his lap, and Joe let him sit out the silence. Eventually, after a slow few minutes, Terry looked up and said, 'I'm not supposed to talk to you. They told me not to.'

'They?'

'The police.'

'If there is something you know that will help me, I'm entitled to know.' Joe reached into his pocket for his voice recorder. He held it up so Terry could see it and said, 'You need to talk.'

Terry's finger scratched at his cup but he stayed silent.

Gina leaned forward. 'Mr Day, if you know something, you need to tell us.'

He looked at her and then at Joe, then took a deep breath.

'All right, I'll tell you. It's about Carrie, and the little girl.'

'Go on.'

He swallowed and then straightened his shoulders as if to brace himself. 'They're alive,' he said.

Joe's eyes widened. 'Alive? How do you know?'

'I've seen them.'

Forty-Six

Sam was left on his own. Everyone else shared small talk and worked their way through whatever paperwork landed in front of them. There were some officers on the telephone, chasing down whatever new information had come in, just to see if there was anything useful, but most calls ended with a polite thank you. The focus was on finding the last person who saw Julie alive, except that no one seemed to know where she had gone once she left her parents' home.

Sam was going back through the files relating to the other missing girls. He was trying to find any reference to a feeling of being watched, hoping to see a similarity to what Ruby had reported, to what he thought he had seen earlier that day. Or, rather, hoping that he wouldn't find anything, so that all he had was a cry for attention from Ruby and someone innocently running away from him in the woods – kids messing about.

Julie's bedroom kept on coming back to him, though. There was no reason why it should, he'd only had a brief look and skimmed through her computer, but something niggled him, like a scratching sound at the back of his head that told him there was something he had overlooked.

He closed his eyes and tried to shut out the disruptions in the room. The tap-tap of fingers on keyboards, whispered discussions, mumbles of telephone chatter. He tried instead to replace it all with Julie's room.

The bed had been to one side of the room when he walked in, with posters on the wall. Some pop stars and animal pictures. If Julie wasn't found, the room would stay like that: a time capsule.

As he walked the room in his head, the next thing along was the dresser, covered in perfumes and powders and photographs, the toy ballerina in the middle. Next, there was a bookcase, and then the computer desk, with a small monitor and a base unit on the floor. There were schoolbooks on the desk, textbooks and dog-eared exercise books. There was an MP3 player to one side.

Was that important? If she didn't have her MP3 player with her, then it reduced the chance that she was snatched silently when she was wrapped up in the music from her headphones. So why hadn't anyone reported hearing her scream or a fight?

Sam took a deep breath. There was something else.

His mind kept on going back to the computer monitor, but it wasn't something on the computer itself. He had read the emails. There was nothing that had jumped out at him. No, it was something *on* the computer.

Sam went over to the corner of the room, where a young female detective was going through all the items seized from Julie's bedroom. Her adolescence had been turned into a collection of clear plastic bags clustered around a desk.

The female detective looked up. She was mixed race, with exotic dark curls tumbling onto her light grey suit, and when she saw Sam, she smiled. 'Hello. I'm Charlotte.' She checked around, as if to ensure that no one else was listening in, and then said, 'I liked what you did to Ged yesterday, about the coffee,' and she pointed towards Ged, who was staring at a screen, his pen tapping on the desk.

Sam relaxed for the first time since he'd joined the squad. 'I've got a thing about bullies, that's all.'

'That's no bad thing,' she said. 'What can I do for you?'

Sam grabbed a chair from a desk nearby and wheeled it over. 'I went to Julie's house yesterday and saw her bedroom. Something has been bothering me about it today. Can I look at what you've taken?'

'I hope you know where to look,' she said, and pointed towards the bags.

'It was near the computer. Every time I try to think about it, I go back to the monitor.'

Charlotte bent down to rummage through the bags. She pulled one out and put it on the desk.

'This was the stuff from around her monitor,' she said, and opened the bag to put them on the desk.

Sam looked through, everything in exhibit bags. They were just scraps of paper mainly, some showing calculations, others showing girlie doodles, with drawings of flowers and love hearts. Then he saw it. It was what had been in his mind, the niggle, the itch.

It was a photograph. It had been attached to the shelf behind the computer screen. A teenage boy, pretty and smiling. But her parents had said she didn't have a boyfriend. There was something about the photograph that was familiar, except he couldn't place it.

'Is this boy on her Facebook page?'

Charlotte brought up Julie's profile on her screen. It was being left open in case someone posted something useful. She went to the 'Friends' page and scrolled down, looking for the person in the photograph. She stopped at a couple, just to check, but then moved on. When she got to the bottom, Charlotte shook her head. 'He's not there.'

He held up the photograph. 'I need to go back.'

Charlotte looked at the photograph and then at Sam. She must have seen his resolve, because she said, 'I'm coming with you,' and grabbed her coat.

*

'Where did you see Carrie and Grace?' Joe said.

'I'm not supposed to tell you.'

'Who told you that? Carrie? Because she's trying to get away from Ronnie?'

Terry shook his head and then looked down. 'I can't say anything.'

'You need to talk, Terry, because this will come out in court, whether or not you tell me now.'

Terry nodded slowly, and Joe watched his resolve slowly build until he said, 'The police told me to stay quiet.'

Joe and Gina exchanged glances. 'The police? Why would the police say that?'

'They said if I didn't keep it to myself, Ronnie would get away with it.'

'Get away with what? If Carrie and Grace are alive, there's nothing for Ronnie to get away with.'

'That's what I said, but they told me not to be concerned, that it was their job to worry about these things, and that it would all turn out right in the end.'

Joe was confused. He knew there was an obsession about figures and targets in the force, but covering up evidence that could free an innocent man was a step back to the seventies.

'Tell me all about it,' Joe said. When Terry clenched his jaw, Joe added, 'You want to tell me, don't you, because that's why you've been watching me, walking to my office and then turning away, because it's bursting out of you, your need to let me know.'

There was still no answer.

'Terry, talk to me,' Joe said. 'Please.'

Terry swallowed. 'Okay, I'll talk.'

'Where did you see them both?' Joe said.

'In the city centre.'

'When?'

'Last week.'

Joe pointed to his dictation machine, which he had clicked on and placed on the small coffee table, the red light showing. 'This is recording now. Just tell me your story.'

Terry took a deep breath. 'I'd gone into town. I go sometimes, just to see people, because no one knows me there, and so I can walk around and be myself.'

Or be someone else, the war hero, was Joe's thought, but he didn't voice it.

'I got the train to Victoria,' Terry continued. 'I was walking towards the shops, and there are some seats in that new part, you know, where it was rebuilt following the IRA bomb, next to the large glass building.'

'I know it. The Football Museum, by the Cathedral Gardens.'

'That's right. Well, I like it there, because there are a lot of things going on, but just behind it is sort of peaceful, because of the cathedral and the music school. So, I was just sitting there, watching everyone, when I heard something behind me. It was a little girl's voice. She was laughing at the fountains they have there, because they just pop up, and they must have surprised her. I turned round, and there they were, Carrie and Grace. She was different though, Carrie.'

'How so?'

'Her hair was shorter and darker.'

'So how can you be sure it was her?'

'It was the little girl I recognised. She's such a sweet thing. Hard to believe that she's their child. Pair of drunks, both of them, but Grace, she is so cute. She has these blonde curls and a lovely smile, because it isn't yet worn down by all the rubbish Ronnie and Carrie will put into her life. And she laughs so much. I would hear it, even on my floor, Grace singing and laughing.' Terry paused as he enjoyed the memory, and Joe and Gina looked at each other, eyes wide.

'How close were they to you when you saw them?' Joe said.

'Close enough to tell.'

'That answer isn't good enough. In distance. Feet and yards. Metres, if you prefer.'

Terry thought about it, and then said, 'Thirty yards.'

'Was it busy?'

'There were a lot of people walking around, but I saw them. They were on the other side of the fountains.'

'So you saw them from thirty yards away, through crowds and the water from the fountains, and Carrie's hair was different?'

Terry scowled. 'That's what the detective said when I told him. He sounded like he didn't believe me, just like you.'

Joe tried not to smile. He knew the question he was about to ask would destroy the case against Ronnie Bagley, because he had learned one thing about witnesses from his own trial experiences, and that is if you challenge them about how sure they are, they will do their best to remove any doubts, because what makes a witness get involved in a case is that they want to be helpful. He glanced at the dictation machine to make sure that it was still recording, and asked, 'But are you sure?'

Terry leaned forward, determination in his eyes. 'Absolutely sure, one hundred per cent,' he said, and then sat back again, his arms folded.

Joe smiled. It was game over. Terry Day would never be allowed to come back from that certainty, and without Terry Day, the prosecution would lose the argument Ronnie had with Carrie, and the threat that he was going to kill her. Joe had to work out how to play it, because if he tipped off the prosecution, there was no guarantee the case would end; they might still hold out for two bodies, just in case Terry had got it wrong. Joe couldn't use Terry himself, because he said too many things that harmed Ronnie. He could leave the recording to the trial itself, and use it to undermine everything, but again, that was a gamble, because the prosecution might be able to persuade the jury that Terry could be mistaken. Identification is a difficult area of evidence, because a mistaken witness can be a genuine witness, but still mistaken, a mantra that had been drummed into juries for decades.

It wasn't quite as bad for Ronnie, because Joe had to create enough doubt, nothing more, but leaving everything to the coin tosses in the jury room was like planning an English summer barbecue a month in advance.

Joe reached for the dictation machine and switched it off. 'Thank you, Terry, for speaking to us. I'm going to try to do something with this. You've done the right thing.'

Terry didn't respond. He stayed in his chair as Joe and Gina let themselves out. They stayed silent as they went down the stairs. It was only when they were back in Joe's car that they spoke.

'What the hell was that all about?' Gina said.

Joe looked up towards the window. Terry was watching. 'I don't know. Someone will be in trouble for this though, for withholding it, because Carrie being alive is one of our defence strategies, and there it is, straight from the mouth of a crucial witness.'

'I'm not sure,' Gina said.

'What do you mean?'

'Would Terry's identification stand up in court?'

'It wouldn't convict anyone. From a distance, with different hair, and through water. Recognition evidence is always easy to disprove. You can turn it into assumptions and guesswork with the right questioning. And when we ask whether the witness has ever been about to say hello to someone in the street but then stopped at the last moment when they realise they have it wrong, the case just crumbles. They say yes, and everything becomes another possible mistake, and if they say no, the jury doesn't believe them, because everyone has done it.'

'But we're not trying to convict anyone.'

'Exactly,' Joe said. 'All we have to do is create some doubt. That will be enough to keep Ronnie out of prison.'

'There might be another way we can use him,' Gina said.

'What do you mean?'

'I've spoken to a lot of killers in my police career, more than you ever will. I've seen how they behave before they get caught. Terry reminded me of one of them, trying to make himself important. Look how he was with his fake medals. That's the kind of man he is, wants to be the centre of everything, but the real Terry Day shone through when he talked about Grace. His eyes lit up, he was animated, distant. He has watched that girl, I can guarantee it, and men like him, well, what do you think?'

Joe was surprised. 'I thought you were against blaming Terry Day.'

'I was, but I've met him now, and know more about him.'

'So you think we make it look like Terry did it after all?'

'Why not?'

'Because we need to have a strategy, not just blunder into questions not knowing which one ours is. Do we believe him? All we have to do is make the jury think that he might be telling the truth. If we try to convince them that he's a liar because he's the killer, that is a higher risk, because the only evidence for that is your suspicion, because Ronnie's daughter is cute. Even Ronnie will agree with that opinion.'

'So what do we do?'

'Simple. We find out why we weren't told about it. I know where I'm going. I need you to do something as well. Find out where Monica is, because I'm uneasy. She hasn't called in sick and this isn't like her.'

'I know, I don't like it either,' Gina said quietly. 'Something's wrong.'

Forty-Seven

Sam was quiet all the way to Julie McGovern's home, Charlotte, the young detective, in the passenger seat. Charlotte tried to start a conversation, just to break the awkwardness.

'I heard that your brother is a defence lawyer,' she said.

'Yes.'

Charlotte waited for him to expand, but when Sam stayed silent she gave up and stared out of the window instead, at the mix of the old and the new, terraced streets and clusters of new housing, where the old grime had been bulldozed away to make space for the new grime. Long strips of houses lined along cobbled streets had been replaced by low-rise redbrick, surrounded by straggly grass, the only colour from dandelions, all connected by alleyways that provided hiding spaces for drug dealers, the streetlights smashed in the darkest corners, featureless tarmac showing the way.

The streets opened out as they got closer, into the long curves of suburbia, the houses getting further back from the road.

'I'm sorry, I've been rude,' Sam said. 'I'm distracted today. There was an incident with my sister last night and, well, it's on my mind.' He turned to her. 'Me and my brother? We don't always see eye to eye over our careers. And he's Ronnie Bagley's lawyer. What are the chances?'

'Does it bother you?'

'Let's just say that I'm sick of having the same argument with him about it.'

Charlotte thought about that, and then said, 'Is your brother honest?'

'Yes,' Sam said without hesitation. 'He fights dirty sometimes, and I don't think he follows all the rules, but he is honest, without a doubt.'

'So wouldn't you rather it be your brother who represents Ronnie Bagley? What if Ronnie had gone to one of the others, who cheat their way through cases and get witnesses to lie, just to get a win? At least this way, everyone plays fair and we get the result the case deserves, whichever way it goes.'

Sam considered that, and then he laughed. 'I've never thought about it like that.'

'There's always another way,' she said.

Sam was smiling as they arrived at Julie's house. He saw that the press had thinned out, down to one television cameraman. The lens swung round as Sam pulled up and he and Charlotte climbed out of the car.

As they headed towards the front door together, a uniformed officer by the gate ensuring that only police and family made it through, they were met by the Family Liaison Officer.

'How is it?' Sam whispered.

'Not as angry as yesterday,' she said.

As Sam got inside, he saw what she meant. The day before had been frantic, wondering where Julie had gone, part anger, part distress. All that noise had gone and been replaced by silence, with her parents sitting in chairs, staring into space. It was all about waiting.

They both looked up at Sam with dread in their eyes, wondering if he was the one who was about to deliver the bad news.

Sam shook his head regretfully. 'I'm sorry. I don't have

any information.' They sat down and Sam pulled out a clear plastic bag from his pocket. It held the photograph. 'You told us that Julie didn't have a boyfriend.'

Julie's parents looked at each other. Sam watched them carefully, to see whether either gave anything away, if one of them held a secret, but all he saw was confusion.

It was her father who spoke first. 'She has never brought a boy home, and never mentioned one.'

Sam passed over the photograph. 'Do you know this boy?'

Julie's father's hands trembled as he looked at the picture. His jaw was clenched as he handed it to his wife, who just shook her head. 'No, I've never seen him,' he said.

'It was pinned to the shelf behind her computer monitor,' Charlotte said. 'Some of the scraps of paper on her desk had love hearts on them.'

It was Julie's mother who spoke up. 'She's a teenage girl. She's bound to have crushes.' Then she frowned. 'Julie has been very quiet lately. We were getting worried, but she's a teenager, and that's what they're like, isn't it? Moody, quiet. We don't know about the boy though.'

'So who is he?' Julie's father said. 'Do you think he has something to do with Julie going missing?'

Sam wondered how to answer that, because the truth was that he didn't know. Except there was something about the picture that troubled him.

'Sometimes we have to eliminate possibilities to see what we have left. That's all I'm trying to do, by eliminating him.'

Sam stood as if to go. Julie's parents stayed where they were. Sam recognised the look in their eyes. They were waiting, and waiting was all their lives would hold until Julie was found. Waiting, wondering, hoping, imagining, dreading, until eventually they will come to one final conclusion: acceptance that Julie was gone forever.

*

Joe paced up and down outside court number four. Gina had gone to Monica's apartment to try to find her, and Joe was waiting for Kim Reader.

The court corridor was quiet. It was almost lunchtime, and the crowds had thinned out to those people stuck at the bottom of the court list. He had a view across Crown Square through high windows, the sun outside filling the steak restaurant with customers and the steps outside the court with office workers looking for some brightness, small clouds of cigarette smoke giving away their positions. There was a noise behind him, voices and then the creak of a door. When Joe turned round, he saw it was a barrister, his wig askew, talking to the client walking behind him, who looked pleased with whatever had happened in there. Kim wouldn't be far behind.

He was right. Kim came out, pulling a small suitcase that contained all her files. As she edged past the defence barrister and his client, they were silent, the defendant's smile turning to a scowl. When she saw Joe, she looked towards the defendant and rolled her eyes.

'He had the best of the morning, did he?' Joe said, following Kim's gaze, the defendant now hugging a young woman in hipster jeans.

'Another final chance,' Kim said. 'If you look closely at the blonde wrapped around him, you'll see a scar over her eye. He did that, with a bottle. She wrote to the court, wanting to take some of the blame, and now they're in love again. It won't last though, and no one knows what she'll have to suffer next time the booze rests on a bad mood.'

'We can't change their lives, Kim. We just show up now and again, and then go back to our own. Don't let it get to you.' He smiled. 'So are you still speaking to me?'

'What, because of your brush off when I rang you this morning, or about your Terry Day stunt?' She returned the smile. 'My heart will survive you, Joe Parker, and as for Terry Day, I'm used to your little games. I just wish Joe the lawyer was more like the Joe the ... well, you know.' She blushed. 'And speaking of violence,' she continued, looking back to the reconciled lovers, 'your eye doesn't look any better this morning.'

'It will mend. And besides, I know who did it now.'

'Who was it?'

'A father of someone killed by one of my clients. I don't think it's going to happen again, but he was the one who put me on to Terry Day.'

'So tell me what Terry Day said, unless you've just come to buy me lunch.'

Joe laughed. 'I suppose I'm sounding a little, what's the word?'

'Focused?'

'Yeah, focused, I'll go with that. But I do need to talk to you about what Terry told me.'

'Couldn't you call the office?'

'No.'

'Why not?'

'Because I want to see your face when you give me your answer.'

'You know I don't play tricks. I thought we knew each other better than that.'

'We do. I know Kim Reader when she isn't wearing a suit, but between nine and five you're different.'

Kim thought about that, and then the defendant walked towards them, his girlfriend hanging on to his arm. 'Can we go somewhere else?' Kim said, and walked the opposite way. Joe followed, the hem of her gown floating upwards like bat wings, the tail of her horsehair wig swishing as she walked. They ended up in a small consultation room, just a table and four chairs. When he closed the door behind him, she took off the wig and put it on the table, before spending a moment straightening her hair.

'Stupid thing,' she said. 'Makes me itch, and there's no point in doing much with my hair, because it makes it a mess.'

'You look good enough,' Joe said.

That brought a smile. 'I thought I was chasing you,' she said.

'Sometimes I want to be caught.'

'And other times?'

'I remember your fiancé.'

That made Kim twirl her engagement ring around her finger. 'So go on, what's so urgent?'

'Is there anything you want to tell me about Terry Day?'

'What are you talking about?'

'Your case is that Carrie and Grace are dead.'

'It's a murder case. I don't think there's any other way you can put it.'

'So why hadn't I been told that Terry Day has seen your two deceased victims since they supposedly died?'

Kim opened her mouth as if to say something but then stopped, her brow furrowed. 'What do you mean?' she said eventually, confusion in her voice.

'Just that. Terry Day saw Carrie and Grace in the Cathedral Gardens last week. And before you accuse me of putting words in his mouth, I have it recorded, and he said he'd told the police. If he did, they must have told you.'

Kim's cheeks acquired a flush, her lips a little tighter than before. 'This is the first I've heard of this.'

'You agree that if Terry is right, or even if he might be right, you've no case? All you have is a woman trying to run away from her drunken and violent partner.'

Kim pulled the chair out and sat down. Joe sat opposite.

'How do you know he's telling the truth?' she said.

'It doesn't matter whether he's or not, does it? If he is, your case is doomed. If he isn't, he's a habitual liar, an attention seeker, so you can't rely on him.'

'I haven't heard this before. It would have been disclosed if I had, you know that.'

'So why haven't the police told you?'

'That is something I am going to find out,' she said, and from the glare in her eyes, Joe knew that someone would be getting a phone call that would spoil their lunch.

Forty-Eight

Sam stepped out of his car, Charlotte just behind him. He fastened his jacket and shivered against a cold wind. They were on the moors, the rolling barren hills that brood over the city.

They were at Gilly Henderson's house, the second girl to go missing. They had been to the other three, and Sam had shown them the photograph of the young man found pinned behind Julie's monitor. Each time the door opened, the parents' expressions had been the same: a mixture of fear and hope, that news of their daughter might be the news they dreaded. The reaction was the same too, part relief, because without the bad news they really expected, their hopes stayed alive, however slim.

Their answers had been the same too – they had never seen him before.

Charlotte joined Sam as they looked down at Gilly Henderson's house. They were parked on a farm track, two dirt ruts cutting through dark coarse grass. There were sheep on the field next to them, and lower down, where the land levelled out, was a two-storey farmhouse under a dark slate roof. The upstairs windows were like tiny peepholes, the bedrooms built into what was once a roof space.

'Are you sure this is the right place?' Sam said. All he could see as he looked around were the dark greens and browns of moorland heather and grass, which dipped and climbed without any trees to slow down the winds, scarred by dry-stone walls and brightened by the occasional glimmer of water, reservoirs fashioned out of the valleys. One way was the climb and then the drop into Yorkshire. The other was the grey sprawl of Manchester, like a dirty stain in the distance against the bleakness of the hills.

'I came here once before,' Charlotte said. 'The girl's father was one of the prosecution barristers in the Grant case. Bill Henderson. A nice man. He said he could retire, but the legal work gave him the safety net so that he could do this, a bit of sheep farming and getting away from it all.'

As Sam looked around, he said, 'It's hard to blame the man.'

'Try this in November, when it's all wind and driving rain. You might think differently,' Charlotte said. 'What do we do if we get another no?'

'We go around Julie's friends,' Sam said. 'If no one knows who he is, then I'm even more suspicious.'

'Perhaps he's just someone cute she saw somewhere, on a website or something? Girls do that kind of thing.'

'Perhaps,' Sam said, although his instinct told him that it was more than that.

They walked down the track to the house and the door opened before they got there.

'I'm DC Sam Parker,' he said. 'And this is DC Glover.' They had their identification ready and both smiled, to make clear that there was no bad news.

It was Gilly's mother. Her hand went to her chest and she took a deep breath.

'I'm sorry,' she said. 'I just thought for a moment, well, you know.'

'We understand,' Sam said softly. 'We came to ask you something.' He pulled out the exhibit bag containing the photograph. 'Do you know this boy?'

252

She took the picture from him and looked at it, peering closely through the plastic bag, before shaking her head. 'No, I don't.' There was noise behind her, footsteps on the stairs, and Sam saw a young woman, like an older version of the missing girl. Gilly's sister. She passed over the photograph and said, 'Rachel, do you know this boy?'

Rachel came up behind her mother and took the exhibit bag from her. She frowned, which turned into a scowl. 'That creep. What does he want?'

'You know him?' Sam said, his voice keener.

'No, not really, but he tried to get to know me,' she said.

'Can you explain?'

'There isn't much to say. He got in touch on the internet, through my profile, said that he'd seen me around, liked the things that I did, horse riding, things like that, but I didn't believe him. It was a bit too creepy. I was flattered at first, but he was familiar right from the start, as if he was too impatient to know things about me.'

'How long ago was this?'

She thought about that, and then said, 'Nearly a year. I think he guessed I was younger, because my picture was an old one. My hair was longer then, and so I looked like Gilly. Perhaps he thought I was her.' Then she seemed to realise why they were asking the questions. 'Is this to do with Gilly? You think he might be involved?'

'I don't know,' Sam said. 'It's just something we're looking at.'

Sam took the photograph back from her. 'Can you remember any personal details at all? His name? Where he was from?'

'He wanted me to meet him,' Rachel said, making her mother's eyes widen.

'Why didn't you say?' she said.

'What was there to say? Some guy said that he liked me and wanted to take me out. It does happen sometimes, you know, and it was a few months before Gilly went missing. What's the connection?'

'What did he say about the meet?' Sam said.

'I can't remember, really. It was a long time ago.'

'What did he say when he first got in touch?'

'Just that he knew me through one of my friends, Claire, but when I asked her, she said that she didn't know him. He just asked to be friends on her online profile, and you know what it's like. It's good to have lots of friends, so she said yes, and then I did too, but he started to get really personal.'

'What do you mean?'

She blushed. 'Just about me. What I like, that kind of stuff.'

'Sexual?'

She glanced at her mother. 'I was going to block him but when I looked he had gone, and I couldn't find him, and so he must have blocked me.'

'Can you check Claire's profile, to see if he's still listed?'

'If he has blocked me I won't be able to see him, but I can send her a message,' she said. 'I'll get my phone.'

As Rachel went back upstairs, her mother turned to Sam, surprised. 'I didn't know any of this. Do you really think he might have something to do with Gilly going missing?'

Sam wanted to say that yes, he did, that something about the picture concerned him, but he didn't yet know why. But he knew that the first rule of dealing with victims is not to raise hopes. Tell the good news when it's definite, and leave the maybes to fade with time.

'We're looking at everything,' Sam said. 'It was just a photograph we found.'

Sam could see that she had spotted his evasiveness, but she stayed silent until Rachel bounded back down the stairs.

'I've sent her a message, to see if she knows anything,' Rachel said. 'I can let you know what she says.'

'I'd rather have Claire's details, so I can speak to her myself.'

Rachel grabbed a piece of paper and, once she had scrabbled through a drawer to find a pen, she wrote down a name and an address.

Sam looked at the piece of paper and thanked them both, and then he and Charlotte stepped back out into the freshness of the moors.

As they walked back to the car, Charlotte said, 'What do you think?'

'It's a link, it must mean something.'

'But how did you notice the picture?'

'I don't know, and that's what's bothering me,' Sam said. 'I had a recollection that there was something significant around her computer but I can't work out what it was that made me notice it. Now I feel like I need to know what it was.'

'It's classic grooming behaviour,' Charlotte said, her voice low. 'Target girls in their teens and slowly wind up the sexual tension, make them share their secrets. Get some pictures from them, intimate ones, and he's got them. Before long, she sets off to meet some sexy guy just a little bit older than her, and when she gets there, it's some sad old man who can blackmail her into doing whatever he wants, because he has all of her secrets.'

'So you think this photograph is just a front?'

Charlotte took it from him and looked more closely at it. Then she stopped and raised her eyebrows. 'Definitely,' she said. 'I don't know why we didn't spot it before.'

'What do you mean?'

'Look at the pictures on the wall behind.'

Sam looked closely at the photograph and tried to work out what Charlotte had seen. The picture showed a teenage boy, his hair a dark trendy flick, his body lean in a T-shirt, brightened by the light from the flash when the picture was taken. In contrast, the wall behind seemed dark, his face and body taking all of the glare.

'I can't see it. Just sports teams. Group shots, celebrating.'

'Yes, but what sort of sports teams?'

'I can't make them out.'

'It's not very clear, but some of the players are holding helmets,' Charlotte said. 'Like gridiron helmets. And on the shelf, there's the tip of a ball, like a rugby ball.'

'Are you sure?' Sam said, peering closer.

'Or is it an American football?'

Sam looked up. 'I think you're right.'

'That's what I see,' Charlotte said. 'That kid is American. It's easy to fake a profile. Just browse around for a good-looking teenager with an open profile and copy his pictures. Make your own profile, upload the pictures as your own, and there you have it, a whole new personality for yourself. He's young and he's good-looking. The rest is just research. Pick your target, find out what they like, and draw them in.'

'But are teenage girls really so gullible?'

'Teenage girls are just like teenage boys. Adult emotions and needs hit them like being barged in the street, because they're all jumbled and confused. So it only takes someone who knows how to give them some direction and they're soon drawn into the trap. I used to work on the sex crimes unit, and it's what all these sickos are like. They see themselves as teachers, all wanting to take their victims from being girls to being women, but when that finally happens they often don't like the women the girls have become, because the women see the groomer for what he is: an abuser. Usually sad little individuals who want to be revered, so they pick on the easily impressed, and make them do things that the victim won't want to be made public. Then they have them. It's not about reverence: it's about fear.'

'But this is more than just grooming,' Sam said. 'He's making them disappear.'

Forty-Nine

Joe looked up as Gina burst into his office.

'What's wrong?' he said.

'It's Monica. She's not at home, and every time I call her mobile, it goes straight to voicemail, as if it's turned off.'

'And she definitely hasn't called in?'

'No. I've spoken to everyone.'

Joe frowned. 'That doesn't seem like her.'

'She's young and in a big city. Perhaps her night got too wild?'

'Does she strike you as the type?' When Gina didn't answer, he added, 'No, me neither.'

'I'm worried, Joe.'

'What do you think we should do?'

'There's no point in calling the police yet,' Gina said. 'What can we tell them? That a young single woman didn't turn up for work?'

'We should call her parents, let them know. Do we have their number?'

'We'll have it somewhere,' Gina said.

'I'm sure she'll be fine,' Joe said, and gave her a smile of reassurance.

'Okay, I believe you,' she said, and then, 'So tell me about Kim. What did your sweetheart say?'

'She's not my sweetheart.'

'She will be.'

'As a matchmaker surely you shouldn't push me towards someone who's engaged?'

'If you're not going to fight for her, fine.'

Joe shook his head, smiling. He liked the way Gina spoke to him. The clerks treated him like a boss. He knew that Gina still saw him as the upstart young lawyer who had tried to upset her investigations.

'Kim didn't know about Terry Day,' Joe said.

'Do you believe her?'

'You knew her when you were still in the force. What was the police view?'

'That she was good when she wanted to be, but she shot her arrow a little too straight, if you know what I mean. We wanted her to back us more.'

'But that isn't her job, is it, and that's why I admire her as a lawyer. Kim can be ruthless, but she is honest.'

'So the police kept Terry's news to themselves?' Gina said. 'That's naughty.'

'But you're not surprised.'

'Only that they thought they could get away with it. When you work for the police, you've got to spot what can come back and bite you. Terry Day was always going to talk. Did they want it to come out during the trial, with a judge barking at them about why they didn't pass it on?' She exhaled. 'So what now?'

'We speak to Ronnie. I'm going to tell him what Terry said, and I want to know whether Mahones knew about it. You know how they work: they will have been speaking to witnesses even before Ronnie was charged. They get a nailed on defence and yet roll over when he wants me. Something doesn't make sense.' He checked his watch. 'And Ronnie should be here soon.'

The phone on Joe's desk buzzed. When he picked it up, he

listened for a moment and then said, 'Send him up.' He smiled at Gina. 'It's Ronnie, and he's punctual, so at least he has one good quality.'

Gina moved out of the way as Ronnie came into the room.

Ronnie was licking his lips and running his hands over his head, smoothing down his hair. His eyes looked wild, almost excited, although they were red, as if he'd been out too late.

Joe gestured towards a seat. As Ronnie sat down, Gina sat on the windowsill behind Joe.

'What's so urgent?' Ronnie said, shuffling uncomfortably in his seat.

'Terry Day,' Joe said.

Ronnie took a deep breath. 'What about him?'

'He's got some interesting stories to tell. One of them will help you, and I thought you might want to hear the good news from me personally.'

Ronnie paled and then looked up at the ceiling. Joe watched the flare of his nostrils, confused at his reaction.

When Ronnie looked down again, he said, 'I told you to leave him alone.' The words snarled their way out.

'But you don't know what I'm going to say.'

'I don't want to hear it.'

'My job is to build you a defence. I've got you one.'

'No, your job is to do what I say,' Ronnie said, his voice raised, banging his hand on the chair arm. 'I'm the client. That's how it works.'

'No, that it isn't how it works, Ronnie,' Joe said, his tone quieter, more measured, a way of disguising the slow rise of anger. 'If you just want someone to do your legwork, you might as well do it yourself.' Joe felt Gina's hand on his shoulder, but he shrugged it off. 'Let me tell you something, Ronnie. I don't care about you. I don't care about any of my clients. That's how the good lawyers are. I care about me, that is all, because I care how I do my job. If you are convicted, all I'll be interested in is whether I did all I could. If I did, then you'll just have to take whatever verdict comes your way. If I've done a good job, I won't be too worried as you head back to Strangeways in one of those white vans.'

Ronnie was silent.

'So don't think that I'll just do as you say, because that would mean me not doing my job properly.'

Ronnie just folded his arms, and Joe banged his hand on the desk in frustration. 'It's your turn to listen, Ronnie,' he said. 'I've helped you today. I've spoken to the prosecutor and told her what Terry Day told me. She didn't know, and so now it affects the whole case, because the prosecutor is on the level, and if what Terry has said means that they can't win this case, she will pull it. So the least you can do is show some gratitude.'

'I didn't want you to speak to Terry Day,' Ronnie said.

Joe stared at Ronnie and then shook his head. 'I give up. It's your life, not mine. I'll get paid and move on.'

'You've changed,' Ronnie said.

'You don't know me,' Joe said.

'I do, better than you think. You don't remember, that's all.'

'What do you mean by that? Have we met somewhere before? Have I represented you before?'

'If you don't remember, it doesn't matter.'

Joe scowled. He wasn't in the mood for guessing games. 'Why haven't you asked what Terry Day told me?'

Ronnie's jaw clenched but he said nothing.

Joe tried to soften his tone. 'Terry Day has said that he saw Carrie and Grace last week.'

There was barely a reaction from Ronnie. Just a flicker of his eyelids.

'It doesn't only mean that they can't prosecute you, it means that your daughter might still be alive.'

Ronnie looked down.

Joe shook his head and sat back again. He glanced at Gina,

who seemed as confused as he was.

Ronnie looked up again. 'I told you not to speak to Terry Day.'

'I can't forget what I've been told.'

'So we're done then.'

'What do you mean?'

'Just that. We're finished.'

Ronnie stood up.

'Where are you going?'

'Would you tell anyone if I told you?'

Joe ran his fingers through his hair. He felt tired all of a sudden. 'No, I wouldn't.'

'I'm going, leaving. I've had enough.'

'Doesn't it mean anything that your daughter might still be alive?'

Ronnie paused at that. He looked at Joe, and then at Gina. 'Where's the other little cutie? Monica.'

'What do you mean?'

'A bit easier on the eye. She had such lovely hair.' He sneered. 'Sorry, *has* such lovely hair. Like you said, I must watch my past tense.' And then he went out the door.

'Ronnie, come back,' Joe called.

All Joe got in reply was the echo of Ronnie's footsteps walking along the landing.

As Joe looked at Gina, he saw that she had gone pale. How did Ronnie know Monica hadn't come in?

'I'm going to call my brother. We need the police involved.'

Fifty

Sam called DI Evans from the car. When she answered, he said, 'We might have something.'

He told her about the link with the photograph. When she hung up, Charlotte said, 'What did she say?'

'She says to follow the trail and keep her informed.'

'So we go to the friend of Gilly's sister?' Charlotte asked. She checked her notes. 'Claire.'

Sam nodded. 'That picture is the link, and whoever is behind the profile went to Claire first and then on to Gilly.'

They drove in silence, through the snarl-up of the city centre, of buses and taxis and shoppers who regretted driving into town, before it turned into the long stretch of suburbia and then a street of semi-detached houses, two-storey, redbrick on the ground floor, pebbledash on the upper, backing on to the green fields of a local secondary school.

'Do we have the right address?' Charlotte said.

'What do you mean?'

'Look around. Rachel Henderson is the horsey daughter of a barrister. This doesn't seem the sort of area where one of her friends would live.'

As they slowed to halt outside the address they'd been given, Sam pointed to a pair of black riding boots outside a door at the side of the house. There was mud on them, as if the owner was letting them dry off. 'At their age, it's the common bonds that unite them. Their differences will become more important as they get older.'

'Very profound,' Charlotte said with a wry grin.

The door at the side of the house opened as they walked up the drive and a redhead stood at the door, her complexion that of someone who spent a lot of time outdoors in cold weather, scrubbed and rosy, her cheeks flushed.

'Can I help you?' she said.

Sam showed her his ID and then said, 'We need to speak to Claire.'

The woman looked shocked. 'Has she done something wrong?'

'No, nothing. I'm hoping she might be able to help with Gilly Henderson's disappearance.'

The woman shook her head ruefully. 'That was awful. Poor Gilly. I didn't know her well, but her sister, Rachel, is a lovely girl. So clever, so bright.' She shouted into the kitchen. 'Claire? It's the police, about Gilly.'

After a few seconds, a girl with a shock of red hair, all tangled and still recovering from the riding helmet, appeared in the doorway. She was wearing jodhpurs caked in mud. 'I got Rachel's message.'

Sam looked at Claire's mother. 'We'd like to speak to Claire alone.'

'I would rather Claire stayed with me.'

'How old are you, Claire?'

She looked at her mother. 'Sixteen.'

'Do you want to speak alone?'

Claire looked at her mother again, and then shook her head. 'No, it's fine.'

Sam handed over the photograph showing the young man. 'Do you know him?'

Claire's cheeks reddened as her mother gave a shrill snort of anger.

263

'Him?' Claire's mother said. 'I knew he'd be in trouble again.'

'So you know this person?' Sam said, surprised.

'No,' she said. 'But you should, because the police know all about him.'

Sam and Charlotte were shown through to the living room, with pink patterned carpets and striped wallpaper, broken only by a paper border in a flower print that wrapped around the walls. There were family pictures on every available shelf, and one wall was taken up by trophies and rosettes.

As they sat down, Sam pointed towards the display. 'You must be pretty good at horse riding.'

Claire followed his gaze. 'I like horses. That's how I know Rachel and Gilly. We use the same stables. They have their own horses, and I just help out, but Rachel knows I can ride well.'

Sam lifted the photograph to show Claire. 'Tell me about him.'

Claire looked at her mother, who nodded her approval. Claire took a deep breath and moved her hair away from her face.

'He got in touch on the internet. He told me he had seen me at the stables, and that I was a friend of Rachel. He told me he liked Rachel, and was sorry for using me like this, but wanted to get to know Rachel through me.'

'How did you feel about that?'

'Used, but that's what happens sometimes with guys, that they like your friend and so they speak to you first, to make the introduction.'

'So what did you do?'

'We chatted, you know, by messages, and then the chat program, and he kept on pestering me to put him on to Rachel.'

'And did you?'

'Eventually. But Rachel didn't like him. She thought he was creepy. He wasn't very happy. He sounded angry on the chat.'

'So who is he?'

'He said he was called Billy. I can't remember his second name.'

'And is he still friends with you?'

'No.'

'You liked him, didn't you,' Charlotte said, her voice soft.

'I liked that guy,' Claire said, and she pointed to the picture. 'He was sexy and funny and seemed to know what I liked. Then the police told me that he wasn't like that all, that he was much older, and smaller. Not even called Billy.'

'What happened with him?' Charlotte asked.

Claire looked at her mother and then at the floor. 'I had arranged to meet him. He was going to take me for a walk, somewhere nice, but, well . . . ' She shrugged.

Claire's mother gave a short, bitter laugh. 'I stopped it,' she explained. 'Claire didn't know that I used to check her internet accounts when she was out, to look for stuff like this. It was disgusting. Some of the things they were talking about. Claire shouldn't know about stuff like that.'

'Mum!'

Her mother waved her away. 'You should be glad I found out.'

'What did you do?' Sam asked.

'They were talking about meeting up and so I called the police, because I knew something wasn't right.'

'How do you mean?'

Claire sat back in her chair, her arms folded. 'She means that guys like him don't like girls like me.'

Sam looked at Claire's mother, who simply pursed her lips. Claire was right, as much as it hurt her.

'So tell me what happened with the police?' Sam said.

It was Claire's mother who spoke again. 'They said that because they had only been talking about meeting up, there was nothing they could do. Nothing had been arranged. How can that be right, that someone has got to set off before they can be caught? It means that my child has to be in real danger before you can stop it.'

Sam agreed with her, but he wasn't interested in a discussion about legal theory. 'Did you tell Rachel about this, that he wasn't who he said he was?'

'My mum told me not to,' Claire said. 'She said I'd embarrassed her enough without telling anyone else.'

Sam closed his eyes for a moment in exasperation. He prayed that hadn't caused a young woman to put herself in danger, because she hadn't been warned off.

'I thought he was interested in Rachel,' Sam said. 'So, how did you two end up talking about meeting?'

Claire didn't reply. Instead, she just played with her fingers and looked down. Her mother filled in the silence.

'Because she put herself on a plate for him,' she said, disgust in her voice now, glaring at Claire. 'Promised herself, boasted about what she would do to him.'

Claire jumped to her feet and stormed out of the room, slamming the door as she went.

Her mother didn't say anything at first, and so Sam and Charlotte let the silence fester, knowing that Claire's mother would eventually say something. They didn't have to wait long.

'I'm sorry,' she said, softening. 'I just couldn't believe how she had put herself in danger. We've given her all the warnings about the internet and strangers, and how bad people can sound good when they're hiding behind a keyboard, and yet she still did it.' She shook her head. 'I was her age once, but it was never like that.'

'The world was never like this back then,' Sam said. 'Thank you for your time. You've been a big help.'

'Have I?'

'Yes. We will be able to trace what happened from your complaint, so that will give us a name.'

'Just one thing,' she said.

'Go on.'

'You said you were here because of what happened to Gilly, and you showed that picture. So you think he might have had something to do with what happened to Gilly?'

'It's just another line of enquiry,' Sam said.

She put her face in her hands. 'You're not saying no, which means that whatever happened to Gilly might have happened to Claire?'

Sam didn't deny it quickly enough, because it was a possibility. Claire didn't have the same link to Ben Grant's case, but that didn't mean whoever it was didn't fill in the gaps with other victims.

Claire's mother started to cry, and Sam decided that it was a good time to go.

They let themselves out, and as they walked back down the drive towards his car, the sounds of shouting could be heard from inside the house.

'May have reopened a wound there,' Charlotte said.

'And got ourselves a lead,' Sam said. 'We need to chase that up as soon as we get back to the station.'

Fifty-One

Joe spent half an hour not doing very much, just twirling in his seat and thinking about Ronnie Bagley. There was something going on that he didn't like, and that he didn't understand. Why didn't Ronnie want to use anything said by Terry Day, even though it should have been the best news for him? His daughter was alive and he would also avoid a life sentence. Was it guilt because he knew Terry Day was mistaken, and if he was that guilty, why didn't he just admit it?

Joe left his office and went to find Gina. She was at her desk, the phone in her hand.

Gina looked up when Joe appeared in the doorway. 'Monica's parents are heading to Manchester. They're worried too.' She noticed he had his jacket in his hand. 'Where are you going?

'Mahones.'

Gina looked surprised.

'They have the info on Ronnie's background,' Joe said.

'Yes, but Mahones?'

'I need to find out about Ronnie.'

'But why? You'll run the case on your terms, not on anything he told them.'

'Ronnie has commented twice about how I should remember him. Now he's walked out on me. And that crack about Monica in the past tense? He wants me to know something, but for some reason he won't come out and say it.'

'Will they let you in?'

'Gina, I left, that's all.'

'You know what I mean. Not everyone leaves like you did.'

Joe smiled. 'Thanks for your concern.'

As he headed out to the street, he didn't have to turn round to know that Gina was watching him from a window. He walked past the small park, looked in, and was surprised to see Ronnie standing and looking towards the office.

Joe muttered to himself, 'You little shit,' and then turned and went towards him.

He wasn't sure what would happen, or even whether Ronnie would talk to him, but Ronnie stayed still as he got closer.

'Tell me about Monica,' Joe said.

Ronnie remained silent at first, but after a few moments he said, 'Everything is your fault.'

'What do you mean, my fault?'

'You were supposed to stop it.'

'You're talking in riddles, Ronnie. What do you mean, I was supposed to stop it?'

Ronnie sat down on a bench and put his hands between his knees. 'Do you know what it's like to lose control over events, when you thought you wanted something, but then someone takes over?'

'Isn't that just life?'

'And death.'

Joe clenched his jaw. 'Is there something you want to tell me?'

Ronnie shook his head. 'No, there's nothing you can do. That time has gone now.'

'What about Monica?'

He shook his head again. 'It didn't mean anything.' He got to his feet.

Ronnie went to walk away but Joe grabbed his arm. 'Tell me about Monica.'

'I don't have to talk to you,' Ronnie said, as he pulled his arm away and walked quickly out of the park. At the gate he turned to shout, 'It's all your fault.'

Joe watched him go, angry, frustrated, and then carried on to Mahones. He hoped the answer would be there.

Mahones wasn't far, he passed it every day on the way to the court, although he made sure he was always on the other side of the road and looking down. He didn't want any chance meetings.

He had trained there, spent two great years as he learned the job, shadowing the more experienced lawyers, and then once he had built his portfolio he was allowed into the rough and tumble of the police station, some fresh meat for the detectives made weary by the constant 'no comment' advice given by the older hands. That was where he had learned his trade, much more than the courtroom, where there was at least a veneer of respectability. In the police station, things could get nasty, with clients angry at being locked up and wondering why some fresh-faced newbie was advising them. And the detectives were meaner, asking how he could sleep at night, acting for the scumbags in the cells. He used to justify himself to them, but eventually realised the question had only ever been rhetorical. He learned that a knowing smirk wound them up more.

Joe found that court was a playground after that. All he had to do was to remember to ask the right questions and enjoy being the interrogator when the detective was in the witness box, where a knowing smirk would not be enough of an answer for them.

It hadn't been the hours that had made him leave though, or career concerns. It had been something else completely.

As he pushed open the entrance doors, he noticed that the reception desk had been refitted. Gone was the low desk from where the receptionist could see everything, and in its place was a high counter, with the receptionist sat low behind it. Joe guessed that it was for reasons of security, because sometimes the clients couldn't stop themselves from pocketing whatever was close by.

The receptionist looked up, too much make-up and dry grey hair exaggerating her weariness, but when recognition struck, her eyes widened.

'Joe Parker!' she said. 'I never thought I'd see you walk through these doors again.'

'Hello, Isla. Neither did I. I'm here about a case, not to cause trouble.'

'Oh, don't worry. All of that was a long time ago.'

He looked around and it suddenly felt so familiar. He'd enjoyed his years at Mahones. It was how it ended that left him feeling sour, because Joe had not only started his career at Mahones. He had fallen in love there too. The full-blown, all-in-until-he-dies kind of love.

Susie was her name. She had joined the firm as a trainee just as Joe was qualifying, so she got to shadow him around the courts. The thing with courts is that a lot of time is spent hanging around, waiting to be called on, so he and Susie had a long time to get to know each other. And Susie had been someone he wanted to get to know, with olive skin and dark hair than curled down to her shoulders, her figure trim, her smile bright and confident.

It was after a long day in the old court at Salford, a grand old building of wooden docks and ornate landings, before it was closed down so everyone could go to the modern building of grubby magnolia paint. They went for a drink, and then another. Susie didn't go home for a week, and within a month, she had moved in.

Unfortunately, being an on-call criminal lawyer kept Joe out too long and too often, and Susie's eyes started to wander. They didn't wander that far. Just two rooms along the corridor, where one of the civil law partners worked. One night, there was a gap between police interviews, and so he went to the office to catch up with some paperwork. When he got there, he felt the full wrench of infidelity, Susie's soft moans instantly recognisable through the closed office door.

He had opened the door slowly, his phone in his hand. He took three pictures before they saw him, Susie on her back on the desk, her shirt and bra on the floor, her skirt hoisted up to her thighs, her new lover standing between her open legs.

He hadn't said anything. There was nothing that needed to be said. He walked out of the room, and that was the last time he had set foot in Mahones. He had a few weeks of doing nothing, except clearing Susie's stuff from the apartment, until Honeywells called.

'How are the two great lovers?' Joe said.

Isla smiled, and then checked around that no one was listening before she whispered, 'Tense. I think his wife is being quite unreasonable in the divorce.'

Joe enjoyed that thought. 'I feel bad about the photographs though,' he said.

'No you don't. I would have been proud of it.'

And she was right. The phone had a decent camera, and he caught them perfectly, with Susie's breasts like two tanned jellies on a plate and Mike's pale legs contrasting perfectly with the dark trousers that were gathered round his ankles, the third picture catching their shocked faces as they turned towards the camera. Joe emailed them to everyone in the firm in a drunken jealous rage later that night, the chain on the door so Susie couldn't get back in. It was the one he sent to Mike's wife that really caused the damage.

Joe had found out how infidelity hurt, and he wasn't going to inflict it on anyone else. It was single women only for him, except that, at his age, there weren't that many around. He guessed he would be waiting until the first marriages started to crumble.

'I need to speak to whoever knows about Ronnie Bagley,' he said.

Isla looked confused for a while, and then said, 'Is he the murderer?'

'He says he isn't.'

'I heard people talking about it. You upset a few people by pinching Ronnie's case.'

'That's no bad thing. Is there anyone in who will still talk to me? What about Matt?'

'Do you want me to see if he's around?'

'Please. I haven't come here for the nostalgia.'

Isla made a call and then turned to Joe and said, 'Go on up. He hasn't moved.' Joe hesitated, and so Isla added, 'Mike isn't in.'

'Susie?'

'Somewhere around, but you can't hide away all your life.'

'No, I suppose not,' he said, and then headed for the stairs.

As he set off, he wondered what he would discover. He was sure that Ronnie Bagley's secrets were buried in the building somewhere.

Fifty-Two

Sam went straight to a computer terminal, Charlotte alongside. No one paid them any attention. Although Charlotte must have shown some strong qualities to become a detective, on the team she was still the junior officer. Sam knew he was even less than that.

Sam logged on and searched for the complaint made by Claire. As the egg-timer icon tumbled on-screen, Evans came up behind him.

'How are you getting on today?' she said.

Sam turned round. 'We're getting somewhere,' and he told her about the link with the photograph.

'A different link?' She thought for a few seconds and then said, 'You two should keep on looking, but we're going to need some more people on this.'

Before Sam could respond, Evans was distracted by a shout from the other side of the room. 'Mary, the prosecution are on the phone.'

'Hang on,' she said, and went over to take the call.

Sam looked back to the screen, still waiting for the information to load, when Evans slammed down her phone. Everyone looked over.

Evans stood up, throwing her chair against the wall.

'Right, confession time,' she said, the words coming out with venom. 'Who's spoken to Terry Day recently?'

No one spoke. A few people exchanged glances and small shakes of the head.

Evans stepped out from behind her desk. She stood in the middle of the room, her hands on her hips.

'Make no mistake, I will ask Terry Day myself, but I'd rather hear it from my team,' she continued, turning round, making sure that she got a good look at everyone. Still no one spoke. 'That was the CPS on the phone. Guess what: Terry Day has told the defence that he has seen Carrie Smith since Ronnie Bagley is supposed to have killed her. And little Grace. Our victims in our murder case. He's certain that they aren't dead.'

There were gasps around the room, pens going down, people looking at each other, eyes wide. Everyone knew how bad this was. Without a potential deceased, there was no murder case.

'I shouldn't have to find out like this, through the prosecution. So come on, who already knows about this, because Terry told the defence that he spoke to someone here?'

She looked around again, daring someone to say something, breathing heavily through her nose, her anger visible from the glare in her eyes.

Then there was a cough. It was Ged, the officer with the muscles, coffee-boy.

Evans whirled round.

Ged looked to his colleagues for support, but they all seemed suddenly distracted.

'I spoke to him, over the weekend,' he said, his voice sheepish.

'What did he say?'

'Just what you said.' He held up his hands. 'Hey, it's not how it looks. He told me that he thought he had seen Carrie, but it was all wrong. Her hair colour was different, much darker, and he had been far enough away to make a mistake.

So I told him that was what it was, a mistake. I thought he agreed with me.'

'He doesn't seem quite so mistaken anymore,' she said, her voice rising a pitch. 'What were you thinking of, for Christ's sake? We spent the weekend persuading the CPS to charge him, and all the time our witness was saying that our victims were still alive.'

'I just thought that there was no point in making a record of it, because the defence would make a lot of it, when really there was nothing in it. It's easy to make a mistake from a distance. He was wrong.'

'It doesn't matter what you think,' she said, stepping closer to him, leaning over him. 'You kept it quiet, and now we've got a police cover-up on top of a witness who is certain the victims are still alive.' Her chest was pumping hard, deep breaths taken through her nose. 'You might have ruined this case now, and Ronnie Bagley could stay free.'

Ged looked down, a flush to his cheeks, embarrassed.

Evans turned away and pointed at Sam. 'Go and visit Terry Day and take a new statement. I want it served on the CPS this afternoon.' She looked round the rest of the room. 'You know how I work. I deal with truth, not results. It's why I joined the force, to get to the truth. I do not want a repeat. Everyone understand?'

There were mumbles of agreement.

Evans went back to her office, and Ged looked for comradeship amongst his colleagues. There was none.

Sam looked back to the screen, refocusing on the link with the photograph, and saw a number of entries that connected to Claire's name. An incident log. A crime report. Statements from the officers who had got involved with the complaint. But it was the crime report that made Sam's eyes widen.

It was a summary of the complaint and how it progressed. It concluded that the suspect had been given words of advice about how he used the internet.

'We need to go now,' Sam said, getting up quickly. 'We will go see Terry Day, but there's somewhere I need to go first.'

'Where?'

'To see my brother. I need to talk to him.'

Sam pointed at the screen. Charlotte gasped. It was name of the suspect, the person behind the internet profile who had made contact with Gilly Henderson using the photograph.

Ronnie Bagley.

Fifty-Three

As Joe walked through the Mahones building, he felt so much of his early career slide back into focus. His nervousness when he first started, the new boy fresh from university and law college. Those boozy nights that ended with him waking up with one of the young secretaries or clerks. Those times had ended when Susie came along.

Like a lot of the law offices in the city centre, Mahones occupied what was once an old grand house, so that the corridors snaked between small rooms that once served as bedrooms, the view outwards through old sash windows. The building smelled of furniture polish, the cleaners attentive. As he walked past the rooms, he glanced in. Some people looked up, and those that remembered him waved. Some of them even shouted after him, but he kept on walking. He didn't want his presence widely known.

Matt Liver had an office at the end of the corridor, overlooking a small car park. Joe wasn't sure what reaction he would get. The last time Joe had seen him, he was pinching Liver's client from him.

Joe knocked on the door and then pushed at it slowly. When Matt saw him, he said, 'You've got a cheek.' His eyes were ablaze behind small round glasses, his chain-store suit too small, as always, so that he looked like he'd grown out of it.

'It's not a social call,' Joe said. 'Look, no hard feelings. Ronnie asked for me. I didn't poach him.'

'Old man Mahone didn't see it like that.'

'I didn't mean to cause you any problems.'

Matt pointed to Joe's bruised eye. 'It looks like you've been making a few enemies this week.'

'It's a long story, and there are some around here who would enjoy it too much.'

'You mean Susie?'

'She's one, for sure. And how is she?'

'Sleeping with one of the partners gives her a power she doesn't deserve, and she doesn't wear it well.'

'She always had greater ambition than me.'

Matt sighed. 'Okay, so what are you here for, if it isn't my wit?'

'Ronnie Bagley.'

'What, you want to give him back?'

'He keeps hinting that he knows me, but I don't remember him. He tells me like it's important, almost as if he wants me to know who he is.'

'Are you sure you don't remember him?' Matt said. 'Haircut Ronnie?'

Joe's mouth opened, as if he was about to say something, but he stopped, because a memory came back to him.

'Haircut Ronnie is Ronnie Bagley?'

'Didn't you know?'

'That was six, seven years ago. I've had a lot of clients since then.'

Joe thought back to the case, because it was one of those that provided light relief for defence lawyers, some oddball tale squeezed in between the usual stories of bad luck and sheer wickedness.

As he remembered it, Ronnie had been a man with a hair obsession, stalking students on the streets down by the university. He carried scissors in his pocket and would clip off a chunk. There had been a few complaints, and he was caught when he was followed and admitted an assault. Joe had regarded it as a good result because they had only been able to pin one on him. He remembered that Ronnie hadn't viewed it so reasonably.

Whatever he had thought back then though, he had wanted Joe to represent him again.

'He's changed,' Joe said. 'I just didn't recognise him.'

'People get older.'

'It explains why he thought I should remember him,' Joe said. He thanked Matt. 'Next time we talk, let's make it more civil. It's good to see you again,' he said, and started to back out of the office. 'I'll go before someone catches me who doesn't want me here.'

'Yeah, right. Next time, stick to your own clients.' He shook his head. 'Look after yourself, Joe.'

'And you.'

He wanted to get away from there. He had the information he needed, although he wasn't sure what it meant. As he walked quickly along the corridor, heading for the stairs that would take him back to reception, he heard a familiar voice. There was a door opening ahead, to the room where the secretaries worked, and Susie was there, holding a file under her arm.

He looked behind quickly, but he knew there was no exit that way. There was no alternative but to walk forward. As he got closer, Susie turned around.

There was a pause as she took him in, that moment of recognition that bought them both a second to compose themselves.

'Joe, what are you doing here?' she said as she closed the door to the typist room, wanting to avoid the gossip that would start up behind her.

'Just a nostalgia trip,' he said.

She pointed at his eye. 'What happened there?'

'Not every client is happy with my work.'

That made her smile, and just for a moment he saw what had brought them together in the first place. There was a glint to her eyes, some fire beneath her demure exterior. It had been too hot for Joe.

'You look good,' he said, before he could stop himself. And he meant it. He had hardly seen her since they split. He had been out when she had collected her things, so he had been limited to glimpses whenever she walked past his office window.

Susie blushed. 'Thank you,' she said, and then she looked towards the office where he had caught her that time, further back along the corridor. Her shoulders slumped. 'I'm still sorry for you finding out like that. I should have told you.'

'I'm sorry about what I did after I caught you.'

'I'd have done the same,' she said.

'How is it going with Mike?'

Susie shook her head. 'His wife finding out made it stressful. It was never meant to be permanent. It was just, well, you know.'

'Arms around you, because mine never were?'

'Something like that.' Her tone softened when she said, 'Why couldn't we ever talk like this before?'

'Because it hurts less now.'

'Okay, I'm sorry. So what are you doing here, anyway?'

'Ronnie Bagley.'

Susie frowned at the name, and then said, 'Oh, Haircut Ronnie.'

'How come you remember that? I was the criminal lawyer, not you.'

'Because he wanted to apply for an order to keep his girl-friend away from him, and he wanted his daughter with him. He came to me.'

Joe was surprised. 'What, Carrie?'

'That's her.'

'Why did he want to keep Carrie away?'

'That was the main problem: he wouldn't say, and so we couldn't do anything for him.'

'You know that he's been accused of killing Carrie, and his child?'

'Yeah, I heard Matt bitching about you,' she said, and then, 'but it doesn't seem right.'

'How so?'

'Because he was scared of her, but he loved his child. It was the way he talked about her.'

'So what happened?'

'He stopped coming in once he realised he would have to pay a lot of money for a lost cause.' She looked at Joe, concern in her eyes. 'Is it something I didn't do? If I'd got the court order, perhaps he wouldn't have been able to kill them.'

'No, it's not that. You know we don't run our clients' lives, we just help them out from time to time.' He smiled. 'Thanks for the catch up, Susie. I've got what I need.'

He turned to go, but Susie grabbed his hand. When he stopped and looked back to her, she stepped forward and kissed him, her lips soft and warm on his, and just for a second he felt his own fires begin to burn. She pulled away, her eyes opening slowly, and whispered, 'We never did say goodbye properly, Joe. You know, one last time, just to spite each other, to get closure.'

He let go of her hand and stepped back. 'You're with some-one else. Infidelity hurts.' And when he turned to go this time, Susie didn't stop him.

'You're a bastard, Joe Parker,' she said.

He didn't try to argue. He was too busy wondering why the news about Ronnie Bagley bothered him so much.

Joe left Mahones and walked quickly back to his office. So Ronnie had been his client a few years earlier, and he wanted him to know that, as if it was somehow important. And what was his jibe before, that it was all his fault? What was his fault?

As he got to his office, he saw his brother's car outside, a young woman in the passenger seat. Joe rolled his eyes. Time for more wisdom from the self-appointed patriarch. When he walked into the building, Sam was sitting in reception.

'What can I do for you, Sam?' he said, trying to hide the weariness he felt.

Sam pointed at Joe's eye. 'What happened to you?'

'Another dissatisfied customer.'

'Have you called it in?'

'No, I haven't, and I won't. It was just one of those things.'

'I tried to contact you last night.'

'My phone got smashed, during this,' Joe said, and pointed at his face. Sam had seemed tense, but that seemed to make him relax. It had the opposite effect on Joe. 'What's wrong?' Then Joe noticed Marion taking an interest in what was being said, and he pointed to the stairs. 'Let's find somewhere more private.'

They were heading along the landing when Gina appeared. Sam looked at Gina, and then back to Joe, his eyes wide with surprise.

'Gina's worked here for a year,' Joe said.

'Hello, Sam,' she said.

'You were there for us when Ellie was murdered,' Sam said. 'You inspired me to join the police, and now you do this?'

'What is "this"?'

'Helping crooks.'

'Helping people.'

'Did you think that way when you were on the job?'

'No, not really.'

'So were you right then, or right now?'

'I see the other side now, that's all. Things aren't always clear-cut.'

283

Joe coughed to interrupt. 'What do you want, Sam? To find out more about Ronnie Bagley?'

Sam's jaw clenched.

'I think we should speak privately,' Sam said, glancing at Gina, as if to say that it was something best kept between them.

Gina put her hand on Sam's arm. 'It's good to see you again, Sam. I'll leave you two to it.'

Both men stayed silent until she was gone, and then they went into Joe's office where he said, 'You're on police time now, so it must be something to do with the job. Are you here to milk me for information again?'

Sam pushed his glasses back up his nose. 'I'm not here for an argument, Joe. If you're still angry, fine, enjoy your bad mood. You play the game more than I do, because my job is to find things out, to get to the truth, whereas yours is just to try to weasel out of it. That's what lawyers do, isn't it, help people weasel out of things? So keep your moral high horse to yourself, Joe, because what I did was nothing compared to things your clients do. But you don't judge, do you, unless it's me?'

'So you've come to justify yourself?' Joe said, sitting down. 'Well, you've done it. Goodbye.'

The brothers stared at each other. Sam still standing, Joe with his arms on his desk.

A few seconds passed before Sam said, 'I'm here about Ronnie Bagley.'

'Fuck off, Sam. I'm not going to tell you about my client.'

'It's not about the case,' Sam said, his voice rising. 'It's about Ruby.'

Joe paused at that. 'Ruby? What about her?'

'Tell me about Ronnie Bagley first.'

'Why is Ronnie more important?'

'I'm worried he's a threat to Ruby.'

'Ronnie? What do you mean, a threat?'

'Ruby was followed. Yesterday.'

Joe didn't like the clench to Sam's jaw. 'Followed? Where?'

'Down the path.'

Joe went to rub his brow, but then pulled his hand away, aware of his bruises. 'What, where Ellie . . . ?'

Sam nodded.

Joe looked down at the desk. It all came back to him in a rush of images: Ellie turning into the path, distracted by her headphones, the hooded man following.

When he looked up again, Joe said, 'Did Ruby know who was following her?'

'No. She didn't get a good view, just saw some movement in the trees, but it was enough to frighten her. She said it was as if the person was trying to keep up with her. She didn't say anything at first, because she knew what Mum would say, but she was being unusually quiet, so Mum got it out of her eventually.'

'So what do we do?'

'I'm going to have a look at some logs from the last few weeks, just to see if there are any reports in the area of a strange man hanging around. But I'm worried about Ronnie Bagley.'

'But if Ruby didn't get a good view, you won't prove that he was the person in the trees.'

'Think like a copper, not a lawyer,' Sam said. 'If we know who the person might be, I can make his life difficult. If it is Ronnie, we'll try to get his bail revoked.'

'Why do you think it's Ronnie?'

Sam let out a long breath. 'So I give up everything and you protect him?'

'No, it's not like that.'

'If I tell you, if it comes to nothing, it doesn't go beyond this room. If we lift Ronnie and you use this in the case somehow, we're finished.'

'We're brothers,' Joe said, 'and if this is about Ruby, nothing else matters.'

Sam stayed silent for a few moments, and then said, 'There is something you don't know. It hasn't been made public yet, but the press will latch on to it soon. There are enough of them hanging around the station.'

'Go on.'

'There are girls going missing. Five of them now. One went missing the other night. There is a link, and that is they all have parents connected to the Ben Grant case. A juror's daughter. A barrister's daughter. CSI. A detective. All these missing girls.'

Joe was confused. 'What, the Ben Grant you arrested? Child killer?'

Sam nodded. 'Your client's dead girlfriend, Carrie, was Ben Grant's most frequent visitor.'

'The girlfriend Terry Day says is still alive.'

'I'm not here for that argument.'

'Okay, I understand, but why haven't you gone public?'

'Because we don't want whoever is behind it to know we've spotted it. And Ronnie is involved.'

'How?'

'The only other link I've found between the missing girls is an internet profile that was used by Ronnie Bagley to groom them.'

'Ronnie, a groomer?' Joe was surprised. 'Groomers go after kids. I didn't think Ronnie was into that.'

'Tastes change,' Sam said, 'because it's all coming back to Ronnie. Ruby says that she was followed, and who has a bigger link to Ben Grant's case than me? I was the one who arrested him.'

Joe felt that instant headiness of fear. The sudden rush of his heartbeat, the fast turn of his stomach. 'Okay, if we're sharing, I just found something out about him. At Mahones, we called him Haircut Ronnie.'

Sam paled. He sat down on a chair opposite. 'Haircut? What do you mean?

'Ronnie Bagley has got a hair thing. Used to snip hair from students and got caught. How don't you know this?'

Sam turned away, his hand on his head.

'Sam, what's wrong?'

'I went to see Ben Grant yesterday. He talked about how he killed his sister because of some hair fetish he had, but when we checked the records it turns out he had no sister.' Sam pulled out his phone. He dialled Evans. When she answered, he said, 'I need to go see Ben Grant again.' When he explained what he knew, it took only seconds to get her approval.

'I've got to go,' Sam said. On his way out of the room, he said, 'Mum's worried. Think about going to see her.' And then he was gone.

As his footsteps receded along the corridor, the silence around Joe seemed heavy. He thought again about the man who had followed Ellie all those years ago. And now Ruby.

The door opened slowly and Gina put her head into the room.

'Everything all right?' she said.

'No,' Joe said. 'Not all right at all.'

Fifty-Four

As they were escorted along the prison corridor, Charlotte said, 'So do you think Grant will have anything new to say to you today?'

'He enjoyed yesterday,' Sam said, cleaning his glasses with a tissue. 'He'll want to see the effect.'

'Are you sure this is a good idea? You seem wound up. He might get to you.'

'He lied to me yesterday. His story seemed to be nonsense, but now I'm wondering if there was more to it. Have you met Grant before?'

'No, and I'm curious.'

'He'll enjoy that,' Sam said. 'He loves the attention. Yesterday was the first time I'd spoken to him since I arrested him, and he was just like I remember. He is like all of a man's wicked side expanded to fill the whole. The thing is, he knows that, and I think it's the part about himself that he likes the most.'

The door was unlocked in front of them and they were shown into the room. Ben Grant was already there, tapping the table with his fingernails, fast and impatient. When he looked up, his eyes focused on Charlotte straight away.

He sat back, his eyes looking her up and down, deliberate, to make sure she saw him. 'I didn't expect you to bring a friend.'

'This is DC Glover,' Sam said. 'We're working together today.'

'You must have a first name though,' Grant said, not looking away from Charlotte.

She shook her head. 'Detective will do.'

Grant curled his lip. 'I'll find out,' he said, and then, 'Too old for me, anyway.'

'And always out of reach,' she said.

Charlotte was tough and confident, although Sam noticed that she pulled her jacket tighter as she sat down, so Grant couldn't look at her chest. Grant must have spotted it, because he tilted his head and said, 'Don't be like that, Detective.' He looked each way theatrically, as if he was checking that they couldn't be heard, and whispered, 'I'll be using you tonight, if you know what I mean. I could have some fun with you, in here,' and he tapped the side of his head with his finger.

'All right, Grant,' Sam said, his voice showing his impatience. 'Pack it in.'

'Oh, but why?' he said, his hand over his mouth, feigning shock. 'Isn't everything better in the mind, where you can live out your fantasies without having to put up with all that contact, that need for affection, wanting to be held like a panting puppy? Tell me, Mr Parker, did you mention me to your wife?' When Sam didn't respond, he winked. 'I reckon not, because that would be like giving in to me, taking your work home. So you just let her sit there, staring at the television, and you didn't want to go near her? You made a mistake.'

Sam opened his notebook as a way of distracting him, but then Grant said, 'What about your sister? Little Ruby?'

Sam tensed but kept his focus on the page.

'Is she still safe? I presume so, or else you wouldn't be here. You'd be grieving again, except then you'd be all out of sisters, and your mother, well, she's too old to try for another little sister for you.' Grant tried to catch Sam's eye, dipping his head right down. 'Or would that be for me?'

289

Sam felt the blood rush to his cheeks, his fists clenched on the page. The room seemed to contract, only Grant in focus, Sam's chest tightening. All he could think of then was Grant, of how he would feel as he went to the floor, Grant's blood wet on his knuckles. The only thing stopping him from leaping over the desk was the knowledge, just nudging him, that it was exactly what Grant wanted.

A soft hand went around his forearm. Sam looked over. It was Charlotte. She gave a slight shake of the head. Don't let him get to you.

Charlotte let go of Sam and said, 'All right, you've got our attention. Now talk to us.'

Grant smirked and said, 'So why do you want to speak to me again?'

'I want to know why you lied to me yesterday,' Sam said.

Grant's eyes stayed on Charlotte. Sam didn't know if he was doing it because she turned him on, or whether he was just trying to make her uncomfortable.

Sam banged on the table. 'This way, Grant,' and he pointed towards himself. 'Talk to me.'

Grant sat back and folded his arms. 'What do you want to know?'

'You told me yesterday how you killed your sister,' Sam said. 'I hope you got off on it. Because I didn't. My inspector didn't either. You never had a sister. So forgive us if we don't waste our time on that. We are a little bit busy right now. I'm sure you'll understand. Like you said yesterday, you've got all the time in the world. Ours is a little more precious.'

Grant laughed. 'I told you, all you needed to know was in what I said to you yesterday, but seeing as you're too stupid to work it out, I feel like I wasted my time.'

Sam bowed his head to him. 'You'll have to forgive me, but I don't have the intellect that you do.'

'Don't be sarcastic,' Grant said.

'Isn't that why you want us here?' Sam said. 'To admire you? So go on, tell me what I'm missing.'

Grant stayed silent.

'All this about my sister,' Sam continued. 'Not just my poor dead sister, but the sister I still have. That's just you telling me that you know about me, which can't be too hard, can it? It's an open world now, information available at the click of a mouse. So you can use a computer.' Sam started a slow hand-clap. 'I'm impressed. But what else is there, Grant? What am I missing?'

Grant's cheeks flushed but still he stayed silent.

Sam looked to Charlotte, who gave a small shrug. They both stood up. 'See you around, Grant,' Sam said, and then turned as if to go, before he stopped. 'No, sorry, I won't, will I, because you're in here, and I'm not.'

'I'm out there with you,' Grant said, his voice low and cold. 'Just you remember that.'

'How are you with me?' Sam said. 'Because you try to get in my head?' He scoffed. 'Bullshit.'

'Do you know what the ultimate power trip is?' Grant said.

'Go on, enlighten me.'

'Sit down again and we'll talk.'

Sam paused for a moment, and then sat down, Charlotte alongside him. 'Our patience is wearing thin.'

They both considered Grant, who glared back at them. Sam had rattled him.

'Have you ever been betrayed?' Grant said. 'Betrayal makes people lash out. Perhaps it affected how I spoke to you, what I said.'

'Who's betrayed you?' Sam said.

'Killing isn't what you think, you know,' Grant said.

'What's this got to do with betrayal?'

'Everything to do with it. So tell me, how do you think killing feels?'

'How do you know I think about it at all?'

'Because you do. Everyone does. You'd like to kill me right now, I can tell. It's only what you would call human decency that stops you. But you wouldn't enjoy it.'

'Why not?' Sam said. 'I can't help but think that I'd enjoy your suffering.'

'No, you wouldn't, because it's all in the planning and the memory. It's the anticipation that gives you the tingle, the excitement of what's going to happen, but when it actually happens, you would be too much in the moment. You can't relish it, because the adrenalin floods in, and so it's like streams of images rushing at you, almost as if it's happening to someone else. No, it's the anticipation, and then the reliving. The actual killing is just a means to an end, a realisation.'

'So what's the ultimate power trip?'

'Letting someone enjoy it with you.'

Sam flinched. The night of Grant's arrest flooded back again. Grant much younger, Sam more raw.

Grant smiled. 'You always knew that,' he said to Sam. 'Right from when you found me, leaving my last little parcel. You've always known that there was someone else there, hiding in the bushes.'

'No, that isn't right,' Sam said.

'Isn't it? I remember how you looked at me. You were scared, your little torch trembling in your hand, but still you looked when you heard something. Your torch twitched that way, but then you remembered me and shone it back. What had you heard? The bushes rustling? Footsteps? Did you put it down to a bird flying off, or was it just the wind, your mind working too quickly, making moving shapes out of night shadows?' Grant started to cackle. 'You never mentioned it, did you? Like a scared little boy. I remember the trial. Do you remember when you were asked whether I was alone? Do you remember your answer?'

Sam swallowed. 'Of course I remember my answer, because it was the truth, the whole truth, and nothing but the truth. There was no one else there. I didn't see anyone. There was no proof of anyone.'

'Proof? Demanding proof is what the guilty say, you know that, because the innocent protest it. So you only go on proof, policeman? You don't rely on hunches or gut instincts, or whatever else you say makes you so fucking special?' Grant tapped his head again. 'But in here, it's not about proof, because you go through it every time you hear my name.' Grant's eyes narrowed. 'I remember your twitch as I came towards you, as I knelt before you. Your eyes flashed to the bushes, because you heard the same thing that I did. Movement. Except that I knew what it was.'

'There was no one there.'

Grant waved his hand dismissively. 'You were never going to admit it. You'd caught the beast, the monster. Why would you spoil it by admitting that someone else had got away?'

'So this is the new tactic, is it, Grant? Deflection? You're trying to lessen your guilt. What for? Some parole bid? Try to convince everyone that you're not the bad guy everyone thinks you are, that you were led astray?'

'Oh, I'm a bad guy, all right. Baddest of them all. It's what I can do to others that gives me the hard on.' He grinned. 'To see someone else act out your own fantasies, some regular person, drawn in and converted, that's the real thrill. I get everything then. The anticipation, the build up, and then the act itself, because I'm not the one in the moment, so I can enjoy it. And afterwards, I get the memories too. But more than that, I get to see the person grow, to change. It's exhilarating. Now that, Mr Parker, is power.'

'You're sick.'

'Yep, a real beast, but there's something you don't know, and that is there is no greater enthusiast than the recently converted, because for all the thrill I get, they get the pleasure of pleasing me too.'

'So you had an accomplice all along?' Charlotte asked.

'Everyone has an accomplice, my dear, that little thing that makes you behave like you do. Sometimes it's your background, or the life you lead, or maybe even those little voices that scratch you in the back of the head, like a symphony to your fantasies, but they're all still accomplices.'

'Okay, was it someone physical?' she said. 'A real person? Is that who betrayed you?'

Grant wagged his finger at her. 'I like you. You're clever. I'm going to have some fun with you later. Tell me, how are you, just so I can imagine you properly? Do you like it rough, someone dominant, holding you down, or are you one of those needy types? Needs a kiss and a cuddle, slow and loving?'

'Who was your accomplice, Mr Grant?' Charlotte said, her voice firmer. 'Ronnie Bagley?'

'Betrayal, remember,' Grant said, his eyes narrowed. 'That's what it was about.'

Sam shook his head. 'I don't understand. Who betrayed you?'

Grant folded his arms. The silence grew until it became obvious that they were not going to get anything else out of him.

'I'll be back, Grant,' Sam said.

Grant kept his eyes on Charlotte. 'What, when the body count goes up?' He smiled. 'I'll look forward to it.'

Fifty-Five

Joe looked up at the house where Ronnie's mother lived. A small stone house with thick stone windowsills and a door that was too small for Joe to fit through whilst standing straight. Ronnie had been bailed to live there and he wasn't answering his phone.

He banged on the door and then paced back and forth as he waited. He needed to find Ronnie. Ruby was in danger and Ronnie was at the centre of it all. Ronnie had wanted Joe all along, but he blamed Joe for something Joe didn't understand.

The house was in the lower part of Marton, nearer the railway line, the town divided by the large hill that created the valley side. The part of the town at the top of the hill had the views and the grand old houses, which was where Ronnie and Carrie had lived. The lower part, along the valley floor, was where all the workers' cottages were, so their occupants were the ones who choked on the smoke in the days when mills and factories clogged up the town.

The door opened and Ronnie's mother stood there.

'Mrs Bagley, is Ronnie in?'

She looked up and down the street and then shook her head. 'He hasn't really been living here,' she said, her voice quiet and shaky.

'What do you mean? He has to live here. That's what the judge ordered.'

'That's between Ronnie and the judge.'

'So where does he go?'

'I don't know. He doesn't tell me anything.'

'We need to talk,' Joe said.

She paused and then turned to go into the house.

Joe followed, squinting in the murkiness of the hallway as the door closed behind him. The house seemed brown throughout. The carpet, the light brown of the wallpaper, the paintwork yellowed through age. When he went into the living room, he spotted the silver cardboard of a cigarette packet and realised that the colouring wasn't just through ageing.

As he sat down, she took a cigarette out of the packet, and the air became murkier still as she lit it and blew smoke into the room.

'You must have some idea where he goes?' Joe said.

She shook her head. 'I don't ask. He doesn't tell me.' When Joe frowned, she said, 'I didn't ask for him to come here. This was your idea, or that girl who called me. She said Ronnie would stay in prison if I didn't help. What could I do?'

'He's your son. We ask the family in cases like this. Why, do you have a problem with him?'

She took a long pull on her cigarette, before saying, 'He's not right. He is ... how can I say it? He's unnatural.'

'What do you mean, "unnatural"?'

'That he has unnatural instincts. Didn't he tell you about them? How I've had to put up with people at my door, shouting about how he upsets people, young women, because he follows them around? Stroking their hair on buses, in shops, watching them outside their houses. He isn't right. Never has been. Ever since, well,' and she paused, before saying, 'well, things have happened.'

Joe looked around the room, small, cluttered with cheap ornaments and photograph frames. Ronnie wasn't in any of them. There was a young woman though. Pretty, long-haired, smiling.

'Who's the girl?' Joe said, pointing at the frames, remembering Sam's words from before.

Mrs Bagley looked over and Joe noticed the clench of her jaw. 'That's Ronnie's sister.' She took another long drag. 'That was part of Ronnie's unnatural behaviour.'

'What do you mean?'

'You need to know what sort of man you're helping,' she said, jabbing her cigarette fingers at Joe, making ash tumble to the floor. 'He isn't right.'

Joe felt his unease gnaw at him a little harder. What sort of person had he helped to put back on the street? 'What happened?' he asked.

'Ronnie used to watch her. His own sister? She caught him, playing with himself, the dirty little pervert. Can you imagine how we felt? My Frank, well, he couldn't cope, so he left, couldn't stand to be in the same house as him.'

'Where is she? Will Ronnie be with her?'

She shook her head slowly, her eyes misted over. She crossed herself. 'I wish he was,' she said. There was a crack to her voice when she added, 'Sally, that was her name. She died. Slipped and fell in the bath.'

Fifty-Six

Sam saw that he had a missed call when the prison guard returned his phone. Even the police had to hand them in. It was DI Evans. He stalled before he made the call.

'That was more than a taunt, about an accomplice,' Sam said to Charlotte. 'And why does it all come back to betrayal?'

'I don't know,' she said. 'Let him have his small victory, because at least we know where he is, locked up and safe.' That brought a smile from Sam, until she asked, 'Was he right though, that someone else was there when you caught him?'

Sam hesitated, just for a second, but it was enough for Charlotte to look surprised. 'So he is right?'

He clenched his jaw. 'No, he's not right,' he said, and then exhaled loudly. 'I don't know, is the truthful answer. I didn't lie in court. I was asked whether I had seen anyone else there. I hadn't. Whether I had heard anyone. I hadn't. Whether I knew anyone else was there. I didn't.'

'So what part did he get right then?'

'The part where I can't rule it out.'

She stopped walking. 'Talk to me, Sam.'

He didn't answer for a few seconds, and then said, 'It was just a feeling. There were some rustles, and the sensation that we weren't alone. And Grant had acted like I had to keep my whole attention on him, coming forward, talking, kneeling in front of me.'

'To give someone else time to get away?'

'Possibly.'

'So Grant did have an accomplice?'

'Maybe.'

'Did you ever tell anyone at the time?'

'I told the inspector in charge of the case, but he told me not to write it down. They had their man, and if the murders stopped because Grant had been caught, what good would it do to speculate? And he was right, because what good would it do? I hadn't seen anything. It was a feeling, nothing more. Why give the defence a get-out, someone else they could blame it on?'

'This job is too hard sometimes,' Charlotte said. 'It's supposed to be about truth, but the truth makes you look over your shoulder and wonder what someone else will make of it. It's almost as though the truth becomes about how you present it and nothing more.'

'So these missing girls could be down to an apprentice,' Sam said. 'Which means that my silence back then led to all of this.'

'Ronnie Bagley is the key,' Charlotte said. 'He's the link we do have. He murdered Grant's most frequent visitor, and he's the one with the hair fetish, just like Grant talked about yesterday. If Grant was playing the part, describing someone else, was that person Ronnie?'

Then something occurred to Sam. 'And how do we know that Grant wasn't just the apprentice, taking the fall for someone else?'

'Why would he do that?'

'Because he was in awe of the person, or because he knew he was caught and so opted for glory instead? Look at him. A pathetic man who gets off on being a somebody. What was he before he was caught? He worked in a factory, just some nobody on a production line. Now? The world knows who he is. The bars keep him in, but they've given him something else too: notoriety.'

'So why now?' Charlotte said. 'Grant has been locked up for a few years now. Then these girls start to go missing. There is a connection with Grant, but why did it start now, and why is Grant speaking now?'

'He talked about betrayal,' Sam said. 'Does he feel betrayed in some way, because he's copped the life sentence and yet his accomplice, or apprentice, or teacher, or whatever, carries on as before? He wants to give him up but can't quite resist teasing us because, for all the betrayal he feels, he still craves the attention.'

'So we need to work out the identity of the apprentice, then we might find out who is behind these missing girls.'

'Ronnie Bagley,' Sam said. 'Who else can it be? Is that why Carrie was drawn to Ronnie, because he was the next best thing to Grant? Now he is supposed to have killed Carrie and their baby. Was she going to betray him? Is that why he killed them, to silence her?' When Charlotte didn't respond, trying to work it out for herself, Sam said, 'I've got to tell Evans where we are.'

Sam called DI Evans and told her about the meeting and what they had found out about Ronnie's grooming, and he heard the urgency in her voice as his tale unfolded.

'We need to find Ronnie Bagley now,' Evans said.

'Where do you want us to start?' Sam said.

'You don't start anywhere,' Evans said. 'We'll do it. You go to Terry Day's house, get that statement,' and then she hung up.

Sam looked at his phone, angry.

'What's wrong?'

'We've been demoted to runners and statement-takers,' Sam said.

The long drive to Terry Day's house was made in silence, both of them annoyed about being sidelined, until Sam realised something as he drove. He got to the traffic lights that would take them to Terry's house, but rather than turning left, Sam looked higher up the hill and then drove straight on.

'Where are we going?' Charlotte said. 'The turning was back there.'

'Bear with me,' he said, driving straight on and then turning a sharp left a quarter of a mile further along. He drove on in silence until they arrived at the end of a terraced street, the stone houses made black by a century of grime.

He stepped out of the car.

'What are you doing?' Charlotte asked, as she joined him on the pavement.

He pointed at the long row of houses running steeply downhill, where it seemed to run out, the end of it being just blue sky. 'Follow me,' he said.

Their footsteps echoed between the two sides of the street as they walked, his shoes as loud leather scrapes, hers as regular clicks. The houses were two-storey, with white stone doorframes and a step in front of the doors, where a few decades earlier they would have been cleaned and polished by tough northern women, their skin made old by hard times and factory smoke.

When they got to the end of the road, Sam stopped. He pointed into the valley that had opened out in front of them, the street coming to an end by a steep verge of scrappy grass. There was a small factory, the sound of a forklift truck loud as it reversed and pulled forward in jerks and sweeping arcs.

'That's where Ben Grant worked,' he said. 'It all came back to me, driving up here, because I haven't worked around here for a while.' He turned to point at a small stone terraced house, the walls dark grey and fashioned out of large pieces of the Pennines. 'That's Ben Grant's house, where he killed his victims, before he dumped them.'

Charlotte paused and put her hands on her waist. 'It looks so ordinary,' she said, her voice quiet.

'That's how they always look,' he said. 'It's been empty since Ben Grant was arrested. Grant owns it but won't sell it. It used to get vandalised, but the neighbours started looking after it, washing off the paint and repairing windows, because seeing it smashed up just reminded them of what had happened. They hope that it'll change hands one day if they look after it, and so they can all move on.'

'Why is this important?' she said.

Sam looked at Charlotte. 'I've been getting phone calls for a couple of months now. I couldn't work them out, because I'm not on the Murder Squad. I was on the financial unit. Ben Grant was a long time ago.'

'What are these calls?'

'Someone screaming, like they're scared, or in pain, but it's muffled. I thought it was from a film, someone playing around with me, because I'd locked them up or something, taken their assets. Now, I think it's connected to this, to Ben Grant.'

'Why do you say that?'

'Because there's a noise in it. I've downloaded it to my computer, and I've tried to play around with it. It's a beeping noise, like the warning beep of a lorry reversing.' He pointed down to the factory again. 'Like a lorry reversing into that factory yard. It's faint, but it's got the same echo, as if it's far away, but with nothing else to interfere with the sound. No other traffic noise. Somewhere quiet, like here.' He pointed at Ben Grant's old house.

Charlotte was surprised. 'Have you still got a copy?'

Sam pulled out his phone and scrolled through his answer machine until he found the file he wanted. He pressed play and passed it to Charlotte.

He turned away as she listened. She was quiet as she passed the phone back to him.

'It's real, isn't it?' she said quietly.

'Now I think it is. Ben Grant would only speak to me. Not

just any copper, but me. And I've been getting these calls. He can't have been making them from prison.'

'The accomplice,' Charlotte said, nodding as realisation hit her.

'I think it's worse than that,' Sam said. 'If Ben Grant was behind this, and the sound was recorded over there, he must have recorded his victims, and so somewhere there must be footage of what he did. Can you imagine how their parents will feel if they find out?'

'So who is the accomplice?'

Sam pointed towards a narrow path that ran alongside Ben Grant's house. 'Follow me.'

They walked until the narrow path turned into a mud track, with a drop on one side, towards the factory in the valley. They crossed two streets like that, just long stretches of housing that fanned out like spokes on a wheel, so that the gardens were smallest at the factory end, the hub of the wheel. Sam stopped and pointed to the house in front of them, a taller three-storey house, with cobwebs and dirt on the windows.

'That's Terry Day's house,' he said. 'Where Ronnie lived.'

Charlotte looked up at the house, and then back along the track they had come down. 'They're close by.'

'Two streets away, except they seem further from the top road, because of the way the streets spread out. It's just a short walk though.'

'So the connection gets stronger,' she said.

'Everything comes back to Ben Grant and Ronnie Bagley. The missing girls. The location of Carrie's murder, Grant's regular visitor. Ronnie has the hair fetish, which is what Grant described to me. He was trying to tell me about Ronnie Bagley, to tease me.'

'And Ronnie wanted to stay close to where he helped Grant,' Charlotte said.

'If he was going to live off the fantasies, he needed to stay close, so he felt closer to them.'

Charlotte turned back to Terry Day's house. 'It looks a dismal sort of a place. What sort of person lives somewhere like that? Perhaps Ged was right to discount Terry's sighting?'

'You watch him when we get his statement, see if you think he's being truthful. Ged was stupid, but I understand why he did it. The first question Terry Day will be asked by the defence is: "Have you seen Carrie Smith since she was supposedly murdered?" The answer will be "Yes". That will be bad enough, but add in the cover-up, and Ronnie Bagley is smiling all the way to his not guilty verdict.'

'So we've been given the job of undoing everything we've done in this case,' Charlotte said. 'As soon as we knock on that door and he tries to convince us that he saw Ronnie's dead girlfriend, it's all over before we ever really got started.'

'Ignoring it won't change that,' Sam said. 'Do the right thing. That's all we can do.'

They went up the stone steps to the door. Sam rang the top doorbell. They both looked around as they waited for the rumble of feet on the stairs, but there was just silence.

'Perhaps it's broken,' Charlotte said, and banged on the wooden door. It swung open as her fist connected.

They exchanged glances. They were going in but something wasn't right.

The hallway was empty. He shouted. No response, except that something told him that they weren't alone. It was a presence, something he couldn't explain.

'Mr Day?' he shouted. 'It's the police.'

The hallway they were in was dim, the only light coming from the street. Ahead of them, the stairs rose upwards, towards the shadows of the first floor. There was a door to their right that was sealed by crime scene tape.

'Ronnie's flat,' Charlotte whispered, following his gaze.

'Do we go up?' he said.

Charlotte made the decision and went towards the stairs. 'Mr Day?' she shouted. No response.

They jumped. There was movement above. Footsteps, light and quick, creaks on the floor.

The solid wooden door closed behind them with a loud click, blocking any light coming in. Sam groped along the wall, feeling for a light switch. When he found one, he clicked it on, but nothing happened. He pulled out his phone and found the flashlight app, which shone a bright square of light. He held it towards the stairs, and as he glanced upwards, he saw the slow swing of an empty bulb socket.

'We have to go up,' he said.

Charlotte took a deep breath, and then nodded her approval.

Sam went towards the stairs, his phone held out in front of him.

Fifty-Seven

He checked his watch. She would be here soon. It was all moving too quickly. The girl didn't seem ready to meet, but the time had to be now. It was what he had been told, that the end was close.

He closed his eyes for a moment as the memories of the night before came back. It was the arousal he was looking for, to make sure he didn't back out. He could leave, he knew that. He was in a van, had wheels. He could drive away and keep going, because this wasn't the ending he had planned. His ending had been so different, had all been for her, because love was like that. Sacrifice.

But he knew he wouldn't do that. He'd gone too far. He'd been reminded of what he would miss and he knew he was too weak. He had always been too weak in relation to her. It was his soft spot, the churn in his stomach, the bounce in his step. He had tried to make it different, but she hadn't wanted that.

He thought of Monica to keep him there. She had been the unexpected one, his treat, a deviation from the plan, and it had been all he had been promised. The feel of her hair in his hand, as soft as he expected, little crackles on his skin, just sparks he could feel. The fast rise of her breasts as she became scared.

His breathing quickened. That was his goal. His arousal kept him there. When it faded, the guilt came at him, almost too fast, like standing in front of a large wave, too powerful to control. He needed the passion to keep his nerve.

He opened his eyes and scanned the streets, making sure that no one was looking. This was the riskiest one. If the police had found out, they would be watching, because he'd given a time and a location. There was no one there. He had chosen a dead-end street, where he could see ahead along plain suburban houses that were far enough back from the road that the occupants wouldn't notice him.

If they did, he was resigned to his fate. He would give himself up, allow himself to be taken. It was the right thing to do.

He wasn't expecting the police though. Like all the rest, she kept the secrets, because he had some of hers. That was how it worked. Get the secrets and get the girl.

Then he saw her. She was there, walking towards him. Tall, gangly, her head down, her arms folded across her chest.

He flashed his headlights. She noticed and glanced upwards and then faltered. Don't stop, he thought. She looked around, like he had told her. This was their secret. Keep watch.

She bent down to his open window and said hello.

'I'm Billy's dad,' he said. 'Did you get the message that I was collecting you?'

'Yes, he mentioned it.' She looked around again, nervous.

'He's excited about seeing you,' he said.

She smiled, quick and nervous. He leaned across the passenger seat to open the van door.

'Get in. We don't want to keep Billy waiting,' he said.

'I'm not sure,' she said.

'Why, what's wrong?'

'I've never met you before. It doesn't seem right.'

'Your family are being protective, that's all, but you're a big girl now. So come on, you're old enough to make your own decisions.'

'Yes, but, you know, it seems dangerous.'

307

'Does Billy seem dangerous?'

'Well, no. He seems nice.'

'Do I seem dangerous? Is that what you're saying?'

She looked flustered. 'No, I didn't mean that. I'm sorry.'

'So there you go.' He patted the seat. 'Come on. Do what *you* want to do, just for once.'

She paused for a moment, and then she climbed in. Her skirt rode up her legs, exposing her knees, her skinny thighs. She pulled at her skirt as he looked.

'Did you do as Billy asked and delete all the messages?' he said.

She nodded.

'All of them?'

She nodded again.

'Don't be nervous,' he said.

He reached across, making her flinch, but he touched her hair anyway, just moved it from her shoulders, exposing her neck.

'Billy is a nice boy,' he said.

'Okay,' she said, her voice timid. 'So can we go?'

He smiled and then started the engine. 'Of course we can, Ruby. Of course we can.'

Fifty-Eight

Sam looked back towards the front door, its solid wood blocking out the daylight, so all that he could see of the brightness outside was what came through the glass pane above.

'Can't we wedge it open?' he said.

'It looks too heavy, the hinges too strong,' Charlotte said. 'The whole place is a hovel. How can he charge rent?'

They were both on the stairs, edging upwards towards the flat where Terry Day lived, both using the light from their phones, but it was a glow, not a direct beam, so that the shadows of doorways stretched and shifted, revealed shapes and then hid them again.

'Mr Day?' he shouted. The words echoed. They waited for a response, but there was nothing.

'He's not here,' Charlotte said. 'We'll come back later.'

'No, he's here,' Sam said. 'I know it.'

'But why do we need to find out now?'

Sam paused as he thought about that. Charlotte was right, there was no urgency. It was just to find out what he had told Joe, to see if there was still a case against Ronnie Bagley. No urgency. They should turn back.

But there was something about the house that told him to keep going. It wasn't just the darkness, or the quietness. It was too still, as if the whole house was holding its breath, watching them.

They both whirled round, startled, when there was a noise, a door closing. He heard it as a click, loud in the stillness of the landing. Sam turned his phone towards the sound, but there was just darkness.

'We should go back,' Charlotte said, fear in her voice. 'Or at least call it in.'

'No, keep going,' he said. 'Something isn't right.' He climbed a step, winced at the loud creak. 'Why doesn't he have lights?'

Sam stepped forward again. The stairs creaked some more, quieter this time, the carpet worn underfoot, loose in some places.

Charlotte reached out briefly, her hand on his back as reassurance. As they got to the top of the stairs, he tried to get the feel of his surroundings. Charlotte shone her phone around to look for a light source. He shone his straight ahead. There was a small corridor to a room further down. A kitchen, it looked like, the light catching the metal edges of drawers. There was a room just before it. The thin gleam of a cord gave it away as a bathroom.

Sam went to it and pulled the cord. Nothing. 'There's no power,' he said.

He felt Charlotte's breath on his neck. 'Let's go back,' she said.

'No, forward.'

'We shouldn't do this alone,' she said. 'We don't know what's up there.'

'And if there's nothing?' Sam said. 'All the trouble for some loner who's run out of coins for the meter?'

'I get it,' she said. 'We keep going so we don't look stupid.'

'If you really can't face going up there, you go back, but I'm carrying on.'

Sam could hear her breaths in the stillness, both of them silent, until she said, 'Isn't there anything up here that we could use to prop open the door downstairs?'

310

He turned to look, but they were immediately put on edge by a noise further up in the house. A groan, and the sound of something heavy being moved, like loud scrapes on the floor.

'What was that?' she said, her voice a hoarse whisper.

'I don't know, but it was that way,' Sam said, and then set off again, his phone in one hand, the other feeling along the bannister. He was now facing towards the front of the house, and his phone caught the shadows of two doorframes, as if the middle flat had no front door, just rooms spread along the landing. He pushed at the first door, ready to shine his torch inside. It was locked.

'Mr Day?' he called again. Still silence.

His hand went around the bottom of the rail and looked upwards. He was at the foot of the stairs that rose to the top floor. They were narrower, steeper. He shone his phone upwards. There was movement. Or was it a shadow created by the beam from the phone?

His breaths were shorter, his stomach turning with nerves, the darkness amplifying his fear.

'I'm going up,' he said, his mouth dry as the words came out.

'I'm going to call this in,' Charlotte said. 'Something's going on here.'

Sam stepped forward as she backed away to make a call. He held his phone out in front of him. The way ahead went up to a glass door on a landing. It was dark behind it, because the glow from his phone reflected off the glass, turning the door into a white sheet. He started to think that perhaps Terry Day was out, and so all they'd heard were the creaks and groans of an old house. But then there was a click.

He pointed the phone forward, more direct, his arm outstretched, looking for the source of the noise. Charlotte was speaking on hers, asking for a uniformed patrol. He took another step upwards but then stopped. A dark shadow appeared behind the glass door.

Sam paused. There was another click, and then the door opened slowly, creaking. A figure stood in the doorway. A man, judging from his height, his hair tousled in silhouette, but he appeared slumped, his head hanging forwards.

'Mr Day?' Sam said, concerned now, no longer trying to alert him. He went up one more step.

There was a screech. The figure at the top of the stairs moved forwards quickly, but it was unnatural, the head still slumped, moving towards the top step as if he was running, except that his feet were dragging. There were noises of exertion and the figure kept on moving.

Sam tried to step backwards as the man seemed to take off from the top step, his arms flaccid, his head towards his chest, tumbling forwards. Sam put his arms up, but it wasn't enough.

His head hit Sam in his chest. He fell backwards, felt the rush of air as his feet lost contact with the stairs, everything happening too quickly. He braced himself for the landing, in that half a second knowing that it could end badly, the weight of someone on top of him, his body at the wrong angle, his head like a spear going towards the ground.

Sam's head hit the wall, and then his shoulder crunched. He gasped in pain but then was smothered as the falling man landed on him. There was wetness on him, sticky but cold. Sam's lungs were fighting to get his breath back, the person like a dead weight.

There was a noise from further above. The same screech he had heard before, except it was angrier this time, running down the stairs, feet moving quickly. Sam pushed at the body but it was too heavy. He heard Charlotte's voice, shouting. His phone had fallen onto the landing, the glow shining upwards. It caught the glint of metal. He tried to move away but was pinned beneath the weight. Another screech and then there was a downward slash. Sam felt heat across his arm, and then it felt like he had been punched in the side, his breath leaving him.

There was more noise. Charlotte shouting, moving quickly. Everything was just shadows. Footsteps on the landing. A struggle. Then there was a scream of pain, of fear, before it was cut short, replaced by a gasp, and then a cry.

Sam tried to make out what was happening but it was too dark. He saw someone falling towards him. In the light from his phone, he saw Charlotte's curls. She landed next to him, making a loud thump, heavy and lifeless. He reached out for Charlotte, to take her hand, to help her, but his hand touched her face. His hand went to her mouth, searching for the warmth of her breath on his fingers. It was faint but still there. His hand moved across her body; her shirt was wet with what he knew was blood.

He looked for his phone. It was just out of reach, further along the landing. He pulled himself out from under the body and pain shot from his shoulder, making him cry out. He collapsed back but he caught sight of Charlotte again and knew he had to keep going. He scrambled towards the phone once more, shards of agony making him gasp every time his right arm touched the floor.

Sam reached the phone. He dialled for an ambulance and then let himself sink to the floor, exhausted, his own view of the world getting fuzzy, his own shirt also wet. The floor seemed to welcome him, and he let reality slip away as he waited for the wail of the sirens.

Fifty-Nine

Joe had been driving back to his office when he got the call from Alice. He had been calling Sam but his phone had been switched off. When Alice told him that Sam had been stabbed, he turned round and raced to the hospital, cursing as he tried to find a place in the car park.

The hospital was like most, a large ugly block of brickwork and glass, blue signs and the hum of air-conditioning fans, although this was at the end of a quiet suburban road, as if it didn't want to let anyone know it was there. The paths around it were busy with nurses and doctors walking between units, along with patients displaying the reasons for their visits. A young man hobbled past on crutches, his foot in plaster. A man in his fifties was attached to an oxygen canister, with plastic tubes going into his nostrils, sitting in a wheelchair, smoking, the purple hue to his cheeks giving away the lie that giving up would help. His habit had already killed him. He was just waiting for the end.

Joe was running as he followed the signs for the A&E department and burst into a waiting room of bright blue carpet and magnolia walls, occupied by the wounded and worried relatives. He saw Alice standing by the wall, clutching a handkerchief, staring at the floor.

'Alice.'

She looked up and started to sob immediately, as if she had

314

been holding on for too long, just waiting for someone to be there so that she could let it all out. Joe put his arms around her, put his hand on her head as she burrowed herself into him. His shirt turned wet as she cried into him.

'What's happened?' he said, his stomach a violent churn of nerves and fear. 'How's Sam?'

She pulled away, wiping her face with the heel of her palm. 'I'm sorry,' she said. 'They said he's going to be all right, but I can't get near him. One of his colleagues was badly injured. A young woman. Stabbed in the chest. They were in a house. They were attacked. Sam was stabbed, but in the shoulder.' She shook her head slowly. 'That's all I know and they won't let me in.'

'They? Police or doctors?'

'Police. A doctor told me that they have treated him. They are just keeping him in a room.'

'Where is he?'

'Near ward six.'

Joe set off walking.

'They won't let you near him,' she shouted after him.

Joe didn't reply. Alice would have backed off when her way was barred. Joe wouldn't take a refusal.

He walked along the hospital corridors, following the numbers, skirting past porters pushing trolleys or patients in wheelchairs. Joe had a scowl on all the way. He hated hospitals. They were all about sickness and weakness. He knew one day it would come to him, but he couldn't face that day yet. Not until he had achieved what he had set out to do in life. Further along the corridor he saw a group of uniformed officers outside a room. It made Sam easy to find.

As he got closer one of them broke away from the group and walked towards him, his hand out. 'Go back. You're not allowed along here.'

'Is Sam Parker in there?' When the officer paused, Joe added, 'I'm his brother.'

315

'I don't care who you are. Go now.' The flat of the officer's hand struck Joe in the chest, rocking him back on his heels.

Joe felt the rush of blood to his head. His brain was telling him to walk, but the anger pumping round his system was telling him not to be pushed around. Before anything else could happen, a detective left the room, and as the door swung open, he saw Sam on the bed.

'Sam!' Joe shouted.

As the door swung closed, Joe said, 'That's my brother. He's a patient in a hospital and I'm going to see him.' He walked towards the door. The officer gripped his arm, his fingers tight around the bicep, but Joe was able to push at the door again.

Sam saw him and shouted out, 'It's all right, let him in.'

Joe shrugged off the arm as the grip slackened and then went inside.

The mood in the room was sombre. There were two detectives with Sam: the female detective he had met at court at the start of Ronnie's case, DI Evans, and a male detective who wore his anger in the tightness of his collar. Sam was sitting on the edge of the bed, shirtless, a large bandage around his chest and his right arm in a sling.

'I heard about the other detective,' Joe said. 'I hope she's all right. I hope you catch whoever did it.'

'So you can get the job of defending him?' the male detective said.

Joe didn't respond. It wasn't the time for the usual argument.

'How are you?' Joe said to Sam.

'Alive.' He looked towards the other two detectives. 'Can I talk to my brother? In private?'

They paused, exchanged glances, and then went towards the door.

'Don't discuss the case unless you've got something you want to share,' Evans said on the way out.

'He's my brother,' Joe said. 'It's not always about the job.'

At that they left the room, leaving Sam and Joe alone.

Sam grimaced as he tried to get comfortable. 'This is all a bit shitty,' he said, his pain evident from the way he gritted his teeth.

'Alice is outside. They wouldn't let her through.'

'Can you tell her I'm all right?'

'Where were you?'

'I was at Terry Day's house,' Sam said. 'You spoke to the prosecutor about Terry seeing Ronnie's girlfriend alive. We'd gone to take a statement after we left you.'

Joe closed his eyes and pinched his nose with his fingers. Sam didn't say anything until he opened his eyes again.

'Did Terry Day do this?' Joe said, and nodded towards the bandages.

'No. Terry is dead. Murdered. We must have got there just after he was killed. His body was thrown down the stairs at me.'

'His body? Jesus.' Joe shook his head and then said, 'Ronnie Bagley didn't want me to pursue what Terry reported, that he had seen Carrie.'

Sam looked confused. 'Why not?'

'I don't know. I couldn't work it out. I told him about what Terry had said, and he became angry, didn't want it coming out.'

'Where is he?'

'I don't know. I've just been to his mother's house and she told me something that might link in to Ben Grant.'

'What?'

'You said that Ben Grant boasted about killing his sister, but it turned out he never had a sister.'

'That's right.'

'Well, Ronnie had a sister who died when she was younger.'

'How?'

'Slipped and fell in the bath.'

Sam's eyes widened. 'Shit,' he said to himself, looking down.

'Is that important?'

'Yes, very.' Sam looked at Joe. 'You know I'll pass this on, because if Ronnie had anything to do with this, I won't protect you.'

'I'm fine about that.'

'But I thought you protected people like him.'

'If Ronnie had anything to do with what happened to you, tell whoever you like.'

'Why the change?'

'You didn't come to my apartment the other night to save a life or anything honourable. It was just a cheap trick, and you know it, expecting me to blurt out what I knew, just because you were my brother. But you were doing it for the wrong reason, because it was just about using me.'

Sam didn't say anything so Joe went to sit on the bed.

'This makes it different,' Joe said, and pointed towards the bandages. 'You joined the police because of what happened to Ellie. I know that, because you've said it often enough.'

'And you went your way, I know.'

'You think I betrayed Ellie?'

Sam stayed silent.

Joe put his head down and closed his eyes. Now was the time, he knew that. What had happened to Sam had some connection to his own case, and a detective was badly injured. Sam had to know.

Joe thought about how he could broach it, the secret he had kept for fifteen years. It had driven him for all those years, and he wondered whether it would drive him less if he shared it. But it wasn't the time for self-doubt. It was the time to share.

He looked up and took a deep breath. 'I became a lawyer for the same reason you became a policeman – because of Ellie.'

'I don't understand.'

'I'm going to tell you something now that I've never told anyone before. You might not like it.'

'Go on.' Sam's voice was quieter now.

Joe swallowed and wished he hadn't started, because now there was no turning back.

'The man who killed Ellie,' Joe begun. 'I saw him, not long before it happened.'

'What do you mean?'

Joe paused as he thought about that day.

'I'd been walking home from school,' Joe said. All the sounds seemed to get sucked out of the room as he spoke, his voice the only noise. 'I wasn't far behind Ellie. She had her headphones on so I couldn't shout to her, but why would I want to anyway? Who wants to walk home with his annoying little sister? I saw her turn into the path, through the woods. There had been someone hanging around near the end, just further along the road. I don't think Ellie saw him, because she was looking down, her head nodding with the music. I knew there was something about him that wasn't right because he was just loitering, as if he was waiting for someone.'

'What did this person do?'

'He followed Ellie. He put his hood up and walked down the path, not long after Ellie had turned down it. I wanted to shout out, because I knew it wasn't right, but I didn't. I was scared, because what if I'd been wrong? Why should anything happen to Ellie? It was just another walk home from school.'

'Shit,' Sam said in a whisper.

'Yeah, shit.'

'Why didn't you say anything?' Sam said.

'Because I was scared. What would people say if they knew I could have stopped it? You can't even think about the guilt I felt. Still feel. It gnaws away at me every day, the desire to just go back and make it different, to shout out, to stop him. Ellie would be alive. Everything would be different. Maybe even

Dad would be alive, because our lives would have been different.'

There was no sound from Sam. It was as if everything had stopped. There was no longer the hum of the equipment in the room, or the occasional click of the radiator. Even Sam's gasps of pain had stopped.

Finally, Sam said, 'But why did what happened to Ellie make you become a lawyer? I don't understand.'

'I see his face every day, in here.' Joe tapped the side of his head. 'I became a defence lawyer because I thought it was one way I might see him again. Because that's what I do every day of my life. I look for him. Every time I walk into a police station to see a client, I hope it's going to be him. If I'm ever in court and a sex attacker is there, I make sure I hang around to see who it is. I call round the police stations every morning and scour the internet for news stories, always looking for his face.'

'Very noble,' Sam said. 'And what are you going to do if you see him?'

'Simple,' Joe said. 'I'm going to kill him.'

Sixty

Alice was quiet all the way home, Joe driving, the daisy chain of streetlights painting moving stripes on her face as they got nearer to her house.

'He'll be all right, you know,' Joe said. Alice turned to look at him, and he saw tears on her face. 'He'll be fine. He's made of tough stuff.'

Alice shook her head. 'No, he's not. He's just had some tough stuff to deal with. That's different.'

She turned to look out of the window again, so Joe let her hide away in her thoughts. He wanted to say that Sam was his brother, that they had a bond, blood and family, but he knew that he'd given up the right to have any kind of say when Alice walked down the aisle to Sam on their wedding day. Joe hadn't even been chosen as the best man. That honour went to a school friend who had hardly been near Sam since the wedding, apart from the occasional Christmas card. The resentment over how he had dealt with Ellie's murder was palpable even back then.

As Joe pulled up outside their house, he expected Alice to head inside alone, but she seemed reluctant. Eventually she said, 'Come inside, if you want. I don't want to be on my own just yet.'

Joe turned off the engine and followed Alice into the house, her steps slow, her shoulders slumped. It was quiet inside. She must have realised what he was thinking, because she said, 'Emily and Amy are with my parents,' before going to the fridge and pulling out a beer. She passed it to Joe, who raised it in thanks, and then she reached for a bottle of wine that was in the door pocket. It was a screw top, and as he took a sip of the beer, she poured her drink into a glass. Her hand shook and then she drank it like she needed it.

'The girls will be back soon,' she said. 'I don't know what to tell them.'

Joe knew what she meant, that the other detective's brush with death had already made it onto the news bulletin, although she hadn't been named. Any story about Sam being a hero would satisfy them for the moment, but as they got older, the memories of Sam being injured would come back to them during the night and remind them that their father had a dangerous job.

'I'm afraid I can't help you,' Joe said. 'I've opted out of parenting so far. I'm sure you'll do the right thing, though.'

Alice looked up at him, and Joe saw for the first time that it was more than shock that was making her quiet. There was fear there too. Her eyebrows were pinched together and her breathing was fast. This was the first time that tragedy had almost visited her family, and Joe saw how it had made her realise what he and Sam had discovered fifteen years earlier, that what feels safe and secure can be ripped apart in an instant.

She sat down and drank from her glass, before saying, 'He'll blame himself.'

'I know. It's human nature.'

'No, it's more than that. He'll believe it's his fault, because he cares too much. I've tried to tell him that it's just a job, that coming home to us should be the important thing, but he doesn't listen. When a case goes wrong, I watch him as he retreats into himself, often for days at a time, as if he's waiting for someone to say that it was all his fault. He can't just shrug

322

it off like most of them seem to be able to do. It's like a mission for him, that no one must get away with anything. Have you ever heard anything like that?'

Joe closed his eyes. He knew all of this. He'd grown up with Sam.

'I tell him he's being stupid,' Alice said, wiping a tear from her eye. 'The thing is, he knows that he is, and it isn't logical, because it is just a job, but his failures gnaw away at him. This will be hard for him to control.'

'His intensity is part of him,' Joe said. 'And he joined the police for emotional reasons, you know that, to atone for Ellie.'

'I just wish he could be different,' she said, taking another drink. 'I can cope with the little things, like the long silences, but they just get longer each time. And then when the silences end, it's just draining to listen to him, because every failing is a symptom of a bigger problem. Like if he goes to the shop and forgets something, it's because he's working too hard or not coping, and not just because he forgot something, like we all do. He'll be impossible now, and I don't think I can take it.'

'Just be there for him,' Joe said.

'And you? No, you'll go, because that's what you do. You just live your life and it seems like no one else matters. Sam can live his life and it will be up to me to pick everything up for him. But what about me? Who looks after me?'

Joe put the beer on the side. He didn't want this argument. Perhaps Alice was right. He knew he was about to walk out on her, but the realisation of her truth wasn't enough to make him want to stay.

'Tell Sam to call me when he's home,' he said, and went towards the door. Then he stopped. He was running away. He turned round. 'Sam isn't the only person who will have things to deal with.'

Alice looked up, her cheeks streaked with tears. 'What do you mean?'

'He was chasing a case of mine. Ronnie Bagley. He went to that house because of something I told the prosecutor, about how the occupant of that house, Terry Day, could help my client. It was just a case, and there will be plenty more, but I almost lost a brother because of it. Terry Day is dead because of it, and a young woman might still lose her life. All from information I didn't have to pass on. So tell me now how I'm able to just walk away, because what if I can't? There'll be no one like you to catch me. So don't make assumptions about me.'

Alice looked into her glass, hurt, angry.

The ring of Joe's phone broke the silence. He turned away to answer it. It was his mother.

'Joe, you need to come home.' She was crying, on the verge of hysteria.

'If it's about Sam, he's fine. He's with his seniors now.'

'No, it's not about Sam. It's Ruby.'

Joe shivered. Alice must have sensed his reaction because she looked up, her mouth open.

'What's going on?' he said.

There was a pause, and when she spoke again, Joe felt the years roll back, to the desperation of fifteen years earlier.

'It's Ruby,' she repeated, and then a sob. 'She hasn't come home.'

Sixty-One

Sam winced as he was shown into the Incident Room, the door banging on his shoulder.

'You could open it for me,' he said, scowling at Ged, who had simply barged through.

DI Evans directed him to a seat in the corner, out of view of the windows. As Sam eased himself into it, grimacing, she said, 'You need to tell us what happened.'

She pulled out a blank police statement from one of the drawers and put it on the desk. She didn't have a pen. Sam knew that she would want to know what he had to say before she committed it to paper.

Sam looked down at the page. 'Shouldn't we be looking for Ronnie Bagley?' he said. 'Why is this so important now? Or is this just about getting a version of events we will present to the world?'

'What do you mean?'

'I'm new to this squad but I've been around. I know how it works. You sent us to that house, and so you want to know whether you're at fault, because all we do is try to deflect the blame in this job. Well, I'm only going to tell it one way, and that's the truth. If you don't like that, I'm not in the mood for changing my mind.'

Evans looked at Ged and then sighed. 'We are looking for Ronnie, but we almost lost one of our team tonight. We might still lose her. Right now, we want to know why. So tell us, so we can catch whoever did this. That is as simple as it gets.'

Sam put his head down. He didn't want to do this. He wanted to go home to Alice and Amy and Emily, take some painkillers and feel sorry for himself. Pain was shooting down his arm and he felt tired, but he knew that Evans was playing it like a copper, and he was expected to fall into line. The one thing he had learned quickly after joining the police was that they exist in ranks, all together, and so if one gets hurt, they all feel it. He focused on Charlotte, and he remembered her groans of pain, how she had been scared as he held her, wondering if she was going to die.

'Like we told you, we were following a trail, a photograph,' Sam said. 'We went to all the families of the missing girls, because there was a picture next to Julie McGovern's computer. A young man. There was something about the picture that troubled me, except I couldn't think what it was. So we touted the picture around to see if I was right, and we got a hit. It was a fake, a groomer's front, used by Ronnie Bagley to contact at least two of our victims. But it was something else that bothered me about it, and I still can't think what it was, because I knew it wasn't right before we discovered the link with Ronnie Bagley.'

'And where did you say you discovered the link?'

'Gilly Henderson, the barrister's daughter. I spoke to her sister, Rachel, and she recognised him, told me how he had tried to befriend her, but she knocked him back. Gilly must have been less choosy.'

'We can't find Ronnie Bagley,' Evans said. 'We are looking but we're coming up with nothing.'

'I think he was Grant's accomplice,' Sam said. 'Grant was taunting us, because he was describing Ronnie Bagley, not himself. It was Ronnie's sister who died in the bath, not Grant's. It's Ronnie Bagley with the hair fetish, not Grant.' Sam grimaced. 'This might all be my fault.'

Ged shook his head on the other side of the room and muttered in agreement.

'How the hell can it be your fault?' Evans said, flashing Ged a glare.

'Because Grant said that he had been betrayed, and when I arrested him, he might have had someone with him, like an accomplice, and I've never said anything.'

Evans looked surprised. 'When did you know this?'

'I never really knew. I was just never sure. It's something I've thought about through the years, because I've always had this worry that I'd missed something back then. Ben Grant didn't try to run or fight. He went to his knees and let me arrest him. I kept my whole attention on him all the time, and so I don't know if there was someone else there, in the bushes, because I was watching him, no one else. And when we visited Ben Grant, he taunted us, told us how he killed his sister, and that he had some obsession with hair, but he was really talking about Ronnie Bagley. And then he said something that struck me as strange.'

'Does this have a point?' Ged asked.

'I don't know, and that's the whole point,' Sam said, getting tetchy. 'Ben Grant was trying to tell me something, I could tell, but it was all wrapped up in cryptic messages and a life story, but then today, he was more direct. He said he was betrayed, and told us how the real thrill was getting someone else involved. He used a phrase, said that the newly converted are often the most enthusiastic.'

'Is that it?'

'Yes, but what do you think he meant by that? I'll tell you. An accomplice. And you know what, I can't rule it out. Which means that if there's an accomplice behind all of this, then it is my fault for not being sure enough back then. Instead, all I had was a nagging doubt. Nothing I knew or could pinpoint, just a doubt. So that is the point.' He sat back in his chair, deflated.

'But it was Carrie who was Grant's friend, not Bagley,' Evans said.

'Carrie was drawn to Grant,' Sam said. 'Was Carrie drawn to Ronnie for the same reason as she was drawn to Grant? Was he the next best thing? But was she about to expose him? Is that why she died? It's one thing lusting after some warped dream, but not quite the same when your partner comes home with blood on his hands. It makes it too close, too real.'

'If we are sure Carrie is dead,' Evans said. 'Terry Day didn't think so.' She sighed. 'This is a real mess.'

When no one tried to argue, she took a pen from her pocket and said, 'Take me back to Terry Day's house. I want to know what happened.'

And so Sam told her. About them walking into the hallway and finding it in darkness. The noises, some sense that they were not alone. The slow creep upstairs, and then Terry Day appearing at the top of the stairs, before his body was thrown towards them.

Evans tapped her pen on the blank statement, still nothing written down. 'So if Ronnie Bagley is the link, was it Ronnie Bagley who attacked you?'

Sam didn't respond at first, as if he was thinking about it, and then shook his head. 'No.'

'How do you know? Have you met Ronnie Bagley?'

Again, another pause, and then Sam sat up straight, his eyes wide, wincing as his shoulder reminded him of his injury. 'No,' he said. 'I haven't met him, but I know it wasn't him.'

'How?'

Sam's mind flashed back to the dark landing. The crumple of Terry's body down the stairs, slow and heavy, and then the faster movement behind. The attacker was skinny and light, but fast and strong. And there was a smell, light and fragrant, like flowers, but musky. It was perfume. The shoulders were slender, and the jawline, visible in silhouette, just flashes against the glow from the phones, was delicate, fragile.

'It wasn't Ronnie Bagley who attacked us,' Sam said. 'Because whoever attacked Charlotte wasn't a *him*. It was a *her*.'

Sixty-Two

Joe ran to his mother's house without locking his car. The street was quiet, just the vague outlines of some kids hovering at the end of the street, and his mother spotlit on her step, a lone sentry, clutching a tissue.

'Joe, you're here,' she said as he got closer. She looked like she wanted to be hugged, looking up at him, expectant, but Joe bristled. He hadn't hugged his mother since that afternoon when Ellie was murdered.

'Talk to me, what's happened?' he said as he went inside, his mother behind him, shuffling slowly. He could smell the booze on her.

'She didn't come home from school,' she said, tears coming now. There was a slur to her voice. He checked his watch. Nine o'clock. It was around the time the day got blurred for her.

'Are you sure you haven't just forgotten something, that she told you she was going to a friend's house?'

'Why would I forget?'

Joe marched through to the kitchen and picked up the bottle of vodka. It was a small one, as if it was some kind of disguise, hiding the problem, because Joe knew there would be more small bottles in other cupboards. 'This?'

'Don't shout at me, Joe,' she said, and then turned away to sit down on a chair in the other room. Her head went into her hands, and Joe felt the hot stab of guilt.

But he didn't apologise. Instead he ran upstairs, into Ruby's room.

It had been a while since he was last in there – he left the whole family thing to Sam – and her room was more grown up than he remembered. There were hair products lying on their sides on the floor, and her clothes spilled out of drawers. Joe noticed a cigarette lighter on a desk by the window. He rummaged for cigarette papers with strips torn from the boxes, to be used as roaches for joints, a hint of drug problems, but there weren't any. At least she had avoided that route so far.

There were pictures of film stars around the walls, although Ruby went for the old ones. A young Marlon Brando on a bike, James Dean leaning against a barn. Just nostalgic cliché shots. He turned on her computer and, as he waited for it to boot up, he looked around the room. It seemed like he didn't really know her, as if she had grown up without him noticing. He realised that he didn't know anything about her. Where she went. Who her friends were.

He went to the stairs and shouted down, 'What time does she normally get in?'

A pause, and then a tear-filled shout of, 'Depends. Sometimes after six. But never this late.'

'And where does she go?'

'Just to see school friends. She doesn't really say.'

Joe clenched his jaw and went back to Ruby's room. How had they come to this? Some pretence of family life, with birthday cakes and collective mourning, when in reality it was broken, so that everyone just lived in their own bubble.

The computer had finished its whirr and chatter and so Joe went to the internet. He went to her browser history and saw the entry for her social networking site. He clicked on it and let it load.

Pictures of Ruby flashed onto the screen and he saw a girl he hardly recognised. Flirtatious, grown up. He went to the messages, looking for something that would give him a hint. It was worse than that. There were messages asking where she had gone, because her friends hadn't heard from her that evening. It was Thursday night, the build up to the weekend.

Joe typed some responses, explaining who he was, and wanting to know if anyone knew if she had anything planned. He paced the room for a few minutes until he saw the screen change. There had been a reply from one of her friends. No. Evythg ok?

He rubbed his face with his hand. He realised then that everything really wasn't okay.

Joe looked around again, for any hint that made it more sinister. Her phone wasn't there, so he guessed she had planned to be out, but then she had been to school, so perhaps she always had it with her.

He saw a photograph on the small dresser near her bed, propped up against her radio-alarm. A young man, a teenager, good-looking.

He went to the stairs again. 'Does Ruby have a boyfriend?'

A pause, and then, 'She hasn't said anything.'

'Okay,' he said, and then went back into her bedroom. He went to Ruby's list of friends, looking for the person in the photograph. He scrolled down her list, wondering how she could know so many people, until near the bottom, he found him.

Joe clicked on his profile. It was the same picture. He looked at his page, and it struck him that there were only a small number of friends. Seven. He knew how the networking sites worked, that once you started, people dragged you in, and soon your page was filled by people you hardly knew. Friends of friends of friends.

He scanned the personal information. Billy Bridge. Likes football and music and fun. Doesn't like authority and being told what to do. Just a normal young man.

Except he didn't seem like a normal young man. There was something not right about it. There were no posts on his personal page, hardly any friends, and no real information.

He tried calling Sam. He had been with Ruby the night before, when he thought she was being followed. It rang out. When it went to voicemail, he left a message. 'Sam, it's me. Call me. It's urgent. We don't know where Ruby is.'

When he clicked off and the room returned to silence, he felt the darkness descend, and the memory of that day fifteen years earlier rushed at him once more.

Sixty-Three

Sam couldn't see Alice as he walked up the path to his front door. The drive was empty, his car still near Terry Day's house, where he and Charlotte had left it.

He went into the kitchen and saw a beer bottle on the side, only half-drunk. He opened the fridge. The wine had been opened, although he couldn't see the glass.

Sam looked for a glass for himself, and as he poured himself a drink, he heard footsteps on the stairs.

Alice walked in, her glass in her hand, and Sam saw that she had been crying. 'Are you all right?' he said.

She came towards him, and so he held out his good arm, the hand holding the glass. 'No hugs, please,' he said, grimacing.

She took his hand and kissed it instead. 'The girls are at my parents' tonight. I don't want them to see you like this.'

'It won't have gone by tomorrow so they'll have to get used to it.'

'It's not just that, because I can't protect them from what might happen to you.'

'What do you mean?'

'I used to worry about you when you were patrolling. But then you were doing the financial cases and so it seemed safe. You're doing this now and so I'll go back to wondering whether I'll get a phone call one night to say that you're never

334

coming home. People die doing your job. I can't cope with that thought.'

'It's what I am,' he said. 'I can't change that.'

Alice went to the fridge to refill her glass, then stared into her wine for a few seconds before saying, 'So it was a false alarm about Ruby?'

Sam faltered as he raised his glass. 'What do you mean?'

'Well, you're here, so it must be all right.'

'What are you talking about?' He put the glass down.

'Ruby,' she said. 'Joe was trying to call you.'

Sam was confused, but then he remembered. 'I turned my phone off when I went into hospital.' He reached into his pocket and pulled it out, turning it on.

'So you don't know?' Alice said, and as Sam shook his head, she put her hand to her mouth.

His phone buzzed. Voicemail. He listened. It was Joe. He didn't call often. Then what he said made his hand tremble.

'Sam, it's me. Call me. It's urgent. We don't know where Ruby is.'

He clicked off his phone and headed back out into the night.

Ruby looked over at the man in the driver's seat. Billy's dad, so he said. She didn't like the way he kept leering at her, looking at her hair, then at her legs. She wished she'd worn trousers.

'Where is Billy?' she said. She knew she sounded sulky, but they had been waiting a long time, the delay broken only by a fast food meal.

He glanced over. She drew her knees together and folded her arms. He made her uncomfortable. Her fingers played with the door handle, but it was locked. He must have heard her do it because he said, 'He won't be long. His gym class must have overrun.' He smiled. 'He'll make it up to you.'

She didn't believe him anymore. Something wasn't right. She was in the middle of Manchester to meet someone she had only ever talked to on the computer, and it was getting dark.

But she was being paranoid. She had seen Billy's pictures, his history. No, everything was all right. Billy just needed to get there.

It wasn't a nice place to sit though. The van smelled of old cigarettes and sweat. Billy's dad was smoking again. She wanted to open her window to let some air in, but he had refused when she'd asked. So she had to put up with the smell of his cigarettes seeping into her clothes and hair.

She glanced across. He looked dirty. His eyes looked tired, surrounded by dark rings. He had strange markings on his hand, like small lines tattooed at the end of his thumb. Six of them.

The thought of Billy kept her there though. They had shared so much. Her secrets, her thoughts, her desires, and he had shared his own. They had been building to this, she knew that, although it had come quicker than she expected. She was excited but nervous, impatient and restless. She didn't want to leave the van. It looked threatening outside, with the orange streetlights lighting the shiny redbrick of the viaduct arches, just the occasional rumble from the railway lines to break the gloom.

Billy's dad craned forward. There was someone ahead, moving quickly. 'Almost here,' he said.

Ruby leaned forward too, closer to the windscreen, relieved now. She almost laughed. She had never met Billy. They had shared internet chats, but never face to face, and so her nervousness turned into excitement, that at last she would meet him.

She could see someone ahead, but he seemed smaller than she expected, his hood up, face hidden, the sleeves too long, so that she couldn't see his face or the broad width of his shoulders.

Billy's dad flashed his headlights. He seemed more excited now, smiling and nodding.

'Who is it?' Ruby said. 'Is that Billy?'

As the figure reached the van, he wound down the window. 'Get in the back.'

Ruby craned her neck to get a view, but whoever it was moved too quickly. The back doors opened and there was a clattering noise.

'Billy?' she said, turning, grinning, excited. 'It's me, Ruby.'

Then Ruby gasped as an arm clamped around her neck. She let out a whimper. 'I'm not Billy, little darling.'

It was a woman's voice.

Ruby struggled, kicking out, crying, her feet hitting the glove compartment, scuffing the dull grey plastic.

There was a glint of metal and then she felt the tip of a knife blade pressed against her neck, just below her ear, pushing into her skin so that it puckered under the point.

'If I cut you there, you will die straight away,' the woman said. 'Do you want that?'

Ruby stopped moving and swallowed. 'I'm scared,' she said. 'I don't understand. Where's Billy?'

'You don't need to understand. This is it. Perhaps the end. It all turns on your brother now. Does he love you enough?'

'My brother? What do you mean?'

'Sam. He's the one I want. For now, you come with us. Will you do that? Will you come quietly and survive? Because if you struggle, I will kill you. You won't be the first.'

Ruby took deep breaths as tears welled in her eyes. She thought of Sam. He would be angry with her. She should have listened. She'd got herself in danger and it was all her fault. Now he was in danger.

'You're not Billy's dad, are you?' Ruby said.

The man laughed. The woman pressed the knife harder.

The man got out of the van and ran round to the passenger

side. When he opened the door, he grabbed Ruby round the neck and pulled her upwards, out of the van. She shrieked but the noise was cut short as she was propelled quickly along the pavement, her feet making soft skipping noises on the floor.

The street they were in got darker the further they went, the streetlights broken. She tried to struggle against him but he was too strong. The woman was behind him.

They arrived at some old metal gates, blocked off by steel plates and with razor wire along the top. They couldn't go any further. She might be able to run, but then he kicked at some corrugated iron next to it and a gap appeared, like a dark gash, just blackness beyond.

'Go in,' he said, and he pushed her hard through the small gap. Her leg caught on something sharp and she cried out, but he didn't stop. Soon they were on the other side and she was being pushed through nettles and grass, stumbling over mounds of rubble, towards a corner where no light reached.

The woman pulled out a telephone and pointed it at Ruby, the flash of the camera making Ruby blink. As she looked at the picture, she said, 'Take her inside. I've got a call to make.'

There was another screech of metal and the dark block of light yielded to a blue glow and the sheen of tiled stairs.

'Keep going,' the man said.

Ruby pulled away from him. 'No, I won't!' But then she was struck by something. Her head hurt and she started to fall. When she hit the ground, the noises were fainter, and as she looked upwards, she could see the stars and the gleam of the moon, much brighter than the shadows and rubble of where she had been taken.

As hands grabbed her again, hard and calloused, she said sorry. To her mother, to her father, the man she had never really known, and to her two brothers, who did their best for her. She had got it wrong and spoiled everything.

As she was taken inside wherever she was, the metal sheet was pushed back into place, and all Ruby saw was darkness.

Sixty-Four

Joe looked up at the sound of a car outside. He went to the window. A taxi, and Sam.

Sam burst into the house, despite his bandages. 'Tell me what you know,' he said, the worry clear on his face.

'Ruby hasn't come home.'

'Have you called the cops?'

Joe shook his head. 'Not yet. This is Ruby we're talking about. I'm just trying to work it all out, so we can convince whoever that it's not just some silly teenager out too late.'

'You think this is attention-seeking?' Sam said.

'Call it what you like.'

'Have you called all her friends?'

'All the ones we know about, but Mum says she doesn't bring many back here.' Joe stepped aside as Sam went past. 'There's no special skill in trying to find her, Sam. I've done all the things you would have done.'

'So where is she?'

'I don't know. I've been for a drive round the usual places. The shops. The community centre. Plenty of kids hanging around, but no Ruby.'

Sam stayed silent for a moment, his tension visible from the clench of his jaw. 'This might be more than attention-seeking,' he said eventually. 'She was followed, you know that.'

'Ruby said she was. That isn't the same as being followed.'

'There was someone in the trees.'

'Or perhaps it was someone running away because you were charging after them?'

Sam didn't respond to that.

'I've gone through her online accounts, her emails, and there's nothing that suggests she's about to do anything stupid,' Joe said. 'Is this another go at us? So soon after it was all about Ellie, and you know how she gets around the anniversary, because it isn't about her anymore. She knows girls are going missing. She might be deliberately making us worry, and she'll come home and be pleased to see us here, her big brothers making her the centre of everything again. How can I ring the police with that possibility?'

'Because there have been teenage girls going missing for a while now, all connected to Ben Grant's case,' Sam said, getting angry. 'That makes Ruby's whereabouts pretty damn important. And where's Ronnie?'

'I don't know,' Joe said. 'I've been looking for him, because our trainee hasn't turned in today and he hinted that he knew something. He said something else too, that I was supposed to stop him.'

Sam pursed his lips, and Joe could see he was deciding how far he could go.

'If Ruby is at risk, we share,' Joe said.

'I think Ronnie might have been Ben Grant's accomplice,' Sam said.

Joe was surprised. 'Ronnie Bagley?'

'Grant talked about a hair fetish. It wasn't his thing, but we think he was taunting us, giving Ronnie away without actually naming him.'

'Ruby might have a boyfriend,' Joe said. 'She could be there.'

'Do you know that?'

'No, I don't. I just saw a picture in her bedroom, propped up against her alarm.'

Sam rushed out of the room, and so Joe followed him, running up the stairs.

As Joe ran into Ruby's room, Sam was holding the photograph. A good-looking teenager, clean-cut, sitting on his bed, posters around his walls.

'Yes, that's it,' Joe said. 'Who is it?'

Sam swallowed. 'It's not who it is. It's what it is.'

'I don't understand.'

Sam took a deep breath. 'This is Ronnie's grooming picture. All of those missing girls – unconnected, apart from the link to Grant's case, and this picture.'

'Oh, fuck,' Joe said. 'Call the cops. Do what you have to do.'

Sam pulled out his phone, but as he did so, it started to ring. He clicked to answer. Joe watched as he listened, Sam's eyes growing wider.

'Who are you?' Sam said, anger in his voice.

Joe watched as Sam listened, sweat prickling his forehead, until he moved his phone from his ear and stared at it, disbelief in his eyes.

'What is it?' Joe said.

Sam looked up. There were tears brimming over his eyelids, but they were of anger, real rage, not sadness.

'They've got her,' he said.

Sixty-Five

Ruby was dragged up some stairs. She'd heard the conversation on the phone, knew that the woman had called Sam, because she'd said his name. So she pulled back, crying now, desperate, but she was hit again, a punch this time, hard on her arm. She wailed out loud. It was an adult punch, harder than she had ever felt, and she began to succumb to the pain.

She couldn't see where she was going. It was dark ahead, lit only by the flash of a torch, the beam bouncing off dirty white tiles, ferns and moss growing through the cracks. Her feet tripped, but her movement was upwards, and she was carried forward by the two people who held her.

They emerged from the stairs into a huge open space broken by pillars, like a large empty factory, except that there was a large gash in the centre of the concrete floor, filled by undergrowth. She looked up. The roof was smashed and broken, the stars visible. There was a flap of wings and something swooped from one rafter to another.

'Where are we?' she said.

'Would it make a difference if I told you?' the woman said.

Ruby didn't answer that.

She was pushed against a metal pillar and her hands were pulled behind her back and tied together with a scarf produced from the woman's pocket.

'Don't think about running,' the woman said. 'I'll run faster than you and kill you when I catch you.'

Ruby nodded, sobbing softly, and then slid slowly downwards so that she was sitting on the floor. She put her head back, the iron cold and hard. As she looked along the length of the building, she saw lights beyond, one end of the building completely open. She listened. She could hear trains, as the steady roll of passenger carriages and the screech of wheels echoed along the vast empty space.

She tried to stay calm. She had to get a sense of her surroundings, because if she was going to get away, she needed to know where to go. The woman was pacing, her hood down, doing something with her phone, as if she was sending a message. Her hair was in a short dark bob, and she looked skinny, her jeans hanging slack on her legs.

The man turned to the woman and said, 'So, this is it. What happens afterwards?'

The woman paused. 'I go to Ben, to tell him.'

'But what about us? Ben will find out anyway. What about our future?'

'We're not doing it for us, you know that.'

'You promised that this would be it, no more.'

She stopped in front of him, her hands on her hips. 'You never quite got it, did you? This was never about you and me.'

'It was for me,' he said.

She shook her head. 'You're being pathetic.'

'You talked about deep love. Perhaps I have that, because it is why I do this. I don't do it for her.' He waved his hand towards Ruby. 'It's for us. This has got to be the end.'

The woman turned away and walked towards Ruby. She knelt down in front of her. She reached out and stroked the side of Ruby's cheek. Ruby flinched and pulled her head away.

'You know this is the end,' the woman said softly.

344

'No,' Ruby said, shaking her head. 'My brothers will hunt you down if you harm me.'

The woman smiled, pity in her eyes. 'They won't find me. And they might not find you.' She leaned forward and kissed Ruby on the forehead, like a sad goodbye. Then she reached in her pocket for a black cloth.

Ruby thrashed her head around as the woman applied the blindfold, but then her vision went dark as the cloth was pulled tight around her head. The woman's perfume filled her nostrils as she whispered in Ruby's ear, 'Darkness thrills, don't you think? You won't know where we will be, but we will be watching you. If you try to get away, it will mean the end of your life. Quick, painless, but you don't want that, do you? You choose life.'

Ruby swallowed and then nodded that she understood. The woman stepped away, her footsteps just light sweeps on the concrete floor. Ruby tried to hold back the fear. She wasn't going to be weak.

There were words spoken, just whispers that Ruby didn't catch, but then she recognised the skip of the woman's shoes down the stairs. They were lighter, more nimble, and the echo was familiar, enclosed, so that the noises bounced. Then there was the metallic scrape as the woman left the building.

She was alone with the man. This was her best chance to get away.

'What do you mean, they've got her?' Joe said.

Sam looked at his phone. 'Ruby. They've taken her.'

Joe couldn't speak.

'Does the name Monica mean anything?'

'Yes. She's the trainee I talked about, the one Ronnie hinted at.' Then Joe closed his eyes. 'We thought she was ill at first and just hadn't phoned in.'

'And now you think she's missing?'

'Yes.'

Sam closed his eyes and took some deep breaths. 'They said Ruby will go the same way as Monica.'

Sam's phone beeped. He looked down. It was a message. A picture message. When he opened it, he swayed, lightheaded, scared.

It was a picture of Ruby, being held, fear on her face. He showed it to Joe.

'Oh fuck, fuck, fuck,' Joe whispered. There were too many facts coming at him, swirling, making his head swim, sweat dampening his forehead. Images of Monica, a young professional starting out, merged with Ruby, all long legs and teenage nuisance. 'Who are they?'

'It was a woman on the phone,' Sam said. 'It was a woman at Terry's house, who did this.' He nodded at his arm. 'She mentioned it, said that it had been good to meet at Terry's house, except that it wasn't supposed to end like that, because this was the way. It's supposed to end with Ruby.'

'I don't understand.'

'It's revenge for Ben Grant. Whoever she is, she must be working with Ronnie.'

'Call the police now,' Joe demanded. When Sam stalled, Joe pulled out his own phone. 'I'll call them if you won't.'

Sam held out his hand. 'No, you can't.'

'Why not?'

'Because of the usual shit these types come out with, that if I do, they'll kill Ruby.'

Those words hit Joe like a punch in the stomach. He felt nauseous. 'So what do they want?'

Sam looked up, and there was something in his eyes that Joe couldn't fathom, some depth of emotion he hadn't reached since Ellie had died. Confusion, loyalty, determination, fear, all crammed into the small creases of tension at the corners of his eyes.

'They want me,' Sam said.

'You? What do you mean?'

'I've got to go to Piccadilly Gardens. If I do what they say, they'll let Ruby go. If I don't, they will kill her.'

'And what do they want you to do?'

Sam put his head down and ran his hands over it.

'Sam?'

When he looked up again, there were tears in his eyes.

'What do you have to do, Sam?'

'They want me to kill myself.'

Sixty-Six

Joe drove quickly to Gina's house, his jaw aching from constant clenching. He had dropped Sam off at a cab-rank, because a taxi would be able to use the bus lanes and cut through the city centre. Once the taxi had pulled away, he had called Gina to tell her that he was on the way. He hadn't told her anything, although he knew that the tone of his voice gave away the urgency. Every traffic light seemed to be against him, and the traffic queued.

His fingers drummed impatiently on the steering wheel. He looked along the line, and then behind, looking for a blue light or the bright battenburg markings of a police car. He couldn't see any. The drum of his fingers got faster and the clench in his stomach got tighter. The lights weren't letting many through. He couldn't wait any longer.

He swung out of the line, grimacing against the flash of lights as oncoming cars swerved to the side of the road to avoid him. The lights were on red as he approached them. He rushed through, ignoring the blare of a horn and the squeal of brakes. He had just one focus: get Ruby.

The traffic thinned as he got to Gina's house. He sounded the horn, two loud bursts. Gina left her house and ran down to the car. Joe set off before she had buckled herself in.

'What's going on?' she said, out of breath, still buttoning her coat.

'It's Ronnie. He's snatched Ruby.'

Gina turned towards him, confused. 'Ronnie Bagley? I don't understand.'

'I'm not sure I do, fully, but I'm starting to work it out.'

'You'll need to explain.'

So he did. About Ruby being followed the day before. About Sam's belief in an accomplice. About the attack on Sam's colleague when they followed up the information from Joe.

Gina shook her head. 'But if that was after school, Ronnie was with us yesterday, when someone tried to snatch her.'

'He's got someone with him, a woman,' Joe said.

'Hang on, the accomplice has got a new accomplice?' Gina said.

'It looks that way.'

Gina was silent for a moment, and then she said, 'So where are we going? And why do you need me?'

'They wanted Sam to go to Piccadilly Gardens. We have to go into the centre, so that we're nearby.'

'But you don't need me for that.'

Joe took a deep breath and fought back the prickle of tears. Stay in control, he told himself. 'I need you here in case Ruby, well, in case . . . ' He trailed off.

He felt Gina's hand go on his. 'I know,' she said, her voice softer. 'I'll always be here for you, Joe.' She raised his hand to her mouth and gave it a gentle kiss, supportive, friendly. It made him break out a small smile.

'I need you to call DI Evans,' Joe said, breathing out, blinking out the well of tears. He didn't cry, hadn't done since Ellie's murder, but he was struggling. The car lights in front of him blurred into red smears.

Gina took out her phone. 'Why, doesn't she know?'

'The caller told Sam not to tell her, and he's scared that he'll do the wrong thing and cause her to be killed. You'll know how to get through to the right people.'

Joe drove as Gina called the police, listened as she dredged up old contacts to make sure the case was given proper priority. When she hung up, he held out his hand for her phone.

She passed it over and said, 'Be careful, you're driving.'

He ignored her and dialled Sam's home number. Alice answered.

'It's Joe. You need to call Sam.'

'Why? What's wrong?'

'I just think he needs to hear your voice.'

Alice started to cry.

'Talk to him, Alice,' he said, and then hung up.

'What's he going to do, Joe?' Gina said.

'They said that they'll let Ruby go if Sam kills himself.'

Gina put her hand over her mouth. 'He's not going to, is he? I mean, that call, to his wife. You're worried.'

'Yes I am.'

As Gina took that in, Joe said, 'There is something else too. It's about Monica.'

Gina's hand dropped and her eyes widened.

'They say they've killed her.'

Gina let out a moan.

They both fell into silence as they got closer to the city centre. As Joe looked across at Gina, he saw the same resolve harden in her that had settled in him. They were going to do this.

Sam kept on looking at his watch as the taxi trundled into Manchester. It was too slow.

Sam closed his eyes and put his head back against the seat. The day was spinning out of control. He recalled his dash through the woods near Ruby's school, and then Charlotte. And now this, all because of an arrest he made eight years earlier, some chance discovery in a park. It should have ended then, but all of this because he missed something, the suspicion of an accomplice always haunting him. His secret, the one he refused to voice.

Why was it happening to him, after Ellie all those years before? It was so unjust. He clenched his hands around his knees. Was it because of the way he did things? Had he got something wrong, was it some kind of penance?

No, it wasn't that, because that was ridiculous, he knew it, the logical part of his brain knowing that things didn't happen for a reason, that they just happened. Except that it was a small voice that was always there, just whispers that told him that things would always go wrong for him.

Sam tried not to think of that. He had to stay focused instead on what lay ahead, to work out how he could get Ruby back. He put his hand over his face, and for a moment the greater blackness, the smothering feel of his palm, was comforting. But he knew it was just snatched respite, because as soon as he relaxed, an image of Ruby flashed into his mind. She was terrified, he knew that, and so all he could do was listen to what they had to say. Whatever Joe did, he would follow their direction. Until then, he was stuck with the deep rattle of the diesel engine as the taxi chugged into the city centre, the journey a constant stop and start through traffic lights.

Sam opened his eyes when he felt the rumble of the tram-lines under the wheels. He was close. He saw the driver glance at him in his mirror, so he looked out of the window. He didn't want any conversation. He preferred the high brick walls of the approach to Piccadilly station.

'Stop here, please,' Sam said, and handed over a note that more than covered the fare. He didn't hang around for the gratitude.

As he stepped out, he looked around. The movement of the city was ahead of him, and he paused for a moment, just to take a look, to see if there was anyone who stood out as different, some static presence in the fast flow of commuters and those who preferred to loiter on the edge of everything. It was dark and the area had become menacing. It wasn't the best part of the city during the day, but at night it seemed to be a stream of people all looking for someone to harm. Young men loitered in bubble jackets and those who were just passing through made their way quickly. He was only a few yards from the bridges under the tracks at Piccadilly, where young woman traded their bodies for a few pounds.

They had told him to go to Piccadilly Gardens, a mix of new stone and flowerbeds and fountains surrounded by shops and hotels and a small bus station. It had long been the meeting point for drunks and junkies and rent boys, but the gardens had been opened out to take away some of the threat.

Sam understood the routine. They wanted to make sure that he hadn't been followed, that he was alone. He didn't want to arrive there in a taxi, his presence heralded. He wanted to sneak in, to see whether anyone stood out, and so as he walked he looked into the eyes of everyone who passed him, looking for the twitch of recognition. Some people looked away. Some held his stare and turned to watch him walk on. Black cabs streamed through the traffic lights and double decker buses coughed diesel clouds.

It opened out as he got to the gardens, the name no longer fitting with the blend of new paving, the only greenery left just small patches of grass and flowers squeezed between the pathways to the glass shelters of the bus station, the traffic a constant clamour. He turned around as he got there, looking for someone watching, but it was impossible to know. He was overlooked by hotels and pubs and offices and shops. Whoever it was could be anywhere.

His phone rang. He snatched it from his pocket.

Sam looked around, trying to see who it might be. They must have seen him arrive. He was searching for the glow of a phone, or someone's hand to an ear. All he could see was the traffic and a stream of people. He pressed his phone to his ear to try to block out the noise.

'Hello?'

'You've arrived.' It was the woman's voice again.

'Where are you?' He was shouting.

'It doesn't matter where we are.'

Sam tried to work something out from her voice. It was almost impossible to hear her, but he wanted a hint about where she might be. He looked around for buses or a taxi, some noise that might appear in the background, just to give him a direction, perhaps shouting from a pub, but there was too much going on.

Then he heard something down the phone. A squeal, getting louder, and then the ding of a tram followed by the screech of the wheels. He turned, trying to spot it, but there were tram-lines from every direction.

'How do I know Ruby is still alive?' he said.

He had to wait before she answered, the tram drowning her out. 'You can take the gamble,' she said eventually. 'She's either alive or she isn't. Tell me though: which is the win? You dying and Ruby living, or you turning coward and burying another sister?' A laugh, mocking and harsh. 'So, are you ready to play?'

He heard the echo again. 'Play what?'

'Our little game of chicken.'

Sam closed his eyes. Adrenalin was coursing through him, making his mouth dry, his forehead damp. 'What do you want me to do?'

'You know already.'

'Kill myself?' A passing man in a suit gave Sam a strange glance as he said it so Sam turned away. 'I can't do that, you know that.'

'So this is the last thirty minutes of Ruby's life.' She sounded like she was running, her words coming in short bursts.

'What do you mean, thirty minutes?'

'That's always the game. Thirty minutes and then it's game over.'

The phone trembled in his hand. He felt the prickle of tears, but they were of anger, almost uncontrollable rage. He had to stay calm.

'So what do I do?' he said.

'You go to Piccadilly station, platform fourteen,' she said. 'You have to do just one simple thing: jump in front of a train.'

Sam shook his head. He couldn't do this. He turned quickly, looking for a hint. 'And you will release Ruby if I do?' he said.

'Yes.'

'How can I be sure you will?'

'You can't, but you can be certain you will hear her die if you don't.' A laugh, and then, 'You need to get moving. There aren't many trains, and thirty minutes is all you're allowed. That's always the game. And you're down to twenty-eight now.'

And then his phone went silent.

As he put it back into his pocket, his heart hammering, he saw a tram approach along the rails that came from Piccadilly station, brightly-lit green and white quivering its way towards him, rocking from side to side.

She had been calling from that way.

He started to run.

Sixty-Seven

Ruby knew that he was on his own. She could hear the pace of his feet, slow and regular, backwards and forwards, crunches on the concrete as loud echoes. It seemed like he was waiting for something. Or someone. The faster, more frantic shorter steps of the woman hadn't yet returned.

'Is she coming back?' Ruby said. She was shivering. It was getting cold and she was still wearing just her school uniform, her bare legs covered in goosebumps.

The pacing stopped.

'The woman,' Ruby said, her voice bolder. 'Why is she so cruel to me? You were nice until she arrived. I don't want her to come back.'

She heard the footsteps turn towards her. Slower, more deliberate. She pushed herself back against the pillar. She felt the vibrations of his feet as he stopped in front of her. She knew he was looking down at her.

There was the crack of bent knees and then she caught his aroma. Sweat and cigarettes. She grimaced as she felt the scrape of his finger along her cheek, and then shivered as he ran his hand through her hair. He breathed heavily through his nose.

'Why do you do it for her?' Ruby said, trying hard to keep the tremble from her voice. She wanted to get him on her side, because she had seen how he had changed when the woman arrived. He became more aggressive, following her lead. Ruby tried to hide her revulsion, she didn't want to make him angry, so she just swallowed hard and let him stroke her hair. Her eyes were closed, although they were still behind the blindfold. He was holding his breath as his fingers ran along the strands, separating them, the curl of his fingers brushing her neck.

'You haven't answered my question,' she said.

'It's love,' he said, his voice a whisper. 'You're too young to understand.'

'I do though. I know about love. That's why I was there, meeting you, because I loved Billy.'

'That was just a silly girl thing, and none of it was real.'

'Yeah, I know that now.'

He didn't respond.

'I'm cold,' she said, and then heard the sound of his jacket being unzipped. As he put it over her, like a blanket, she ignored the smell and savoured the warmth. As her legs tingled back to life, she realised it had another use. It concealed her hands.

Ruby tried to move her wrists until they found an edge on the pillar, the base rough and bubbled by rust. She moved her arms slowly, so that he couldn't see what she was doing.

'Will you take off my blindfold, please?' she said. 'If I'm talking to you, I want to see you.'

There was just silence.

'Please,' she said.

He knelt down again and she felt a pull on the knots. As the cloth was pushed up, everything loosened and the night came back into view, making her blink, despite the darkness.

He was on his haunches, saying nothing, just looking.

'Thank you,' she said, and tried to smile. 'So what do you mean about love?'

'It's about sacrifice,' he said. 'About doing something to let the other person go free. That's real love.'

'I don't understand.'

'I said you wouldn't.'

'So educate me,' Ruby said. 'What's your name?'

He paused for a few seconds, and then said, 'Ronnie.'

'And what is she called, the woman?'

He didn't answer for a few seconds, as if he was working out whether he should answer, but then he said, 'She's called Carrie. And over there is our baby, Grace.' He pointed towards the corner of the building.

'I can't see a baby.'

'She's asleep, wrapped up warm.'

'So Ronnie, what do you mean about sacrifice?'

He sat in front of her, cross-legged, and reached forward to touch her hair. Ruby fought the urge to pull away, and so instead she closed her eyes, tears brimming on her lashes, the smell of his hands in her nostrils, dirty and unwashed, as he stroked and caressed.

'I was going to go to prison for her,' he said softly. 'Men do that for Carrie. She's special.'

'What do you mean?'

He shook his head. 'It sounds stupid now, but we set it all up so that everyone would think I had killed her. We smeared some blood and then Carrie went away. I acted suspiciously, shouted things, did badly at work. We thought the police would come round sooner, that her family would call them, but she was seen by someone and so I handed myself in, told the police I'd killed her. I was going to go to prison so that Carrie could make a fresh start, go live somewhere else, but, well . . . ' He shrugged.

'That's extreme.'

'We had to do it that way.'

'So what went wrong?'

'I couldn't go through with it. I thought I could handle prison, but I couldn't. I got your brother to be my lawyer. He

357

would remember me, I thought, because he's helped me before. I know how it works with lawyers, that they all talk between themselves, and so the rumours go round and reach the police, and so the police would know that even my lawyer thought I was guilty, even if the jury freed me. All I would have to do was sit it out for six months and then I would be free. I'd be able to join Carrie again, and it wouldn't matter about the things we'd done, because everyone would think Carrie and Grace were dead, and that I'd got away with it. They'd stop looking for her. But everyone had to believe they were dead or it wouldn't work.'

'And the plan didn't work?'

'That was your brother's fault, Joe. He set me free. When they let me out, Carrie said we had to carry on, because it was a sign.'

'Carry on what?' Ruby said, her voice breaking. 'What had you been doing?'

Ronnie pulled his hand away from her and rubbed at the homemade tattoos on his hand. Six lines. He stood up and moved away.

'What are you going to do to me?' she said.

'It's not time yet,' he said. He swallowed, the clench of his jaw showing as a lump in his cheek.

'But why are you doing it for her?' Ruby said. 'If you don't want to do it, you look like a mug.'

He just stared, and for a moment Ruby thought she had gone too far. She braced herself for the blow, but then he smiled, almost regretful, and she felt her hopes rise that she was getting him on her side.

'Untie me, please,' she said. 'Let me go. I won't tell anyone. Come with me, if you want. I'll tell everyone how it was all her fault.'

'It's too late for that. I've told you everything, but it doesn't matter. This is the end for you.'

There was a clang from down the stairs, movement of the metal plate, and the fast steps of someone running upwards.

He quickly reached forward and pulled her blindfold back down. She was in darkness again.

The woman was back, Carrie, and she sounded out of breath and more excitable when she said, 'It's on. He's on his way there. This is it, Ronnie. The end.'

'What happens now?'

She laughed, high and wild. 'I go outside, because then I can see him do it. Sam Parker, dead. Think what Ben will say.'

Ruby put her head back against the pillar and her lips curled in distress as her tears started to soak the blindfold.

Sam was running but he wasn't dressed for a sprint. His tie flew over his shoulder and his suit jacket flapped backwards. His right arm was still strapped in the sling and the movement made him grimace with pain. But he had to keep going.

He faltered as he got to some traffic lights, his shoes slipping on the new stones. There was a bus turning to his right. He thought he could make it and so he made a quick dash, rushing into the road. He heard the judder of brakes and then a horn, but he didn't stop to apologise.

He looked down at his phone, glancing ahead to make sure he wasn't about to run into someone, slowing slightly to dial Joe's number. When he answered, Sam was panting. 'They're somewhere near Piccadilly.'

'Where? Do you know?'

'No, but whoever it was could see me in the gardens. They're close by.' Sam threaded his way through the crowds, ignoring the shouts and threats whenever he bumped a shoulder or knocked a bag.

'Are you sure?'

'She told me to go to the gardens. Now she's told me to go to Piccadilly. She knew when I was there. She will know when I'm at the station. She's close, I know it.'

'Is that where you're heading?'

'Yes. I'm going to get Ruby back. We've got less than half an hour now.'

'What do you mean?'

'She says that she'll kill Ruby after thirty minutes if I don't jump in front of a train.'

There was a pause, and for a moment all Sam could hear was the thump of his shoes on the pavement and the strain of his breath as he ran. Then Joe said, 'I've called Evans.'

Sam slowed to a halt, his chest pumping hard with exertion. 'I told you not to,' he said, panic in his voice.

'I can't let you do this. You can't sacrifice yourself.'

'Why not?'

'Because you've got a wife, and two beautiful girls. And think what it would do to Mum.'

'I've made my mark,' Sam said. 'I've created life, lived some good years. It ought to be Ruby's turn.'

'Bullshit, and you know it,' Joe said, getting angrier. 'They'll kill Ruby anyway. They want you dead. Why would they release Ruby?'

Sam didn't respond. He just stared at the crowds ahead of him, and the glass of Piccadilly station at the end of a slow rise past food shops and newsagents.

'How can we explain that to Mum?' Joe continued angrily. 'That she's about to lose a son, and probably a daughter? Stop and think, Sam. What would you do if it wasn't your sister?'

'I'd leave it to the police.'

'So why won't you?'

'Because I need to do something!' he shouted.

'But it doesn't have to be the only thing. You do what you need to do, Sam, but stay alive. You don't have to be a martyr for anyone. It won't change anything. I'm going to tell Evans where you'll be.'

Sam nodded slowly, taking deep breaths to maintain some semblance of control. 'All right, but I'm going to follow their instructions. I'll follow their trail and let you know where I end up.'

'I'm coming there myself. I've got to help you. Don't do as they ask, Sam. Don't do anything stupid. Wait for me.'

'There's no time to wait. I've wasted five minutes already,' and then he clicked off.

Sam tried for a sprint, his legs protesting as he ran, his lungs straining, his throat raw from panting hard breaths. It was hard up the slope, and he slowed down as he approached the station entrance, pausing with his free hand on his knee, leaning over, sucking in more air, sweat across his forehead. He glanced up. The station was busy, the bars, cafés and shops filled with people who had stretched their working day into a drink with friends. His eyes flitted from group to group, looking for the loner, the woman standing on her own, watching him. She would have just arrived, because she was somewhere quieter when she called. Or was it someone else who would be there, watching? He gritted his teeth in frustration. All he saw were bored commuters and some people who were starting to enjoy their drinks too much.

He rushed forward to the departures board. There was a train due at platform fourteen. It was in a separate part of the station, along one platform and up a level. He took a deep breath and broke into another run. He barged past people with shopping bags and briefcases, and someone spilled a coffee.

There was a ticket collector ahead, barring his way, a queue of people leading to him. Sam reached into his pocket for his police identification. He flashed his card and rushed past him, not waiting. A hard push sent him out of the way. There was a shout, and someone grabbed at his sleeve, but Sam yanked his good arm away and started running again. He expected to hear the sound of running feet, but instead he got the unmistakable beep and fizz of a walkie-talkie. He wouldn't be alone for long.

He ran onto the long moving pavement that crawled to the upper level, past the dead-end platforms lined with the red livery of the long-distance trains. There were shouts behind him, but Sam ignored them and kept on going to the bridge that would take him down to platform fourteen, weaving through commuters. He missed out steps as he skipped down the stairs, until he landed on the hard concrete of the platform. There was a train further down the track, rumbling towards Oxford Road. He'd missed one.

He sucked in air, his heart beating fast, sweat pouring down his face. He looked around. It was quiet. There was an old man sitting on a plastic seat, hunched up in an old coat, and three women with shopping bags chattering, glancing briefly as he stared at them.

Then his phone rang again. He looked at the number. Withheld.

'Yes?'

'You're there. Good.'

'Where are you?' he shouted, turning quickly. Then he realised.

He walked to the edge of the platform. It was for the through-trains and the station was above the rest of the city, feeding trains across Manchester on old brick viaducts. It was mostly dark ahead, the view towards where the bright lights of the city centre petered out. There were some offices and apartments and the high-rise of student flats, along with the stream of orange lights from a road that seemed empty apart from the flow of black cabs. There was no one walking, it wasn't that type of area. There were large patches of darkness, where derelict brickwork spoke of decay, spaces used for prostitution and drug dealing. This was why she had chosen this place. She could see him. But he would never see her.

'So what do I do?' he said.

She was moving again. 'Like I told you. When a train comes in, jump in front of it. Then Ruby goes home. Just twenty minutes now. Time is slipping by.'

'There has to be another way,' he said.

There was a noise in the background, some shuffling, and then, 'No, please, stop, don't hurt me. No, no, no,' and then a scream, a short burst, a lungful of terror and desperation, loud and shrill, and Sam could hear the tears in it, the fear, but it was cut short by a slap. It became muffled as something was pushed into her mouth, like screeches through cloth. He had recognised it though. It was unmistakable. It was Ruby.

Sam closed his eyes. He didn't want to think about what they were doing to her, of how damaged Ruby would be afterwards, if there was an afterwards for her.

'How can I trust you to let her go?' he said.

'You can't,' was the reply. 'But you can believe me when I say that I will kill her if you don't do as I say.'

Then the phone went silent. He looked at the handset, disbelieving, and then looked out over the city again. Where was she?

The three women had edged away from him and had stopped talking. When he looked at them, they turned away. Then he was distracted by the sound of heavy boots. As he looked round, he saw the bright green coats of cops.

Transport cops.

Sixty-Eight

'They're somewhere near Piccadilly,' Joe said, accelerating. 'We don't have much time.'

'What, he's seen them?' Gina said, surprised, wiping tears from her cheeks, the news about Monica hitting her hard.

'No, but they saw him in Piccadilly Gardens.' He got closer to the car in front, craning his neck, looking where he could overtake, but it was all traffic bollards and lights and further queues ahead. His knuckles were white from gripping the wheel, tight and throttling.

'Why Monica?' Gina said. 'What has she ever done to Ronnie Bagley?'

'I don't know,' Joe said, as he stared grimly out of the windscreen. 'I should have protected her.'

'You can't think like that. He was just a client.'

'Accused of murder. I should have been more vigilant. I should have remembered him. That's why he wanted me, because he had used me before, and it was a big thing to him, that I remembered him. Why was that?'

'But it's not just Ronnie, is it? Who's the woman? If Ronnie has an accomplice, do we have a name?'

Joe glanced over. 'I'm not sure Ronnie is in charge.'

'How do you mean?'

'Think about it,' Joe said. 'You were right, Ronnie was with us around the first time someone followed Ruby. So someone else must be involved, helping with the hard stuff. The snatching. The pursuing. And what did we find out today about the woman Ronnie was accused of killing?'

'Carrie? That she's still alive.'

Joe nodded. 'Terry Day told us that he had seen Carrie and Grace. What was Ronnie's reaction?'

'Anger.'

'Didn't that surprise you? He's wanted for murder, and instead of relief that his case is going to go away, or happiness that his daughter is alive, he got angry, told us not to pursue that line of defence. Not long afterwards, Terry Day was murdered. Sam said that it was by a woman. What does that tell you?'

Gina frowned. 'I don't know.'

'That Ronnie didn't want anyone to know that Carrie was still alive,' Joe said, and banged the steering wheel with his hand. 'Why would that be? If he was working with someone else, why does it matter if Carrie is alive or not? Sam thought that he might have murdered Carrie because she'd found out what he was doing, snatching teenagers, people linked to Ben Grant's trial, and so he silenced her. But why would that bother her? She was Ben Grant's most frequent visitor. There are rumours about her being involved with him. No, she wouldn't feel revulsion.' He frowned. 'I think it's something different.'

'I'm sorry for being slow, Joe, but I haven't caught up with you yet.'

Joe stayed silent for a few moments as he negotiated a roundabout, through the grime of the inner city, where new office blocks sheltered behind high railings, bright glimmers against the decaying redbrick and long grasses.

'Remember the Moors Murders?' Joe said, once they had rejoined the stutter of traffic lights. 'Myra Hindley was the key to Ian Brady's ability to snatch children. Everyone talked about how lovely she was, genuine, those suckers who campaigned for her release. And you notice how they were all men, drawn in by how beguiling she was. But weren't those the qualities that persuaded those children to get in the van, to end up with Brady? Would they have got into a van with Ian Brady if he had been on his own? No, of course not.'

'What, you think that Carrie was Ben Grant's Myra?'

'Doesn't it make sense? Sam thinks there may have been an accomplice. Why not Carrie? Rumours of romance. Frequent visits. She's the one who's in charge here, because she misses it. The buzz, the thrill.'

Gina shook her head. 'She was a woman, a mother. She wouldn't do that.'

'Myra Hindley did.'

'Because she was under Ian Brady's spell, his influence.'

'And perhaps Carrie is still under Ben Grant's. Hindley and Brady were separated by being in prison and eventually she was less under his influence. It broke the link. Carrie has never been separated from Grant, not truly. There were regular visits to prison. And what did Sam say about how the girls were taken? Through the internet, online grooming. Why can't that be done by Carrie? Wouldn't she know how to make young girls want more? Do you think Ronnie does?'

'But why pretend to be dead if she's working with Ronnie?' Gina said. 'Sam might be right. Ronnie might be the main person and has got a new accomplice. Perhaps Carrie was always just a friend to Grant and she found out more than she wanted? Has she disappeared to get away from Ronnie, because of what he is?'

Joe was silent as he considered that, except that every time he had a clear thought, images of Ruby flashed into his mind, what Ronnie might be doing to her. He shook his head. He couldn't think of those things. He was going to find her. That was the only way he could think.

Joe went to his phone again. He scrolled through his dialled numbers, looking for one from the day before, his eyes flicking upwards all the time at the traffic. He found the number he wanted. He pressed dial and waited.

It was his client from the day before, from the meeting in the Acropolis.

'Joe, you're keen,' he said. 'When do you need the info? I've been asking around for you but no one has said anything yet, but I see these people now and again. You know how it is. No one clocks on, there's no register.'

'No, it's not that,' Joe said. 'Same case, different query.'

'Fire away. I still owe you.'

'Where would you take someone near Piccadilly if you were going to harm them? Somewhere quiet, but near the railway lines?'

'Hey, what is this? Are you recording this, Joe?'

'No, I'm serious. It's for something that is happening right now, and it's urgent.' There was silence, and so Joe added, 'I don't care what you've done in the past. I'm your lawyer. I just need to know.'

Joe lowered his phone so he could steer through some lights and change gear. When he put the handset back to his ear, his client said, 'That's easy, if you're talking hypothetically.'

'Pretend I am.'

'Mayfield station.'

Joe was confused. 'Mayfield station? I don't know it.'

'You will when you find it, because everyone who has ever caught a train from those outer platforms has seen it. Large abandoned train station. Not been used for sixty years, but it's all still in there. The platforms, the ticket office, even the rails as you get near to the Piccadilly tracks. It's like someone just closed the doors and walked away. And so people have been taken there. It's quiet, it scares them, gets them to talk.'

'Thank you,' Joe said, and ended the call. He looked over to Gina. 'Did you get that?'

'I know where it is,' Gina said, and pointed to the right. 'Turn down there at the next lights and keep going.'

The lights were on green. They would change soon, and so he accelerated towards them, pulling hard on the wheel as he got through, the lights just going red. His tyres squealed, drawing a cheer from teenagers nearby, and then he scrolled through his contacts, trying to keep his eye on the road ahead at the same time, looking for Sam. He needed to let him know.

Joe hoped he was in time.

Sixty-Nine

Sam cursed as the two transport cops approached. He didn't need this, not now. He looked at his watch. Fifteen minutes left. Their fingers were tucked into their equipment belts, like some cowboy cliché. There was a small man who walked quickly and a bigger one behind, his stomach pushing some of his white shirt out from underneath the belt.

Sam pulled out his identification. 'It's all right, I'm on the job,' he said as they got closer. He needed to get rid of them.

'Yes, we know,' the smaller one said. His colleague stood behind him, all wide chest and scowl, head pushed back, making his jawline disappear into the fat of his neck. 'The ticket collector you pushed out of the way told us that. What's going on?'

Sam licked his lips and tried to think of a story he could spin. 'I'm expecting a suspect to get off here very shortly,' he said. 'If you stand here with those uniforms on, he won't.'

The two transport cops looked at each other. 'Who's the suspect?'

Sam shook his head. 'I can't tell you. It's too sensitive.' He faked an apologetic smile, but he could feel his tension giving him away.

'But how do you know he's going to get off here?' the cop said. 'And why is there only one of you if it's such a big deal?'

'Because we don't know where he's going,' Sam said, his

frustration getting the better of him. 'We know he's on the move, but if he comes into the city, he'll probably get off here.'

'And if he does?'

'I follow him. That's why I'm on my own.'

'So why the rush back there?' the cop said, pointing up the stairs.

Sam tried to stay calm. They were persistent. 'Because he wasn't going to let me through and a train was about to come in. What if I had missed him because of some ticket stamper? I have to alert people further along if I see him. Once we have sight of him, the reinforcements will arrive.'

'Are these passengers safe?'

Sam nodded. 'Absolutely.'

The two cops looked at each other, making small twitches with their mouths.

'Okay,' the smaller one said, spreading his feet for his final burst of authority. 'Just let us know next time so we can help. And be nicer on the guards. They deserve better than that.'

'Yes, I'm sorry,' Sam said, letting them have their moment. He waited for them to go and then returned to the platform edge. He stared at the lights and the darkness, there in equal measure. Somewhere out there was Ruby, and somewhere out there must be whoever had her, watching him.

He closed his eyes. Memories of Ruby flooded in. That was what he was searching for, some good memory that would give him the strength for what he needed to do. It was hard for the thoughts of her to settle though, because it was all a swirl, the images of Ruby all mixed in with memories of his own life. His children, asleep in his arms. His wedding. Alice in the morning, all dozy, or wrapped up in winter, the tip of her nose turned red by the cold. It was Ruby he was looking for in his mind, but all he got was sadness. Even when she was born, there was always Ellie's shadow, his parents' joy tinged by the awareness that she lived because someone had died. What lay

370

ahead? More heartache? It had been two years after Ellie had died, his parents in their forties. When Ellie died, it had been the first time he had seen his father cry. When Ruby was born, it had been the first time he had seen his father look truly scared. It wasn't the responsibility, he knew that now. It was the fear that tragedy might visit them again.

That stress had killed him in the end. Sam understood that when his own children arrived. It sent his father to a stroke, his mother into a bottle.

Ruby. Little, awkward Ruby. Always too tall, a little quirky, but always a smiler. She was making life hard for herself, getting into scrapes and not trying enough at school, but Sam knew that she was just trying to get some attention from her mother. That was how teenagers worked. She would grow out of it. She might even make a success out of something, bring some new life into the world, like he had. His mark had been made by his two beautiful girls. Was it Ruby's turn?

His phone rang. He looked at the handset. It was Alice. He closed his eyes. He had to be there for Alice, and Emily and Amy.

He looked back at the monitor showing the departure times. There was a train due in two minutes. He breathed out slowly. She could see him. Whoever she was, she would know what he did. He glanced down to his feet, just on the safe side of the yellow line painted along the platform. Three feet away, that was all. Just keep walking, as simple as that. He was the one she wanted, for the arrest of Ben Grant. It wasn't about Ruby, so why would they kill her if he did as they asked? He thought he heard his daughters shouting for him. He tried to shake it away. He was saving someone. Sorry would never be enough, but they might understand one day.

There was the slightest rumble under his feet. Just a tremor. He looked to his left. He could see the headlights from the train beginning the sweep towards him. It was early and travelling fast. A tannoy pinged, and then there was the recorded voice, announcing that the train didn't stop at the platform.

Sam stepped closer to the edge. Just a foot away now. The tracks were oil-blackened, trails of paper strewn across the sleepers. The noise got louder. He looked back towards the train. It was rocking from side to side on the rails. Five carriages. The engine wasn't slowing down.

His stomach gave a violent churn. He thought of his daughters, how they would grow up without a father. Alice mourning. But they would know why he'd done it. Would that make them hate his memory more? How would Ruby cope with the guilt?

His eyes shot back to the tracks. They were vibrating, the large brackets holding them together starting to sing. The train was getting closer. The noise was too loud. He grimaced. The time was now. Soon it would be past him and Ruby would be gone.

His legs started to strain, wanting to make the leap, his body rocking, ready to go. He shouldn't do it, he knew that, but one part of him said it was the right thing to do. Sam looked up, to his city. Red lights and streetlights and the soft speckles of stars over the orange glow of his hometown. Taking it all in for the last time. There was the sound of a horn. Someone shouting behind him. He looked down. His toes were over the platform edge.

Then he saw something below. Someone step from the shadows. A small glow.

He stepped back quickly as the train screeched past him, the clatter of the wheels deafening, the rush of the carriages blowing his hair.

He had seen someone. He knew it. And now he had to get to them before it was too late.

372

Seventy

Ruby sat upright at the clang of the metal door and the fast movement of feet. She had been rubbing the cloth that bound her wrists against the cast-iron base of the pillar. It had become slack so that she could pull her wrists away more. She stopped when she heard the movement. Ronnie had been quiet but something had changed. There was something about the speed of the footsteps that frightened her. She rubbed faster.

'He didn't jump,' Carrie said as she burst from the stairwell. She sounded angry, her words echoing, and she was still pacing, backwards and forwards, short angry steps. 'The coward watched that train go past. He knew what it would mean if he didn't jump, and just watched it go by.'

The footsteps came closer to Ruby, quick and urgent, and then Ruby yelped as she was slapped across the face. She was still blindfolded so hadn't seen it coming.

'Hey, don't do that,' Ronnie said.

Ruby's head sagged forward, blood on her lip, but she'd heard Ronnie. He had sided with her.

The coat slipped from her. The floor was cold against her legs. It must have exposed the bindings around her wrists because Carrie said, 'You little bitch,' and grabbed Ruby's hair, making her yelp. 'What have you been doing?' She tugged at the cloth around Ruby's wrists.

Ruby started to cry. 'I'm sorry. I was uncomfortable. I'm not going to do anything. My arms were aching, that's all. Don't hurt me, please.'

Carrie turned away and barked at Ronnie, 'Get some rope from the van.'

Ronnie didn't answer. He just walked away, and as his footsteps disappeared, the woman got closer to Ruby and hissed in her ear, 'You want to know what's going to happen? I'll tell you. Your big brother is going to kill himself, and I'm going to watch him do it, because if he doesn't, I will kill you. And don't think this is some kind of idle threat, because you are not the first.'

'You can't do that,' Ruby said through her tears. 'And what do you mean, I'm not the first?'

'It's not hard to work out, a clever little girl like you. The ground around here is full of people like you, silly little girls who thought life was just about fun, when you don't understand the greatest thrill of all.'

'But why? I don't understand. You were once like me. Will I end up like you?'

'You won't get that lucky, even if you get out of here. You think you know about grown-up stuff, because I've seen the messages you sent to Billy.'

Ruby flinched as Carrie moved loose strands of hair that had fallen over her face. It wasn't meant to be caring, Ruby knew that. It was supposed to let Ruby know that she was powerless, that Carrie could do what she wanted.

'But you don't really know,' Carrie continued, her voice soft, but spoken with a quiet threat. 'You pretend that you do, but that was all stuff you've picked up from the internet and books. It's not the same as the real thing, because you don't get that bond, something so deep that you will do anything for them. And I mean anything. Not just the dirty promises you made, even though we both know that you wouldn't have done any of it, because it was just fantasy. What I have felt is something beyond the reach of most people.'

374

'What, with Ronnie?'

Carrie laughed. 'No, not with him. He's just a stop-gap, someone to help me get what I want.'

'I can't talk with the blindfold on, because I'm scared,' Ruby said. 'Just pull it down, please, just so I can see.'

There was a pause, and then Ruby felt hands on her head. The blindfold was pulled down.

Ruby blinked. She was finally able to get a proper look at Carrie. She would have been pretty once, but looked like she had gone skinny and didn't wear it well. Her cheekbones were prominent, her eyes wide and tired-looking, with dark rings and tight skin. Her lips were pressed tightly together, the tension pulling lines around her mouth.

'Thank you,' Ruby said.

'So what do you want to say?' Carrie said.

'I don't know,' Ruby said, sniffling. 'I just want to know more. Why me?'

Carrie tilted her head, and then she grinned. 'So you think it's all about you?' A laugh. 'It's not about you. It has never been about you, little Ruby.'

'So tell me, I don't understand. I don't want to be here, because I'm cold and I'm scared, and now it's not even about me.'

Carrie reached forward and stroked Ruby's hair. 'Is there anyone you would do anything for? Your brothers? A friend? Your mother? Or is everything about you, little Ruby, baby of the family?' Carrie shook her head. 'No, probably not, but that's where we're different.'

'How are we different? Teach me.'

'You've got promise, Ruby. You know how to manipulate. But that's not going to work with me, because I know the tricks. Nice try, though.'

Ruby looked up as Ronnie came back into the building, holding a length of tow rope.

Carrie stood up. 'Tie her tighter this time,' she said. 'I'm going back outside. It's nearly time for the next train.'

Ruby watched as Carrie walked away, disappearing into the dark mouth of the stairwell, her footsteps fading until she knew that it was just her and Ronnie. She tried a smile, although it was hard. 'Don't tie me, Ronnie, please. I won't run away. I'm cold and my arms hurt.'

He shook his head. 'I have to. Carrie said.'

'She told me that she doesn't love you,' Ruby said. And then in a whisper, 'All of this is for someone else. Not you.'

'Do you think I don't know that? But I love her, and that's all that matters. You're the last one. Then we go.'

'What do you mean?'

'Run away, where no one will find us.' He wrapped the rope around Ruby's wrists.

'What, like the last plan, when you were supposed to be her killer so that she could run away?'

As he yanked on the rope, making Ruby cry out, her wrists bound together tightly, he said, 'See this hand?' He showed Ruby his right hand, the small lines tattooed between his thumb and finger. 'Six of them. One for each of them. But I've more to put on, and soon there'll be another line. For you.'

Ruby's breath quickened and tears ran onto her cheeks. 'Please don't do it,' she said, her voice breaking, her attempts to get Ronnie on her side coming to nothing.

He pushed Ruby to the floor. She was on her side, her hands bound behind her back. Ronnie pulled the blindfold back down.

She tried to work out where he was, where the next threat was coming from, but all she could hear was the steady rhythm of his breaths.

He was watching her, and she wondered if the blackness ahead would be her last view of life.

Seventy-One

Sam turned to the watch the train speed into the distance and then looked back to the street below. He had seen a light, he knew it.

There were footsteps behind him. The two traffic cops.

'What the fuck are you doing?' the taller one screamed at him.

Sam didn't answer. He knew what he had thought of doing and it scared him. The closeness of the train, but just the hint of a distant light had made him pull back.

His phone rang. Withheld number. Sam turned away to answer. It was her.

'You didn't jump,' she said, her voice hostile. 'You're running out of time.'

He stepped further away from the transport cops. 'Yes, it wasn't the right time. You haven't given me enough assurances about Ruby.'

'Ruby will die. Take that as an assurance. You haven't got time to be so demanding. You had thirty minutes. That's always the time limit. All the others died.'

Sam took a deep breath, panic welling in his chest. 'But why would you do that? It's me you want.'

'So fucking jump!'

'It's a tough thing to do,' he said, his voice rising. 'I've got children. Responsibilities.'

'What about the life you can give to your baby sister?'

'You bitch. You evil fucking bitch!' Passengers on the platform looked over at him and then turned away when he caught their gaze. The smaller transport cop put his hand on Sam's arm but Sam yanked it away. He cupped his mouth around the mouthpiece. 'If you hurt her, I will come after you.'

'No you won't, because all you will feel is guilt. Cowardly Samuel Parker. He does everything right. Nice wife. Two lovely little blonde girls.'

Sam felt the colour drain from his face. It felt like he was standing in water. 'You leave my girls out of this.'

'Why should I? We're not negotiating. And maybe I won't stop at Ruby. I might just keep on going until all that's left is you. Cowardly Sam. Wrapped up in remorse and guilt. You'll have no life. You might as well go now.'

'Why are you doing this?'

There was a pause, and then there was more snap to her voice when she said, 'Because when you take something so special from someone, you get it back. It's the great rebalance.'

Sam scoured the street below as she talked, looking for the same light, unsure if it had been just a reflection from streetlights. But it might have been her phone. He kept his head down but used his eyes to scan the area below the platform. Then he saw it, just a faint glow. He was right. A phone in the darkness lighting up someone's face.

'Who are those two in green with you?' she said.

'Transport cops,' he said, as he looked back along the platform. Sam was walking away from them, and he could hear them on their radios.

'I told you to be on your own.'

'When I look like I'm about to jump from the platform, don't you think they'd be interested?'

'The next train is four minutes away. You need to be under

378

it. If you're not, Ruby will be dead in five minutes, and then I work my way through your family.'

'You said thirty minutes. There's ten left.'

'You didn't jump. That incurs a penalty. And Ruby's cold. She wants to go home. You can do that.'

'Wait, don't go!' Sam shouted. 'Who are you? At least let me die knowing the answers.'

A laugh. 'You know who I am.'

He closed his eyes. He did.

'Carrie.' He stepped towards the edge of the platform. As he looked, he could see the glow of her phone lighting up the shadows.

'Well done, Detective,' she said. 'You would have showed promise.'

'Why are you back with Ronnie? I don't understand. He must be violent towards you.'

She laughed. 'He's not violent. He's never hit me.'

'But the blood?'

'I know you're playing for time, but you won't stop the train.'

When Sam didn't respond, she said, 'The problem with people like you is that you don't see the creativity. The blood was a plant. Draw some out with a syringe, squirt it on a wall and then smear it. It was his idea, to make you think he had killed me, so that you would believe him when he said he had done it, bursting into the station. We knew you'd get all excited and only see one thing.' There was a sigh, and then, 'It was his silly idea. The one thing I did for him. He thought that if he made it look like he'd killed me, I would run away and stop serving my beautiful Ben.'

'So these murders, these young women, they were your idea, to please Ben Grant?'

'You've locked him in a prison but I can keep him free.'

'But you were going to stop, because you were going to disappear.'

379

'No I wasn't. I was just going to leave Ronnie. He made it perfect, because then everyone would think I was dead. Who's going to look for a dead woman?'

'But your darling Ben wasn't happy about it,' Sam said.

'What do you mean?'

'Don't you know? He tried to give you up this week.'

There was silence on the other end of the phone. Sam was trying to distract her, to prolong it, just to somehow hope that it would put off whatever they had planned for Ruby.

'Ben wouldn't do that,' she said, and Sam detected a rise in her voice, some of the gloating replaced by anger.

'He did exactly that, because you betrayed him, and he did it the cowardly way, by giving me clues that would lead me to Ronnie, but once we got to Ronnie, we got to you. You brought his games to an end, you see, by letting Ronnie do what he did, handing himself in to let you get away, because if you go, he thinks you're leaving everyone behind. This new start didn't involve Ben, he knew that, because you made sure his accomplice was locked up, until my brother freed him. Is that why you've carried on, because Ronnie is free?'

She started to laugh, loud and shrill, and he could hear it echoing from where she was. 'You think Ronnie was Ben's accomplice?' Another laugh. 'I was in the bushes back then, Sam, not Ronnie.'

Sam's mouth dropped open. 'You?'

'Yes, me. I watched how you took him, my darling Ben. We were doing special things and you took it all away from me. Cast your mind back, Sam, because I can remember it as clear as yesterday, because I play it in my mind all the time. The night you took Ben from me, I was watching you, Sam, and you were a coward then, your little torch trembling, scared that Ben was going to jump up and hit you.'

Sam didn't respond. Instead, he thought back eight years. The rustle of the leaves. The light footsteps.

'Ben did that for me,' she continued. 'He gave himself up so that I could go. That is why Ben would never give me up.'

'He thought you'd betrayed him.'

'No, he would have realised soon, when I wrote to him. Then I could serve him again. Ben did it for me. Ronnie tried to do it for me, until your brother did his work and set him free. You need to do that for Ruby. If you love her as your sister, you would do it. But you won't, because deep love is something you wouldn't understand.'

'Understand?' Sam said, incredulous, angry. 'Don't try to make it a romantic thing, Bonnie and Clyde. Ben Grant has all the power. You have none. And if he loved you, as deeply as you think he does, he would let you go. That is love, that is sacrifice.'

'I saw him sacrifice himself, back when you arrested him.'

'And how far did that get him? Locked up in a cell as you sleep with someone else, have his child, and then prepare to run away? And you wonder whether he was angry with you?'

There was silence on the other end of the phone, and then she barked the words, 'Just jump, to save Ruby,' and hung up, leaving Sam looking at his handset, his hands trembling. He looked to where he had seen the glow but it had gone.

He jumped, startled, when his phone rang again. It was Joe.

'Joe! Have you found anything out?'

'I've been trying to get hold of you. How long have we got?'

Sam looked at the departures board. 'Two minutes.'

'Try Mayfield station,' Joe said. 'They might be there. We're on our way.'

Sam turned round to the transport cops. 'Where's Mayfield station?'

One of them pointed to the dark space where Sam had seen the glow. 'Right there,' he said. 'The line to Eccles used to run through it. No trains for sixty years now. We have to go in there sometimes to clear out the tramps.'

Sam looked. It was dark, foreboding, as if a blanket had smothered the streetlights and brightness of the surrounding buildings. But there was something else too that hadn't been there before. Flickers of light, flashing beams in a black space, a void that the city lights didn't quite reach.

A tannoy announcement broke his thoughts. The next train was due. Sam focused on the building. Now he knew what it was, he could see the shape of the roof. Long ridges, broken in places, and the streetlights picked out where the windows used to be. The more he looked, the more he could see it for what it was. Mayfield station. Dormant for longer than he had been alive, just a shadow behind the bright lights, empty, a void where nothing passed through anymore. No trains. No people.

Then he saw lights. Beams crossing through gaps in the roof. Two people with torches. There was someone there now.

Sam put the phone back to his ear. 'You're right. That's where they are. I saw her. She can see me too, but I don't think she knows I've spotted her.'

'We're not far away.'

'You've haven't got time.'

Silence for a few seconds, and then, 'Don't do anything stupid.'

Sam didn't answer.

There was a commotion behind him. Sam looked. It was DI Evans running along the platform, her identification out, two other detectives behind her, more out of shape, panting.

'She's at Mayfield station!' Sam shouted, moving towards them. Evans looked. She must have seen the torch beams because she raised her hand and pointed back along the platform.

Sam went to follow her, but she barked, 'No, you're too involved. Stay here.'

He stalled, then turned on the spot, exasperated. He looked

back to the view of the old station, a light breeze ruffling his hair, and then his gaze fell back to the tracks, in the direction of the oncoming trains. He didn't have long to work out what to do.

Seventy-Two

'Is it near here?' Joe said, craning forward towards the wind-screen, driving past the bright taxi ranks of Piccadilly, a queue of black cabs to one side, the long stretch of streetlights along a glistening empty road ahead.

'Just ahead, there on the right,' Gina said.

Joe saw where she was pointing, a large block of brick and dereliction. He skidded to the side of the road, his trims scraping along the kerb, opening his door and switching off the engine at the same time.

'Come on! We haven't got much time.'

They ran towards Mayfield station, their steps loud in the wide, empty street, audible even over the steady rumble of idling taxi engines and the ping of the railway announcer from the station above the arches. The orange of the streetlights gave the glaze of the redbrick a deep glow.

As they got to the corner, Joe saw why it had been used as it had by those who sought peace and quiet. It was the size of a football field but two storeys of Victorian brickwork high, with the main part of the station like a grand old house and the platforms hidden behind walls and stretching into the distance. The front was covered in displays for fleapit music concerts, fly-posted and repeated along the side, foliage making its way through some of the cracks. It would make people cross the road rather than walk past.

'How do you get in?' Gina said, looking frantically around.

'I don't know,' Joe replied. It was hard to see any access. The roof was crumbling, with the rafters visible in places, but the exterior looked solid, with bricked up window spaces and thick walls. As he looked, his eyes went to the high arches opposite, his attention attracted by the rumble of a train. There was a train platform, high and exposed, people watching them. Then he saw Sam, who was pointing straight ahead.

'Sam's there,' he said, pulling on Gina's arm.

When she looked round, she said, 'Thank God. He hasn't jumped. Now let's find Ruby.'

'Which way?'

'We can't get in through the front, so we need to find another way,' she said, and then she set off running again.

'Where are you going?'

'Down here, where Sam's pointing,' she called, racing down a street that ran alongside but disappeared into darkness, the streetlights broken.

Joe sprinted to catch her, to get ahead. It wasn't chivalry. Gina had been a cop and didn't need his protection, but Ruby was his sister and he owed it to her to be first through the door.

The thump of their footsteps became louder as they got further away from the lights, echoing between the high walls of the station and the student accommodation that rose tall next to it. Joe was trailing his hand along the bricks as he ran, worried that he would miss something in the gloom: some loose bricks or a well-hidden doorway. The brooding shadow of the building gave way to the night sky, and so they were running past the wasteland around it, still protected by a high wall.

Then he stopped.

'Hang on,' Joe said, urgency in his voice. 'The wall runs out here.' He took some deep breaths as he felt along with both hands until they clanged onto a heavy metal plate. As he looked up, he could see the blades of razor wire against the sky.

But then he saw something else: a flash of light, moving. Torch beams. 'We need to get in there,' he said, pushing against the metal plates.

'I'm calling the police,' Gina said.

'I'm not waiting for them.'

As Gina spoke on the phone, Joe ran his hands along, looking for a weakness. His hands clanged against the metal, solid, unmoving. Then it changed. He looked round at Gina, her face barely visible in the darkness. His hand had struck corrugated metal. The sound had been different, a higher pitch, thinner metal, but more importantly, there had been movement. It hadn't been much, just a swing inwards, but it had been enough.

Joe pushed against it harder, and then there was the loud scrape of metal across stone and the corrugated sheet moved.

'There's a way in,' he said.

Joe didn't wait for Gina to reason with him. He pushed harder at the metal. He ignored the noise and eased his body into the gap. He strained and grimaced until he was through, and held it so that Gina could join him.

They stood there in the dark, trying to get some sense of where to find the way inside. The sounds from the street had gone and the view ahead disappeared into bushes and trees, nature reclaiming the space. There was a low wall at one side and the steady bubble of a stream. There was only one way and that was into the blackness ahead.

Joe saw the flashes again, through the holes in the roof. 'We need to keep moving,' he whispered.

'We could use our phones to light the way.'

'No, they might see us. We need to surprise them, so that they don't do anything rash. I don't care where they go. I just want Ruby back.'

They moved forward slowly, feeling with their feet as they went. The ground was uneven, with small mounds of rubble and tangles of undergrowth. Leaves stroked his face, and he waited all the time for a hand to reach out for him.

The darkness got deeper as they got closer to the building, which rose in front of them, blocking out the glow from the streetlights and station on the other side. Gina grabbed the back of his jacket so that they wouldn't get separated. His footsteps were light and careful, but still he felt like he was shouting his arrival, from the race of his pulse to the short gasps of his breaths.

He didn't see the piece of metal sticking out, a long-discarded strip left to rust on a pile of stones. It caught his shin, cutting at the skin, making him shout out in pain.

There was a pause as they stood there, Joe grimacing, unsure if they had been seen. Then a torch flashed from one of the windows upstairs, lighting them up, making them squint into the glare.

They'd been spotted.

'They're here,' Ronnie shouted, panicking, running back to Carrie.

'Who's here? Where?' Carrie said.

'Joe Parker, and a woman from his office.'

'Shit.' A pause, and then, 'This is it, Ronnie. It's over.'

Ruby started to cry, but they were tears of hope. Joe had come for her. Then she pushed back against the pillar. There was someone in front of her. She could hear the breaths, close, watching.

'What is it?' Ruby said.

Ruby yelped as the blindfold was pulled off. She blinked her vision clear and then looked around. Carrie was in front of her, on her haunches, breathing heavily, looking scared.

'Your rescuer is here,' Carrie said. 'They're going to be too late though.'

'What do you mean?' Ruby's lips quivered as she spoke. 'No,

please, I'm scared. Just let me go. You can run. Get away. I'll tell them you spared me.'

'No,' Carrie said. 'Sam hasn't suffered enough.'

Carrie reached into her pocket and produced a sheet of clear plastic. It looked strong, thicker than a shopping bag. 'If your brother wants to find you, he can.'

Ruby screamed, shrill in the large space, but it was cut short as Carrie forced the plastic sheet over her face and pulled it tight. Everything was blurred, out of focus, except that she could see the snarl of Carrie's mouth as she pressed. She tried another scream, but it caught in her throat and she was unable to take a breath.

Seventy-Three

Joe heard the scream, short and loud. It hit him like a grab to the throat, making him gasp. 'Ruby!'

Gina pulled at his arm. 'Come on,' she said, and set off running, scrambling over rubble, weeds and discarded metal.

Joe followed, grimacing at the pain in his leg. Gina was heading for the darkest spot, pulling out her phone, pressing the button to provide a glow. The light bounced as she ran, making the shadows of the undergrowth shift and move on the walls.

Gina tripped on something, her phone tumbling out of her hand, but Joe kept on going, dragging her up by grabbing a handful of her jacket as he went past.

The overhang of a large doorframe seemed to loom ahead, and so Joe ran at it, not knowing if he would meet something solid. His hands were out in front of him, ready for the impact. He grunted as he hit more metal, but there was movement. He pushed hard with his shoulder, shouting, snarling. The metal scraped on the ground as it moved, slowly inching open. Gina joined him, pushing hard, grimacing.

'Someone's placed a rock behind it,' Gina said, straining.

They made a space big enough to squeeze through. Joe went first, shedding his jacket as it snagged on the rough edges, and then he held the metal back so that Gina could get through.

Once on the other side, Joe tried to get his bearings. It was dark, but he could see stairs that went upwards, the faint glow from the top picking out the long bar of a handrail. There was the steady drip of water from somewhere, the noise bounced around the tiled stairwell, and there was a faint glow at the top. Joe set off, using the handrail to guide him upwards.

'There's only one way,' he said, and then shouted, 'Ruby!'

There was no response.

He started to run.

Sam heard the scream. It changed everything.

He looked along the tracks. The next train was coming in, swaying on the tracks, screeches and bright lights, rumbling towards him, but that didn't matter anymore. Ruby needed him.

He ran along the platform, ignoring the pain from his shoulder as he went. Evans and the others were gone. The train got closer. As he looked along, the platform was busy, a train on the opposite side spewing out passengers who had come in from the northern stations. There were guards and more transport cops and people with suitcases. He needed to get past them and beyond the train. They would slow him down.

Sam looked back towards the train. It had cleared the end of the platform and was now moving along, faces visible at the doors ready to be disgorged. He dodged people on the platform, weaving in and out, his breaths coming faster, not used to the exertion. He barged into someone, catching his injured shoulder. He cried out in pain as the other man went to the floor. There was a shout but Sam kept on going.

He looked across. He could see where Mayfield station ended and spilled out into the night, its mouth cavernous. Where there had once been an offshoot into Mayfield was just empty land that led to the tracks that fed into Piccadilly. Sam looked down at the rails. They were black and oily apart from the sheen on the top of the rails. There was a line of paving slabs on the other side, tight against the wire fence that over-looked the long drop to the street below. But it gave him a clear run and ended on the right side of the tracks.

He took one last look along the platform. The train was close but slowing. He could do it.

Sam jumped down from the platform, his shoes slippy on the oil of the sleepers. Someone screamed behind him. He didn't stop. The train blared a horn and the brakes screeched louder. It was closer than he realised, the lights bright in his eyes. His feet found the sanctuary of the paving line as the carriages flew past him, the wind making his hair fly up and his face contort into a grimace.

He couldn't stop to think about the train. He took one more look at Mayfield, at the flicker of torch beams through the crumbling roof. There was more movement there now.

He started to run.

His feet were slipping but he didn't hesitate. He was above the line of the streetlights as he went, moving quickly, not wanting to look down, only a wire fence stopping him from falling. There were trains pulling in ahead, but they were on the other lines.

He looked over at Mayfield again. He was running along its length. He could get in that way.

His chest ached, his legs in pain, but he strained for one last burst. He could do this.

Ruby thrashed her head around, kicking out with her feet, trying to stop Carrie from getting a firm hold with the plastic. It was tight on her face, smoothing out her skin.

'Just stab her,' Ronnie said, behind Carrie, his voice frantic. 'It's taking too long.'

'I want Sam to see that the little bitch knew what was happening.'

'We've got to go.'

Carrie turned as the shout of 'Ruby!' came from the stair-well. The plastic sheet slackened. Ruby took a breath, a long gasp, and then she lashed out with her feet, shrieking, sending Carrie sprawling backwards.

'You bitch!' Carrie snarled.

Ruby screamed again. 'Joe, Joe!'

Carrie scrambled to her feet and pulled out the knife from her pocket. It was a dagger, long and sharp, jagged edges catch-ing the glare from the torch that she had dropped onto the floor.

'Ronnie, have you got your knife?' Carrie said.

'Yes, here,' he said, holding it up.

'When they get up here, kill them.'

Carrie grabbed Ruby under her arm, her bound wrists making it easier to lift her. 'Come with me.'

Ruby tried to pull away, until the knife jabbed under her chin, cutting her, making her yelp. Blood trickled onto the tip of the blade.

'You either come with me or I skin you right here,' Carrie hissed at her, and then pulled at her arm again. Ruby went with her this time.

'Where are you going?' Ronnie shouted, as Carrie started to run, prodding Ruby forward with the knife in her back.

'She's the only negotiating chip we have.'

'What about me?'

'Kill those bastards and then join me.'

'And if I don't?'

Carrie paused, and then said, 'Sacrifice yourself, like Ben did. If you love me, you would.' She turned back to Ruby and gave her another jab in the back with the knife. 'Now run.'

Ruby felt herself propelled along as Carrie hooked her arm through hers, so that the knife was pressed against her ribs.

They were heading for the exit, towards the railway lines.

*

Joe's legs were aching, his chest heaving from running when he got to the top of the stairs, but he wasn't going to stop. He burst into a large open area, the station platforms, the rail sections overtaken by weeds and bushes that grew high in the middle.

'Ruby!'

'There,' Gina said, pointing.

There were two figures ahead, running towards the exit, huge and open, the glow of the rail lines and buildings beyond like a beacon. The lights of a train went past. Joe recognised Ruby. The long skinny legs. Why didn't she turn to run away, fight back?

Joe set off running again, the way lit by the moon that filtered through the roof spaces, although it didn't reach the sides, where the walls seemed lost in shadow. He could hear Gina trying to keep up with him, her exertion coming as short gasps.

They skirted past the old ticket office, still intact, a ghost, and towards the long stretch of the platform. Ruby and someone else – Carrie, he presumed – were framed in the light that came in from the tracks outside, like two small black figures heading out of the darkness. Where was Ronnie?

Joe felt like he was gaining, but Ruby was forty yards ahead, maybe more, and every muscle in his body was telling him that he couldn't run anymore, the gash on his leg sending shards of pain through his body with every pound of his foot. But he couldn't stop, he knew that.

Then there was movement to his right. Someone in the shadows. A flash of metal, and then a shout, a roar of anger, and the rush of someone towards them.

Joe gasped as a moving shoulder caught him, sent him sprawling to the floor, his arms jarring as they broke his fall. He looked towards Ruby; she was getting further away. Then he heard another roar, and saw a shadow appear over him, the arm raised, the metal of a knife blade catching the light. Joe raised his arms to protect himself, with no time to scramble away, waiting for the thrust of the knife, and agony, and terror.

There was the rush of someone else. Gina. She led with a fist, catching his attacker on the jaw, knocking him to one side, falling, the knife skittering across the floor as he hit the cold concrete of the ground. Then she was on him, panting with exertion, pushing his arm up behind his back so that he cried out in pain.

Joe recognised the voice as Ronnie's. He looked at Gina, who was sitting on him.

'Go after her, Joe!' she shouted. 'I've got him.'

Joe didn't need to be told again.

He scrambled to his feet and set off running. Ruby was in the open now, heading straight for the tracks. He wasn't going to make it.

Sam saw them emerge out of the old station, Ruby and Carrie, heading towards the railway tracks, their outlines visible through the bushes and long grasses that had taken over the entrance.

There was no way forward. There were just the tracks, some electrified, but he realised that Carrie wasn't stopping, that she would know that they couldn't get out that way. She was taking Ruby to the tracks.

Sam couldn't keep up the pace. His police work had become deskbound, all those accounts and bank statements, and with one arm strapped up, it was too hard. Tears started to stream from his eyes. He wasn't going to get there. He was about to lose another sister. He wanted to say sorry to her, to his mother, because of what she would endure again. Another funeral. Another dead child. He should have jumped, he knew that now. It had come to this, because he thought he could save her.

He slowed to a halt, his good hand on the wire fence, and

watched the small silhouettes make for the train line. He was panting hard, his lungs aching, his legs burning with exertion, and he wanted to throw up, angry that he had let her down.

Then he saw something else. Another train, a relentless unstoppable line of passenger carriages heading for one of the other platforms. There was a ping of a tannoy behind him. The train was approaching the station. Carrie and Ruby were running towards it. He had to get there first.

He set off running again.

Ruby was screaming with fear as they ran towards the lines. The woman's arm was locked around hers and the knife was sticking into her side. Grass and weeds thrashed at her legs.

She tried to pull away, but Carrie thrust with the knife, going in a few inches, making her sag to her knees. Her shirt became damp and sticky.

'Keep running,' Carrie snarled at her, yanking on her arm again.

Ruby ran, becoming lightheaded as she bled, succumbing to the terror and pain. She was running on instinct alone, fear keeping her legs moving, in spite of the searing agony from the fresh wound between two ribs, the ache of her lungs, the chafing on her wrists as the rope rubbed.

The railway lines were close. She could see them ahead, a mesh of metal and concrete and overhead wires.

'Nowhere to go,' Ruby said, her words coming out as short gasps.

Carrie ignored her. Ruby tried to slow down but Carrie just kept on pulling at her, driving them forward. The bright metal of the railway lines was right in front of her and Ruby expected Carrie to veer away, to run alongside where she could see a path, but instead she stepped over the first set of rails and then onto the oil and gravel of the next, the concrete sleepers slippery.

Ruby tripped and stumbled, falling onto the rail, her body over the metal, knocking the breath from her lungs, unable to break her fall with her arms tied behind her back.

'Get up, get up,' Carrie shouted, and pulled at her, making her arms strain behind her back.

Ruby cried out in pain and scrambled to her feet, her knees bloodied now, snot and tears blending with the sweat on her face. She felt sick from pain and crying. She couldn't fight anymore. There was nothing left except a desire for it all to end.

There was a noise ahead, vibrations under her feet, the glare of headlights in the distance.

'There's a train!' Ruby screamed, her knees sagging. 'We've got to go.'

'No,' Carrie said, and gripped Ruby round her waist.

Ruby wriggled, made alert by a new terror. 'We've got to get off the tracks!'

Carrie gripped tighter.

'No, we can't stay here,' Ruby said, and she fought to pull away, desperate, screaming, stamping at Carrie's feet, kicking back at her shins, but Carrie was holding too tightly.

'This is for Sam,' Carrie shouted in Ruby's ear, anger in her voice, not fear. 'I want him to find you like this, so that he knows you felt terror at the end.'

'But we'll both die.'

'I've no life left. I'm ready.'

The train was getting closer. There was the sound of the horn, loud and strident. Another blast. There was the ear-splitting screech of brakes, the thump and thud of carriages coming together, but it was going too fast, too close. Ruby struggled again, turning, thrashing, fighting, but Carrie's arms were clamped tight. The noise was deafening, the lights making her look away. The rattle of the tracks sent vibrations through her legs, almost sending her to the floor again. She screamed but it was lost, and so she wailed her goodbyes. To her mother. Her brothers. She screamed that she was sorry for everything and then closed her eyes, waiting for the collision, praying that it would be quick.

Sam wouldn't make it, he knew it. He was shouting as he ran. Shouting for Ruby, just a silhouette against the train headlights. The screech of brakes, the blast of the horn. It was going too fast.

One final burst, his chest aching from effort, his hair stuck to his forehead by sweat, Ruby outlined in the glare of the lights, braced for impact, turned away, Carrie holding her. He was just a few feet away, his whole world filled by noise and lights and fear and screams and the blast of the train as it tried to slow down, but it had been going too fast, was still too far from the station.

He reached out with his good arm. It was one swift movement, no time to think or work it out. His arm went around Ruby's and he pulled hard, falling to the floor, Ruby coming with him, his strapped-up shoulder about to take his weight. He cried out in pain, but it was lost in the roar of the train as it went past, his back jarring on the rails next to it, winding him, the brakes still making the wheels scream. There was just the flash of the passenger carriages, Ruby not with him, lost amongst the shadows of the train.

Then he lifted his head to look further along the tracks, back towards the station, where the train was coming to a stop, and he saw her, thrown against the fence like he had been, blood and grazes on her face where she had landed on the stones. Her hands were tied behind her back.

Then she lifted her head, panting, crying, and then Sam started to cry too, through exhaustion, through relief, tears pouring down his cheeks. He had saved her. No, the bound wrists had saved her, had allowed him to use her arms like a hook and just yank her away, throwing her to the side.

He heard the sound of footsteps and someone shouting Ruby's name. He lifted his head. It was Joe, running alongside the tracks, his tie flying over his shoulder, blood on his shirt, his trousers torn. When he got to Ruby, he sank to his knees and pulled her in to him, his eyes skywards, sucking in air. Ruby put her arms round his waist and shuffled her legs to get closer to him. She was going to be all right.

'Carrie?' Sam shouted, and he looked back along the tracks. There were pieces of cloth on the gravel next to the train, but they were glistening, and he realised that they were pieces of Carrie, her body dragged along and shredded like tissue. Beyond, he saw people running towards them, the bright green of the transport cops.

Sam lay back and let the cold stones cool him. He looked at the stars above, his chest rising and falling rapidly.

It was over.

Seventy-Four

Monica's funeral was a week later, after the postmortem had been done, along with one by the defence pathologist, the legal procedures now concluded. Ronnie Bagley had gone back to Mahones. They had sent their regrets for Monica by way of flowers and a letter, but Joe knew that they were doing what he would have done by taking on the case. It was what they did, Joe and Mahones – deal in misery, help the wicked. Joe had come face to face with it and he questioned whether he could still do it, but he knew he would. It was the world he had chosen, for better or for worse.

The funeral had been difficult. Joe had met her parents. They were good people and said that they didn't blame Joe, but he knew there was an undercurrent of resentment, that if she had worked somewhere else, then she would still be alive, that it was her short time in Joe's department that had killed her.

They were at Southern Cemetery, a spread of large grass squares peppered by gravestones on one of the main roads out of the city. Buses and cars rumbled in the distance, but it was quiet as Joe faced forward, the area tranquil and reflective, towards the open space in the ground that would be Monica's resting place.

Monica's family was grouped closer to the grave, Gina with them, but Joe hung back, Sam alongside him.

Joe turned to Sam. 'Thanks for coming.'

Sam nodded. His arm was still strapped across his chest and he had a few more grazes and bruises than before, but he was alive. Ruby was alive. 'I had to be here,' he said. 'I feel as responsible as you do. If I had known Carrie was there back when I arrested Ben Grant, none of this would have happened.'

'Ifs and buts,' Joe said quietly, and they both looked towards the coffin that was next to the grave. The vicar was saying something but Joe was too far away to make it out.

'I didn't know any of these people,' Joe said, and pointed towards Monica's brother, her old university friends, her parents trying to support each other. 'She had a whole other life, and then for a short time she crossed over into mine, and look how it ended. All so pointless. A waste.'

'Have you spoken to anyone?' Sam asked. 'A counsellor, or a doctor?'

'Why?'

'For the stress of what happened. We have people in the force who can help us, but for you there'll be nothing.'

Joe shook his head. 'I'll deal with it, the same way I deal with everything.'

'By keeping it bottled up.'

'That's right. The only thing I have to worry about is the bottle cracking. If I go see someone, the whole lot comes out and I have to learn how to deal with it. My way, it's all locked away where it can't hurt anyone.'

'I went to see Ben Grant,' Sam said.

'Why did you do that?' Joe said, surprised.

'To make sure that he knew it was over. He is nothing now. Carrie is dead. Ronnie Bagley will go to prison. Ben Grant will probably never get out.'

'Should I take any solace from that? It's hard to see anything good in this as I look at Monica's parents right now.'

'I did it for me, and Ruby, and maybe in part for Ellie, because it was someone just like Ben Grant who took her away.'

'I can understand that,' Joe said. 'I know I should feel something good, because Ruby's still alive, but it's too hard. And there's that poor little girl, Grace. Her mother is dead and her father in prison.'

'She'll be brought up in a good home,' Sam said. 'Foster care for now, but wherever she ends up, she will be better there than she would have been in that poisonous environment.'

'It's not the same as being with parents.'

'Doesn't that depend on who your parents are?'

Joe didn't answer that, and instead said, 'How did Grant respond?'

'He didn't. He just stared at me, but I could see from the glare in his eyes that he knew the same as I did, that he had nothing left except a small cell and a lot of contempt. There are no more games for him to play.'

'So what now?' Joe said.

'Nothing. It's over.'

They both stood in silence for a few moments, until Joe said, 'We're going to pay for a bench in the gardens opposite the office. Monica used to sit there sometimes. It will be a way of remembering her.'

'But then life just goes on,' Sam said.

'That's the way it is. The memories stay with us though. We remember Ellie. We will remember how we nearly lost Ruby. It's just more weight to carry with us.'

'Come with me,' Sam said.

'Where?'

'You know where,' Sam said, and set off walking.

Joe caught up with him and together they walked along a tarmac path, past neat rows of black granite decorated by gold letters. The child graves were furthest away, marked out by plastic windmills and toys that hung from the branches of the trees. The council had tried to take them down, complained that they were spoiling the visual tranquillity, but how can you interfere with the grief of a parent?

Ellie's grave was at the end of a row. As they got closer, Joe saw the fresh white roses in the flower holder – Ellie's favourite flower.

Joe stood over her grave and took a deep breath. Black granite, like most of the rest, but it was the words in gold that hit him. *Eleanor Parker. Much loved daughter and sister. Died 19 May 1998*. That was all it said, but what else could it say?

Flashes came back to him, of Ellie walking towards a woodland path, her college bag on her shoulder, her headphones on her head, the wires from her Walkman trailing out of her bag. And then he saw the man further along, loitering, his hands thrust into the pockets of a grey hooded sweatshirt, the hood tight around his face, even though it had been a hot day. He should have shouted, because he had sensed the danger, but he hadn't. He had stalled, scared, and watched as Ellie disappeared into the trees. She had looked up briefly as she went past him, and then as she carried on, he had followed her.

Tears welled up in his eyes. He reached out to touch the stone.

'I'm sorry, Ellie,' he said. It was what he always said.

He let the sun dry his tears. Sam didn't say anything to him as Joe tried to stop them, but when he wiped them away more tears replaced them, along with memories of Ellie, her golden hair flying in the breeze on those summer walks they had taken, the family complete, he and Sam wrestling on the grass, Ellie all laughs and shouts.

He stayed like that for a few minutes. He looked to the ground. She was down there, a few feet under, and he had to force himself not to think like that. That would not be how he thought of her.

It was getting harder to remember Ellie though, because her face was being replaced by Ruby's. When he remembered Ellie, he started to see Ruby.

He took a deep breath and wiped his eyes.

He felt Sam's hand on his shoulder. 'When you told me about Ellie's murderer, that you look for him every day – is that true?'

Joe nodded.

'And you are going to kill him?'

Joe nodded again.

'Then we'll lose you too, because you'll end up in prison, with people like Ben Grant. Why not channel your efforts into it the right way? Become a prosecutor?'

Joe shook his head. 'I do what I do. This is the way it's always going to be.'

'And us? Me and you? Having a detective for a brother?'

'You're not thinking of leaving the force, are you?'

'Of course not.'

'So we'll be fine,' Joe said, and he smiled. 'We're brothers. It should mean something.'

Sam returned the smile and started the walk back to the huddled group at Monica's grave.

Before Joe turned to join him, he touched Ellie's gravestone. 'I won't forget,' he whispered. 'I'll make it right.'

Don't miss Joe and Sam's next chilling case

THE DEATH COLLECTOR

Joe Parker is Manchester's top criminal defence lawyer and Sam Parker – his brother – is a brilliant detective with the Greater Manchester Police force. Together they must solve a puzzling case that is chilling Manchester to the bone ...

Danger sometimes comes in the most unexpected guises. The Death Collector is charming, sophisticated and intelligent, but he likes to dominate women, to make them give themselves to him completely; to surrender their dignity and their lives. He's a collector of beautiful things, so once he traps them he'll never let them go.

Joe is drawn into the Death Collector's world when he becomes involved in a supposed miscarriage of justice, and when the case becomes dangerous, Sam is the first person he turns to. In this gripping thriller, danger lurks for not only the Parker brothers, but also those closest to them.

Out June 2014

NEVER SOMEWHERE ELSE

Alex Gray

When three young women are discovered strangled and
mutilated in a Glasgow park, it is up to DCI Lorimer to find
their killer. Frustrated by a lack of progress in the
investigation, Lorimer is forced to enlist the services of Dr
Solomon Brightman, psychologist and criminal profiler.
Together they form an uneasy alliance.

But when a homeless man is brought in for questioning,
the investigation takes a bizarre turn. Soon Lorimer has to
scratch the surface of the polished Glasgow art world
and reveal the dark layers hidden beneath . . .

'Gray never rushes her story, preferring to slowly, delicately
build a multi-layered, international web of drama and
deceit that requires the concentration levels to stay
on high from the first page until the last'
Daily Record

THE SURROGATE

Tania Carver

A sickening killer is on the loose – a killer like no other. This murderer targets heavily pregnant women, drugging them and brutally removing their unborn babies.

When DI Phil Brennan is called to the latest murder scene, he knows that he has entered the world of the most depraved killer he has ever encountered. After a loveless, abused childhood, Phil knows evil well, but nothing in his life has prepared him for this.

And when criminal profiler Marina Esposito is brought in to help solve the case, she delivers a bombshell: she believes there is a woman involved in the killing – a woman desperate for children . . .

'With a plotline that snares from the off, and a comprehensive cast of characters, Carver's debut novel sets the crime thriller bar high. A hard act to follow'
Irish Examiner

THE DEVIL'S EDGE

Stephen Booth

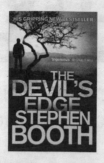

In the heart of summer, in the dead of night, something wakes you. The house is quiet. The children are sleeping. The kitchen is empty.

Except for the body on the floor.

A series of brutal home invasions is terrorizing the Peak District. Until now, the burglars haven't left a clue. This time, they've left a corpse. But as the death toll rises, two intrepid cops begin to suspect that the robberies – and the murders – are not what they seem. Beneath the scorching summer sun, a dangerous game is in play ... and a merciless killer is hiding in plain sight.

'One of our best storytellers'
Sunday Telegraph